Violent BEGINNINGS

USA TODAY BESTSELLING AUTHORS

J.L. BECK & C. HALLMAN

Copyright © 2020 by Beck & Hallman LLC

Editing by Kelly Allenby

Cover Design by C. Hallman

Cover Image by Wander AGUIAR :: PHOTOGRAPHY

All rights reserved.

No part of this book may be reproduced in any form or by any electronic or mechanical means, including information storage and retrieval systems, without written permission from the author, except for the use of brief quotations in a book review.

PROLOGUE

Markus

*B*lood. It coats everything with warmth. Each rivulet is like a brush of paint against a white canvas. It surrounds me. Drowning me in its darkness. I did this. I killed her. Staring down at her beautiful face, I realize I'll never be able to see her smile, never be able to hold her hand in mine again. Her blue eyes will never shine with excitement at my presence. I'll never hear her say my name again. She is gone.

My insides twist as if someone is trying to twirl them with a fork.

You did this.

You killed her.

I look away, but the blood is still there.

There is no escaping what I've done.

"We have to go, Markus," my friend, Anthony, calls, his voice filled with panic.

I can't move, can't breathe. Police sirens echo in the distance, but the dooming fate they bring doesn't faze me. All I see is her face, her pale, cold skin, her lifeless eyes. Her name forms on my lips, but I can't get the word out. Not that speaking her name would make her answer. Not with a bullet lodged in her skull.

"Markus! Let's go. She's dead." Anthony speaks a truth that I feel in my soul. I can barely get my body to move; my legs feel like jello. All I want to do is lie here beside her and cradle her body against mine.

She's dead.

"We have to go, Markus. If they catch us, you'll go to prison for sure. Moretti will kill you!"

Somehow, I manage to get my legs to move. Pushing off the concrete, I can't pull my gaze from her.

Dead. Gone. My future. Taken in a second.

I feel a tug on my shirt and realize Anthony is physically pulling me toward the car. Part of me feels I deserve to go to prison and pay the ultimate price but the fact I am still breathing, and she is not, will be my suffering.

On unsteady feet, I stumble backward, letting Anthony pull me to the car. The sirens grow louder, and I feel pain and anger. Anger that she was here when she shouldn't have been, anger toward myself, and to the fuckers that shot her.

By the grace of God, I make it into the SUV, and we race away just as the first sight of lights flash across the rearview mirror.

"Did you know that girl?" Anthony huffs from the driver's seat, his hands trembling as he drives.

I contemplate telling him, yes, but it's none of his concern. The plan was to keep her sheltered from the darkness that followed me.

"No," I reply dryly, feeling the sting of tears in my eyes. Peering out the window, I blink the fucker away. Men don't cry. They don't show weakness.

"Oh, well, it looked like you knew her. I've never seen you like that..."

"I didn't," I growl, because again, admitting such a thing would only make me look weak. Still, deep down inside, I admit the truth. I more than knew her. She was a part of me.

I might not have pulled the trigger, but I killed her just the same.

I killed the love of my life, and I'll have to live with that so long as I remain breathing.

1

FALLON

Sacrifice. That sums up my life. Like a cow before going to the butcher, I'm being prepared for auction, where I'll be placed on a block for a group of men to purchase me like I'm inhuman, nothing more than an item.

I've tried to prepare myself for today, knowing what's to come. At least on the outside, I attempt to look like a warrior, while on the inside, I'm a leaf shaking in the wind, barely hanging on.

I've been held prisoner for the last three days. They grabbed me off the sidewalk while I was walking home from a college class. In the dark, no one heard my screams or saw me, overcome with fear, afraid about what would happen next, fighting as they shoved me into the back of the van. I push those memories into the recesses of my mind.

I want to forget the small, cold cell I was kept in without clothes or a blanket. I want to forget it all. The worst part was the dark. There was no window or light in my cell—only darkness. Sometimes bugs would crawl on me, but I couldn't see anything.

Now, light and noise surround me. It's overwhelming. The four other girls are crying, some sobbing uncontrollably. I pride myself on not crying in front of the men who are about to sell us.

I've cried enough in the last three days to last me a lifetime. I'm done crying. No amount of begging or pleading will convince these monsters to let me go.

Naked as the day I was born, I stand with the girls, each one of us different from the next. We've only just met since we were kept alone before today, but alone or together, I already feel a connection to each one of them.

Kindred spirits by our captor's makings, knowing we share one and the same fate.

"Put this on," one of the men growls and hands us each a scrap of clothing. Mine is a white lace fabric with gold trim.

I look at the *dress* in my hand, if you can even call it that. It's barely enough to cover my privates. It looks like the kind of lingerie a woman would wear under a wedding dress. I almost laugh at the thought.

Objecting isn't an option, so I do as instructed. Pulling it over my body, I hope to feel a little more human, but I don't. If anything, I feel even more like a cheap hooker than I did before.

Goosebumps pebble my flesh, blanketing me. I feel bare—exposed, and I hate it.

The girl beside me lets out a ragged sob, and I turn just enough to look at her. Her hair is black, sleek, and straight. I don't gawk at her or look at her body, but I can tell she is on the slimmer side and young. Most likely barely of age.

Tears stream down her cheeks, and she is shaking so badly her entire body is vibrating.

"Stop crying, whore!" one of the men orders. "If you think it's bad now, wait until after the auction. I'd love to hear your cries then."

His voice makes me shiver and leaves me feeling sick to my stomach. Suddenly, I'm grateful that I didn't eat anything. Even though I was hungry earlier, I couldn't bring myself to take a single bite from the stale sandwich they brought me.

The guy suddenly looks past me and nods. "Finally. I thought we were gonna have to send them out without a shot."

Shot? What are they talking about now? Just as I ask that question in my mind, a woman appears at the side of me. A woman in scrubs with a hospital ID card clipped to her hip.

I look up and meet her gaze, expecting to see fear, compassion, or shock, but I find none of those in the depth of her green eyes.

Only indifference. Like she doesn't have a care in the world.

"What are you doing?" I ask when she stops right in front of me.

"Don't talk, please," she answers in a flat voice.

She keeps her eyes down like she doesn't want to look into my face while she pulls out a small box from her oversized purse. Flipping the case open, I count five syringes inside.

"Hold her arm," she orders one of the men.

A moment later, my arm is being grabbed and held still so the woman can clean a spot with an alcohol wipe before injecting me with whatever is inside the syringe. Funny, she cleans my arm, worried I might get an infection but fails to care what is happening to all of us.

"What was that?" I ask, hoping she'll at least give me the courtesy of telling me.

"Birth control," is all she says before moving on down the line of girls.

"Men buy you for fucking, not breeding." The guy who was holding my arm chuckles and releases me with a shove.

He walks away, moving onto the next girl, and a spot in my chest starts to ache for the girl beside me. I don't know her story, how she came to be here, if it was of her own choice or someone else's. I don't know the circumstances that gave her this fate, but I want to help her.

"Hey…" I call out. "It's okay. Everything is going to be okay." I try to reassure her.

She looks over at me, and I notice then that her eyes are green and framed by thick lashes that are soaked. The skin around her eyes is swollen from the constant crying.

"I... I want to go home." Her bottom lip trembles as she speaks, and her chest rises and falls so dramatically I know she is close to having an anxiety attack.

"My name's Fallon," I tell her, attempting to distract her. "What's yours?"

The girl looks away for a second before looking back. "Julie," she replies after a moment. I'm not sure how to comfort her because while I'm not showing it, I'm scared out of my mind on the inside. I have no idea what will happen to me after tonight.

Where will I go? Fear of the unknown is the only thing I have.

"It's okay to be scared, Julie. Everything is going to be okay," I assure her, even though we both know it's a lie. But what else am I going to tell her? What can I do to ease her mind, even if it's just a little?

Shaking her head, she sends pieces of dark hair across her face. "It's not going to be okay," her voice cracks with raw pain, "aren't you scared? Afraid of what will happen to you tonight?" Her questions make it hard for me to swallow.

I try not to focus on the future or what will happen tomorrow. It's not promised for any of us, especially not under these circumstances.

"Yes, I'm afraid. I'm terrified, but I can't let that fear own me. I won't."

"Then you're stronger than me," she shamefully admits.

"How did you end up here?" I ask, not wanting the conversation to end yet.

I've been stuck inside my head all day, trying to figure out my next step. Now that I'm here, I know the decision has already been made for me.

Her lip trembles and her eyes become glassy once more. "My

father. He owed some money to the wrong person, and because he couldn't pay, they took me instead."

Heartbreaking.

Her response reminds me that we're all fighting our own invisible battles, merely trying to get through today so we can see a better tomorrow.

"What about you?"

"I..." I've tried not to think about the circumstances that have gotten me to this point. At nineteen, I never thought I would find myself in a situation like this, but I can't undo what is already done. "Someone grabbed me as I walked home after class."

Julie nods. "What do you think they'll do with us after the auction?"

She whispers the question almost as if she knows the fate that lies ahead but is too afraid to see it with her own eyes.

I shiver involuntarily, fear coiling tightly in my gut. A man willing to buy any one of us isn't going to take us home to merely clean his house and cook for him. He's going to use us, over and over again, leaving us a shell of the person we used to be. Nothing innocent will come from whoever purchases us.

"I don't know, but I don't think it will be anything good," I reply honestly, licking my dry bottom lip. My throat tightens, and the fear I've been trying to swallow down and keep at bay starts to rise up again.

I've mentally prepared myself to be raped and caged by the man who is going to buy me, but what if it gets even worse?

What if I'm tortured?

What if he kills me?

The questions swirl, taking the shape of a tornado.

After the woman is done administering the drug, she takes her bag and leaves, as if this was just another day at the office for her.

The men come back around and start putting collars around our necks like we're fucking dogs. The collars are heavy, made out of thick leather with metal rings on the front and back. They tighten them to the point of being uncomfortable and secure them with a small lock on the side.

Next, they put metal cuffs around our wrists and attach those to chains, which are hooked to the front of our collars.

Julie starts to sniffle. "This is wrong. How can they do this to us? Chain us up like animals and auction us off?"

The girl beside Julie leans over. "Be quiet, or you'll get us all in trouble."

"I don't want to be quiet. I want to go home." Julie starts to sob once more, her chains rattle as she struggles against them.

Despair and anguish are all I feel, along with deep sadness.

I look down at my own body and feel immediate shame. I can't believe I'm doing this. Even after a few days, I think this has to be a bad dream. A nightmare I'm about to wake up from.

I'm so lost in my own head that I barely notice Julie breaking out of line and running toward the door.

"No!" I yell after her, but it's already too late.

"Where the fuck do you think you're going?" The man closest to the door snatches her by the hair and pulls her back viciously. He slams her body to the floor violently, like a rag doll, and it takes every ounce of self-restraint I have not to rush to her aide. If I struggle or try and save her, I'll be risking my own life. *Is it worth it?* The smart thing to do is turn the other cheek, ignore what is taking place even though it's right in front of me. That's not me... to turn and look the other way when someone else is in trouble, but what more can I do?

The other two men in the room laugh, the sound making my stomach churn. The poor girl is pulled from the floor by her hair while a man twice her size rears his fist back and punches her in the stomach.

No! I scream inside my head, desperate to help her, but too afraid to move.

She doubles over, practically folding in half, and cries out in pain before spitting blood all over the guy's shirt.

"Fucking shit! Rick, how many times do we need to tell you not to damage the girls on auction day?" A guy with dark hair and menacing eyes, who seems to be in charge, questions with disgust as he walks into the room and inspects Julie.

She continues spitting up blood while hunched over, her slender arms wrapped around her middle like she's trying to hold herself together. All I want to do is go over there and wrap my arms around her, but I'm rooted in place, knowing the consequences will be grave if I do.

She doesn't deserve this. None of us do.

"I can't sell her like this. Take her back to one of the cells. If she's still alive come the next auction, we can sell her then, but the difference is coming out of your paycheck, idiot."

He dismisses her like she is worth less than the dirt beneath our feet.

Tears prick at my eyes, but I refuse to let them fall. The Rick guy grabs her by the arm, his thick fingers dig into her skin, and she cries out. He starts to drag her away, and my throat tightens when her eyes meet mine.

Fear and just overall sadness reflect back at me. I knew she was scared, knew she wanted to go home, but all she had to do was make it through tonight. Then she could've made a run for it and escaped. Now, I feel she'll never escape, and that leaves my heart bleeding.

I'm dragged from my dreadful thoughts when a man's voice comes over the speakers announcing the start of the event.

"Gentlemen, can I have your attention, please. Our auction will begin momentarily. Tonight, we only have four girls for sale, but believe me, it's quality over quantity. Enjoy, and may the highest bidder win."

The sound vibrates through me, and the words hit their mark

dead on. It's now my turn to start shaking, the fear almost overwhelming me.

Four men walk into the little room we're in a second later. They gawk at us, slimy smiles on their faces, and you can basically see the wheels turning in their heads. If given the chance, they would take from us right now. Without blinking their eyes or caring. Each one takes a girl. The guy I get walks over to me and grabs the chain connecting my collar with my hands, tugging me forward and off-balance.

"You're lucky you're a virgin because if you weren't..." He licks his lips and drags his gaze down my body. When he speaks next, he's leaning into my face while I lean back, trying to put as much distance as I can between us. "I would have fucked you good before sending you off." His rancid breath fans against my cheek, and I have to stop myself from puking, swallowing the bile in my throat.

The darkness in his beady eyes tells me he isn't lying, and the pressure of the collar on my neck becomes tighter as I try to escape him.

"A little fucking slut, that's all you are. A fuck toy." He tugs me out of the room. In that singular moment, I question if I can do this without losing myself. I know I'm strong, but how strong do I have to be to survive this? If I ever do escape this mess, will I be the same person I was before?

I already know the answer is no. Whatever is going to happen, I don't think I will ever be the same. I will never again be the college student whose biggest concern is her grades. I will never be the careless daughter who gets annoyed by her mother calling twice in one day. And I will never be the little sister who is jealous of her sibling getting to travel the world.

Yes, I know I will never be me again. The real question is, who will I be after this?

That question lingers in my mind as I'm led out onto a stage like a dog. The shining bright lights above make it hard to see anything, but I can hear the hollers and catcalls nearby. Feel eyes on every inch of my exposed skin. My lips start to tremble, and I squint against the harsh glare of the lights, looking for an escape, a way out.

There is none.

As my eyes adjust to the brightness, I scan the crowd, over the men eager to get their pound of flesh. In the midst of all the chaos around me, my gaze clashes with that of a man across the room. The world stops. My lungs expand, and a different kind of fear grabs onto me. Its claws sink deep into my skin.

He's a man with eyes as dark as the night, and a soul that's just as dark.

2

MARKUS

A ghost. That's what I see when I spot her on the auction block. The spitting image of a girl I once knew, once loved. The air expels from my chest, and I almost drop the drink I'm holding in my hand. The voices and movements around me become silent.

Hair the color of spun gold, and even from a distance, I can see the color of her eyes, ocean blue, just like... *Victoria.*

I suck in a breath, noticing how uneven it is. I haven't let myself think her name in so long. I've tried everything to keep those memories buried. To keep her buried. Not that I want to forget her but thinking about her is simply too painful. The guilt is overwhelming.

I look at the girl again. She looks to be barely legal, more proof that it isn't her. The question still remains: why does she look so much like her?

The crowd of men congregates around the stage as the girls are each put up on a little pedestal. The space fills with whistles and loud hollers while rage seeps slowly into my veins. These events aren't my kind of thing, and generally, I ignore the women on stage, not caring how they got here or what's going to happen to them. It's easier that way. Not to think about them as people. I know it's fucked up, but it's the world we live in.

Unfortunately, I can't bring myself to do that today. I can't ignore the woman who looks so much like my past. I can't let anyone touch her or have her.

She has to be mine, no matter the cost.

The four girls on stage look wide-eyed and shocked, their bodies shaking, and the chains around them rattling with every move they make. There are collars around each of their necks, and a chain hangs down that's connected to their hands.

My eyes are glued to the Victoria lookalike. She is the only one not crying, even though she is clearly scared shitless. I can see her knees knocking together from across the room.

The host starts talking, introducing the blue-eyed beauty I'm about to buy. "First up is this long-legged blonde, her name is Fallon, but of course you can name her whatever you want. She is untrained but well worth the money since she is untouched."

Fallon... I whisper to myself, trying out the name. It feels foreign on my tongue, but that doesn't stop my desire for this woman from growing even stronger.

"We'll start the bidding at ten thousand."

Shit! I didn't plan on bidding. *Where is my fucking ticket?* Frantically, I search every one of my pockets until I find the folded-up paper with my number on it.

In the time it takes me to find my ticket, three people have already put in their bids. Unfolding my damn piece of paper, I lift it up in the air, waving it like a white flag of defeat. The auctioneer looks up and points to me. "Forty thousand."

"Fifty!" One of the men up front yells.

I take a few steps closer to the stage before making my next bid. "One hundred thousand."

She's it, the one I want. It's been years since I've been with a woman, but if I were to ever find someone, to touch, to be with again, it would be her.

"What really happened?" Julian insists, refusing to accept her lie.

She shakes her head, her eyes bouncing between Julian and me.

"We will discuss this further," Julian finally turns his attention back to me.

"There's nothing to talk about. I'm taking some time off. Lucca is more than capable of stepping up." It's true. Lucca is one of our best men and has been handling way more shit lately. He will do just fine.

Julian looks like he wants to strangle me, but with Elena latching onto his arm, I know he can't deal with me right now. It's the perfect combination, really.

"Call the car for me," he orders. I give him a slight nod and pull out my phone.

Julian turns his full attention to the small, barely dressed Elena next to him. She never lets go of him as they walk away, heading toward the exit.

After I call for the car, and we part ways, I make my way to pay and pick up my prize. I'm unsure how to feel. Part of me is worried by the pull I feel toward the girl, while the other part of me is frenzied with need. I have to have her.

The payment process goes through quickly. As soon as the money transfer is approved, I'm being led back to my purchase.

The door opens, and I hear a strangled scream echoing down the hallway. It's the kind of sound someone makes when they are hurt and trying not to scream, but the pain is too much to bear, and their instincts take over.

All I can think is... if that person wants to live, they better not be touching what's mine.

I grit my teeth so hard my jaw quakes. Speed walking down the hall, I turn the corner into the open space behind the stage. Something overtakes me, and my blood freezes in my veins when I spot Fallon on the ground.

A man twice her size looms above her, digging his knee into her chest.

His hands are fumbling to unlock the chains around her wrists while she struggles to push him off. I can see her tiny nails sinking into his flesh with vengeance.

She's a fighter.

Swinging back his arm, he hits her across the face, backhanding her into the concrete. It's then that I completely see red. I cross the room in a flash, wrapping my arm around his throat. I put him in a chokehold, then use my other hand to twist his head sharply. I don't think, I simply react. The crack of his neck fills the room with deafening silence, and his body goes slack in my hold almost immediately.

I don't feel remorse, pain, guilt. Nothing.

Pushing his body to the side, he falls onto the ground next to Fallon. His face is tilted to the side, and his mouth is open, a look of terror stuck permanently on his face. I drag my attention away from him and back to her.

She sucks in a shaky breath, her chest moving rapidly as she struggles to get air into her lungs. Her eyes are wide, and some small veins inside have ruptured, making the white part blood red.

Staggering above her, my chest heaves as war rages inside of me. I want to bring that fucker back to life and kill him again, this time a little slower. I've never felt this way before, never felt this possessive need.

"What the fuck?" Louis, the guy who escorted me backstage, yells.

Turning on my feet, I glare at him. My fists are clenched, and I'll kill him too if I have to.

"Yeah, what the fuck? I already paid for her, and I paid for what I saw on stage! If I wanted someone beat up and broken, I would have found a girl on the nearest street corner. Is that how you do business here?"

His face pales. "What? No, not normally, but I mean, you didn't have to fucking kill him. We could have just knocked some of the price off or something..."

Or something? This guy must think I'm a fucking idiot.

"Fuck you," I spit. "Would you rather I tell everyone else how you fuck people over and deliver damaged goods as soon as you receive payment?"

"No, no, we're good. Just take her. I'll deal with this mess." He gestures to the dead fuck lying on the floor.

"Damn straight, you will." I dismiss him altogether before turning my attention back to the woman on the floor. "Give me the key for those. I'll keep her chained up for now."

He steps around me and kneels down next to the guy with the broken neck. He pries a set of keys from his hands and tosses them to me.

Leaning down, I undo the chain on the front. I try not to let my eyes linger on her exposed skin. Her barely-there dress, which looks like lingerie, has been pushed to the side, causing her nipples to peek out, and my dick is already at war with my zipper. Better to look away as much as I can so I don't lose control and fuck her in the back of my car, not that it would matter if I did.

She doesn't struggle while I move her restraints around. Of course, I don't have my knee pressed into her chest, either.

Rolling her over slowly, I pull her arms back and re-hook the chain to the collar, so her hands are tied behind her back. Her dress is pulled up in the back as well, exposing her perfectly shaped ass. I want to rip my shirt off and tug it down her body so no one else can see her.

No one else should be looking at what's mine.

But I don't have time for that. I need to get her out of here as quickly as possible. I shove the small key into my pocket for safe-keeping before I grab her and lift her up with me.

Hauling her off the floor, I throw her over my shoulder like a sack of potatoes. Louis gives me one more disapproving look about killing his friend but doesn't dare open his yap. He knows I'm right. He shouldn't have touched her.

Knowing Fallon's ass and pussy are on full display the way I'm carrying her, I quickly make my way out of the building. Thankfully, without many people seeing her or any further mishaps. I use the side door that leads straight to the parking lot. Cold air wisps around us, making her shiver in my hold.

Grabbing the car keys from my pocket, I hit the key fob to unlock the car, and pull open the door with my free hand. I hate how light she feels and how she doesn't even struggle or say anything. It's almost as if she has accepted her fate.

Where is the fighter I saw just moments ago? I'm sure she is in there somewhere, ready to come out at any given moment. Placing her in the backseat, I lay her down, facing the trunk. I stare at her for a moment. She looks so fragile, a piece of glass that might break with the slightest movement. I shouldn't have bought her, but I had to.

"If you try anything stupid, I'll gag you and put you in the trunk. Stay like this, and don't move unless I instruct you to," I order, my voice a little harsher than necessary.

"Okay." She nods, her voice hoarse from screaming.

I give her one final once over. I know her face is already swelling, and I bet she'll have a killer headache from her head bouncing against the concrete. I'll have to give her something for the pain later.

Climbing into the driver's seat, I start the car, wondering where the hell I'm going to take her. For a moment, I just sit there, weighing my options. If I take her to my place, I have to keep her chained up because there isn't a secure room to put her in.

Fuck, the thought of keeping her tied to my bed to use whenever I want makes my cock harder than steel. I know I'm a sick fucker, but I didn't even know that part of myself existed until this very moment. I've killed people without batting an eye, tortured men until they told me whatever I wanted to hear, but I've never taken a woman against her will.

I've never bought someone or owned someone like I'm going to own this woman. And that thought excites me more than I'm willing to admit.

I wouldn't be that cruel to keep her chained up. Especially since I plan on keeping her long term, and in order to do that, trust is going to have to be built. I want her to want me the same way I want her, and that won't happen if I keep her chained up like an animal.

I think a little while longer, considering my options. Julian has a few safe houses. One is a cabin up in the mountains, secluded and away from the rest of the world. If she escapes me, which I doubt she will, all that surrounds us is nature. There won't be anyone coming to her rescue, not out there.

Choosing the cabin in the mountains, I put the car in drive and head out to the highway.

It will be perfect not only for its secluded location but especially since I know it has a cell in the basement.

"What's your name?" I ask after we've been driving for a few minutes.

"Fallon," she whispers, almost inaudible.

"I already know that. What's your last name?"

I need to make sure she's not related to Victoria before I let this go any further.

"Brice," she says hesitantly.

Brice... I tap my fingers against the steering wheel. I've never heard of anyone by that last name before, but I'll still have someone look into her when we get to the safe house. I have to be sure. I know just the person to do that.

Although, I'm sure my brother will not be happy that I'm contacting him for a favor.

I think further on questions I should ask her like this is a fucking date, and I didn't just pay one million dollars for her body.

"Where are you from, Fallon?"

"Sun Valley." She doesn't offer any more than the bare minimum.

"Have you always lived there?"

"Yes." A second passes, and then she asks the question that dooms both of us. "What are you going to do to me?"

Gripping the steering wheel a little tighter, I grit my teeth and answer her truthfully.

"I don't know yet."

I just don't fucking know...

3

FALLON

Fear zips through me and down my spine with the intensity of a lightning bolt.

"I don't know yet." That singular statement sets me off and straight into a full-blown panic attack.

He doesn't know what he's going to do to me? It doesn't matter that he saved me from that man back there. He doomed me to a much worse fate when he bid on me and won.

With my eyes squeezed shut, I try to focus on my breathing. It's much harder than one would think, though, given my circumstances.

As I lie here in the backseat, every bump we drive over pushes my face further into the seat. My arms throb, and my cheek hurts as it rubs against the leather.

I think about my situation. I don't have to know this man to know he is bad. I can feel it. The darkness rushes off of him in waves, leaving everything in ruins when it's gone. That's the aura he gives off, and the way he looked at me before pulling me off the ground and away from that man. A man he killed with his bare hands without blinking or showing a shred of remorse, I shiver at the reminder. Sure, I would've wanted that sick bastard of a man to die anyway, but the way he did it without a care, like he was tying his shoes. It told me everything I needed to know about him.

I won't lie. For a moment, I felt there might be some good in him. The way he looked at me when I was struggling to breathe. It was almost as if he had a heart, like he was more than what everyone around him saw.

There was a sliver of compassion in his gaze for me, concern... or so I thought.

Then he opened his mouth and voiced that his only concern was for his purchase not to be damaged. I realized quickly that I was his property, nothing more, and I needed to keep that fact in mind. He wasn't saving me, and he didn't buy me just to let me go. He was going to use me, hurt me, and there was nothing I could do about it.

After what seems like an eternity, we turn onto what has to be a dirt road. The car shakes as the tires move over the uneven gravel. The restraints dig into my skin, especially around my neck, and I can't stifle a groan much longer.

When we finally come to a stop, I'm almost certain some of my skin must be bleeding, or at least it feels like it.

My captor gets out of the car and opens the back door, reaching inside to pull me out. He is not any gentler than he was when he put me in the car, and I have to bite the inside of my cheek to stop myself from crying out in pain.

My limbs are stiff and sore, my wrists are rubbed raw, and my cheek throbs, pulsing with pain as if it has its own heartbeat from that guy hitting me.

He throws me over his shoulder like I'm a sack of potatoes and carries me into the house. It's probably of no use for me to look around, to take in the location I'm at, but the part of me that wants to escape him, run away and be free tells me to, so I do.

Lifting my head, I take in my surroundings as much as I can.

Trees. All I see are trees, no matter what direction I look. I have no idea where we are, but clearly, it's somewhere secluded. Mountains are a short way off in the distance, the setting sun making it hard for me to make out all that is around me.

Stopping on the porch, he fumbles with the key. The door creaks open a second later, and then he walks inside the house. The light flicks on, illuminating the area. Even though the brightness hurts my eyes, I open them. I need to see where he's taking me even if there isn't any way to stop it.

Craning my head back as far as I can, I scan the area.

We've entered the living room. To my right are two large couches angled in front of a fireplace. My head moves on a swivel as I dart to look left and find a modern looking kitchen with a dining area attached.

Everything is clean and decorated nicely with a rustic flair that reminds me of the inside of a cabin. Maybe that's what this is. I didn't get a chance to see much of the outside of the house with it being dark and all. A secluded cabin on the side of a mountain makes sense.

I tuck my head against his back as he takes me up a set of stairs, his feet slapping against the wood. It feels like I'm being carried to my funeral because, in a matter of minutes, a part of me is going to die.

He is going to rape me. Which is scary for more than one reason.

The auctioneer announced I was a virgin, which I'm not. It hits me then, paralyzing fear.

What if he realizes that and gets angry? It's not my fault the guy who kidnapped me lied, but I'm the only one here, the only one he can let his anger out on.

He drops me unceremoniously onto the bed.

I land on my side and bounce against the soft mattress. I can't even enjoy the softness beneath my body because all I feel is pain. He rolls me over onto my stomach, and I hear him rustling with the key. A moment later, he undoes the chain holding my wrists back. Relieved, I drop my arms down to my sides and let out a soft sigh. "Here is what's going to happen, Fallon. I'm going to undo the cuffs and the collar around your neck so you can take a shower. If you do anything stupid, I will hurt you. Really hurt you. Not like what that guy did back there, but worse. There is a cold and empty cell in the basement, and I don't mind putting your nametag on that door. Got it?"

"Got it." I nod my head yes, savoring the softness of the sheet rubbing against my cheek.

He uncuffs me like promised. Then takes the collar off. I want to rub my skin where the leather and metal used to be, but I force my hands to remain at my sides.

"Get up," he orders gruffly.

My movements are labored and sluggish, but I manage to stand and turn around slowly. As soon as I do, I wish I hadn't. He's standing so close; I can feel the heat of his body like flames licking against my skin. He's tall, so tall that I have to tilt my head up and back to see his face. His own amber-colored eyes scan my face, almost like he is studying me, analyzing every inch of it.

"What's your name?" I ask quietly.

He doesn't say anything for a long time, just stares at me. When I'm certain he isn't going to answer me at all, he finally says, "Markus."

All I can do is nod. I don't know what else I can ask or say. I don't have to ask the most obvious questions. *What do you want with me? Will you let me go? Why me?*

I'm not stupid. I can answer those myself.

He wants me for sex. He will not let me go. And he chose me because, from the four girls on that stage, I was the most appealing to him.

"Go take a shower," he points toward an open door on the other side of the room, "leave the door open, and come out naked when you're done."

I swallow down the lump in my throat and give him another

small nod before I scurry away and into the bathroom. I almost close the door out of habit but stop myself when my fingers touch the smooth wood. I don't look back to see if he's watching me, not when I can feel his eyes on me.

Moving out of view, I turn the shower on. While I wait for the water to turn warm, I take in my surroundings. Just like what I've seen so far of the house, it's nice, but nothing fancy. I suppose I expected a man who drops a million dollars in one night to live in a mansion or at least a lavish house.

Which leads me to wonder if this is even his place or someone else's?

Not knowing what he plans to do with me worries me more than anything. Part of me expected him to screw me in the back of his car. I was shocked when he did nothing of the sort.

When steam starts to fill the room, I step into the shower. Sighing loudly, I forget about Markus, and where I am. I practically melt beneath the spray of the water and take my time washing every inch of my body, trying to get the stink of the auction out of my skin. I wish the soap could wash away the memory of the last couple of days.

I'm a little surprised when after a few minutes, he doesn't come in to check on me. Then again, where would I escape to anyway?

I finish up my shower and turn off the water. I shiver when my feet make contact with the cold tile and quickly grab a fluffy towel that's neatly folded on the rack above the toilet. The cotton towel feels like a luxury as I dry myself and wrap the towel around my shivering body. My gaze catches on my reflection in the mirror, and I barely hold back a gasp.

I've been through the wringer, yes, but I didn't think I looked this bad. There are ugly red marks on my throat from the collar and blue handprints around my neck. My cheek doesn't look much better, swollen, black, and blue. A vein must have popped in my right eye since the white is mostly blood red now. I already don't look like myself, and I'm sure by the time I leave here, I'll be a completely different person. *If I ever leave.*

Blinking away the tears that have formed in my eyes at my own reflection, I force a ragged breath into my lungs—no more tears. Pulling myself together, I walk toward the door.

My steps falter, and I stop in the doorway and find Markus sitting on the edge of the bed. He looks to be lost in thought, probably trying to decide his next move. Looking up from the floor, his gaze collides with mine. It's intense and all-consuming. The kind of stare that makes you weak in the knees and has you making stupid choices.

Annoyance pinches his brows. "Do you not know how to listen? I said to come out here naked. Does that look naked?" His tone is mocking as he points at my towel-covered body.

Rugged is easily the best way I could describe this man. Dark, disheveled hair and light stubble shadows his angular jaw. He's definitely handsome, but more in a, I'll kill you after our date way. I don't want to cross him, that's for sure.

"I'm sorry, I was cold." I drop the towel, and his eyes do a quick once over, stopping on my face and lingering there. I'm not shy about my body, and unbeknownst to him, I'm not that inexperienced either. I've been with a couple of guys, though it's been a while for me.

"Come here," he commands, and my feet move on their own. I stop right in front of him, but apparently, that's not close enough. "Closer."

He spreads his legs and motions for me to step in between them. Stepping forward, my knees hit the edge of the bed. It feels like a trap, one I've just walked right into it. Lifting a hand, he ghosts his fingertips over my stomach, leaving a trail of goosebumps in his wake.

Those same hands travel up to cup each of my breasts, and I'm ashamed when he grazes his thumb over my hard nipple, and I feel a spark of pleasure in my belly. I blame it on nature. My hormones or body don't understand what kind of man he is; my body is merely reacting to a handsome man touching my naked skin.

"Turn around," he orders.

I slowly spin around, letting him inspect every inch of my body, knowing that's exactly what he is doing. After all, he paid for me, so why shouldn't he? His fingers move shamelessly over my most private parts like he owns them, and I guess in his mind, he does.

"You are beautiful," he murmurs. "I'm going to enjoy you very much."

His words make me shiver. I know sex is a part of this. Probably the most prominent part to him and realize he will take it whether I want him to or not, but I'm not ready. Then again, I guess no one can prepare themselves to be raped.

"But not right now. Put these clothes on," he adds.

For a moment, I think he is joking, but when I turn back around to face him, I find a pair of owl-print pajamas laid out on the bed beside him.

Regardless of this being a trick or not, I don't want to disobey again.

Something tells me that Markus's patience is not to be tested. Moving to the side, I lean over and grab the clothes off the bed. Curiosity has me wondering if he usually has women's clothes lying around. Everything about him and this place is off-putting.

Maybe he brings women up here all the time? My thoughts twist, and soon I'm wondering what he does with the others? If there are even others? Does he sell them? Kill them? Oh god, I'm going down a hole I cannot come back from.

I slip into the cotton pj's quickly, and for the moment, they make me feel normal again, even though I know for certain all of this is as far from normal as it gets.

Markus pushes off the bed, and the room seems to shrink with his stature. Unconsciously, I take a tiny step back.

"Take the pill and drink at least half of that glass of water." He points to the nightstand, where I find both. He reminds me of a caveman more and more, ordering and pointing, expecting me to listen to him without question.

"What is—"

"Do it," he says more sternly this time, his gaze slicing me down the middle.

As badly as I don't want to take the pill, I know there is no way around this. It's the pill or something far worse, and I'm not ready to go down that path. I'll have to pick my battles, and this one isn't worth fighting over.

Defeated, I pick up the white oval pill and place it against my tongue and swallow it down with nearly the entire glass of water. Markus watches me, a look of satisfaction appearing on his face.

"Now, get on the bed on your knees, and put your hands behind your back."

I hesitate for a few seconds, but the deep growl rumbling in his chest has my legs moving a second later. I climb on the bed and crawl across it, coming to rest on my knees like he instructed with my hands behind my back. The position is uncomfortable and will make for restless sleeping, but again it's this or... I think back to what he said in the car—a dark, cold cell.

The air shifts with every move Markus makes, and I think I could feel him behind me even if I couldn't hear his footsteps approaching. I dare to sneak a peek over my shoulder and find he is holding a rope instead of the chains. That makes me feel a little better.

It might not be comfortable having my hands tied behind my back all night, but it will certainly be better with the rope than metal cuffs, a collar, and chains.

"Eyes to the front," he barks when he notices I'm watching, and my head snaps back like my body is already used to being ordered around.

He wraps the rope around my wrists a few times, looping it in between, and then he tightens it somehow. The rope digs into my already tender flesh, but I bite my tongue to prevent the groan from escaping. This is not the time to complain.

I need to be smart about this. I need to make sure I don't anger or annoy him. And most importantly, I need to earn his trust. That's my only chance of getting out of here.

He latches onto my upper arms from behind and lowers me to the mattress, so my head is on the pillow, and I'm lying on my side.

A moment later, the light turns off, and the room descends into complete darkness. Panic seizes me the second the space goes dark. My eyes are wide open, but I can't see a thing. In a flash, I'm back in that cell... alone, and cold, so fucking cold. My heart races as I hear Markus move around the room. Somehow, his presence is the only thing keeping me from going off the cliff and diving headfirst into a panic attack.

The bed dips, and I can feel him climbing into bed, lying down in the spot next to me.

Our bodies aren't touching, but I can still feel him, his body heat radiating toward me. I can smell the thick manly scent of his cologne and hear the even rhythm of his breathing.

I'm not alone. I'm not in the cell. I keep telling myself until I'm calm again. Ironically, I'm not much safer now, but somehow it feels safer. I guess after being isolated and alone, even the company of a criminal is better than nothing.

Wiggling my body a few inches, I try to get comfortable enough to go to sleep, but the movement only makes it worse. *I wonder if he would consider restraining me in a different way?*

"Is there any way you could loosen the rope?" I ask before I can stop myself.

"No," he answers gruffly.

A moment of silence passes between us, and another million-dollar question is burning on the edge of my tongue. Like the idiot I am, I ask, "Don't you want... you know, to have sex?"

He sighs, almost as if he's annoyed by my presence, which makes no sense to me. He bought me to have me here, and yet he is annoyed that I'm speaking or even alive, it seems.

"Not tonight, but don't worry, soon you'll be on your back, begging and pleading for me to stop. Now, if you're smart, you'll shut up and go to sleep."

I don't ask any more dumb questions after that. My eyes drift closed, and I force myself to go to sleep. I'm tired, exhausted as hell. Problem is, I'm too damn uncomfortable and scared to even think about sleeping.

Minutes pass slowly, and I'm about to beg him to untie me, anything to ease the ache in my shoulders, but I don't.

That thought is slowly being washed away and replaced by a warm fuzzy feeling spreading through my veins. The pain in my limbs eases, slowly seeping out like venom until it's completely gone. Weightless like a cloud, I think my body might float away into the night sky. Only for a brief moment do I realize I shouldn't be feeling this way.

I should be scared and in pain, but I'm none of those things.

"What did you give me?" I mumble, but I'm not sure if the words actually come out right.

"Go to sleep," he growls, without an explanation. And this time, I do.

4

MARKUS

The sun peeks through the curtains, and for a long moment, I simply lie there. It's been so long since I allowed myself the pleasure of sleeping next to another person. Not in a sexual way, but in the physical sense of being next to someone. In fact, I hardly ever sleep, and yet I did just that last night. For the first time in years, I fell asleep and didn't wake from a nightmare.

I'm not sure why, but I would pin it on having everything to do with the petite woman lying beside me. Gently, I roll over, paying careful attention to my movements. I don't want her to wake yet, as I still need to call and hear what my brother has found out.

With ease, I lift my head from my pillow and let my gaze roam over her body. I felt a slight flicker of guilt over giving her the pill last night, but I wasn't sure I could handle her fighting me. Plus, her head and arms must have been aching, and I know the pill took all of that away, giving her a moment of reprieve.

The pajamas she's wearing might hide her body well, but I know what is concealed beneath already, and I cannot unsee it. Carnal need hits me like a bull directly in the groin.

A strand of her spun gold hair tickles my skin. I'm unsure why, but I lean into her, wanting to bury my nose in her hair. Inhale her scent. It's wrong. She isn't of grave importance to me, and there is no way Fallon is *her*, but I still want to breathe her in. Even if it's just pretend.

My nostrils flare as I inhale deeply. Just as I had assumed. She smells clean, like soap and something else. A faint scent of lavender catches in my nose, and I inhale her a little deeper, wanting to taste her on my tongue and feel her wiggle beneath my body.

Fuck. I chalk it up to being forever since I've gotten laid, and that's why I'm so drawn to her, and she looks just like *her*—a spitting image. I remind myself instantly that she isn't Victoria. She is dead, gone, and all because of me.

Easing away from Fallon and forcing distance between us, I shift off the bed, and it creaks beneath my weight. Grabbing my phone from the nightstand, I cast one last glance over my shoulder before walking out of the room. Quietly, I close the door behind me.

There isn't anywhere she can go, not while she's tied up in my bed. Heading into the kitchen, I make my morning coffee. The house remains stocked at all times, the pantry full, and the house ready to live in with little notice in case there is ever a need to come here right away.

That's what made it the perfect location to come to, well that, and it's secluded and away from wandering eyes and ears.

I'm still not sure what I'm going to do with her. Complete control is something I shouldn't be given access to. The thought makes me insane. I want her to be submissive, begging, and pleading for me.

Before I can sink down that rabbit hole, I tug my phone from my pocket and call Felix. I only sent him an email last night, so I'm not sure if he'll have even looked into her yet. Or if he is going to do this for me at all. We didn't separate on good terms, and it's been a while since we've seen each other. I wouldn't be surprised if he doesn't answer the phone either.

He picks up on the second ring. "Markus, my long-lost brother. I'll be damned."

"Felix, how have you been?" I ask, trying to keep the conversation casual, though we both know this is anything but a casual call.

"Sipping on Pina Coladas in Tahiti. How have you been?" Surprisingly, his question seems genuine, as if he really wants to know if I've been doing well.

"Same, pretty much."

"I'm sure." He chuckles.

"Look, I'm sorry I haven't called in a month, and now I'm asking for a favor out of the blue, but I really need to know."

"I saw her picture," is all he says, and I know he understands.

"Everything checked out. She is who she says she is. Fallon Brice, nineteen, born and raised in Sun Valley to small-time politician Paul Brice and his wife Marlene Brice, maiden name Brown. Two daughters. No other relatives. There is no connection, Markus. At least not on the surface. I can dig deeper—"

"No, it's fine." I feel both relief and anger. She has no connection to Victoria. It's simply a fluke of nature. Or maybe it's the universe taunting me. Probably the latter, I deserve this; after all I've done, I'm sure this is her memory haunting me.

"So, Fallon has a sister?"

"Yes, Amelie Brice, twenty-one, is currently studying abroad."

"Okay. One last thing. What do you mean, small-time politician?" I don't need someone with connections coming after me.

"Used to be Mayor of his town back in the day when his daughters were younger, but some drug scandal made him resign. He owns a little convenience store now. Fallon worked at the store until recently, then she left for college. Her roommate reported her missing two days ago."

At least her roommate cares enough to notice she is missing. It doesn't matter, though. They won't find her, not hiding here.

"Good, thank you. I mean it."

"I guess I'll wait for you to call next time you need something." He sounds a little snide, which I deserve. I've been ignoring his phone calls, and now I'm the one that reached out needing a favor.

"Why don't we meet up soon? I wouldn't mind seeing your ugly face." As soon as the words are out, I regret saying them, and not because I don't mean them.

If I meet up with my brother, I will have to either take Fallon with me or leave her somewhere alone. Neither would be a good idea.

"Yeah, let's meet up. I'll call you when I'm back in the US."

"Sounds good. Thanks again, talk soon," I tell him and hang up the phone.

Knowing everything checks out as she says means she didn't lie to me. It also means she has no connection to Victoria. Still, every time I look at her, that's exactly who I see.

Her smiling face. Her sparkling blue eyes. I can almost hear her soft laugh like a breeze blowing through the trees. She was mine for an instant, and then the very life I live now took her away from me.

Damnit! I slam my fist angrily onto the counter. Pain lances up my arm, but it's nothing compared to the pain I feel in my chest at the reminder of her memory.

The feelings I am experiencing are out of control. I've never done something this insane. I always think things through and never show my emotions because if you do that, you might as well be giving your entire game away. Emotions mean you have something worthy of caring for, something that someone can take from you, and that's what I've gone and done.

I've bought something, someone technically, and now I'm like a goddamn lion guarding his prey so no one else can have her.

Indecision weighs heavy on my mind as I drink my black coffee and prepare some breakfast for Fallon. I still don't have the first fucking clue what I am going to do with her. I just know I can't let her go. I want her too much. Want to possess her, touch her, own her. I've never wanted a woman like I want her, and not understanding the reason behind it is driving me insane.

Going through the pantry, I find some oatmeal. I cook it and place it at the breakfast nook with a glass of orange juice. I'm not anywhere close to being domesticated, but I can cook a fucking meal.

I walk back upstairs and into the bedroom and stand at the foot of the bed, staring at her, watching as she sleeps peacefully, knowing that I'm going to disturb that.

I'm going to take everything in her life from her. Whatever she had in the past is gone. Now, I'm her past, present, and future.

She is my property, and though she may not be Victoria, she brings all those feelings I thought were gone, that I never thought I would experience again back to life, and part of me is angry at her for that.

I know it's completely irrational. Borderline insane, but I want to punish her for it all the same. Inflict pain because that's what she's doing to me, even if it's unintentional. It's not her fault she looks like her, but I don't care. Someone needs to pay.

Having waited long enough, I pad over to the side of the bed and give her a shake. Her skin is cool to the touch, almost as if she's cold. When she doesn't wake right away, I shake her again, this time a little harder.

With a startled gasp, her lips part, and her eyes flutter open. Confusion hits her first, followed by fear. It's prominent in her features, and her blue eyes bleed into mine as the memories of yesterday return. There's a wealth of secrets in those deep blues, and I'm going to sink into them and expose them all.

It takes a moment for recognition to appear, and then she

seems to release a breath, sucking in another, her chest rising and plunging as if she is trying to calm herself.

"I'm sorry, I forgot where I was," she croaks, her voice full of sleep. I try and make myself not care that she is frightened but I can't, so the second best thing is to shut my emotions down altogether.

"I'm going to untie you, lead you to the bathroom, and then we're going to go into the kitchen so you can eat your breakfast. Remember my warning from last night?" I narrow my gaze, noticing the light dusting of freckles across the bridge of her nose.

I wasn't lying last night when I told her she was beautiful. Even bruised and scared, she looks like an angel. A heart-shaped face, full lips, and blue eyes that could make any man weak in the knees. She's young too; there is still an innocence about her, which only adds to the appeal.

I shouldn't allow myself to wonder how she ended up at the auction in the first place, but I do. They usually kidnap girls for those things from vacation spots or clubs. Wherever they can find young girls that won't be missed right away.

Innocent and naive. They can get them to do anything they want. College is not their norm. My guess is she was at the wrong place at the wrong time.

"Yes, I remember," she finally answers quietly.

I'm apprehensive in believing her but want to test her and see what she does. Untying her from the bed, I do my best not to brush against her skin. The warmth of her body calls to me already, and god knows I'm fucking attracted to her. I haven't had sex in forever, so it wouldn't take much for me to snap at this point.

I don't fully believe her submissive nature. Even now, the way she is acting is odd, I just woke her up, and instead of screaming and begging for me to let her go, she says she forgot where she was? It's strange and not typical of a captor, captive situation. Something is off about her.

With her arms released, she stretches them above her head, most likely trying to get the blood pumping back into them.

"Bathroom," I growl, pointing toward it.

She nods and shoves to her feet faster than necessary.

I can see her falling before she does, and I catch her around the waist, seconds before she is about to hit the floor and tuck her into my chest. The drugs I gave her last night might have left her feeling a little woozy this morning, but that doesn't stop me from lashing out at her.

"Are you trying to kill yourself?" The words come out as a deep rumble from my chest as I peer down at her. I'm a good foot taller than she is, forcing her to crane her neck back to look up at me. I won't deny her tiny little body pressed against my bare chest is probably the best thing I've felt in forever. It's almost like she was made to fit there perfectly.

"No... I'm sorry. I'm just unsteady on my feet," she replies but doesn't make a move to push me away. Either she's stupid or unaware of the danger she is in.

I could kill her with the snap of my fingers, which I've already proven. Subdue her with no effort and take what I want, and yet she stands here molded to my body, unwavering, without a plea falling from her lips.

My cock hardens in my low hanging sweatpants, and I know if I don't push her away, I'll end up fucking her right here and now. As tempting as that is, I'm wary about the way she is acting. It would be stupid of me to give into my most primal needs with her without seeing the full picture. Grabbing her by the arms, I give her a light shove, putting distance between our bodies. Distance is good and exactly what I need. It lessens her stupid intoxicating scent from entering my nose. It removes her soft little body from molding into the harsh pieces of my own.

I don't want to be her missing puzzle piece or her savior. I want to own her, want her complete submission. I want her to be mine and understand the extent I'm willing to go to keep it that way.

"Good, because you're no use to be if you're dead," I hiss.

Her big eyes grow a little rounder, but she doesn't seem bothered by my brashness. That's got to change. I need her afraid and not so accepting of her fate.

"Go to the restroom before I change my mind and tie you back to the bed for the rest of the day." I shoo her away. Hesitantly, she walks away and into the adjacent bathroom.

She doesn't even attempt to close the door behind her. In fact, she hasn't tried to escape or begged me to let her go. She hasn't even asked to call her parents or roommate to let them know she is okay.

Every order I give her, she obeys, and there is something wrong with that.

She shouldn't obey me.

She shouldn't blindly accept her fate, but that's how she is acting.

The flushing of the toilet and the running of the faucet drag me from my thoughts and back to the present.

Walking into the room, she stops before me and peers up at me like I'm her master. That's not really something she should want me to become. I can promise her that.

"Kitchen," I say gruffly, irritated that I've repeated myself when I already laid out the plans for her. In fact, I'm irritated in general.

Angrily, I trudge out of the bedroom, down the hall, and into the kitchen that opens into the living room with her on my heels.

When we reach the kitchen, I point to the chair and take the spot directly across from her. Pulling the chair out, she sits and stares down into her bowl of oatmeal for a moment before grabbing the spoon. She eats without question or complaint, even though I am certain the food is cold by now.

"I have questions." I tap my fingers against the wood table.

"Yes?" She peers up at me, spoon partially in her mouth.

I notice then that her eyes are framed by thick, long lashes the color of sand. Creamy white skin, with a soft kiss of glow from the sun. I wonder if she would taste like her, if she would let me kiss... I shove the thought away before it can take root and clench my hands into a tight fist. I want to punch something, hurt someone. I'm not sure how, but I keep myself from doing either thing.

Focusing on my breathing alone, I ask the question I'm most curious about,

"Why haven't you tried to escape? Begged me to release you? You haven't even asked if you could call your parents. I'm sure you know how suspicious that makes me, right?"

Something close to fear flicks across her gaze and then disappears.

"If I asked you any of those things, what would be your answer?" She counters.

My gaze narrows to slits. "No."

She lifts her chin just a little. "That's exactly why. I'm not stupid. I already knew you wouldn't let me do any of those things, so there was no point in asking. You bought me for a lot of money, so of course, you won't let me go. Begging will get me nowhere, besides maybe irritating you more. Then there's the fact that you're twice my size, and we're in the middle of nowhere. The chances I would get away from you are also slim to none, and I'll probably just end up dead or hurt in the process of either. The best thing to do is to behave and listen, hoping that you won't kill me or hurt me too badly."

My teeth grind together, and I'm a little pissed at how smart and reasonable she is.

Buying her, I expected her to be timid and scared. To beg,

plead, and do everything in her power to run away. My expectations were obviously off.

She is a politician's daughter, all right. Assessing risks and trying to do damage control. Everything she said makes sense, but that doesn't mean I can trust her.

She'll have to do better than that.

5

FALLON

You win some, and you lose some, but I'm pretty sure I'm going to be signing my own death certificate if I don't shut my mouth soon. *Be smart, Fallon.*

Markus is looking at me like he wants to murder me, and the weight of his stare makes it hard for me to swallow down the heavy globs of oatmeal in my mouth. Somehow, I manage and finish breakfast without another word. He offers me a glass of water, which I take without question. For some odd reason, I'm beyond thirsty.

Maybe it's the after-effects of whatever drug he gave me last night. I want to be mad at him for giving it to me, but being able to go to sleep without pain was heaven.

I try not to stare or make eye contact with him, but it's hard when he's right there, literally in my face with a body sculpted from stone, and a look of complete disinterest on his Adonis face. He didn't want sex last night, which was shocking, but a blessing as well, which leaves me to wonder if he didn't want that, what did he buy me for?

Perhaps the sex will come later?

"Get up," he orders gruffly.

He's all about ordering. There is no asking. No chance to object or ask a question. I scamper to my feet like a soldier, nearly knocking the chair over. All he's done the entire time I ate my cold breakfast was stare at me while drinking what I assume is coffee. He made nothing to eat for himself, unless he ate before waking me up.

Maybe he doesn't eat breakfast?

I don't know why I care... he's my captor. I should be hoping he dies, planning out my escape, not worrying if he's eating breakfast or not. Maybe I want him to eat with me to make this seem more normal, to create an illusion of this being anything besides what it is.

The chair scrapes across the tile as he shoves it backward and stands. It takes everything in me not to cower. My knees wobble, knocking together. He's such a large man that it would take little effort for him to hurt me, and even if he hasn't done so yet, I need to remember that he has the power to.

He takes one mammoth step toward me, and his massive hand reaches out and wraps around my wrist. The contact of his skin on mine sends a zing of heat across my flesh. His touch is branding, like flames of fire licking at my flesh.

"You don't have to hold onto me. I already told you I will not run," I spit when he stalking back toward the bedroom, dragging me behind him.

"I don't care what you told me. I don't trust you," he snaps back almost angrily.

Uneasiness churns in my gut and becomes full-fledged apprehension when we reach the bedroom. Releasing my wrist, he turns on me and narrows his gaze. I can almost see his thoughts processing right before my eyes.

What's he going to do to me?

"I want you to strip out of your clothes and turn around to face the door."

I bite my tongue to stop myself from asking a question that

will most likely get me backhanded into next week. With shaking fingers, I slip my fingers into the waistband of my sleep shorts and shove them down my legs slowly. I've gotten used to being naked. At first, when I was taken off the street, it took me a while to grow accustomed to it. I used my hands to cover my most intimate parts, but that didn't last long. The men would threaten to beat me if I tried to cover myself, so I got used to being naked quickly.

But being used to it and liking it are two different things, and all over again, I find myself feeling exposed. I move slowly to remove my shirt. Having sex with a man I don't know, who will most likely kill me or throw me away like I'm trash when this is all over, isn't what I wanted to be doing, but I have no choice.

I'm not sure why I do it, maybe to torture myself a little more. I don't know, or maybe to see if he's really as cruel as I think he is, but I glance up at Markus as I grab the hem of my shirt. Our gazes lock just as they did when I was on that stage, and I see something in them, something that is hidden, locked away in the dark amber waters.

It's a carnal need, a want, and fascination.

He doesn't want to hurt me; he wants to possess me, to own me, and that's just as scary of a thought. His nostrils flare, and his eyes dilate while impatience fills the rest of his rugged features. I drag my gaze back down his body, trying not to check him out in the process—chiseled muscles and an eight pack. He's obviously committed to a rigorous workout schedule. I can't deny that he is attractive, but he's dangerous too.

"Are you going to remove the shirt, or would you like me to rip it from your body? When I tell you to do something, I want it done immediately." The deep growl he admits makes me shiver. My nipples harden at the sound, becoming tight little peaks.

I hate that even as I tremble with fear swirling in my belly, my body is still attracted to him. Clearly, the body doesn't understand the fear that the mind does.

I tug the material off and over my head without a word and toss it to the floor. Letting my arms hang down at my sides, I do the one thing I shouldn't. I turn my back on the enemy and face the door. I can only pray he doesn't beat me or hurt me in any way.

A breath passes, and then another. I wonder what he's going to do next. What will happen? The anticipation is killing me.

Finally, Markus moves. I can hear his feet shuffling over the floor, and then he's directly behind me, the heat of his body laps against mine like waves against the shore.

Grabbing both my wrists, he pulls them together, twisting my arms at an angle as he ties them behind my back with the rope all over again. It feels like a knife is being plunged into my stomach, and I cannot stop myself from asking the most important question of all,

"What are you going to do to me?"

With the rope digging into my skin, and my hands bound behind my back, he grabs me by the shoulder and leads me over to the bed.

"I bought you for a purpose, so don't you think I should use you?"

Use me. That's what he's going to do. Use my body.

"Yes, I suppose." I gulp, trying not to sound as worried as I feel.

A man like him will take my fears and twist them, turning them into the truest of nightmares. Spinning me around, so I'm facing him again, he lifts me by the hips and places me on the edge of the bed. My throat tightens when his hands remain at my hips and trail down my sides slowly.

His hot breath caresses my cheek, and the smell of soap and cinnamon clings to my nostrils. Clean, intoxicating. I stare at a spot on the floor, waiting for the inevitable to happen, for him to take me and use me as he sees fit. I brace myself for the pain that I know will come.

"Are you scared of me?" His voice is gentle, like a soft breeze. I look up and directly into his eyes. "Should I be?"

There is a pregnant pause as if he is unsure as well. His gaze catches on something behind me before returning. "Yes, you probably should, and you should definitely fear the things I want to do to you. The things I *will* do to you."

"Will you hurt me?"

"That depends on you. Are you really a virgin?" He grabs me by the chin, forcing me to look at him.

The lie sits heavy on the tip of my tongue. I could lie and tell him yes since it's been a while, and I've only been with two guys. I'm sure I could pull it off. Maybe then he would be gentle with me? Take his time?

Somehow, I doubt it, but there is a sliver of hope.

I'm afraid to speak the truth but know the truth will get me closer to him. A man like him will see through my lie, so even as afraid as I am of him knowing I'm not, I'm more afraid of what lying will bring me.

"No," I tell him, feeling defeated.

He gives me a smirk that looks more devious than happy. "Good. Because there's no way I can be gentle with you. I want your mouth around my cock. Have you ever sucked a cock before?"

All I can do is nod my head as I'm left completely speechless when he reaches for the waistband of his sweatpants and shoves them down his legs.

My gaze widens and travels down his torso and over two thighs of steel, stopping on his hardening cock. It's impressive in size and girth, and I worry if I'm going to be able to fit it in my mouth.

Before I can get lost in that sea of worry, I feel his hand trailing down over my thigh.

My legs seem to spread all on their own, giving him access while my core tightens with anticipation of the unknown.

I'm at his complete mercy, and though I'm afraid, I'm curious enough to want more. My attraction to him is instant, and even if I were to fight and beg him not to touch me, he still would. He bought me, and I wasn't at all naive about what would happen if I was bought. I knew my body would be used.

Warmth fills my belly, and in an instant, he's cupping my sex. I wince, biting my lip to stop myself from reacting as two thick fingers enter me at once. My channel stretches to accommodate his digits. A light sting and fullness follow but soon disappear when he pumps in and out of me slowly.

With one hand between my legs, he takes his other hand and fists my hair, tipping my head backward.

Leaning into my face, he growls, "I'd apologize for what I'm about to do, but we both know I'm not sorry. I paid a million dollars for you, and I'm going to make it worth every fucking penny."

Fear licks my insides at the coldness of his voice and the iciness in his eyes as he removes his fingers, leaving me needy and hot, as he guides me to my knees in front of him. I feel ashamed at the way he makes me feel, and my cheeks burn with heat.

He pulls my face to his groin, and I open as wide as I can. He gives me no warning as he slides inside, barely fitting, forcing me to open wider. My jaw aches at the intrusion, and when the head of his cock nears the back of my throat, I gag.

I swear the sound turns him on more because his cock literally twitches in my mouth.

Tears well in the corner of my eyes and break free, trailing down my cheeks in tiny rivulets. We've only just begun, and I already feel completely used.

"Fuck. Don't you dare stop." He bares his perfectly straight white teeth, looking more animal than human.

All I can do is remain where I am, bound, and at his mercy. With his hand in my hair, he fucks my face, roughly pressing his cock to the back of my throat over and over again. I plead with my eyes, wondering if he would stop if I asked him to, while knowing he's going to take from me until there is nothing more to take.

"Yes, just like that. Suck harder," he snarls and tightens his grip. It's unbreakable but doesn't hurt, which surprises me. I want to shut off the feelings rushing through me, but it feels like he's reaching inside of me and grabbing onto them, pulling them out of me with his fingers.

Using my tongue, I run it on the underside of his cock, causing him to groan with pleasure. My heart skips a beat, and I'm not sure what it says about me, but I want to hear him make that sound again. I want to please him. I want him to keep me, want me.

Focusing all my attention on him, I hollow my cheeks out and suck harder, continuing to move my tongue at the same tempo as before. His hips move faster, and from the way his body tightens like a bow, I know he's getting close to his release.

"I bet your fucking wet, wishing my cock was inside you, filling your tight cunt."

"Mmm," I mumble around his length.

Staring down at me, his gaze darkens, the cool amber in his eyes becoming almost black. His top lip curls as if he's going to release a roar, and a second later, he stops mid-thrust, holding his cock at the back of my throat. It's like someone has overtaken my body because I shouldn't enjoy this, not one bit. I should be pushing him away, crying, and pleading, but I'm not. There is something wrong with me for enjoying this.

Tears slide down my cheeks, and saliva dribbles out the corner of my mouth and down my chin. I must look like a mess, but somehow, Markus looks at me like I'm the hottest thing he's ever seen.

"Swallow," he demands, and a moment later, I feel his hot release fill my mouth.

The salty tang of it burns against my tongue, and swallowing it is the last thing I want to do, but I wouldn't dare disobey him.

Pushing my pride aside, I do just that. I swallow around the tip of his mushroom-shaped head and look up at him as I do. He looks thoroughly satisfied.

After he empties every drop of his release into my throat, he drags his cock slowly out of my mouth, rubbing the tip over my lips before pulling away.

I suck in a shaky breath, feeling lightheaded.

As if I'm a child, he grabs me under my arms and picks me up, laying me on my stomach on the edge of the bed. Squeezing my eyes closed, I'm not sure what is going to happen next. I'm ashamed that I wanted to please him, and even more ashamed that a part of me liked it.

With my ass now exposed to him, I'm pretty sure he is going to fuck me, but instead, I feel his fingers slip between my legs and over my wet folds.

"Fuck, I knew you'd be wet. You like being my fuck toy, don't you?"

I shake my head, burying my face into the mattress, wanting to deny him as long as I can. He merely chuckles at my reaction and slips two fingers inside my tight channel again.

Warmth fills low in my belly at the intrusion. Before, I winced when he entered me, but this time, I'm soaked, my core tightening, basically begging to be fucked.

Like a musician playing his favorite song, his fingers work dutifully, moving in and out of me at a relentless pace. They're slippery as they enter me, and the glide of his thumb over my clit draws me closer to the inevitable.

In that singular moment, I forget about everything.

My body becomes soft, melting on his hand as if I'm butter. I can hear how wet I am, and I both love and hate it. I don't even know this man. He could be a serial killer for all I know, but caution gets thrown to the wind because all I care about is reaching the finish line.

"Come for me. I know you want to. I can feel it, feel your tiny pussy trying to push me out." The deep, robust baritone in his voice makes my toes curl, and my entire body tightens. Like a firework, my fuse is lit, and I'm headed toward the sky.

Exploding around his finger, I clench down, letting the warmth and pleasure consume me. I allow myself to let go. However, as fast as the pleasure came, it also leaves, taking with it the fog that clouded my mind.

Markus must feel the change in me because he gently removes his fingers. My folds are slick with my release, and I hate the feeling. Hate knowing he was the one who did this. Part of me wants to cry, and the other part of me wants to lash out.

Why would he touch me like that? Why not just use me? It would be so much easier for me to hate him if he didn't touch me, if he didn't give back to me.

There is a tug against the rope binding my wrists, and then I'm free. My arms fall uselessly beside me on the bed, and I let out a heavy breath.

My heart aches in my chest, and my cheeks burn.

"Go clean yourself up," he says, dismissing me.

It takes me a moment to gather my wits and get my arms to work, but when I do, I scurry to the bathroom like the floor is on fire while holding back tears I know will surely come.

6

MARKUS

Guilt. An emotion I don't often experience. I've done things in my life, bad things. I've killed people, hurt, and tortured them. I've stolen, lied, and cheated. I've ruined people's lives, and I've rarely felt guilt over any of that, but here I stand, feeling guilty over using the woman I spent one million dollars on.

As if she didn't know what was coming. As if I didn't realize I'd react the way I did.

It's been so long since I've been with a woman, so long since I touched one or allowed one to touch me. As soon as I felt her fiery mouth around my cock, and the wetness between her thighs, I lost it. The carnal want and need overtook me.

The pleasure was all-consuming, and being the gentleman I am, I thought returning the favor was the right thing to do. Now, I think that was a mistake. She can't think I care about her or her feelings. Because I don't, I can't, I won't.

I need to keep the line drawn. To make sure she knows her place and purpose with me. I've never gone soft on anyone or anything in my life, and she will not be an exception.

Pulling some random clothes out of the closet, I hold them

and wait for her to finish in the bathroom. As soon as she steps back out, I shove the pile of fabric into her hands.

"I have some shit to do. Come with me," I tell her, but before she can move on her own, I grab her upper arm and pull her along with me. My patience is running thin, and I don't have it in me to wait around.

Ignoring the heat and softness of her skin, I drag her through the house, down the stairs, and into the basement. Her entire body is shaking when we get downstairs. That shaking only intensifies when we reach the cell.

It's stupid, but glancing over at her, I notice how pale she is. All the blood has drained from her face as she surveys the small concrete, windowless room. Looking so scared and pitiful, I almost spin around and walk her back upstairs. *Almost.*

Then I remember how important it is to prove my point, to show her she is nothing but my property. Nothing but my possession, something I will do as I please with.

"It's soundproof, so no one will hear your screams," I say like she needs anything else to scare her.

Patience isn't my strong suit, so when she doesn't enter the cell straight away, I push her through the doorway and watch as she stumbles forward, barely catching herself. Turning around quickly like I might attack her, our gazes collide. She's pleading with me without words. Begging me not to leave her here.

As if it were going to be that easy.

Ignoring her puppy dog eyes, I slam the door in her face. I lock her in and force myself to climb up the stairs, putting as much distance between us as I can get. *Damn her!* Her tempting body and soft eyes. She's a reminder of everything I will never have.

Feeling like I'm about to come apart at the seams, I know I need to find something to do. This aggression needs to come out somehow, and I don't trust myself to let it out on her yet, not without doing some serious damage. I don't want to hurt her, not really, but I'm not myself right now. *What are you doing, Markus?*

When I told Julian I was going to take some vacation time, I wasn't even sure what that entailed. All I knew was that I wanted the girl on that stage, and I wanted to go somewhere away from people with her.

However, now that I'm here, I'm questioning everything. I wonder if I can even handle this. It's been years since I was with a woman and even longer since I slept beside one. I'm not good at being kind, and I've never had to care for anyone but myself.

Walking into the kitchen, I stop in front of the sink and stare out the window that overlooks the backyard. There are a bunch of logs that lay unsplit on the ground just a few yards away from the house.

A little fresh air would do me good and help clear my head. Physical exertion usually helps relieve the aggression, but there is nothing and no one but Fallon out here. I suppose I could find an ax and finish cutting up the logs scattered outside.

You didn't come all the way here to be an outdoorsman.

Nevertheless, I walk over to the door and slip my feet into my boots.

I find the ax easily, hanging up on the side of the house above a stack of already cut firewood. I grab it and start working. One log after the next, I chop through the wood like it's nothing but butter.

I work through the whole pile, the muscles in my arms starting to burn, my heart rate picking up, I channel all of my anger into each strike, and I finally feel like I'm getting a bit tired.

I'm almost done stacking the firewood next to the house when movement catches my eye on the far corner of the property. It's just some leaves rustling, which could be anything.

We are far out, and I didn't hear any cars approaching. No one knows where we are, and this is one of Julian's safe houses. There is almost no way someone followed us here. It has to be an animal... but what if it's not?

Briefly, I contemplate running inside and grabbing my gun from the safe. I didn't think I'd need it, and I felt safer without it lying around. A gun would be the only way Fallon could win in a fight against me. I figured it'd be safer to take an equalizer like that out of the equation.

Deciding on taking a risk, I walk to the edge of the property armed with an ax instead of my usual gun. When I get closer, my hunch is confirmed when I find a fresh track of footprints in the dirt. *Motherfucker.*

Tightening my grip on the ax, I follow the tracks. It doesn't take me long before I see someone moving in the distance. The guy is trying his best to get away from me, but I easily catch up with him.

He looks over his shoulder, seeing me approach. I raise the ax like a fucking Viking warrior charging into battle, ready to strike. I expect him to pull out a gun, but he continues running like a little pussy. "Please!" He yells out seconds before I drop the ax and tackle him to the ground. He struggles slightly, waving his arms around, making it clear he has no kind of fighting skills.

Who the fuck is this guy?

He isn't a cop nor anyone the mafia would send. If I believed in coincidences, I would say he is here by chance, but I don't.

Keeping my knee pressed between his shoulder blades, I lift my upper body up, so I can search him. He has three things on him. A phone, his wallet, and a fucking camera. I shove all three items in my pocket.

Getting to my feet quickly, I drag him up with me and slam him against the closest tree. He hardly fights, and I wrap my hand around his throat, pinning him in place.

"Who are you?" I demand. His eyes go wide, and his mouth opens, but it seems like he can't get anything out besides a little wheeze. I loosen my grip just enough for him to talk.

"I'm nobody. I was just walking," he explains, but I can tell it's a lie.

"Wrong answer," I growl.

Grabbing his shirt, I shove him away and quickly pick up the ax from the ground. "You're going to walk a few feet ahead of me. If you try to run or do anything else stupid, I'll chop off your head."

"O-Okay, okay." He stumbles over his feet. He's a skinny guy with shaggy hair that reminds me of a surfer. He's also much younger than me. Probably closer to Fallon's age. Which leads me to wonder? Is this guy her boyfriend?

"That way, back to the house. You know, the one you accidentally stumbled upon even though there isn't another house for ten miles in either direction."

He walks without another word, which means I'm right. He isn't here by chance.

By the time we get back to the house, I'm a little more relaxed. Whoever he is, he came unprepared and without backup.

I make him go into the house and force him to sit on a chair in the kitchen. He doesn't even fight me. He looks way too scared to do anything, really.

He only speaks when he sees me picking up the rope. "You don't have to do that. I'm not lying."

I take a step toward him. "I don't believe you."

His eyes flicker to the door, and he tries to run. I shove him back down by his shoulders and tie him to the chair before I get out the items he had on him.

Flipping open his wallet, I pull out everything inside.

"So, Christopher Wheeler... Wanna tell me why you're here?"

"Look, man, I'm not lying. I'm no one. A nobody—" My fist connects with his jaw.

His head snaps to the side, and blood flies through the air. Before he gets the chance to recover from the first punch, I follow up with two more. If only he were honest. He's going to die anyway, but I could end it sooner if he told the truth.

"Please, stop! I'm no one." His voice is shaking, and I'm pretty sure he is about to cry.

"Who sent you?" I ask between punches. "Tell me, now!"

"I-I don't know! He just sent me to take some pictures, that's it!"

"Who is he?"

"I don't know. I swear. This guy contacted me by email. He transferred me money and gave me this address. Told me to get him some pictures of a blonde girl. I'm guessing it's his girlfriend or something, and he wanted to catch her cheating."

"When? When did he contact you?" I'm about to shake the fucker to death.

"This morning. He said it was urgent, and he paid me a lot of money, so I drove here right away. I figured it was easy money."

Easy money? Does this idiot not realize who he is dealing with? Does he not realize he is going to die for that money?

"Did you get any pictures? If so, did you send them to anyone yet?" I ask while digging out the camera. It's small and compact but has a retractable lens that allows clear long-distance shots. I turn the thing on and look at the little screen on the back.

I almost groan when I see the pictures he's taken through the window. Pictures of Fallon—naked. *My Fallon.* Now, he is going to die.

"I got some pictures, but I haven't sent them yet."

"Good." I nod approvingly.

The kid's eyes light up with hope. "Does that mean you're going to let me go now?"

I chuckle at his question. "No, kid, unfortunately for you, there is no leaving."

Matter of fact, I might be the only one leaving this cabin alive.

7

FALLON

I wrap my arms around myself and pull my knees to my chest as close as I can. The cold seeps into my bones down here. I think the worst part isn't the chill but that I'm not sure when he's coming back, or if he's ever coming back.

My nose wrinkles as I breathe through my nose. Death clings to the air, the walls, every inch of this room. I would know it even if it wasn't for the puddle of dried blood on the floor. Even if it wasn't for the unpleasant stench. I can feel it. Feel the poor souls who died in this room lingering within it.

I hate this place more than anything. I hate him for leaving me here, and I hate myself for wanting him to come and get me. Hate myself for being weak.

Resting my cheek on the top of my knee, I let the tears that have been threatening to fall escape. I refuse to let myself cry in front of him, but here, alone in this windowless cell, I can be the helpless and scared girl for a little while.

There is some hope. At least he left the light on and gave me some clothes. It's one minor act of kindness, but I'll take it. I hate the dark so much, I would have given anything for that not to happen. I would've dropped to my knees and begged for it.

After a short time, and when I'm sure that he will not come back, I put the clothes he gave me on. It only takes the edge off the coldness in the room, but it's better than freezing to death. It's a true prison down here.

With nothing to do, I return to the small bench in the corner.

Hours pass, or maybe it's just minutes. I have no way of knowing how long I've been down here and nothing to pass the time. Only my thoughts are keeping me company, and those are my enemy right now.

When I finally hear the lock disengage and the door creak open, I scramble to my feet. I let out a groan when I realize my legs have fallen asleep. My knees almost give out as the pain of my legs waking up shoots through my muscles.

My limbs tingle as I force them to work and hold up my body weight. I feel like a dog who is excited to see his owner after being away for hours. I should sit back down and pretend to be uninterested in his presence, but my eagerness to get out of this cell is overpowering.

All that excitement vanishes in a blink of an eye when I look up and see his face. The evilness etched into Markus's dark features makes me take a step back. Like the night sky, he's impenetrable, beautiful, but deadly. He looks vicious, like a shark that smelt blood in the water, and he's tracking the prey it belongs to.

Speaking of blood, as I drop my gaze, my eyes catch on his knuckles, which are bloody and swollen. My tongue feels heavy at the sight, and a lump forms in my throat. Fear roots me in place. *What happened?*

"Move!" He half growls, half hisses.

Darkness clings to his vocal cords. What is happening? When he left, he was angry, yes, but he looked nothing like he does now, like an unhinged beast.

When I don't immediately move, he grabs my wrist, his fingertips burn into my skin while he pulls me to the door. My feet slap harshly over the concrete. Something tells me I should run the other way, or at least beg to stay in this cell.

I'm not sure what's going on. All I know is that for the first time since he took me, I'm scared for my life.

Forcing my feet forward, I bite my lip to stop from whimpering. Complaining isn't going to help me at this point. Nothing is. If he plans to hurt me, which I'm sure he does, then there is nothing I or anyone else can do to stop him. When we reach the kitchen, he stops dead in his tracks. The forward momentum of my body causes me to crash directly into his back.

Whirling around, he curls his lips and stares down at me like I'm the enemy. And in a lot of ways, I guess I am.

"I'm going to give you one chance to answer this question and one chance only. If you lie to me..." He leans into my face, his eyes bleeding into mine. "If you lie, I will know, and I promise you, you'll regret it."

I nod because that's all I can do.

"Is anyone looking for you or waiting for you back home?"

"N- No... I mean. I don't know. Maybe my parents? I don't know if they realize I'm missing. I don't know if anyone knows I'm missing. I've been gone for a few days. Maybe they went to the police? Or my roommate, maybe. I don't know," I ramble, trying to find the words he wants to hear.

I cannot hide the tremble in my voice, and that makes me feel weak, so incredibly weak. Deep in my gut, I know something bad is going to happen. Danger and fear cling to the air, making it hard for me to breathe.

Does he believe me?

"I want to make it very clear to you what will happen if you try to escape me...if I find out you have a boyfriend." I don't get a chance to respond because, in an instant, we're moving again. He grabs me by the arm, and this time, his hold is like an iron shackle. Cold and unrelenting.

I'm unsure of where we're going or what he is planning on

doing next, but too afraid to open my mouth and ask. Entering the living space. I know something is off. There are random items on the floor, a wallet, a camera... an ax.

Markus releases me and takes a step to the side. It's then, in his shadow, I see a man tied to a chair in the center of the kitchen. His entire face swollen, blood dripping from the various lesions on his cheek and lips.

"Oh god..." My voice fills with horror, "I think I'm going to be sick."

Markus pounces on me, his vast body engulfing mine like a raging inferno of sin and power. He slaps a hand over my mouth, stopping me from talking. The warning glare he gives me without speaking a single word leaves me trembling.

With his hands so close to my nose, I can smell the blood. The metallic odor has another burst of fear running through me. I plead with my eyes for him to stop all of this, but his stare is an icy jagged rock headed straight for my heart.

"Do you know him?" he demands.

Even if I could answer him, I wouldn't. I can see how unhinged he is and know that no matter what my answer is, he will not listen. He's past reasoning. *Feral.* Like a rabid animal.

My eyes dart over to the man. I can barely see his face, but from what I can see, both his eyes are black and blue. Immediately, I understand why Markus's knuckles are swollen and bloody.

I don't recognize the man tied to the chair. I wonder where he came from and how he got here? Did Markus just pluck him off the side of the road? Was he kidnapping him while he had me locked away in the basement? Bile rises in my throat.

It was already obvious that Markus is an evil man. I knew it the moment he placed his bid on me, but this right here was the nail in the coffin.

I knew what I was getting into when I walked on that stage,

but this man... I don't know his story or association with Markus, but I don't like where this is heading.

The human in me said I had to do something, or at the very least, say something. He pulls his hand back, leaving the skin around my mouth cold and wet. He must have left blood on my face. I realize in horror.

Markus walks away, leaving me standing a few feet away. My knees are shaking so much, I'm not sure if I can hold myself up much longer. He stops when he is right next to the tied up man and turns back to face me.

What is he going to do?

"Do you know him?" Markus asks again, pronouncing each word carefully as he walks back over to the man. His voice is a deep growl that wraps around my throat, squeezing the life out of me. I look away from the unknown man and slowly lift my eyes to Markus, who is now standing beside the man, his eyes piercing mine.

I answer him with a shake of my head. The faintest smile appears on his lips, and it's like the grim reaper is staring back at me.

Before I can say anything or tell him to let the man go, he pulls out a knife. The blade catches in the light, and I bite my lip to stop a gasp from escaping.

I'm not even sure where he got the knife, and I don't really care. All I care about is what he plans to do with it, and with the look of murder in his eyes, I wouldn't be...

The thought evaporates into the air in an instant when Markus grabs the handle of the knife and jams it into the man's legs all the way to the bone.

An ear-piercing scream fills the air, and my lungs seize inside my chest. I stare at Markus with a look of shock and terror. While he looks at me with pure glee.

Who is this man?

"Are you sure you don't know him?"

I shake my head profusely. Why won't he believe me? I'm so afraid of what he'll do next. Markus is unstable, like a volcano ready to explode and destroy all that's around him.

"Why don't you let him go? I don't know him. I don't even know where I am. No one knows I'm here..." I try to hide the quiver in my voice, but that is even less likely than Markus letting this guy go.

Markus snaps, his face filling with rage.

"Let him go?" he roars, grabbing the handle of the knife and tugging it free from the man's leg. The chaos has to end here, I tell myself, but it doesn't.

He brings the knife level with his eyes and peers at it, almost curiously, watching the blood slide down the blade and drip onto the floor. My stomach churns, and I think I may vomit. Speaking incredibly calm while continuing to examine the blade, he says, "He had a fucking camera. He's somebody, and I'll bet you know who he is, or at the very least, you know who sent him."

The way he's staring at the knife makes me wonder if he would use it on me. Is he going to stab me next? I wouldn't be surprised if he did.

"I don't," I whimper like a wounded animal.

"Wrong answer," he growls and moves lightning-quick, taking the knife and stabbing the man in his other leg. I flinch because I thought it was going to be me that got the knife plunged into her skin.

The unknown man lets out another muffled scream, and I can see the pain etched deep into his features. Tears slip from his eyes and down his face, mixing with the blood that dribbles from his nose.

He looks as hopeless as I feel.

"Markus, please... I don't know him," I try to reason with him, even though he's past reasoning. What kind of person would it make me if I didn't? The sides of his lips tick up, and the smile he gives me is anything but charming—it's pure carnage. It's like staring the devil directly in the eyes and expecting to live.

Stalking toward me, he wraps a hand around my wrist and pulls me into his chest like a rag doll. "You think I'm stupid? You think I don't know a liar when I see one?"

He doesn't give me a chance to answer him before he twists me around, forcing my back against his chest. I'm facing the nameless man now, and I can feel the tears in my eyes threatening to break free and run down my cheeks.

Wrapping an arm around my middle to hold me in place, he slips his hand into my sweatpants, and I freeze. My entire body becomes an iceberg.

What is he going to do?

His thick fingers move down over my smooth skin, trailing lower and lower while my heart races faster and faster in my chest. When he makes contact with my mound, I almost scream. The only reason I don't is that I'm sure that's what he wants, to terrify me, to get a reaction out of me.

"You like this, don't you? Seeing me so close to the edge. That's why you won't tell me? You want to see how close I'll get before I completely lose it?"

My bottom lip trembles, and I'm about to tell him, no, that this is wrong, that he needs to stop and let this man go, but two fingers slide between my folds and find my clit. The world around me spins.

It's wrong, so wrong, and beyond fucked up, but the moment his fingers touch my clit, all the fear and terror turns into something else. His touch, no matter how cruel, tugs me off the edge of losing myself in fear and dread.

Heat creeps up my body, and I'm on the verge of pushing it away, but with every stroke of his fingers, it becomes more and more impossible. If I'm honest with myself, I don't want to push it away. I want to lean into it, run toward it, because the alternative is pure terror.

Instead of falling off the cliff and into a full-blown panic attack, I let Markus pull me back. I let the heat spread through my body until I'm on fire, burning with the intensity of the sun. His fingers move faster and faster, and I can feel my body growing wetter, my toes curling. I'm climbing, rushing toward the surface. The pleasure consuming me.

Markus's furious breath fans against my ear, and my nipples form into hard peaks. Tears slip from my eyes while my body is caught in limbo between right and wrong, pleasure and pain.

"So fucking wet and ready for me." His words drag me from my mind. I hadn't even realized I'd closed my eyes until now. When I open them, I see the man watching us.

Reality hits me like a bucket of ice water—shame, guilt, and deep-rooted fear rush back.

"No... I don't want you," I lie, shaking my head as if that would make me more convincing. I'm so ashamed of myself. So disappointed in how weak I am.

I want him. I want him badly, despite all the things he's done, but not like this. Not with this other man watching us. No, Markus is so thirsty for an answer, he's willing to hurt anyone. I don't want his violence. I want his pleasure.

I don't even know how I do it, but I gather up every ounce of willpower in my body. Having had enough and wanting to be done with the sick twisted games, I twist. Taking him by surprise, I'm able to break from his hold and rush toward the couch.

That's my mistake. Giving my back to the predator. He's on me in a flash, his hand in my hair, pulling me backward. My scalp burns at the contact, and I collide with his firm chest, the air expelling from my lungs with the contact.

"Liar," he grits out and nips at my ear hard enough to draw blood.

The world shifts as he shoves me forward and face-first into the couch. The sweatpants I'm wearing are ripped down my legs violently. I struggle to breathe and turn my face to the side, my cheek resting against the cold leather.

"I'll fuck the truth out of you then."

Opening my mouth, I go to tell him again that I'm not lying, that I really don't know who this man is, but my voice vanishes when I feel the hard head of his cock pressing against my entrance.

"Tell me the truth..." He growls in warning, giving me one last chance, but I have nothing to confess. And even if I did, I wouldn't be able to get a word out. My tongue refuses to work, and my entire body trembles uncontrollably. Nothing I say will convince him otherwise.

He's going to use me, take from me, hurt me.

An eternity ticks by, and I gasp as he slams into me with the intensity of a bullet train. My lips part, and a gasp escapes. He's huge, bigger than I've ever had, and he forces his way inside me without mercy. It's like I'm being ripped in two. All I can feel is the leather beneath my cheek, and his hard body pressing into mine.

My core tightens around him without care to my brain's thoughts. One of his mammoth hands moves to my hip.

With bruising force, his nails skin into my skin, holding me in place like I'm wounded prey that he's going to devour. His other hand snakes to the front of my body, slipping between my quivering thighs. Devilish fingers find the tight bundle of nerves hidden between my folds.

The rough pads of his fingers press against my clit, and I can't stop myself from moaning out loud. It's like my body is betraying me, and I want to fight back, tell him I don't know this man, that I have no idea where he came from, but I can't...

Sinking more of his body weight on me, he molds our bodies

together as if we're two pieces of clay becoming one. Fear, anger, and pleasure blend into one when he fucks me, the slap of our skin echoing all around us.

His fingers maintain the same tempo as his hips, and everything fades away. The man in the room, the cell that's waiting for me downstairs, and all the other worries I carry. All gone. I'm left drenched, flooded with arousal.

Even though I know this is fucked up, that I mentally shouldn't want this, especially not with this beaten and bloody man in the room, I can't stop him, and nor do I want to.

"*Mine.* You're fucking mine, and no matter who comes for you, that will never change. You can lie to me, you can try to run, but I will hunt you down and drag you back here. You will never be free of me. Never."

The words he speaks don't even reach my brain. I can't comprehend them at the moment. All I know is that I can't let him stop. *I can't.* I need what he's going to give me, the pleasure and pain. I'm an addict for his pain, for his anger.

"Lie to me," he grunts, bringing his mouth to my ear. "Lie to me again and see what happens."

Hot breath fans over my ear and throat, my muscles quake, and my nipples harden from the friction of my shirt against the leather with each thrust.

Releasing his hold on my hip, he grabs a fistful of my blonde hair and tugs my head backward. The skin of my scalp screams, the pain searing through each strand as his grip tightens. "Look at me. Look at me and tell me you don't know him," he roars.

Like an obedient slave, I look up. "I-I... don't..."

The worst part of all is that even with the pain, I still know I'm going to come... hard, harder than I've ever come before.

My lungs deflate in my chest, and my eyes flutter closed. A tsunami of an orgasm overtakes me, pulling me into the deep abyss. Like a rag doll, I sag against the cushion and let him use my body to the fullest, and he does. He fucks me with punishing need, at a pace that's frightening, that has me clawing at the couch and mewling like a cat in heat.

His own movements become jerky, and he releases his hold on my hair and grips me by the hips with both hands. Holding me in place, he pumps into me a few more times, each thrust driving a blade of anger into my chest.

A second later, he releases inside my tight channel with a roar that shakes the walls. It's violent, and all I can do is let it happen.

He collapses on top of me, his weight pushing my body into the couch.

"Tell me who he is?" he pants, pressing his lips to the back of my head.

"I... I don't know. I swear. I've never met him before. I'm not lying to you." I'm completely out of breath, but somehow, I get the words out this time.

As fast as he entered me, he's pulling out, plunging me into icy waters at the loss of his body heat. Hate burns in my chest and tears sting my eyes.

Why did I let this happen? I could easily tell myself that I didn't have a choice, but I chose to enjoy it. I chose to let him make me come. Shame consumes me, replacing all other emotions. There is something wrong with me. I just let him fuck me in front of some random man who he beat up.

He fucked me, used me because he assumed I was lying. I feel raw, and that feeling only grows as his release slips out of me, dripping onto the floor and down my thighs. It's a reminder of what I let him do. I should've fought him, should've begged him to stop, but I orgasmed. I fed right into his darkness, feasting on it as if I was starved.

I'm going to be sick.

I'm about to push off the couch when I hear footsteps behind me. Turning, I peer over my shoulder and find Markus holding a gun in his hand. The shiny metal catches in the light. My eyes bulge out of my head, wondering where the hell the weapon came from and what he's going to do, but before I can jump to stop or protest, he pulls the trigger.

The noise is deafening, and my ears ring and remain that way even after the man slumps back in the chair, a bullet hole through his head.

The air turns to ice in my lungs, and my whole-body freezes. I stop breathing, stop blinking, stop moving. All I can do is stare at the man on the chair.

What just happened? This has to be a dream. A nightmare, actually.

That's all I can think about. It's not real. It's a movie, some kind of special effect. The man is going to sit up any minute now, wiping the fake blood away. Seconds pass, maybe minutes, and still, nothing happens. My lungs burn, and I realize I'm still holding my breath.

I try to suck in a bit of air, but I feel like there are nails in my airways. My throat constricts, making it hard for me to breathe or swallow. I blink, trying to wake myself up, trying to leave this horrible nightmare behind, but the man is still there, sitting in the chair with a hole in his head.

This isn't a dream, Fallon. This is reality, your new reality.

Everything around me moves in slow motion.

Markus turns to me, lowering the barrel of the gun to the floor. There isn't an ounce of remorse in his gaze. It's almost as if he doesn't care that he just killed someone. Like it's normal for him. It hits me then.

He killed someone.

Shot them dead, right in front of me.

"Now you know what will happen if you ever try to escape me. If you ever think you can lie to me and get away with it. Next time, I won't fuck you... I'll just kill you."

Shock ripples through me with the effect of a lightning strike.

I know it because I feel nothing of the world around me. It's like I'm disconnected. Someone has pulled the plug on my body. The ringing in my ears continues, and all I can see is the man slumped over, his brain matter splattered against the wall.

I can't unsee the evil in Markus, and that is as terrifying as the dead man before my eyes.

8

MARKUS

I've completely fucking lost it. Lost my mind—lost touch with reality. I've gone off the deep end, and there is no way to bring me back. Fallon is in my blood, beneath my fucking skin, and I can't shake her. I can't claw her out.

The thought of her lying to me, of her knowing that fucking bastard, consumed me. I had to claim her right then and there, had to show her who was in control. Looking at her shocked expression now, a sliver of guilt forms.

I want to focus on the now, the part of my life I can control and change. I don't feel guilt for killing that fucker, nor do I feel bad for saying what I said to her. I need her to be afraid. I need her to know who is running the show. This was inevitable and had to happen. Nonetheless, the guilt is still there, sticking to my bones.

I shouldn't have taken her so roughly. I should have controlled myself better. But all I saw was red. Fury consumed me to the point of no return. Then, I shot him like I was out hunting a deer. Like I've done so many times before, but today was different. Today she was here, watching me, seeing the darkest parts of me.

I don't regret killing him, but I wish I hadn't done it in front of her.

I knew that Fallon was innocent. Death had never touched her until now.

Staring at her, I find her blue eyes glazed over, fear hovering just beneath the surface. This is going to break her, crack her wide open. To this day, I've never forgotten the first death I witnessed, and neither will she. This day will forever be ingrained in her mind.

"Fallon," I call, my voice rougher than intended.

She doesn't blink, doesn't even acknowledge me.

Fuck. As badly as I feel the need to clean her up and feed her, I've got to get rid of this body. I've also gotta clean the kitchen wall, but I can't do either of those things unless I put her back in the cell downstairs.

Even with my threat, I can't trust that she won't try to run the first chance she gets. Any rational person would run after witnessing what she did.

Knowing that she will not respond to my words, I walk over to her and pull her pants back up. Her body is stiff and unmoving, but the moment I slide my arms beneath her to pick her up, she recoils like my touch physically burns her skin.

Anger replaces the guilt I felt moments ago and floods my veins. It's an oxymoron, really. I want her to be scared, want to keep her in line with fear, but I also want her to want me. Want my touch. It's a contradiction. Two things that will never go together, yet it's exactly what I want.

I try cradling her against my chest, but she's struggling against me, trying her best to get away, to put a few inches of distance between us. She has no idea I'll never allow such a thing. The only way she will ever be able to escape me is through death.

Switching my hold on her, I throw her slender body over my shoulder and grab a blanket that's hanging off the back of the couch.

I half expected her to pound against my back, to scream for me to let her go, but I get none of those things. Her silence is so much louder, and I'd almost rather have her raging than quiet. All she does is struggle in my grasp, wiggling like a worm to break free.

By the time we get to the cell, she has calmed down a bit. Her body is draped over mine limply, and she doesn't fight when I slide her down my front and place her on her feet. She wobbles, her knees knocking together. Grasping her forearm, I try to steady her, but she tugs her arm from my hand.

Clenching my jaw, I ignore her behavior. She's in shock and needs a moment to gather her thoughts. I'll give her that, but I won't tolerate her not allowing me to touch after today. She belongs to me, and she needs to realize that.

Using the blanket, I drape it over her shoulders. She grabs the corners and tugs the blanket tighter around herself while stepping away from me. She doesn't stop until her back is pressed up into the corner of the room. Her gaze is trained on me with every move she makes, almost like she is scared to take her eyes off me.

"I'll be back soon," I say, softly.

She doesn't respond, doesn't nod, or even blink. It's like she is frozen in shock, stuck in her mind, where the fear I created is holding her prisoner.

Even though everything inside of me tells me to stay, I turn and walk to the door.

She doesn't stop me or beg me to return to her side. She says nothing, and that annoys me more than it should. The heavy metal door falls shut behind me when I step out into the hall, and a distinct ache forms in my chest. I rub at the spot, wanting it to disappear. Admitting fault isn't something I do often. I don't fuck up. I'm good at what I do. It's why Julian made me his second in command.

This time, though, I know I've fucked up. Took things too far.

I let my emotions rule my actions, and that's a mistake I'm going to pay for.

Regardless, I can't change what's already done. I can't turn back time and bring him back to life. I can't make Fallon look at me the way she did before.

I remind myself of how our story started. This would never end with a ring and a happily ever after. I knew it the moment I saw her. I didn't pay for a partner. I paid for a woman that will do as I say. A woman I can do with whatever I want.

It seems I've gotten more than I bargained for.

Ignoring the ache in my chest the best I can, I make quick work of untying and dragging the dead body outside. Using some gas from the shed out back, I set the corpse on fire. The smell of burning flesh tickles my nostrils. I don't even flinch. Death and mayhem no longer bother me. The only thing that does was the look in Fallon's eyes when I did it.

While his remains are burning, I go back inside and clean the kitchen.

I mop and bleach every surface from the top to the bottom until everything is sparkling clean. *Just like new.* I take the dead guy's possessions and the cleaning supplies outside and throw them into the fire. I don't really need to cover my steps. No one will think to come out here, and if they do, I'll get rid of them the same way I got rid of this bastard.

Stripping out of my clothes, I add those into the flames. For a moment, I just stand there, hypnotized by the dancing of the flames and the heat kissing my naked skin.

I think about what the guy told me, how he was here to take photos of Fallon. She claims no one is looking for her, and I believe her, but it sounds a lot like someone is. The thought of her having an ex-boyfriend, someone looking for her, makes my blood pressure spike.

Yes, I know there were others before me, hence her not being a virgin, but there will never be another. There is me and me only, and I hope that I have made that clear tonight.

I don't know what the future holds or what I'm going to do with her, but I will never allow her to be with someone else. I'll kill the unlucky bastard and fuck her in a puddle of his blood. Not that she'll ever get the chance.

She is mine, my property, and only I get to touch her.

When the flames start to die down, I make my way back inside. I pass the couch where I fucked Fallon earlier, and all the blood rushes back into my cock. I'm a sick fuck. I can't believe I'm getting hard just thinking about it while Fallon is downstairs, probably scared to death.

There is seriously something wrong with me.

I scrub myself clean in the shower before getting dressed and finding a new outfit for Fallon to wear. I leave her clothing on the bed and walk downstairs.

Unlocking the door, I push it open slowly. Fallon is still in the same corner where I left her. The blanket wrapped around her tightly like she is keeping it over her body as a protective shield. Her seafoam blue eyes are open and trained on some random spot on the concrete.

Keeping my movements slow, I step into the cell. She doesn't look up, not even when I step right into her line of sight. Dropping to one knee directly in front of her, I force her to acknowledge my presence, but instead of looking at me, she turns her head and closes her eyes.

That guilt I felt earlier pulses with life. I'm such a fucking prick for buying her and subjecting her to this madness. For losing fucking control. Julian would laugh his fucking face off right now if he were here to witness my fall.

I want to be both the gentle breeze and the sinister storm for her, but how can I be both?

"Are you ready to come upstairs, take a shower, and maybe eat something?"

One beat passes, and then another. Slowly, she nods her head but makes no move to get up. I'm not used to asking questions. I'm the one giving the orders and following through with the punishments if the jobs don't get done. So, dealing with her is taking every shred of patience I have, but I know I can't act like I normally would.

Heaving out a sigh of frustration, I ask, "Are you going to walk, or do you want me to carry you?"

"I'll walk," she whispers, as if the thought of me touching her scares her enough to snap out of her shocked state.

She pushes off the floor and to her feet. I rise to my feet with her, motioning to the door and for her to walk in front of me. I see her throat move as she swallows hard. She doesn't like the idea of turning her back on me again. Smart girl.

She's been warned. When she runs, I will give chase, and when I catch her, it will be anything but poetic.

Against her better judgment, she does as she's told and walks ahead of me. With her shoulders slumped down and her head bowed, you can tell that she is thoroughly defeated.

Her feet move slowly up the stairs, but I try to be patient with her and not say anything. When she reaches the top, she stops altogether as if she is waiting for direction.

"Go to the bathroom," I tell her, and she continues moving toward the bedroom.

Her eyes stay trained on the floor, and I just want her to fucking look at me. "I want you to take a shower while I make some dinner. Do you understand?"

She nods again, but this time I'm not satisfied with a simple nod.

"Look at me," I demand.

She turns around hesitantly before lifting her eyes to mine. The moment our eyes connect, I wish I hadn't made her look at me. There is a heavy sadness in the depth of her blue eyes. A sadness that is only overshadowed by one thing... *fear.*

I can't imagine what she thinks of me now. How monstrous have I grown in her mind? It was the plan all along, and it must stay that way. I will keep her as mine until she is no longer of use to me anymore, until her worth has expired, and then I'll...

Cowardly, I can't bear to finish that thought.

The thought of killing her feels like someone is plunging a serrated knife into my chest. I've killed women before, but it's been on rare occasions and only in situations where it was absolutely required.

"Do you understand?" I repeat, needing her words.

"Yes, I understand." Her voice comes out soft and shaky but at least she is talking.

"Good, go take a shower and clean yourself up. It will make you feel better." She, of course, doesn't respond, not that I expected her to.

I watch her walk up the stairs to the bedroom, and when she disappears from view, I turn around and head back into the kitchen. There isn't anything fresh here, only canned and dried goods, but it will do for now. We won't go hungry.

After searching through the cabinets, I end up preparing a simple pasta dish with tomato sauce, parmesan, and canned chicken. I just finish draining the spaghetti when I hear Fallon descending the stairs. Peering over my shoulder, I catch sight of her wearing the overly large men's gray T-shirt I left out for her.

My mouth fills with saliva and it's got nothing to do with the food. The thought of fucking her against the counter, dirtying up her clean body all over again, makes my cock turn to steel.

No! A voice counters in my brain. I'm reminded of how emotionally unstable she is right now and how even if I am a shit person, she still needs to eat and sleep. Coming closer, her movements become slower, and her eyes flicker to the kitchen chair, where hours ago, the guy was tied up. There's no evidence of that now, but she knows he was there. She knows I killed someone in this room.

You can't unsee what's already been done.

"Why don't you go sit on the couch. I'll bring you a plate."

I don't have to tell her twice. She sighs in relief and heads to the couch. I load up two plates and bring one, along with a bottle of water. She takes the plate from me and starts eating right away. At least I don't have to force-feed her, which was something I was prepared to do if need be. I get my own plate and a beer from the fridge before I join her on the couch.

She doesn't acknowledge me, pretending to be too busy eating.

"No gourmet food, but you don't seem to mind," I point out.

She shrugs her shoulders. "I'm a college student. I live off ramen noodles most days." Even though she is speaking in a monotone voice and doesn't look at me, I don't miss how she just gave me a sliver of information willingly. That shouldn't excite me. I shouldn't care about her life or what she did before the day of the auction, but I do. I want to know more about her, find out all her secrets. I want to crack her open and peer inside, peel back the layers of who she is.

"I might make a run to the grocery store for some fresh food tomorrow or the day after. Is there anything you are allergic to?"

She shakes her head. "No."

I almost ask her if there is anything she wants me to bring her, but then I remember her opinion doesn't matter to me, or at least it shouldn't. Asking her if she wants anything would make her seem like more than just a warm body for me to use, and I'm not about to cross that bridge. She finishes all her food and places her empty plate on her lap.

"Just put it on the coffee table. Let's go to bed. I'm sure you're tired."

As she puts the plate onto the table, I can see her hands shake. The porcelain wobbles slightly before it touches the smooth wood.

Getting to my feet, I hold out my hand to her, but she just

looks at it like I'm trying to drag her to hell. Maybe I am, or maybe I already have.

It takes a few minutes before she places her hand in mine. I pull her up gently and walk her up the stairs and to the bedroom.

When I tie her up, I leave her hands in front of her body, so she'll be a little more comfortable tonight.

"Do I have to sleep in the bed with you?" she asks softly, looking everywhere besides my face. "I can sleep on the floor." Her words bother me more than I can explain. The fury that had simmered down returns full force like a raging bull.

"You will sleep in this bed with me, or you will sleep in the cell naked and with the light turned off. Which one do you prefer, princess?"

"I want to stay up here," she answers, her voice breaking at the end, and I know she is about to cry.

"Lie down then. Do you want something to help you go to sleep?" I offer, but she shakes her head right away. She awkwardly crawls into bed and curls up onto her side.

I tie her ankles together before I strip down to my boxers and climb into bed.

Turning off the light, I pull the blanket over both of us as I settle into the spot next to her. It takes a few moments for my eyes to adjust, and I can just about make out her blonde hair and delicate shoulder. She is turned away from me, quiet as a mouse, until a tiny sob escapes her.

Fucking Christ. Why does that bother me so much?

Huffing in frustration, I reach for her. Wrapping my arms around her slender body, I pull her into mine. She goes stiff before trying to wiggle out of my hold. I pull her closer until her back is pushed up against my chest. For good measure, I throw my legs over hers, rendering her completely immobile.

When I have her wrapped up like a cocoon, she loosens up slightly, but it isn't until minutes later that she finally gives in. Instead of trying to get away, I can feel her relax into my hold.

Maybe I'm imagining things, but when she turns her head and moves her shoulder slightly, I almost think she is cuddling into me.

Not long after that, her breathing evens out, and I know she's going to sleep. Only then do I allow myself to close my eyes and drift off into a dreamless sleep.

9
FALLON

They say things get better with the start of a new day. That yesterday's sorrows fade with the rise of a new sun, but I think that's a lie. You can't forget the bad that happened the day before. Not when it plays on repeat like a record in your mind. Not when the man holding all your fractured pieces together is the cause for such evilness. I knew Markus was bad. I knew he was evil. I even knew he was a killer, but knowing and seeing are two different things.

I'd seen him kill before, but that was different in my mind. He killed someone bad, someone who'd hurt me. Hurt all the girls. An evil even greater than Markus himself... or so I thought. Witnessing the true darkness he harbors ignites a new fear.

No matter what I do, I can't forget the feral look in his eyes. I can't forget how little he cared when he raised the gun and pulled the trigger. It was like the man wasn't even a person at all, but instead a nuisance. A fly that wouldn't stop buzzing.

But the worst feeling of all is knowing how I acted, that I came. I gave in to his touch, enjoyed the way he took me roughly in front of that man. I knew who Markus was; I just didn't know I was capable of such things.

All night I stayed cocooned in his warm arms, feeling hopeful and safe, but it was a false sense of hope, safety. I'm not safe with him; he's proven it again and again.

I'm so ashamed of myself. I shouldn't have accepted his kindness. I shouldn't let him soothe me. Nothing good will come from this.

"Are you hungry?" His voice startles me, and if I wasn't wrapped up like this, I would have probably jerked to a sitting position. The thundering of my own heartbeat fills my ears.

"Yes," I whisper and wait for him to release me.

We get up, and he undoes my restraints. I'm glad he tied my wrists together in the front last night. Even with him adding ropes around my ankles, it allowed me to sleep much more comfortably.

Markus puts on his jeans and a shirt, and I avert my gaze. I don't want to look at him or be attracted to him. I'm ashamed enough that my body betrayed me and that I let him fuck me over the couch while that now dead man watched.

Once dressed, he leads me downstairs. "Go sit in the living room, and I'll make us some breakfast." He points in the direction of it. I do just that and meander over to the leather sofa, folding my legs beneath my body.

He prepares breakfast in the kitchen. I can hear bowls clanking together and the stove turning on, but I keep my eyes trained on the fireplace in front of me.

I don't want to look into the kitchen because I see a man with a bullet lodged in his skull every time I do. I see vacant eyes staring back at me. I see death. And I see Markus looking at me like I'm next.

It's probably not healthy, but I'm just going to try to forget about it. If I don't look at the kitchen, maybe I can force the memory to the back of my mind or pretend that it never happened.

Fat chance. Those images will haunt me for the rest of my life.

A few minutes later, Markus appears with two bowls of cheesy grits and two cups of instant coffee. I eat and drink everything he gives me, even though my stomach is tight with knots. I know I need to eat to keep my strength up.

I have to survive, to make it through this. Eventually, I'm going to have to escape Markus, and I can't do that if I'm broken and weak.

Silence settles around us. I'm finding it impossible to look at Markus for more than a second. I bet he thinks I haven't noticed the change in him. He's being overly nice, almost caring, as he takes my bowl back into the kitchen and returns with another cup of coffee.

Bringing my lips to the rim of the cup, I wonder if his behavior could be a sad attempt at him being sorry. I wonder if he's really remorseful about yesterday or if he's playing games with me. If he really is sorry, what exactly is he sorry for? Buying, drugging, and fucking me without my permission, or torturing and killing a guy? Perhaps both? Filling my coffee cup up and providing me food isn't exactly an apology.

It's doubtful he would ever apologize.

"I think some fresh air would do you good. We're going to go for a walk. Find some clothes and boots upstairs in the closet and get ready while I clean the kitchen."

"Oh... okay." I look up from my coffee and at him for a brief second before looking back down. I wasn't expecting that at all.

Going for a walk? That seems too normal. Maybe going for a walk is code for taking you out to shoot you. Then again, he shot someone inside the house yesterday, so he clearly has no qualms with cleaning up blood.

Walking back up the stairs, I head straight to the bedroom.

I stop in the doorway and look to my right and down the hall. There are more doors further down the hall, two actually. They're most likely an office or bedroom and bathroom. I bite the inside of my cheek and stop only when I taste the coppery tang of blood on my tongue.

I can't... I'm not risking checking those out yet.

Soon I won't have a choice. Time is running out.

Before I can change my mind and make a mistake I won't come back from, I walk into the bedroom. Going through the closet, I notice that there is an equal amount of male and female clothes. A couple lives here or *used* to live here. Maybe this isn't his house at all? Maybe it's someone else's? Maybe he killed the people who lived here? Or maybe he's working with someone? The questions surrounding this man stack up right before my eyes.

I find a pair of jeans and a sweater. As well as thick socks and brown boots in the closet's corner.

As I strip out of my clothing, I dare to look down at my body. The way Markus handled me yesterday, claiming my body with such raw, primal power, I wouldn't be surprised if there were bruises branded into my skin.

Dragging my gaze down to my hips, I'm not even surprised when I find just that—fingerprint-sized bruises mar my skin, each one a shameful reminder of what I allowed to occur. Bile rises in the back of my throat as I remember the way he took me, owning my body, claiming it not like a lover would claim a woman but like a beast determined to remind me who I belonged to. I shake the thoughts away. I'm disgusted enough with myself. I should've fought more, begged and pleaded more. Not orgasmed.

I dress in a flurry, wanting to hide all proof of what happened. If I'm not reminded of it, then it never happened.

Once I'm completely dressed, I turn around to walk back downstairs, but I crash into a wall, and by *wall,* I mean Markus. My cheek presses into his chest, and I take a step back, trying my best not to breathe his manly scent into my lungs. I don't want to enjoy any part of who he is because doing so makes me feel like I'm doing something wrong.

This is wrong, Fallon. All of it.

"Sorry," I blurt out.

How can someone so big move so quietly?

"Ready?" he grunts, unfazed by the fact I plowed into him.

"Yes." I hold my arms down at my sides, even though I want to cross them protectively over my body. As I follow Markus down the stairs, I let myself look at him and realize he is now wearing boots and a hoodie, both of which he wasn't wearing before.

That only reminds me of the mystery of this place and where all these clothes I'm wearing are from.

"Is this your real house?" Curiosity is finally getting the better of me. I can only hope it won't get me killed. He stops mid-step, and I almost run into him again. Maybe I need to stop walking so closely.

Peering over his shoulder, he glares down at me. "No, I brought you here mainly for convenience, and because there is a cell in the basement, which I don't have at my house."

His frank words shock me, but at least he's honest. With nothing else to do with my hands, I shove them into my pockets.

"So, you know the person who owns this place or..." I'm waiting for him to tell me he murdered them or something.

"If you're wondering if I killed the person who owns this place, the answer is no. I more than know him. You could say he's my *boss*."

Well, that's a surprise.

"What kind of work do you do?" I know it's a stupid question before I finish the sentence. Markus doesn't sell cars or sit in an office all day. His boss has a cell in a house located in the middle of nowhere.

"Are you sure you want me to spell it out? I'm sure you can put the pieces together and come up with your own conclusion."

Markus leads us outside, and I decide to not push him by asking any more questions.

If I'm honest, I'm quite surprised. I didn't expect him to let me outside, let alone without having the chains attached to my body. *Is he no longer afraid that I'll run?* Or is this a trap? Maybe he brought a gun and is planning on shooting me if I run. Yes, that is much more likely.

Gulping fresh air into my lungs, I take a moment and check out the scenery. *Trees.* There are trees everywhere. It's like someone took the house and dropped it into the middle of a tree plantation. Seeing for myself that there is nothing but forest for miles makes the fear of it all really set in. There is no one to help me, no one to save me. I'll bet there are no neighbors for miles. Markus doesn't offer to take my hand, almost as if he's testing me.

Testing to see if I'll run, like I would be stupid enough to do that. Instead, he cocks his head in the direction he wants to go before heading off that way. I shove my hands deeper into my pockets, thankful that he didn't try and hold my hand. Every time he touches me, I'm zapped into another dimension and seem to forget all the bad he's done.

I don't like how my body reacts to him or the heat that stirs in my belly when he looks at me. This cannot end any differently than it was supposed to all along. I have to remember the task at hand. What's really important here.

I follow behind like a lost puppy, taking in the sights and sounds around me.

The birds chirp, and the sun hangs high in the sky. The warmth of it against my skin is like a beacon of light in complete darkness. It's only been a few days, but it feels like forever since I've been outside and felt the sun's rays on my skin or the wind in my hair.

For the first time since arriving here, my lips turn up at the sides, and though the motion feels foreign, I'm smiling, letting the fresh air and sun push me through another day.

I do my best to keep up with Markus, but one of his steps equals two for every one I take, and after only a few feet, I fall behind. He's almost at the edge of the large backyard before he realizes how far behind I am. Turning around, he stares at me, his eyes narrowed to slits. He's watching me, hunting me. A shiver runs down my spine, and the knots in my stomach coil tighter. I say nothing, though, and neither does he.

When I reach him, he looks away, and I pause beside him, looking down at the ground where he is looking. There is a pile of ashes near our feet.

My throat tightens, and my heart gallops in my chest.

"What happened?" I ask moments before I spot the remains within the ashes. "You burned his body."

I know I'm answering my own question, but I need to hear him confess to it. It's like him admitting it makes it more real, even though the proof is right before my eyes.

When I look away and back to Markus, there is no remorse in his liquid amber eyes. There is, however, cool indifference. I don't understand. How can he just shoot, kill, and burn someone without caring? Without being eaten up with guilt or pain? He's someone else entirely, and if I look too closely, I'm afraid of what I'll find. I'm not cut out to deal with a man like Markus, but what other option do I have?

Without saying a word, he moves again.

I take one more glance at the gray powdery residue in front of me, hoping that this won't be my fate. I wonder if he would really do it. There is no denying he *could* but saying and doing are two different things. As we walk, more questions appear in my mind and burn the edge of my tongue while trying to escape.

When we stop again, they pass my lips like word vomit, "Do you kill people often? Do you like it?"

I know I should keep my mouth shut, but I want to know. In my mind, this will all be easier if I see him as a monster instead of a man that makes me melt every time he touches me. Perhaps if I hear him say it, I can convince myself that he made me do all these things.

That he made my body react to his touch, that he made me want him.

Markus looks different in the sun. More human, and less dark growly beast. His dark brown hair shines, and his skin has a soft glow to it. When he turns to me, I almost gasp—the feral look in his eyes takes my breath away.

"You should've realized by now that I'm not a good man. I bought you at an auction and killed a man seconds before taking you. Don't act so surprised. You know I'm a monster, and if it makes it easier for you to sleep at night, I'll tell you. Yes, I kill often, and yes, sometimes I enjoy it. It comes with the job."

"What job?" The words squeak past my lips.

Markus's lip tips up at the side. He's giving me what most would see as a lopsided grin, but what I see as a sinister smile that hides the devil beneath.

"You're full of questions, aren't you?"

"I just want to know more about you," I confess.

The smile slips off his face as fast as it appeared. Taking two gigantic steps, he stops in front of me. Every part of me says to take a step back, to drop my gaze to the ground and cower like an injured animal at his feet, but I can't, or maybe *I won't*.

Amber pieces of glass shine back at me, and he plucks a strand of hair from my shoulder and rubs it between his fingers, almost as if he's examining the fragility of it.

"If I wanted you to know things about me, I would tell you. You don't matter to me. I bought you to fuck you, not to listen to you talk, and certainly not to get to know you."

I'm not sure why, but his words slice through me, cutting me clean in half. It's not like I expected him to say he cared or wanted to get to know me. That would be wishful thinking, but at the same time, I guess I expected anything but what he said.

"I'm sorry... I just thought—"

He shakes his head. "Nothing. You thought nothing. The only reason you're out here now is because I know keeping you in that cell in the basement would break you, and I don't want you broken, yet. So, while it might seem like I'm being kind, and maybe even sweet..." He leans into my face, and I'm hit with the scent of mint and an undertone of coffee.

My bottom lip trembles and my eyes well with tears.

I will not cry, not in front of him.

He analyzes my face for a moment, dropping the lock of hair before continuing, "I'm not. You're alive because I want you to be. Your one job is to provide me with a spot to park my dick at night, so don't get it twisted. My caring for you has everything to do with keeping you alive so I can fuck you and nothing to do with wanting to get to know you. This isn't going to become anything, and you'll be lucky if you get out of this unscathed."

I swallow down the ache that's forming in my chest. It doesn't matter if he doesn't see me as an actual human being. It doesn't matter than I'm just a warm hole to sink into.

When I finally leave this place and him behind with it, which I will, I won't even blink. I won't look back. Markus is a monster, and it's time I stop trying to make this into a fairytale that it will never be. I need to stop trying to see the good in him, especially when there is none. There is just a massive black hole of nothing where his heart should be.

"If I don't matter to you, then why did you kill that man the other night? Why didn't you just let him go?" I fire back. What could possibly be his excuse?

Markus's nostrils flare, and I swear he wants to murder me. The look in his eyes tells me he's completely done with my shit. It's a miracle I've made it as long as I have. I'd have run by now, but there's something I need from him, and also, I don't want to die.

"I killed him because, *one*, you're mine. *Two*, I paid good money for you, and I don't plan on wasting that money. *Three*, you're fucking mine. He came here, showed up uninvited, intending to get close to you. He's lucky that death was the only thing he got." The possessive tone of his voice frightens me.

He really does only see me as an object and not a breathing, living person. Before I can speak another word, he's stepping closer to me. I shrink back, but there isn't anywhere to go.

"Let me ask you this. Would you still be speaking the same tune if I allowed him to touch you, hurt you? He could've been anyone. Could've come here to kill you, to kill us both. You think I'm the darkest monster in the forest?" He lets out a sad chuckle and looks away for a moment before looking back at me, his eyes hazy. "You have yet to see true darkness or pain. Those other girls that were bought at the auction, they're going through a much worse fate than you ever will. Show some fucking gratefulness."

My throat tightens, and my heart clenches in my chest at the thought.

Without a doubt, he is right, but I don't want to admit it. The thought of comparing my situation to there's... it seems wrong.

I've been trying to push away the memory of the other girls, the one who wasn't sold, the one who was so scared. The one I couldn't save... I grow silent, and my thoughts fester. I couldn't save them, just like I can't save myself.

There is no escaping the situation I've put myself in. There is no way out of this mess. I'm at a dead-end road with nowhere to go, and nobody is coming to save me.

10

MARKUS

*A*s soon as the sun creeps through the blinds, I'm rolling out of bed. Like sleeping beauty, Fallon remains in a deep slumber, her blonde hair splayed out across the pillow, her pink pouty lips formed into almost a permanent frown. A frown I put there.

I want to trace her heart-shaped face with my fingers, to mesmerize the way it looks in this instant. Almost content. When awake, she is wary and afraid. As badly as I want to, I don't allow myself the opportunity to do that. I've got shit to do.

Grabbing my phone from the nightstand, I slip out of the bedroom and into the hall, closing the door behind me softly. Yesterday, I texted Felix the information about Christopher Wheeler, explaining everything I could about this whole fucked up situation. I want to know who sent him and why so I can piece the puzzle of who is looking for her together.

I tell myself I'm doing it to cover my bases, but deep down, I know it's more than that. I want to know who is looking for her and why? How did they know she was here? Is she in danger from something other than me? Then there is the irrational jealous side of me that wants to know everything about her, so I can kill any fucker that touched her before me.

As if he's reading my mind, my cell buzzes in my hand, and when I look down, I see *restricted* flashing across the screen. Only one person calls me restricted.

"You got anything?" I answer gruffly, moving a few steps away from the door. I'm not ready to let Fallon know that I'm trying to figure out who she really is. She'll find out when I'm good and ready.

No matter what she tells me, it still feels like she's hiding something, and I'm going to figure it out for myself.

"Hey, loser, good morning to you too."

"Cut the shit. This is important, Felix."

"Yeah, everything you do is important, hotshot. Don't get your panties in a bunch, let me work at my own pace. I have nothing yet. I didn't really get the chance to dive into the stuff you sent me. The police are looking for the girl, though. They have no leads, which means whoever found you at that cabin either followed you there or put a tracker on your car."

"Fuck." I run a hand through my hair in frustration.

I was so consumed with Fallon last night that I forgot about looking for a tracker. There's no way I would have missed someone following me all the way out here. It has to be a tracker on the car.

"If I hear anything, I'll call you. Otherwise, expect to hear something from me soon regarding the information you already sent." I grind my teeth together with impatience.

I hate waiting, but it is what it is.

"Great, talk later," I say and end the call.

I don't even have time to pocket my phone before it's ringing again. Lucca's name flashes across the screen. I'm tempted to ignore the call. If Julian needed something, he would call me, so Lucca calling me means that it's personal.

"What?" I bark into the phone.

"Well, good morning to you too." His cheery voice filters into my ear.

I should've sent his call to voicemail.

"What do you need? I'm assuming it's not regarding Julian. If he had a problem, he would've called me himself."

"Things are fine with the boss. He's not the reason that I'm calling."

"Then why are you calling?" I ask, impatience dripping from each syllable.

A second passes, and then another before he finally speaks, "I need a favor." The way he asks makes it seem as if he doesn't want to ask at all.

I tip my head back and look up at the ceiling. "I'm on vacation, Lucca. Can't your *favor* wait till I get back?" Whenever it is that I decide to come back.

"Look, I know you're doing your own thing right now, but I'm holding this fucking place down and what I'm asking is small compared to what you dropped into my fucking lap."

Asshole. "You're more than capable of being second in command. Now is your time to prove yourself."

"I am proving myself, which is why I'm calling you. I need you to go check on someone for me. I would do it myself, but Julian has me on Elena duty and doing a bunch of other shit. The family comes first," he mutters the last part.

It's too fucking early to make decisions like this, much less before I've had a cup of fucking coffee. Like a bear, I want to growl and tell him to go away, but Lucca is a friend, a brother, and I know he wouldn't call me if he didn't absolutely need something.

Men like us don't call in favors. We don't ask for help at all, so in a way, he's allowing me to see his one and only weakness. If I was a betting man, which I am, I'd say it is a woman.

"Who is she?"

Lucca chuckles. "Don't worry about the specifics. I'll text you everything."

I roll my eyes. "It's a woman, you don't have to try and cover your ass. I'm not going to tell anyone." And I won't. I don't care what the men do outside of working for Julian; as long as they're faithful to the family and do their job, we have no problems.

It's never been in my cards to take a woman, and Lucca has never shown much interest in the whores at the brothel. I suppose I now know why.

"It is, but I don't want her involved in this life. The person who has been watching her has gone MIA. All I need is for you to check and make sure she's okay. That's it. You don't even have to make it known that you're there to check on her. In fact, don't. It'll be easier if she doesn't know at all."

"Does she know you're watching her, or is this a one-sided thing," I say, poking fun.

I can practically see the smirk on Lucca's face when he speaks again.

"She knows. Just wait for the text from me, okay?"

"Sure, 'cause I got nothing better to do with my time than sit around waiting for your ass."

Laughter echoes through the speaker. "Admit it, you don't."

"Whatever." I shake my head and hang up.

Shoving my phone into the pocket of my sweats, I contemplate going downstairs to make some coffee before waking Fallon but decide to sneak back into the room and check on her. As soon as I open the door and step into the room, I spot a pair of blue eyes staring back at me.

"Good morning," I greet, walking over to the bed. Again, I tied her hands in front of her body, knowing the position would be the best for her to sleep in, and even though she won't admit it, I know she's thankful. As I undo the rope, Fallon watches me cautiously.

"When will I get to sleep without being bound?"

"When I can trust that you won't try and run or kill me in my sleep," I respond without so much as a blink. "Which is probably going to be a while."

"You think after what you said to me the other night, and what happened, I would still run?" Her voice comes out as a whisper, and I can practically see the events from that night playing back in her mind.

I drop the rope onto the bed and reach for her hand, noticing how much smaller it is in mine. The warmth of her touch ripples through me. She doesn't tug her hand out of my grasp, which surprises me. It's like she's accepted this sick fate she's been given. It's too bad I don't quite believe that.

"When faced with a choice, I think you would always choose to run from me. It's what any logical person would do. Try to escape the monster before the monster gets you. It's eat or be eaten in my world."

Fallon nods as if she understands. She doesn't have the slightest clue, but that lesson is for another day. Right now, I have other plans.

"Take off your clothes," I order once we're in the bathroom.

Apprehension flickers in her eyes, and she slowly tugs her hand out of mine and reaches for the nightshirt she is wearing.

"If you want to have sex..." Her cheeks tint red. "I'm still a little sore."

Her confession makes my cock swell with blood. Of course, she is still sore. I took her like a wild fucking animal, throwing caution completely to the wind. I hadn't been with a woman in a while, and the women I'm used to fucking are accustomed to that type of sex. The whores in the brothels don't care if you fuck their ass or pussy. If you take them too roughly or make them bleed. They just care about the cash they get after.

I hate making the comparison, even if it's just in my head. I paid for both Fallon and the hookers, but Fallon didn't get the money. She didn't even do this willingly. She gets nothing in return besides living in a nightmare.

It's me that's the same in this comparison.

Paying for flesh. Being selfish, cruel, and uncaring. Even worse, I don't feel bad about it. The world is unfair. I'm not a good person, and Fallon should know that by now.

"I paid a lot of money to use you wherever I want. If I wanted to worry if someone was sore, I'd get a girlfriend. But hey, if you're that worried about it, I can use your ass. That hole isn't sore, is it?"

Fallon's blue eyes go incredibly wide, and I can almost guarantee she is squeezing her butt cheeks together in anticipation. She opens her mouth to say something, but no words come out. I'm a fucking bastard, but all I can do is chuckle at her response.

She should have it through her thick skull that I don't give a shit what she thinks or how she feels, but she doesn't. She still thinks there is some good in me, even after I killed the guy in front of her.

"Take your clothes off, or I'll do it for you," I repeat.

My words snap her out of her shocked state, and she springs into action, pulling her shirt and sleeping shorts off. I take a moment to gawk at her naked body—perky tits with dusky pink nipples, my gaze trails down to a smooth belly and over her hips. My gaze lingers on the faint bruises along her hips, yellow and green colored...bruises I put there.

It shouldn't fucking bother me that I bruised her flesh or hurt her in any way. She's mine to do whatever I want with, but it does, it fucking does, and I hate admitting it.

Turning my back to her, I twist the knobs and turn on the shower. I wait a few seconds for the water to get hot before I motion for her to get in. She steps under the spray while watching me out of the corner of her eye. I can only imagine what she is thinking right now.

Probably worried that I'm going to fuck her again.

Stripping out of my own clothing, I join her in the shower. Her entire body tenses, and even more so when my steel hard cock brushes against the swell of her perfectly-shaped ass. I want her, crave her body, and it doesn't help matters when she looks like the one and only person I've ever let down in my life.

"Relax," I coo into her ear and run my hands over her shoulders, massaging them lightly. "Turn around and close your eyes."

She moves hesitantly but follows my command. As soon as she is facing me, her eyes flutter shut. I know she's scared, and she has every right to be, but I want her body to trust me, even if her mind can't.

I could still fuck her even if she didn't trust me, but it would be difficult, and I'd rather fuck a woman who wants and craves my touch than cowers and cries every time I come near her.

Grabbing the shower gel, I pour a generous amount into the palm of my hand. Moving my hand over her smooth milky skin, I slowly massage the soap in, working the tension out of her muscles as best I can without hurting her. A soft sigh slips from her mouth, and the sound goes straight to my cock. Almost as if she realizes the effect the sound has on me, she tenses up, and her eyes pop open.

Staring down into a pair of crystal blues, it's as if I can see right through her. See her fears, her pains. She's like glass, and I'm the proverbial hammer that's going to shatter her.

"It's just a shower. Relax, you have nothing to be afraid of," I assure her, even though I don't have to.

Her pink lips turn down at the sides, forming a frown. "You. You told me to be scared of you and what you are going to do with me," she repeats my own words back at me.

I shake my head. "Yes, but not now. I'm not going to fuck or hurt you right now."

Fuck me. I sound like a complete bastard.

Fear flicks across her face. "No, but you will later. You already told me I don't matter, that my feelings don't matter."

I did, and I wasn't lying. Her feelings don't matter, she doesn't matter, not in the sense that she thinks she does.

"I'm many things, but I'm not a liar. I'm not going to pretend I care about you when I don't, and when I say I won't hurt you, I mean, I won't hurt you *physically*. Like I said before, I didn't buy you because I wanted a girlfriend. If that were the case, I could have anyone. I bought you because I want to fuck you continuously until I've had my fill." It's not a lie, but it feels like one. It also makes me feel like a complete asshole for saying it.

"So, I'm basically a live-in whore who doesn't get paid?"

The way she spits the words back at me only makes me feel worse. Anger eats away at my resolve. She isn't in control. I am. She doesn't make the rules. I do.

"You're whatever I want you to be." My voice booms through the small space. "Would it make you feel better if I pay you? Or would that make it worse?"

Her eyebrows furrow, and she opens her mouth as if she's going to respond, but clearly thinks better of it and closes her mouth a moment later.

Obviously, my response is sufficient since she has nothing more she wants to say. The conversation fizzles to the back of my mind. Continuing, I wash her entire body, cleaning every crevice and inch before easing her beneath the spray of water to rinse away the soap.

The water cascades over her skin, and the droplets shimmer like diamonds. Beauty. She is beauty, and I'm the bastard that's taken her and placed her in a cell of steel. A cell that she will never break free from, so long as I live.

"Turn around, so I can wash your hair."

Squirting shampoo onto my palm, I move on to washing her hair and massage the soap into her scalp. I love watching how she melts beneath my fingertips. Taking a step back, she collides with my chest. This time, she doesn't shriek or even tense up.

Progress.

Fear in this situation is required to some degree, but I'm starting to realize that I want her to trust me. I want her to seek my body for protection, for warmth. I want her to want me.

"That feels so good," she murmurs.

Leaning forward, my lips brush against her ear. "That's the point."

"I didn't think you could be gentle," she confesses.

"I can be a lot of things under certain circumstances." I rinse my hands and grab her by the hips to turn her around, so I can rinse the soap out of her hair.

Steam fills the bathroom, making it feel like a sauna. Fallon lets me rinse her hair without resistance, and when I'm finished, I wash myself quickly.

I can feel her eyes on me, watching my movements. It doesn't bother me she stares. In fact, it's fascinating, especially since I know mentally, she doesn't want me. It only shows me that regardless of what she says, some part of her is interested in me.

Once we're both clean, I shut the water off, and together we step out onto the bathmat. I dry her from head to toe and then help dry her golden locks.

I head out into the bedroom, making a beeline for the closet. Looking through the clothing, I find some clothes and bring them out to her. She stands there for a long moment, staring at the clothes in my outstretched hand.

Then she looks up at me. "You really don't... you don't want sex?"

I pull on a pair of sweats and meet her gaze. "Not right now."

"Not today, you mean?"

"Not *right now*," I repeat sternly. "Now, put on your fucking clothes. I don't have time to argue with you. I've got shit to do."

Her eyelids flutter against her cheeks, and she looks as if she's trying to hide her shocked expression from me through them. Of course, she doesn't believe me. I hardly believe myself. Every time I think I'm going to keep myself in line and be strong, I feel a piece of my hard-exterior break free. I don't want to admit it, but she has a special hold on me, and it's more than her looking like Victoria.

If I'm honest, I have hardly thought of Victoria since I laid eyes on Fallon. I expected her to be a constant reminder; maybe that's why I wanted her so badly. I subconsciously wanted to punish myself. But now that she is here, I only see her, only Fallon.

Taking the T-shirt I handed her, she pulls it over her head, her perfect body disappears beneath the cotton. I watch her pull on panties and leggings while I get myself dressed.

"What is it you have to do today?" she asks when we are both dressed.

"I'm going to find out how someone could track us here, and you are going to help me."

11

FALLON

Breakfast consists of oatmeal and canned fruit. Markus doesn't eat as usual but pours himself a cup of coffee, so I don't feel as if I'm the only one doing something.

As I shovel food into my mouth, I think about the kindness he showed me this morning. How he washed my hair and body without asking for anything in return.

Everything told me it was a trap, but as I finish my breakfast, and he doesn't jump across the table to take me like a savage beast, the thought fades. I find myself squirming in my chair as he stares at me across the table. Beneath his gaze, it feels like I'm under a magnifying glass, each move and word spoken, always given a second look.

Watching him murder that man without blinking made me see him in a new light. I was sure I couldn't hate him anymore, that I couldn't become anymore frightened of him, and then he did that. My body and brain were confused by him, pulled in two different directions by his whiplash behavior. I didn't know if he was going to be kind or use me, and that left me on edge.

Now he's worried we are being tracked, and I am too. How did that man find us? Why did he have a camera?

"Let's go." Markus interrupts my thoughts, and I look up from my bowl and discover that he's finished his coffee. I peer down into my bowl and see I still have a little left to eat.

Looking back up, my lips part. I'm ready to tell him I still have some to eat when I find his features hard as stone. He's on a mission today, and I'm along for the ride.

"Okay," I murmur and shove out of my chair, making it scrape loudly against the floor.

Markus walks around the table and grabs me by the wrist. His hold is firm, his fingers branded into my skin, and even though I'm tempted to pull away, I know better than to try.

"You don't have to hold onto me. I'm not going to run."

He drags me to the door and releases me, giving me half a second to put my shoes on. "I know you won't. Not if you value your life, but one can never be sure enough."

If I was here for anything else, I would probably run—run until my lungs burned, and there was enough distance between us—But I can't run. I can't even consider escaping because doing so would defeat the purpose of me being here.

As soon as my shoes are on, Markus is dragging me behind him and out to the car. He acts like the vehicle is going to disappear before we can reach it.

I stop myself from saying something stupid.

He releases me again and takes a step back. "We're going to search for a tracker. The outside first, then the inside. I need your little hands to reach into spaces I can't since I don't feel like taking the entire car apart."

I almost miss his instructions, becoming entranced by the sun shining high in the sky. Warmth envelopes me, and it's like being hugged by the sun.

"Are you done wasting time?" Markus grunts.

My brows pinch together. This man reminds me of a grizzly bear more and more. Majestic and awe-like from a distance, but vicious and violent up close. There's a reason they tell you to play dead when captured by a bear.

"I was just admiring the shining sun. It's so nice outside." I place a hand above my eyes to block the sun out of my eyes and crane my head back to examine his face.

He could use some sun too. Maybe then he wouldn't be such an asshole?

Markus doesn't even blink. There is no emotion whatsoever on his face, and I don't understand how he can turn it on and off so easily.

"Start searching the car, or I'm taking you inside and putting you in the basement and doing it myself."

The thought of the basement makes me spring into action and start inspecting the outside with him. He points out multiple spots for me to reach while he gets onto the ground and searches underneath.

After a good ten minutes of searching, he tells me to start on the inside. I open the car door and get to work looking through the vehicle.

Starting in the front seats, I find nothing and quickly move onto the backseat. I stick my hand between seats, under seats, and everywhere else my hands will fit but come up completely empty. We must be at it for a good thirty minutes when Markus finally gives up.

When I step out of the car, I find Markus standing there, arms folded across his chest, making him seem even more mean and menacing. I'm not surprised by his demeanor.

"I didn't find anything," I tell him. The heat in his stare is enough to burn me to the ground. He's looking at me like I'm the villain here.

"Did you bring anything with you?" he accuses. I blink, and this time I'm surprised.

"Did I bring anything with me?" I snap, seriously wondering

if he is all there in the head or if he just sees red and reacts later. "Are you kidding me? I was basically naked. Where could I have hidden anything?"

A light bulb must go off in his head because the harsh contours of his face soften a bit. He grabs my hand and starts pulling me back inside the house.

For a moment, I'm scared he is taking me back to the basement, but instead, we are heading up the stairs and into the bedroom.

He releases me, leaving me standing in the center of the room.

"Don't move," he orders before disappearing into the walk-in closet.

The sound of the chains rattling makes me cringe, and he appears a moment later with them in his hand. Suddenly, I'm reminded of that day all over again. I'm reminded of what it felt like to be weighed down by those things.

It doesn't hit me what he's doing until he starts looking over the chains.

The tracker could be on them, but why? Who put it there?

When he doesn't find what he's looking for, he moves onto the collar.

He feels the inside of the cheap leather, running his fingers over the inside. Shaking his head, he flips it inside out and shows it to me.

"Right here in the collar is the tracker. I should've known," he growls angrily as he tosses the collar to the floor along with the chains. An aurora of distraught surrounds him, his fingers slice through his hair in frustration, and his face turns dark.

Fear nags at the back of my mind. "Maybe we should leave since the people from the auction know where we are. If they sent that man, who is to say they won't send someone else?"

I'm afraid of someone else showing up here, but more than

that, I'm afraid of seeing Markus as crazy as he was the night he killed that man in the kitchen. I don't know if I can handle something like that happening again. I don't want to witness any more people dying. Plus, if I can convince him to go to his place, then I'll be one step closer to finding what I need.

Markus grins, but as always, it's not a smile. It's more like the devil smiling when he tells you that you've earned a lifetime of residence in hell.

"Let them come. I'll slaughter them the same way I did the other. However, I doubt they will come here now. After tonight, they will know that I found the tracker and most likely piece together that I killed the other man. They won't fuck with us again. I'm not afraid, and if I'm not, then you have no reason to be either. So long as you're with me, I will kill anyone who tries to hurt you." I'd believe him if he wasn't the one holding all the power. If he wasn't the one threatening me left and right.

"You mean you'll protect me from anyone but yourself..." I whisper.

"I don't want to hurt you, Fallon. I want to own you. Own your entire fucking body, make it so the only thing you can think about is me. The only thing you crave is me. Don't get it twisted, though..." he steps into my space and pinches my chin between two fingers. His thumb brushes over my bottom lip, and he looks down at me hungrily, as if he could devour me right this second without thought.

"I will hurt you if I have to. I don't want to, but that doesn't mean I won't. In life, you have to do things you might not want to do. Listen to me, and you will be fine. Fight me, and you'll be in a world of hurt. The choice is yours."

He releases my chin, and my skin burns where he touched me.

The choice is mine? I've never heard a bigger lie than that. I don't have a choice in this, and I never have. The day they picked me up off that sidewalk, I was destined to be here. Destined to get the job done.

I can only hope Markus discovers my secret after I'm long gone.

12

MARKUS

You mean you'll protect me from anyone but yourself... All afternoon that sentence has played on repeat in my mind, a constant reminder of how selfish I am with her. I could easily release her and let her go back to her mediocre college life.

That would be the right thing to do, the good thing, but I never said I was good, and I certainly didn't pay a million dollars just to let her go. If that were the case, I could've set the money on fire.

I'm going to get my fill of her, use her, and keep her until I see fit. Even then, the thought of letting her go doesn't sit well with me. I try to distract myself from the thought of her leaving. It's not happening, not for a while at least, if ever.

After burning the collar and the tracking device, we spend the afternoon outside. I cut wood while Fallon sits and watches me. She attempts to act like she isn't staring at my shirtless chest, watching the rivulets of sweat drip down my body, but I catch her more than once with a lustful haze swirling in her blue eyes.

Afternoon gives way to evening, and we return inside for dinner. I let Fallon make a casserole, and she takes her time doing it. When she puts it in the oven, I stand, shoving my chair across the tiled floor.

Fallon turns and looks at me, her pink lips parted. Surprise at my sudden movement flickers in her eyes, but she doesn't say anything.

"Come upstairs with me."

It's not a question. I'm not asking her to do it. I'm telling her she is doing it. She gets the point and walks over to me.

I gesture for her to walk ahead of me and watch her ass as it bounces as we make our way up the stairs. My cock, of course, hardens in my jeans, but I ignore it. I need to focus on the task at hand, seeing if she will follow my directions or disobey me.

At the top of the landing, she heads for the bedroom without further direction. I smirk, enjoying how easily she bends to my will, knowing exactly where to go.

Once inside the bedroom, she stops and whirls around on me, her arms now crossed over her chest. Her brows are pinched together, and she seems confused.

"I made dinner. I thought you might want to eat that before..."

"Sex?" I answer.

She nods, and I smirk. "We aren't having sex. I want you to sit on the edge of the bed and remain there the entire time. I'm going to take a quick shower."

Shock blossoms in her eyes, and she moves to do just as I instructed, looking up at me through her long lashes once seated. She's damn beautiful, and maybe in another universe, she could be something else to me, but here, in the now, she is my very expensive fuck toy.

I unbutton my jeans and shove them down my legs. The afternoon sun felt great beating on my skin, and my muscles feel less tense after splitting wood. I can feel Fallon's eyes on me as I walk into the bathroom and turn on the shower.

I don't have to warn her what will happen if she's not there when I get out. Reminding myself that this is a test and that if she fails, it's her own fault, I step into the shower.

I wash my hair and body quickly, but also make sure I go slow enough so that if she is planning to do something, she has a little bit of time.

By the time I'm done in the shower, I'm prepared to have to chase Fallon down buck-ass naked, but I'm surprised to find her sitting on the edge of the bed, right where I left her. Her azure eyes move upward, drinking me in, and my cock twitches against my leg... She's a siren, and I'm drawn into her compelling gaze.

She passed. She had the chance to run, and she didn't. There is a small jolt of pleasure coursing through my body at that realization. I want her to trust me and for me to trust her. It's stupid for me to want her trust, or for her to even trust me, but I want it, nonetheless.

I dry off and get dressed in some sweats.

"Let's go eat dinner," I declare, and like a toy soldier, she jumps to her feet.

"You acted like you expected me to run away," Fallon whispers.

"That's because I did."

Fallon's gaze falls. Maybe she thought I'd started to trust her, but I haven't. If she is smart, she will run the first chance she gets because if I have it my way, she'll never be free of me.

∽

SHE CLIMBS into the bed and extends her arms out to me.

I grab the rope from the nightstand and wrap it around her wrists so it's binding but not digging into her skin. I still don't trust that she isn't going to make a run for it.

"I'm not going to run. If I was going to, I would've already."

I look up from her wrists and at her heart-shaped face. Her

eyes look like little sapphire jewels. "This is for your protection, not mine."

"What do you mean?"

Pushing on her shoulder, I ease her back against the pillow. Her face is still a mask of confusion and remains that way as I pull the blanket up, shut the light off, and nestle into the spot beside her. I toss my arm over her middle and spoon her, molding us together like clay. She sucks a sharp, almost fearful breath into her lungs. She reminds me of a spooked horse right now, willing and ready to fight. She won't win this battle, though.

After a moment, she settles against me, the tension in her body seeping outward. A second later, she clears her throat.

"What did you mean, Markus?"

For a moment, I contemplate not telling her. It will only scare her more, pushing her further away from me, which is the last thing I want. I want her to trust me, to need me, but I also need to make it apparent what happens to her if she betrays me or crosses the line.

Burying my face into her hair, I inhale deeply. Her scent calms me and makes me wonder if I can do better, be better. It's nonsense to think such a thing. I've been a stone-cold killer since Julian's father asked me to work for him. Some five-foot, blonde-haired, blue-eyed woman isn't going to sway me away from that life.

I'm a monster. That's all I'll ever be, all I want to be.

Our differences don't stop the possessive need, though, nor do they make me want her any less. Holding her tighter, I find her ear and press my lips to her thundering pulse beneath it. I kiss the sensitive flesh, wanting to do so much more than that.

"In a way, it protects you because if you were to get away from me, all bets are off. You are mine, and not only will I kill anyone who tries to take you away from me, but I will also punish you severely for trying to leave."

Silence, aside from our shallow breaths, surrounds us. I hate myself for the things I'm going to do and the things I've already done, but even if I could go back in time, I would do it all again. This is who I am.

"Does that mean the only way out of this is death?" Her voice is so low, it's almost a whisper. A lump suddenly develops in my throat.

She still believes that there is a way out of this?

"It means there is no way out."

My response might be cruel, but it's the truth. Fallon will never escape me. She became ensnared in my web, sealing her fate in my life the moment she walked across that stage and met my steely gaze.

13

FALLON

I can't believe how nice he has been to me. As nice as it can get, considering he bought and uses my body as he pleases. He might be controlling, careless, completely insane, and unreasonable, but at least he isn't unnecessarily cruel to me. *Yet.*

He feeds me, dresses me, and lets me sleep in the bed. He doesn't hurt me physically, and he treats me like a human. I've been thinking about the other girls a lot during the last few days, even though I try not to because of the way guilt and shame make me feel.

The men treated us like animals before the auction, and none of us expected a different treatment after they sold us. Like Markus said, the other girls face a much worse fate than me, and I have no doubt about that.

I take one last look at my reflection. The bruises on my face are almost gone, and my eye looks normal. My hair is freshly washed but uncombed, and I could use some good Chapstick, but other than that, I look like me again. I just don't feel like me.

When I exit the bathroom, Markus is standing next to the door, leaning against the wall like he's been waiting for me. I'm a bit startled but not at all surprised. He's like a shadow, always a few feet behind me.

"I'm going into town for some supplies. I can't trust you yet, so you're going downstairs while I'm gone. Grab some pillows from the linen closet," he orders, pointing toward a narrow door next to the bathroom.

"Can I ask you a question?"

I'm learning that asking questions isn't the best thing because I rarely get an answer I want. Still, I have to ask this one because it's burning a hole in the back of my mind.

Markus shrugs. "You can ask anything you like, but there isn't much I'll answer."

"Do you know what happens to girls if they are not sold at the auction?" I ask as I'm getting out the pillows.

His lips form into a thin line. "What do you mean? Why wouldn't a girl be sold?"

I nervously chew on my bottom lip. "There were five of us when the night started out. One girl was so scared, she tried to make a run for it. That guy, the one you... killed," I clear my throat, suddenly feeling like I've got a lump lodged inside, "he hurt her, she was bleeding badly. The other man took her away. Do you know what happened to her?"

"She's probably dead." He shrugs, answering like he is telling me what's playing at the movie theater today. "If she isn't, they probably sold her to a brothel or to someone outright for less money than she would have brought them at auction."

His words hit me like a punch in the gut. He basically just confirmed my worst fear.

Clinging onto the pillows, I follow Markus down the stairs in silence. I'm actually looking forward to being alone for once since all I want to do right now is cry. Cry for the girl who is probably dead.

At the bottom of the stairs, Markus stops. "Go pick a book."

He motions to the small bookshelf next to the fireplace. "I'll be gone a while since the next town is hours away."

Still shocked by what Markus just told me about the girl, I move around the living room on autopilot. I don't even look at what book I grab. I simply add it to the grip I have on one of the pillows and walk down to the basement with Markus following behind me. When I reach the cell, I shiver. This place is so dark and cold. Lifeless—just like that girl.

Back in the cell, I drop the pillows in the corner and plop down on them. Markus stands in the door for a few moments, his gaze lingering on me as if he is having second thoughts about leaving. It would be nice if he took me with him, but I'm dazed by it. I'm his captive, not his girlfriend, as he likes to frequently remind me.

"I'll be back later," he finally says. The door closes behind him, and the sound of the lock clicking in place follows right after.

Only then, when I'm alone again, do I let the tears escape.

~

I CRIED for a while until I finally picked up the book just to keep my mind off things. Again, I wonder why he is acting kind to me. Why give me a book and pillows?

Everything he does and says is a contradiction. He says he doesn't care about anything I want or feel, but in the same breath, he is worried about my comfort. It doesn't make sense.

I'm almost at chapter eight when I hear the lock disengage, and the door opens. Markus's large body fills the doorframe a moment later.

"Come on, I'm hungry." He frowns. Apparently, the time outside has darkened his mood.

Scrambling off the floor, I drop the book and try to keep up with him as he leaves the cell. He climbs the stairs like he is in a hurry, and I wonder if he is really that hungry or if something else is going on.

"Put the groceries away and fix something to eat. I have some work to do that can't wait," he tells me while taking a seat at the kitchen table. I try not to stare when I see the laptop sitting on the table. It's the first time I've seen it, and I can't help but wonder what kind of stuff he has saved in there?

Could it be... The question trails off in my mind when Markus scoots his chair in. It reminds me of the man sitting in the same chair, struggling to get loose, and scooting the chair across the floor in the process.

All those memories come rushing back, and all I can do is stand there. Frozen in place, I stare at him sitting at the table, only a few feet away from where he shot that man in cold blood.

"You need to get over that," Markus growls. "Yes, someone died here. It's done and over with. There is no need to worry. I bleached the place. It's all clean, now do what I told you to." He doesn't even blink, and I wonder if he's even human. If there is even a part of him that shows empathy and guilt. Does he even care? *All clean?* Does he think I'm worried about it not being sanitary? Does he really think *that's* my problem?

"Fallon, I'm losing my patience," he warns, and I know there is no getting out of this.

"I'm sorry..." I look anywhere but at that wall because it reminds me of everything that Markus is. It takes all the kindness he's shown me and shits on it.

"Don't be sorry. Just do what I told you to," he barks, and the coldness in his voice touches me in the tips of my toes.

Something foul must've happened to put him in such a bad mood.

Forcing my legs to move, I step into the kitchen and toward the shopping bags piled on the counter. I'm a twisted knot, my insides churning, but manage to unpack the groceries even with my hands shaking.

"Do you care what I cook?" I ask when I'm finished stocking the fridge.

"I'll eat whatever."

"Okay, I'll fry some chicken." I get the chicken, broccoli, and some potatoes back out to prepare.

Not wanting to ask any more questions, I look for everything I need. I quickly find a cutting board, spices, and a pan. Then, I spot the knife block next to the stove.

It doesn't even dawn on me that he is giving me access to a weapon until the heavy butcher knife is nestled against my palm.

Glancing up at him, I find his eyes are already on me, and his lips are pulled up into an unsettling grin. "I'll have you disarmed twice before you have a chance to nick me with that, so don't even think about it. It won't end well for you."

"I wasn't thinking about attacking you," I say truthfully. "I'm just surprised you let me handle a knife, but I wasn't thinking about stabbing you with it. I'm not like you. I don't think I could ever hurt someone."

"You'd be surprised what you're capable of when your life depends on it."

"Maybe," I murmur, looking at the shiny blade.

"You don't think you would try to slit my throat if I was treating you differently? If I was starving or beating you every day? If you had to choose between my life or your life? I can guarantee that you would try to kill me in a heartbeat."

I swallow, my mouth suddenly dry as the desert. "I don't know."

Truly, I don't know. I have never been put in a situation like that, never been pushed to my limits, having to fight for my life. Could I kill someone so easily? No, but he's right. If it was my life or his, then I would do everything I could to save myself.

"Don't overthink it. Anyone smart would try to kill the person hurting them."

"I don't want to hurt you," I whisper, and it's the truth.

I don't want to hurt him. Not even after all that's happened to me while being here with him. I'm not like him. I'm not capable of hurting or destroying. Markus and I are nothing alike. He is darkness and agony. I'm light and happiness. We're on two different spectrums of the universe.

"You don't have to feel guilt over it. I'd expect you to hurt me. Hell, part of me is just waiting for you to act out. To try and poison me or attack me."

I can't help myself. I let out a laugh. "Poison you? Where would I get poison? And attack you? I'm not stupid. I know you'd have me subdued in a second flat, so I'm not about to waste either of our time with that."

I look from the cutting board and find a small, what could be considered a figment of my imagination, smile tugging at his lips.

"Every time I think I have you figured out, you show me a different side of you. You're something else, Fallon."

The way he says my name makes my belly heat. It's a stupid reaction, one I should not have toward him. I can't control my treacherous body when he is near or when he acts with kindness. It's like beneath the armor, he is a different person altogether, and the weight of the world, his world, has caused him to build up high walls.

I wonder if I'll get the chance to see who he really is? If I'll break through that steel armor plate he wears like a second skin before I find what I need and escape.

The universe tells me, no, but a small, tiny part of me hopes I do because even if I don't want to admit it, there has to be something decent that lives inside of him.

Otherwise, I'm sure I'd already be dead.

14

MARKUS

When I wake up the next morning, Fallon is plastered against my side. Her tied hands are pulled against her chest like she is praying. Vulnerable. Fragile. A treasured jewel. That's how she looks to me. It's wrong, fucked up even, but I stare at her, watching her sleep for a few blissful moments. Only in sleep is she not scared of me.

I wonder briefly if this is what Julian felt when he signed the contract for Elena. The magnetic pull to something he shouldn't want but can't give up. An addiction of sorts. I'm aware that Fallon is slowly becoming that to me.

The more time I spend with her, the more I grow invested. It's getting hard to brush it off, to act like it's nothing.

Sometimes, I think she can see right through me. See the act I'm playing. She never calls me out, though, and thankfully so, because I'm not sure what I would do if she did. I have to keep up an image, have to keep her in line. I fell for a woman once before in my life, and it shattered me when I lost her. There is no room for love in the mob. It takes everything you cherish most and grinds it right into the ground.

The idea of physically hurting her makes my chest quake and

my heart hurt. I want to possess her, fuck her through the bed, and over every surface in this house. I want to protect her and control her, but I don't want to hurt her. That much, I know.

Like a baby kitten, she nuzzles into my chest, seeking comfort. She knows I'm her only protection. It's almost laughable. I bet if she was awake right now, she'd be losing her mind.

In her pretty eyes, I'm the enemy, a cruel bastard that's unhinged and willing to kill anyone that stands in my way. She doesn't know that's all I've ever known, and the way it has to be. It's kill or be killed in my world.

I'm just about to roll out of bed and head downstairs to make some coffee when her bare thigh brushes against my morning wood. It's the briefest bit of contact, a mere graze, a completely innocent movement, but I'll be damned if it's not enough to set me off.

As if the universe is testing me and one time isn't enough. She does it again, following the movement with a soft little groan that slips from her plump lips.

I don't know why I continue to deny myself the things I want. I paid a million dollars for her. I should be able to take her whenever and wherever I want. However, that mentality doesn't seem to stick.

When it comes to sex with her, I need her willing, hot, and begging for my cock. I don't want to take anything... I want her to want me as badly as I want her.

That's what makes this even more complicated. I want her to want me, want her to need me while knowing that this is a ship that will never make port. Caught up in my thoughts, I fail to notice she's now awake and startle a bit when my eyes connect with hers.

HER GAZE IS MOLTEN LAVA, as if she is feeding off my own lust. She licks her lips, and I swear to fucking god, pre-cum beads the tip of my cock. I've envisioned those lips wrapped around my cock so many times in the last few days. It's going to happen again soon, but right now, I need something else...

"Are you still sore?" I don't even recognize my own voice.

"Not really," she replies, her teeth sinking into her bottom lip.

I'd like to fuck her hard and fast. That way, I can disconnect from the feelings being inside of her bring out of me, but I don't want to hurt her.

"I want to try something." I inch back, so I can grab her wrists.

She watches with curiosity as I undo the binds and drop the rope to the floor. Rubbing at her wrists and ankles, she looks up at me through thick lashes. Her eyes are still a little sleepy, giving her that, I just rolled out of bed look.

"What are you going to do to me?" Her voice cracks as I sit up and move to hover above her. She flashes her pussy at me as she moves up the bed, bracing herself against the pillows. A pussy that I've been dying to have my tongue in since I saw her on that stage.

"Anything I want." I grin.

Since arriving here, I've just been pent up with need, my aggression and possessiveness overshadowing and taking over my most basic instincts, making it hard for me to slow down for anything.

I have yet to go down on her, mainly because it's not something I often do. Eating pussy out is reserved for lovers, those you care about. Anytime I had sex, it was to get my dick wet and nothing else.

However, I find myself wanting to taste Fallon now. I want to be feasting on her pussy, take my time, and savor every morsel like it's my last meal. Savor her.

Bracing myself on my knees, I place a hand against her knee and gently push her legs apart. I nearly groan. She's wet for me. Her folds glisten with arousal.

"You want me?" I ask, even though the evidence is right in front of me.

"Yes... but I want..." She looks away, almost bashfully.

"Oh no, you don't," I command and grab her by the chin, forcing her to look into my eyes. She can hide from the rest of the world, but she cannot hide from me. "You have no reason to be shy now. Tell me what you want."

Her lips press into a thin line, and she seems to hesitate before opening her mouth to speak again. "I was thinking maybe. This time you could be gentle with me."

Is she asking me to make love to her? That's almost laughable, *almost*. And I say almost because looking at her face, at the flicker of fear in her eyes, I know that's exactly what I need to do. I haven't made love in a very long time.

All I know how to do is fuck. No kissing, no slow and steady. No passion or sweetness.

Fucking. Plain and simple.

"Why?" I stare at her for a long second, and she gazes back at me cautiously, half expecting me to tell her no, I'm sure.

"I just... it would be nice," she explains. Nice? Nothing about me is *nice*.

I consider her request. She hasn't asked for much since I brought her here, and she is not asking for much now. Could I do slow? Could I give her this, or am I so far gone? I'm honestly, not sure.

"Are you asking me to make love to you?" My voice comes out thick.

Her throat bobs. "No. I don't think you're capable of such a thing but slow. Slow, I think you can do."

I grin devilishly. "You underestimate me, sweetheart."

Giving her no warning, I shove her shirt up to her abdomen and toss them over my shoulder

Her breath catches in her throat at the swift action. I drop to my stomach in front of her. Shoving my way between her creamy thighs, I lift her by the ass and bring her pussy to my face.

It's smooth, velvety even, minus a tuft of hair that resembles a landing strip. My cock twitches in my sweats at the sight. Arousal coats her folds, glistening in the morning light, and I'm ravaged. Completely fucking ravaged.

Leaning forward, I bury my face between her folds, my fingers digging into her ass, holding her right where I want her as her scent and sweet arousal fuel me.

Forcing myself to slow, I trace her pussy with my tongue, loving the little gasps and whimpers that elicit from her pretty mouth. I can't wait to listen to her scream, to tell me exactly who she belongs to. *Mine.*

"Who do you belong to?" I growl between her folds, alternating between licking and nipping at her swollen clit.

Fallon's hands fist the sheets, and her hips buck upward, seeking pleasure she knows only I can give her.

"You." I reward her by moving down to her entrance and tonguing her pussy. I swirl the tip of my tongue around the outside and dip in and out until I know she can't take it another second.

She's so wet now, I can feel her arousal on my face, and I love it, want more of it.

"Markus... please... oh god, please," she cries into the quiet room, pleading for her release, and I'm more than grateful to give it to her.

Parting her folds, I flutter my tongue against her clit and dig my fingers into her ass, holding her in place, so she can't escape me. Driven by the need to make her come and explode against my tongue, I devour her.

"Don't stop! Please, don't stop..."

I'm merciless in my assault, and all it takes is a few seconds for Fallon to crest. Her tiny hands release the sheet and make their way into my hair. Using her nails, she digs them into my scalp and holds my head in place. Lifting her hips, she literally grinds her pussy against my mouth like she can't get enough, and I almost chuckle. When I'm between her legs, the world around us falls away. Nothing matters except the joining of our bodies.

Trembling, she lets out a raspy sound—the noise is like a lightning bolt straight to my cock. Fueled with the need to feel her tight pussy around my cock, I remove her death grip on my head and shove off the bed, pushing my sweatpants down my legs.

Climbing back on the bed, I hover above Fallon, moving between her still spread legs.

"Take your shirt off. I want to see your body."

Reaching for the hem of her shirt, she leans forward and pulls it off. She tosses it to the floor and looks up at me. Her cheeks are heated, and her chest rises and falls so rapidly you would think she was running a marathon.

Her dusky pink nipples are hard peaks, begging to be sucked. Leaning forward, I take one into my mouth and swirl my tongue around the bud. There is nothing like the way she tastes—like sweet honey and vanilla. Her scent surrounds me, and all I want to do is bury myself deep inside her, but I tamp down the need, reminding myself that I want to take this slow, show her I'm capable of more than just fucking.

Releasing her tit with a loud pop, I pepper kisses across her chest and collarbone before taking the other nipple into my mouth. I lap at it, giving it the same amount of attention as the other. Fallon arches her back off the bed, pressing her chest into my face, and I wrap my arms around her and pull her into my chest.

My cock is caught between our bodies and slips between her slippery folds. I'm burning with need; the flames of desire threaten to consume me, and I know I can't hold off any longer. I need to be inside her—now.

As if she feels the same, Fallon claws at my back while lifting her hips at the same time. It's such a feeble attempt to guide my cock inside her.

Fallon lets out an airy plea, "I need you."

"You have me," I growl, easily guiding my cock to her soaked entrance.

I grit my teeth as I slowly sink the tip into her tightness. My chest heaves, and I swear I'm going to explode at any second. Eyes trained on hers, there is almost an overwhelming need in her depths. Easing her back against the mattress, I fill her with another inch.

The feel of her hands on me, clinging to my body like she can't get enough. It's a shock to my senses, to my resolve. Something, I wasn't quite sure what it was, squeezed at the organ in my chest—guilt, anger, sadness. It could've been any of those things. I wasn't sure, and I didn't want to think about it or feel it, but Fallon had that effect on me, making me feel things I shouldn't.

Unable to hold off any longer, I slide home. The head of my cock hits her cervix, and my balls come to rest against her ass. It's a snug fit, and she squeezes me like a glove. We both let out a sigh of pleasure, and then I start to move.

My movements are slow at first, but soon I gain speed, thrusting in and out of her. We climb the hill of pleasure together, our breaths mingle, and our hearts clash in our chests, beating to the same rhythm. When Fallon starts to fall apart at the seams, her muscles quivering, her head tipped back into the pillows, and her lips spilling delicious sounds, I allow myself to let go.

My movements become a little faster, and I can feel it... my release is on the cusp of us.

"I'm coming," I grunt, slamming a fist into the mattress beside her head.

Fallon wraps her arms around my neck, spreading her legs wider. A second later, the pressure becomes too much.

My toes curl, and I stop moving altogether, becoming as stiff as a board. Warm spurts of cum spill inside of her, and I let my eyes fall closed to bask in the feeling. The sound of my heart thunders like a galloping horse in my ears.

Out of nowhere, warm lips press against mine. It's a soft kiss, full of hesitation, but it's a kiss. I feel the heat of it deep in my bones. A piercing breath fills my lungs, and it's like I've been tossed into an icy pond.

Why would she do that?

Anger replaces the blissful feeling in an instant. I blink my eyes open and find Fallon peering up at me, her eyes wide, her cheeks pink, and her forehead sweaty.

She looks scared and flinches as I pull out of her and climb off the bed. She kissed me. She fucking kissed me. I haven't kissed a woman since...

Anger prevails, owning me.

"I'm sorry... I didn't... I don't know why I did that," she tries to explain.

"You don't know why you did it?" I mock and turn around to face her.

I'm seething. It's like she's ripped the fucking rug out from under my feet. I thought I had everything figured out, fucking planned, and then she presses her warm lips against mine, dooming me to an eternity of thoughts I shouldn't be having.

Shaking her head, she causes strands of blonde hair to fall across her sweaty forehead.

"I'm sorry. It didn't mean anything."

A growl lodges itself in my throat. "Of course, it didn't mean anything."

I want to say more, to tell her never to do something so stupid or careless again. I want to say something cruel to push her back down, to keep her in place, but I can't make the words come. *It didn't mean anything.*

No, it didn't, because if it did... I didn't even want to think about the results of such an action. The easiest thing to do was to drop it and move on. I'd make sure it never happened again.

"Forget it. It's time for a shower. I've got a job to do today. Move it," I order through my teeth, waiting impatiently for her to start moving.

Her throat bobs, and her brows pucker together. She's confused and maybe even a little hurt, but she's doing a damn good job of hiding it.

She climbs off the bed and walks over to me slowly, her eyes trained on the floor. I'm half tempted to grab her by the arm and drag her into the shower. I don't want to talk, and I don't have the patience to deal with her bullshit.

Her timid gaze finds mine. "I'm sorry, Markus."

Sorry? She is apologizing for kissing me when all I want her to do is drop it. She needs to forget it ever happened, so I can forget about it.

"I don't want your apology. I want you to forget it ever happened, and I don't want you to ever try something so stupid again. Now move before I put you in the shower, and don't even think I won't because I will."

With big eyes, she squeezes past me and into the bathroom.

I follow behind her, telling myself that it was nothing, just a kiss, just sex.

None of it means anything, and especially not with her.

15

FALLON

I'm so stupid. Stupid and careless. I still can't believe I kissed him yesterday.

Why did I do that? It was dumb and irrational, and I should've thought it through before doing it, but he looked so vulnerable. Drawn into his orbit, I wanted to taste his lips, see if they tasted of the same amount of sin that he spoke. It was a mistake.

My lips tingle every time I think about our kiss, well, the kiss I gave him. He didn't react, didn't even kiss me back. He turned to stone the second my lips touched his, and I knew I made a mistake. I mean, I knew it before, but I *really* knew it then.

He pulled away, and any closeness I thought we had gained was gone. He retreated back inside himself, a broody, angry scowl overtaking his features.

Then I apologized like a fool, and he all but slapped me in the face with his verbal hemorrhage. Now, I'm standing behind him in the shower while he is under the hot spray. I want to protest but press my lips firmly together.

Ignoring me, he washes his body and hair in record time while I try not to look at him or notice his perfectly sculpted muscles. His body is etched from stone, sharp angles, and ridges —a true Adonis and as cold as one too.

He's been ignoring me since yesterday, barely muttering a word unless necessary. It angers me more than I care to admit, even to myself. He's the only person here, so if he doesn't talk to me, I talk to no one. The loneliness is enough to make me hurdle myself off the side of a cliff some days.

When done, he turns to face me, and I almost don't meet his gaze, but I'm not a coward. Looking up at him, I see his face is a mask of pure indifference. I can't read him, can't tell what he's thinking. All I know is I really shouldn't have kissed him.

"Get on your knees. I want to use your mouth," he demands suddenly, his voice even, deep, and emotionless.

"No." I lift my chin in defiance. My voice comes out meeker than I would like, but the word itself does the job. I might not be able to leave this place, but I won't have him command me like that anymore. I won't give in this time. If he wants this, he'll have to force me.

"No?" He raises his eyebrow. "You don't get to say no."

"That's where you are wrong. You can force me to do stuff all day long. You can force me to my knees, but you can't make me want it."

In one swift move, his hand is in my hair, fisting it. My scalp burns, and I let out a tiny gasp when he pulls me into his face. I stare into his eyes, and barely controlled chaos reflects back at me. He wants to hurt me. I can see it, taste the danger on the tip of my tongue.

"You think I wouldn't force you?" He cocks his head to the side, and I know I'm close to seeing a new side of his evilness. A darker side.

Before I can answer, he pushes me down to my knees. The impact on my knees vibrates through my entire body, and I grit my teeth to stop from whimpering.

His free hand wraps around his already hard cock. "Open your mouth."

"I'll bite you," I hiss through my teeth.

A predatory grin appeared on his lips. "I'll pull every single one of your teeth out if you bite my dick."

He is lying. He has to be.

"I guess that's what it's going to be then," I say, calling his bluff.

His grip on my hair tightens, and I wince at the sting on my scalp. It feels like he's pulling my hair out. For a split second, I wonder if I was wrong, if he wasn't bluffing. Would he really hurt me like this?

The moment passes, and the air in the shower grows tense. If he hurts me, then he does. I can't stop him. Releasing me with a shove, he growls in anger, curling his hands into tight fists. I let out a startled gasp.

"Finish up and get dressed," he snarls and briskly gets out of the shower. "You're going back to the cell. Maybe a night or two in there will remind you what your place here is. I've got to go somewhere, anyway."

He has to be mental if he thinks locking me in that cell will get me to bow down to him. For a whole second, I stand there just staring at the tile. I hear him pad out of the bathroom, and I manage to snap out of it. I wash my body then. Rinsing quickly, I start on my hair and hurry through the process.

I'm just rinsing my hair out when Markus's voice booms through the space. "You've wasted enough of my time this morning. Get out of the shower."

I twist the knobs, turning off the water. I stand there for a moment and wring my long hair out. "Just drying off," I reply, not letting my annoyance mixed with fear show in my voice.

"You can dry off in your cell. Get the fuck out here." I can hear him stomping across the room. I wouldn't be surprised if he was coming to get me.

I hurry out of the shower and grab a towel. I don't even have the towel wrapped around my body when his large frame appears in the doorway.

"Hurry the fuck up," he growls impatiently, crossing his arms over his broad chest while his eyes are shooting daggers at me.

I'm shivering and not because I'm cold. I can't help but think I might have pushed him too far. On shaking legs, I clutch onto the towel with a death grip and scurry across the bathroom naked. The next two seconds happen in slow motion.

My wet feet touch the cold tiled floor, and in an instant, I lose my footing. Even though time seems to slow down, I'm unable to stop what's happening.

It's like a movie playing right before my eyes, only I'm not watching it. I'm the lead, and Markus has the supporting role, standing a few feet away from me, watching me fall.

My feet slide out from under me, and my arms flail in the air. I'm looking for anything to reach out to grab on to, but my fingers catch nothing but air.

Wide-eyed, I see the same shock reflecting back at me in Markus's eyes. The anger has disappeared altogether, and he looks... scared.

My body slams to the ground a split second before the back of my head does, and before I can even register any kind of pain, I'm out.

~

THE NEXT TIME I open my eyes, I almost forget what happened. I'm a little disoriented when I find myself in bed, untied, and with Markus hovering over me.

There's a sharp pain that radiates outward across the back of my head and a throbbing, dull pain right behind my eyes. I'm about to ask what the hell happened, and then I remember how I ungracefully slipped on the floor, hitting my head.

Ugh, no wonder it feels like someone tried to crack my head open.

Using my hand, I probe at the back of my head, finding the tender spot easily. A hiss passes my teeth as the pain intensifies.

"Don't touch it," Markus growls, still sounding angry and irritated. "I've already cleaned the wound."

"I'm sorry," I murmur, not sure why I'm the one apologizing since this is definitely his fault. Maybe it's just my basic survival instinct telling me to do everything I can to make him less angry. After all, anger is what got me into this situation to begin with. "I should have been more careful—"

"Stop. I don't have the patience for this." He sighs loudly, and I don't want to look at him. Don't want to see any more of his anger, which is burning out of control like a forest fire. "I have somewhere I need to be, and since I don't want to come home to you dead in the cell, I'm going to have to take you with me. You're no use to me if you aren't alive."

I drop my hand back down on the bed. "Gee, thanks."

"Get up and get dressed. We've got to go," he orders, ignoring my sarcasm.

Pushing my still very naked body into a sitting position, I let my legs dangle from the side of the bed. My head is already spinning, but I still plant my feet on the floor and stand up.

I regret that move immediately. Dizziness overcomes me, and the room starts turning around me. My knees go weak, and I reach out my arms to hold on to something. This time, I'm actually able to grab onto something.

I curl my fingers into the soft fabric of Markus's shirt just as he grabs my hips to steady me.

"Fuck. Sit back down," he commands, pushing me back down.

I close my eyes and take a few deep breaths, forcing the queasiness away. Markus briefly disappears into the walk-in closet, returning with a handful of clothes a moment later. I try to stand up again, but Markus shakes his head warningly.

"Don't move." Kneeling in front of me, he helps me into a pair of panties, leggings, and socks. Pushing himself off the floor, he continues helping me with the bra and shirt. His touch is gentle, almost careful, as if he is scared, he is going to break me on contact. It's strange to see such a big man that you know is capable of great violence and destruction be kind. I've seen his worst. Am I now seeing his best?

When I'm dressed, he slides his arms under my body and tucks me against his chest. Instinctively, I throw my arms around his neck, clinging to him. He cradles me to his chest as we walk downstairs, and I can't help but hug him even closer.

The scent of soap and man wafts into my nose, and I inhale a little deeper. I shouldn't enjoy his scent or let it calm me, but I do.

Letting my head rest on his shoulder, I nuzzle my face into his chest, reminding myself he is only treating me like this because I'm injured. And I'm only acting like this because I hit my head. I don't want him, and he doesn't want me.

Whatever twisted attraction this is between us, it can only end one way... with me leaving him. As soon as I find what I need, I will leave and never see him again.

16

MARKUS

Every time I look at her, I feel a little more guilty than I did before. If it wasn't for me rushing her, trying to get her into the basement faster, she wouldn't have fallen.

Granted, she pissed me off with her defiant behavior, thinking she could tell me no—like she had a fucking choice. She made me want to take her against the shower wall without care, but I didn't have to act out.

What if she had fallen and actually cracked her head open?

Yesterday she kissed me and now this. She finds a way to push me to my limits daily without even knowing it. Keeping her is starting to be more trouble than it's worth.

"No shoes?" she asks as I carry her outside.

I did that on purpose. No shoes and she is less likely to make a run for it. Plus, it's not as if I'm planning on letting her out of the car.

"You don't need shoes. You're going to keep your ass planted on the passenger seat the entire time we're out, got it?"

"Got it," she murmurs into my shirt.

Her slender arms are slung around me like I'm her life

preserver. In a way, I guess I am. It's fucked up, but I'm what's keeping her alive. If anyone else had bought her...

I quickly shove the thought down before it has the chance to manifest into blinding rage. No one else touches her. Fallon is mine to touch and mine alone. I'll kill anyone that touches her or tries to hurt her.

I deposit her into the passenger seat and watch her buckle up before closing the door and walking around the car. I keep my eyes trained on her the entire time, just in case she gets the crazy idea of taking off. It would be stupid on her part. She won't get far, but if she did, she would only be hurting herself more.

Getting behind the driver's seat, I turn on the car and start to pull out of the long and winding driveway. Fallon stays quiet, folding her hands in her lap, she leans her head back against the headrest. The last time she was in a car with me was the night I brought her here. That night seems forever ago.

Glancing from the windshield and over at her, I watch her eyes flutter shut.

"Don't go to sleep. You need to stay awake for now. That's the whole reason I brought you along."

"I'll try." She yawns and sits up straight.

Tightening my grip on the steering wheel, I drive us through the countryside, periodically glancing away from the road and over at her. I don't want her to get the wrong idea, to actually think I *care* about her on any other level than keeping her around for sex.

I won't let this become something more than that. I'm not a good man, and I'm not capable of giving a woman anything but the darkness inside of me. The good in me died the day *she* did, and no one, not even Fallon, can reach that part of me.

We drive for a short while, entering a town with one gas station, a grocery store, and a McDonalds. Without looking at Fallon, I already know that she is going to ask me something. She's too curious for her own good. Most would shut up and enjoy the ride. Fallon isn't like that, and I'm positive that's why I'm partially drawn to her.

"Where are we going?"

"Don't worry about it. Just sit there and be quiet."

"I thought you said I couldn't go to sleep," she grumbles under her breath, crossing her arms over her chest. "I don't know if I can sit and be quiet without falling asleep. Can we talk about something else then?"

"No," I growl, my impatience shredding with each word I speak. "I didn't bring you to talk."

"No, you brought me to make sure that I don't fall asleep and never wake up. You brought me because you don't want your sex toy to die before you can get your full use out of her."

"Drop the fucking attitude and shut up."

I hate how angry I sound, but she has a way of pushing every single one of my fucking buttons, and it's hard enough keeping myself in check, making sure I don't show her too much emotion or say something that she might twist and turn around on me.

Her lips press into a thin line, and I'd bet all the money I have in my bank account that she wants to say something. She knows I'm not messing around, though. If she pushes me too far, who knows what I'll do. Not even I know where my limit is when it comes to her.

Pulling into the first fast-food joint we pass, I head for the drive-thru.

"I hope I don't have to tell you what's going to happen if you say or do something stupid."

"You're going to kill me?" she says, almost as if she is bored of my threats.

"No," I shake my head, "not you. I'm going to kill everyone inside this restaurant, and I'm going to make you watch while I do it."

The blood drains from her face, making her look ghostly pale.

I can see her delicate throat working as she swallows whatever she was about to say down.

She doesn't make a single sound or even look toward the drive-thru window as I order us each a coffee and sandwich. Once we have our food, I park the car in the back of the parking lot, so we can both eat, and hand Fallon her burger. She takes it but doesn't unwrap it.

Pinning her with an icy glare, I say, "Eat."

She tenses. "I'm not really hungry. I just want to sleep."

"Well, you can't. You need to eat something, and then I can give you some Ibuprofen."

"Yes." She sighs. "I know. I just don't have an appetite right now. I'll try, though."

I eat my own burger quickly and sip at my coffee since it's scalding hot, and I don't feel like burning my lips off. Fallon nibbles on her sandwich, taking little bites as if she's a bird. I check the time on my phone.

Lucca said I needed to be at a certain house by a certain time, so if we're going to be on time, we need to leave within five minutes.

Fallon continues to pick at the burger, staring at it like it's poison. "My head hurts, and I'm tired, and I get pretty cranky when I'm tired." She looks over at me with a tiny smile on her lips.

I hate the way her smile makes me feel. Like fucking joy and happiness. I don't know how she can even manage to smile in this situation. Tears would be more acceptable.

She continues, "I'm grateful that you brought me with you... and for lunch."

I know where this is going, and I'm going to pump the breaks on it right the fuck now.

"Stop," I snap, "I'm not the good fucking guy in this story. Just because I didn't leave you on the bathroom floor and gave you food doesn't mean I'm a decent person. You're still alive because you're a good fuck, and nothing more. Don't twist things. I'm not the knight in this story. I'm the fucking villain, and if you don't stop with the bullshit, I'll show you just how dark things can get."

Her brows furrow, and where I thought fear would fill her eyes, I instead find confusion and maybe even a little anger. "I wasn't saying you were good. I was saying I'm thankful for your help and for feeding me. It sounds to me like you're the one twisting things."

I don't even think, all I do is react when I reach out and wrap my hand around her throat. She jumps, a startled gasp escaping her lips, and her sandwich falls to the floor. My hold is tight but not hurtful, which is surprising since I feel like strangling her right now.

Her pulse hums beneath my fingers.

"I'm not going to take your talking back anymore." I give her delicate little throat a warning squeeze. It would be so easy to finish her off, to end this before it can become something bigger, but I can't do it. I'm not even sure I could if I wanted to. The idea of seeing her eyes vacant, her body unmoving. It squeezes the life out of my fucking heart. I'm cruel, and I've done some bad shit but killing an innocent for nothing. That's not me.

"When I release your throat, you're going to shut up and sit there. I don't want to hear a peep out of you. Understand?" I sound like I've swallowed a bucket of gravel.

The warning hits where it should, and she nods, shifting her gaze down fearfully. I release her throat and pull my hand away. Fallon shifts in her seat, but only slightly, and remains staring at the floor as if she's been punished. Hopefully, she takes my warning as a promise and keeps her mouth shut the rest of the ride. For whatever reason, she acts as if she has less reason to fear me, and I can't have that. I need her to understand who is running the show.

Putting the car in reverse, I pull out of the parking spot and back onto the road. I follow the GPS directions, and thirty minutes later, we arrive.

I park exactly where Lucca instructed me to. I check the time again and realize I've barely made it. Lucca was very specific about me being here at four-o-clock sharp.

"What are we—" I glare at Fallon, cutting her off mid-sentence. She presses her lips together and flares his nostrils like a bull. If she's smart, she'll keep her mouth shut.

Looking away from her, I drag my gaze back to the road.

A few minutes later, a school bus pulls up right in front of the street corner I'm supposed to watch. Great, now I can't see a fucking thing. It's always something, I swear.

Luckily, the bus swiftly takes off again. That's when I see her. Red hair, gray jacket, slender figure, petite—just how Lucca described her.

But that can't possibly be her? This girl is just a kid, no more than maybe fifteen or sixteen-years-old. *What the fuck?*

Lucca doesn't have a sister, at least not that I know of. They don't look like they are related at all, not with her fiery red hair. So why the fuck is he watching her? My stomach churns at the thought. Lucca is a good guy, by mob standards, that is.

We've done some fucked up shit in our line of work, but we don't deal in underage girls. We don't recruit from the streets as young as some others do. Some families shove guns into ten-year-old boys' hands and have them do their dirty work. Julian won't stand for shit like that, and neither do I.

Fucking up kids' lives, that's a whole other kind of evil, an evil that I'm not okay with.

Lucca has some explaining to do. Whatever is going on with this girl better not be what I'm thinking. I let the girl walk down the sidewalk a few feet before I put the car in drive and start following her slowly while keeping my distance. I don't want to draw attention to myself. She doesn't seem to notice me, and when I get closer, I can see why. She has earbuds in her ears, probably blasting so loud, she can't hear a thing.

The girl turns into the front yard of the house Lucca told me she would go to. So far, everything he has said lines up. I stop the car once more, watching her pull a key from her jacket pocket and unlock the door.

"Oh my god, you're going to kidnap her," Fallon shrieks. "Y-you can't! She's just a kid. I'm not... I'm not letting that happen—"

"What are you talking about?"

"Y-you... you..." She looks like she is struggling to breathe, her chest rising and falling rapidly. Is she having a fucking panic attack? I need to diffuse the situation before it explodes in my face.

"Calm down, I'm not kidnapping anyone," I tell her, but it's like the words don't reach her at all. Her chest is heaving, her eyes are wild, and I'm pretty sure she is hyperventilating. Shit.

Grabbing her shoulders, I turn her to face me. "Look at me. You need to snap out of it." Her eyes are so wide they are almost round. Her breathing is rapid and shallow, but her eyes slowly focus on me again. "Take deep breaths."

I start to show her how to do it. Sucking air in through my nose and exhaling through my mouth. She copies me, matching each breath until her breathing returns to normal.

"There you go, just keep breathing like that. No reason to freak out."

"I thought... I thought you were going to kidnap her," she admits.

"I gathered that much." I let go of her shoulders and twist away from her, so I'm looking out of the windshield. "I might be a monster, but even I have limits. I won't touch a kid, and I'll kill anyone who does."

"Then, why are we here? Who is the girl?"

"That I don't know yet," I say through clenched teeth, irritated by the way she doesn't believe me and angry by Lucca sending me here in the first place.

As I pull out of the neighborhood, I keep glancing at Fallon, who is looking out of the window in silence. At least she is not freaking out anymore. It's not until we are back on the highway that I see her head loll to the side.

"Hey," I shake her arm, "no sleeping."

"I know, I know. I'm trying."

"Tell me about your family," I urge. I know this is a terrible idea, but I've got to keep her awake.

"Um, my mom and dad own a little store in the town I grew up in. I worked there before I went to college."

"You liked working there?" I ask, surprising myself by how genuinely interested I am in the answer.

"I guess." She shrugs. "It was fine. My sister always hated it." I don't miss the way her voice takes on a sad note.

"Why did your sister hate it?"

"She thought it was boring, maybe even a little beneath her," Fallon says, a smile on her face like she is laughing about some inside joke. "She was always the wild child. Adventurous, never sitting still, and always up for anything. She left as soon as she turned eighteen."

"Where did she go?"

"Europe. She went to France to study but dropped out and moved in with her boyfriend she met there. I don't think she was ever planning on coming back. I haven't seen her in a long time. I miss her..." She looks out into the distance. I get the feeling that there is something more about her sister that she isn't telling me, probably a falling out with the parents given the situation.

"I'm sure you'll see her again soon," I say without even thinking about the meaning of those words. Shit. I should have kept my mouth shut because she won't see her sister soon; she might not see her sister again at all.

Not if I have my way, which has always been the plan.

17

FALLON

Three days pass in a blur, and we slowly fall into a weirdly normal routine. The tether of trust between us seems to grow. I'm pretty sure it has everything to do with the other night. Ever since he talked me off the edge of a panic attack, and we just talked like humans, things have been different, better.

I saw something in him that day in the car. It was like for the first time, he allowed a small sliver of who he was to shine through all the broken, dark pieces of who he made himself out to be. After that day, it made maintaining the hate I had for him hard.

I've never been the type to hold onto negativity, but it is hard not to hate him with the way he treats me sometimes. I often wonder if this is all a front, if Markus said and did things to keep me in place. Part of me stupidly thinks he would never hurt me, mainly because every threat he has made has been an idle one.

He's all over the place, some days hot and other days cold, which is frustrating as hell. I can't gauge his mood because I never know which way it's going to go.

Every night we have sex, and of course, he makes sure I climax.

It makes me feel incredibly guilty that my body is drawn to him, that when he is inside me, I forget what we are to each other and where we are. I crave his touch, even though admitting it makes me hate myself a little bit. He's my captor, the man who paid a million dollars to fuck me. However, he wants. I'm not supposed to want him.

Except I do. When he's inside of me, he's a different person, and I forget about all the shitty things he's said and done. It gives me hope that maybe everything he's said is a lie, that there is a kinder person beneath the grumpy, angry, violent exterior he shows to others.

Nothing has changed in our nightly routine. He ties my hands together, securing them in front of me, and tucks me into his side each night, wrapping an arm over me that resembles a thick steel band. Even if my hands weren't tied, it would be a huge risk to try to escape his hold.

Each night I fall asleep, I feel a little more guilty for nuzzling into his chest and inhaling his scent, but he holds me in his arms, encouraging me.

I do everything he asks of me, cleaning the kitchen after meals and helping with the laundry. I don't get to go anywhere in the house alone, but at least he doesn't tie me to the bed and only come and see me when he wants to fuck me.

Staring into my cup of tea, I watch him out of the corner of my eye. He sits at the small kitchen table, working on his laptop. It's ridiculous how normal he makes this all feel.

It's as if we're a real-life couple without technically being one, minus the fact he paid a million dollars for me.

SOMEHOW, I need him to trust me enough to take me to his place because I don't think I'll find what I'm looking for here. This isn't even his house. *Ugh.* Somehow, I need to make him trust me enough to take me to his home.

He needs to think that I'm under his spell, willing to do anything he wants. I tap my fingers idly against the counter. I'm not sure how many days have passed since the auction, but this is taking longer than expected. How can I speed up the process? I don't have the time it would take to convince him that everything is good, that I'm worthy of his trust.

I need to get into contact with them now. To let them know I'm still alive and need more time. How I'm going to do that is beyond me. I haven't seen a phone inside this house, and Markus's cell has a six-number code on it. All I have is their phone number, which they made me memorize while they held me in that awful cell.

Markus looks up from the laptop and right at me, and my heart clenches in my chest. I feel guilty all of a sudden and for no reason. I haven't done anything. *Yet.*

I know what has to be done, but doing so will ruin everything. We've got into a pleasant rhythm with no fighting, and I almost feel bad doing something, knowing that I'm tossing all that effort out the window. Everything seems *normal,* and I'm going to destroy it all, but I have no other choice. I have to make that call soon.

"Bring me a glass of water," Markus orders, his deep voice startling me.

I jump at the sound, and the tea in my hand sloshes out the side of the cup and onto the counter. Damnit. I'm basically giving myself away here.

Deep breaths.

Swallowing down my anxiety, I go to the cupboard, get out a glass, and fill it with water. I squeeze the glass hard, trying to stop my hand from trembling as I walk over to the table and hand him the cup.

He takes it and blinks slowly, watching me. His fingers graze mine, and I shiver at the contact.

"I have to go to the bathroom," I blurt out.

"Okay..." his gaze narrows, "then go."

I scurry across the living space and into the bathroom. I don't even have to go pee, but I need to get away. I need a breather, even if it's just for a moment.

I take a few minutes to collect myself before I exit and return to the kitchen.

"What's wrong with you? You're acting weird," Markus points out, having my nerves right back where they were ten minutes ago.

"I just don't feel well," I lie, "I think I'm about to get my period."

Markus makes a weird face as if periods are the last thing he wants to talk about. Typical guy. At least he seems to believe me.

"Are you ready to go to bed?"

"Yes. I know it's early. You don't have to come with me. Or I can just lie down on the couch for now."

"It's fine. We'll go." Picking up the glass of water, he chugs the last bit and gets up. Shutting his laptop, he grabs it and heads for the stairs. I follow close behind, feeling both grateful and nervous about another day coming to an end.

"Wait here," Markus orders when we reach the bedroom door.

I stop in my tracks and watch him curiously.

Markus continues walking down the hall and opens a door. He disappears inside what I've assumed was another bedroom until now. When he reappears, the laptop he was carrying is gone.

"What's that room?" I ask before I can stop myself. To my surprise, he actually answers me.

"My office."

I nod and follow him to the bed. We both strip down to our underwear. I stopped wearing pajamas a few days ago at Markus's request, or should I say order. Either way, I don't mind since I prefer sleeping naked, anyway.

Sitting down on the edge of the bed, I hold out my hands for him to tie them together, but he stuns me yet again when he shakes his head.

"Just lie down. Your wrists and ankles are red. I'll give you a break tonight."

I stare down at my wrists in shock. Yes, my skin has been angry and red looking lately, but I'm still not convinced that this is the only reason. Is he testing me?

"Okay."

We both crawl into bed and under the blanket. As we assume our normal positions, my mind is reeling. I can't figure out if this is a test or if he is starting to trust me. His arm snakes around my body, and I bury my face into his chest.

I let his words run through my mind again... *I'll give you a break tonight.* Does that mean he'll tie me up again tomorrow? If so, that means tonight will be my only chance to try to find a phone. Maybe there is one in the office.

Just one quick call. That's all I need.

Closing my eyes, I try to even out my breathing without actually falling asleep, and then I wait. I wait for what feels like two hours until my eyes start to droop, and I can't keep myself awake any longer. Only then, when I am certain Markus is asleep, his breathing evening and his body unmoving, do I move. Slowly... so very, very slowly, I scoot away from him.

With every inch I put between us, my heart slams against my ribcage faster and faster. I'm so scared, terrified of what may happen, what he will do to me if he discovers I'm no longer beside him in the bed.

Everything inside me says to stop, to lie back down, and cuddle back into his chest, but I can't. I have to do this. I have to take this chance. I've already taken long enough, another day without letting them know I'm still here and alive.

When I'm finally out of bed, I feel cold, and it's not just the loss of body heat. It's not the fact that I'm standing here in nothing but my panties, my bare feet on the cool wood.

It's knowing that if he catches me, whatever we had developing between us will be gone.

That kind of coldness is much worse than the physical one. It's the kind of cold that you feel in your bones and deep in your gut. The kind that you know can freeze your soul to death.

Forcing my feet to move toward the door, every step feels like a step toward death. The door creaks a tiny bit as I open it, and of course, it sounds like a marching band in my head. I stop for a minute, making sure the sound doesn't wake him.

When the room remains silent, and Markus's large body unmoving, I continue.

I step out of the room, tiptoe down the hallway, and come to a halt in front of the office door. Reaching for the doorknob, I wrap my fingers around it and turn. The door pushes open with ease, but my stomach is in knots.

Panic builds, gripping me by the throat. In this instance, I cannot think about the consequences if Markus were to catch me.

I need to do this. I need to make that call.

I will never forgive myself if I don't.

18

MARKUS

Fallon has been acting off all day, and I can almost guarantee she is up to something. I caught her glancing at the office door like it holds the holy grail inside. She doesn't think I saw her, but I did. I caught the slight flicker of interest in her eyes.

I knew she was going to try. I knew it the moment I let her crawl into bed without tying her up. And still, as I feel her inching away from me slowly and slipping out of the bed, disappointment settles deep into my bones.

I wish she wouldn't do this. I wish she would have just stayed in bed with me. Obviously, she needs a reminder of where we stand; she needs to see what happens when you betray me. I've made myself clear in every instance.

My disappointment bleeds into anger with every second that ticks by. I stare at the mattress, at the spot beside me that she should be sleeping in. I'm pissed that I was starting to trust her. Then the moment I give her a slice of freedom, she does this.

I climb out of bed slowly and walk to the door. Pushing the bedroom door open, I walk out into the hall. On nimble feet or as nimble as a six-foot-two, two-hundred-fifty-pound man can be, I approach the office door. It's closed just as I left it, giving away no signs of change, but I know better. I know she is in there.

Preparing to burst through the door, I grab the handle and turn it, only to realize it's locked. My anger intensifies by a million.

"Open the fucking door, Fallon!" I growl, beating my fist against the wood.

The door rattles against my closed fist, and my patience is withering away with every second that passes. She betrayed me, took my trust, and threw it back in my face. Taking a step back, I look at the door, which still isn't unlocked.

"Fallon. Open the door, or I'll open it myself," I warn.

"Just... I'm sorry..." I hear her say, but they're not the words I want to hear, and the damn door is still locked. Anger surges through my veins, and I see red.

Lifting my foot, I kick the door in. The wood splinters, and the lock snaps, sending the door into the room and against the wall.

Chest heaving, I stalk forward. What I see pushes me over the edge. I knew she came in here for something, but part of me didn't think she would have the balls to do anything. But somehow, here she is with the phone in her hand.

Her skin pales, and terror erupts in her eyes.

She looks afraid, and she should be. The things I want to do to her right now. They would make her run away screaming.

"You really shouldn't have done that." I'm close to losing it, and I'm not sure what would happen if I did. I need to put her in the basement to get her out of my sight.

"I'm sorry..." her plump lips tremble, "I was calling my parents. I wanted to tell them I was okay..." She is lying, I can tell right away. I've done enough interrogations to tell the difference, and Fallon is a shitty liar.

I clench and unclench my hands a few times, feeling the need to release the aggression out on something, anything. One hit is all it would take for me to hurt Fallon. I could bring her unimaginable pain, force her to tell me who she was really going to call, but physically inflicting pain on her isn't something I can bear, and that only makes me angrier.

"Do not lie to me. I'm not stupid. This was a test, and you fucking failed it." Stalking forward, I grab the phone out of her hand and toss it down on the desk. I'm not sure if she succeeded in making the call, but it doesn't matter.

She won't get another chance to escape me.

"I just wanted to call my parents," she repeats once more.

Tears shimmer in her blue eyes, but she doesn't realize that her tears only enrage me more. I want them gone, to squish them beneath my thumbs. Paying her pity act no attention, I grab her by the arm and tug her forward. Her legs wobble, and she nearly trips over her own feet.

"You can't possibly expect me to believe that you were calling your parents. I'm not stupid, Fallon." I pull her forward, crushing my chest against hers. I should fuck her right now, right here against the wall, fuck her until she begs me to stop until she can no longer stand, and I have to hold her body up for her. Until my cum is leaking out of her and down onto the floor.

I should punish her with my cock, but I can't trust myself not to take it further, so instead, I'll punish her by leaving her alone in the cold basement. She'll have all the time in the world to think about what she did, and I'll have time to calm the fuck down.

"I told you not to try to leave. I told you, you are mine and will remain here until I say so. I warned you, Fallon. I warned you!"

Tightening my grip, I drag her behind me and head for the basement.

"Please, Markus... I'm sorry. You have to believe me. I wasn't trying to leave. I wasn't..." Stopping dead in my tracks, I release my hand on her wrist and grab her by the hair. My fingers thread into her soft locks, and she lets a soft whimper slip past her lips when I crane her head back and force her gaze to mine.

"I don't want to hear your excuses," I snarl. "You betrayed me. I don't care what you planned to do. You shouldn't have been doing it, to begin with. Now, shut your fucking mouth before I find a better job for it besides talking."

Her eyes are filled with fear and disappointment. I'm just not sure if it's herself or me she is disappointed in.

I release her hair, grab hold of her arm once more, and continue our walk down to the basement. The basement temperature is about ten degrees lower than upstairs and will make for a very uncomfortable situation.

She'll remain alive, but she'll be exhausted and cold by the time her punishment is done.

Opening the cell door, I shove her inside and release her arm. She stumbles backward on unsteady feet, catching herself before she can fall. I grit my teeth and clench my fist, digging my nails into my palm to stop myself from reaching out to steady her.

I shouldn't want to help her.

Shouldn't want to protect her. She broke my trust; she did this to herself, yet I still want to help her. No. I won't be made a fool of.

"Welcome to your new home," I sneer.

"Please, Markus." She peers up at me, her eyelashes fan against her cheeks, and I can barely make out her features in the darkness.

However, what I can see makes me sick to my stomach. I swallow down the protectiveness that starts to build up at the fear and anxiety overtaking her features. I'm showing her exactly who I've been all along. The only difference is she's seeing me for that person for the first time tonight.

No. No! She will not control the situation. She will pay for breaking my trust.

"Shut your mouth," I roar.

She flinches as if my words have physically smacked her, and I need to get away. Leave this room before I do something I can't take back, or worse, before I take her into my arms and run back up the stairs.

Turning on my heels, I walk toward the door. I've made it all of two feet before she starts to sob. The sound makes my ears ring. She's openly crying, allowing me to see how weak she is. Does she not realize how stupid that is?

"Please, turn the light on!" She lets out a strangled sob.

The fear in her voice reaches out and grabs me by the balls. *Fuck.* I look at the light switch, stare at it, and then another sob fills the room.

"Please, Markus! Please, don't leave me in the dark. I'll do anything." I hear tiny feet shuffling over the floor and twist around to see that she is now a few feet away.

She risks getting close to me when she knows how angry I am with her? Does she have a death wish? The way she is looking at me right now. It makes me want to reach out and take her into my arms. *Don't. She deserves this.* I remind myself.

"Don't do this to me, please. I can't handle the dark."

Her pleads hit me right in the chest, and I can't ignore them. I flick the light switch on and walk out of the room, slamming the door shut behind me. I lock it and stomp up the steps angrily. Even though I can no longer hear her cries, I know she is crying. Her heart-shaped face stricken with fear and the tears in her eyes...

Stop! I force myself to stop thinking about her and walk to the alcohol cabinet in the living room. I don't bother grabbing a glass and instead grab the bottle. It won't be a glass night tonight. Twisting the cap off, I bring the bottle to my lips and take a long pull from it.

The whiskey burns all the way down my throat, leaving a path of fiery hell in its wake. I take the bottle and myself over to the couch and sag down on it. I take another drink, and another, wondering if I'll have to drink this whole thing before I can stop thinking about her.

I don't know why I'm so angry over her breaking my trust. I should've expected it, but I was stupid. I stupidly wanted her to stand by me, to be loyal because she wanted to be, that she maybe wanted whatever was taking place between us. I wanted her to want me. In the end, all it did was make me look like a fool. I won't be as stupid next time. I won't fall for her lies.

Shaking my head, I take another drink. My throat is numb, and my insides are warm now. The world around me is swimming, and I wonder how much time has passed. Then I hear it—the ringing of my cell phone from upstairs.

Like a newborn calf, I push off the couch on unsteady legs and nearly eat the floor a few times. I almost chuckle to myself as I walk upstairs with the bottle in my hand. By the time I reach my phone, it's no longer ringing.

Grabbing the device off the nightstand, I see that I've missed a call from Lucca. My anger is immediately redirected at him.

What the fuck has he been doing?

I enter my code and call him back. Taking another gulp of bourbon, I put the phone on speaker and listen to it ring.

"Hey," Lucca coolly answers.

"What the fuck, dickhead? What took you so long to return my text and calls? You ask me to do you a favor, and then I don't hear from you again?"

"Whoa, calm down. There was an accident at the mansion the other day. Elena got hurt, and Julian has everyone working night and day to find her father."

A tinge of guilt develops but doesn't latch on. I do feel a little bad for leaving Julian, but I haven't taken so much as a day off since I started working for his family when I was sixteen-years-old. I deserve this, even if it's not a typical thing to do when working for the mob.

"Oh, well, a text message wouldn't have hurt," I grumble and take another drink.

Lucca chuckles. "You sound like a clingy girlfriend."

"You sound like a stupid fuck," I retort, and my words slur a bit. Obviously, the alcohol is catching up with me. My eyes dart to the alarm clock on the nightstand. Just a little after ten. I feel so fucking old, and drunk. What's the next step, the nursing home?

"Are you drinking?"

"Yeah, what's it to you?"

"Not a damn thing. Wish I could have a drink myself, but I've got to stay on my toes. Julian would have my head on a platter if I got drunk."

"Yeah, yeah. Don't be doing anything to piss him off. You don't want to see him when he loses his fucking mind. It turns into a bloodbath real fast."

"Right. I called because I wanted to see if I could come by the cabin in the next few days and talk. It's something I can't really speak about over the phone."

I blink slowly. "Is it about her? The underage girl? This better not be what I think it is."

"She's sixteen, Markus, and it's not like that. I'm not a fucking creep. I'm not going to fuck her. Even if she was twenty, I wouldn't touch her." I'm not sure if he's trying to convince himself or me, but it's not working. I see right through his fucking lies.

"Yeah, sure, whatever," I mumble. Right now, I don't care about anything. I take another gulp of whiskey, emptying the rest of the contents into my mouth. Frowning at the bottle, I contemplate going back downstairs to grab another.

"I'll message you when I'm on my way, okay?"

"Yeah," I hiss and fall back onto the mattress. "Wait... I could use your help with something. Since you're going to come here anyway."

"Okay?" He sounds a little uneasy, probably because I hardly ever ask for help.

"Fallon, the girl here with me, the one I bought at the auction..."

"Yes. You're speaking in blocks, Markus. Spit it out." Impatience fills his voice.

"Fuck you!" I growl and continue, "I need to teach her a lesson. I'll send you a text and tell you exactly what I want from you when you get here."

"Whatever you need, I got you."

It should bother me he's willing to do anything I ask, even to an innocent woman, but it doesn't. Not today.

Fallon needs to learn her place and learn that no matter how much time passes or how attached I grow to her, she will always be mine and that I will always hold the power in this fucked up relationship we have.

"Talk later," he says, and ends the call.

I drop the phone onto the mattress beside me and stare up at the ceiling. My vision is blurry, and my ears start ringing.

As soon as my conversation with Lucca is over, my thoughts return to Fallon.

She did this to herself. She betrayed you... I tell myself, but somehow it doesn't lessen the pain I feel in my chest. It doesn't lessen my want to bring her upstairs and wrap my arms around her, to fuck her until she is a mess of my cum. She won't learn her lesson that way, though, so I hold myself back.

I let the alcohol pump through my veins and overtake my senses. Eventually, my eyes drift closed, and my mind shuts down. I fall into a fitful sleep, but even in my dreams, I can't escape her beautiful face and soft cries.

FALLON

I try to abate the shivers and tears, but I can't. I can't get them to stop. I haven't since he left me here two nights ago. He's been coming to bring me food and to let me use the bathroom, but he doesn't even look at me, and he barely speaks at all.

I'm still naked beside the pair of panties I'm wearing.

The only thing to keep me warm is the blanket and the two pillows that were down here from before. The book remained here as well, but my mind is too scrambled to even attempt to read. Plus, my constant crying would make it hard to see the words.

The tears slip freely from my eyes and down my cheeks, leaving wet tracks behind. It was a mistake to think I could go into that office and make a phone call without him knowing.

I knew it was a trap, knew he was testing me, and I still did it. But I had to try, and I did, but unfortunately, I didn't succeed. Another shiver wracks my body, and I shake like a leaf in the wind. The cold down here isn't normal. It pierces your insides, making it impossible for the warmth to ever return.

At least he left the light on, but that was only after I begged and pleaded with him. I felt so weak doing so, but the thought of being in the dark for days, I couldn't fathom it.

Sighing, I bite the inside of my cheek to stop my lips from trembling. However, it doesn't stop my teeth from chattering. Curling up on the two pillows, I wrap the blanket tightly around my body and let my eyes drift closed. I'm exhausted, so exhausted. I've barely slept while down here, and I don't think I will be able to until my body completely shuts down.

I know whenever sleep comes, it won't be restful. Time seems to drag on when you're cold. Eventually, I stop sobbing, and my entire body becomes numb to my surroundings.

I'm not sure how much time has passed, but I feel myself sinking into a fitful sleep when the sound of approaching footfalls meets my ears.

My eyes flutter open and my heart jumps in my chest. Suddenly, I'm awake again, my eyes darting around the cell. Is it time for food again? Is he coming to let me out? It's false hope since I know there is no way he will bring me upstairs, but I want to think he will because it makes me feel better and gives me a sliver of warmth when nothing else does.

The door creaks open a moment later, and Markus appears on the other side. His entire face is cloaked in a mask of complete darkness. A shudder works its way down my spine as a new kind of coldness washes over me.

I notice then that his hands are empty, which means he is not here to bring me food.

Markus is watching me like a predator watches its prey, waiting for the perfect moment to strike. Unsure if I should say anything, I remain quiet and unmoving. It's like I'm seeing a side of him I've never seen before, and if I'm not careful, I won't survive.

My stomach tightens into a ball of nervous knots. My entire body trembles, and I'm struck with terror. I've never been more afraid of Markus than I am right now.

What's he going to do to me?

As soon as he's close enough, I can smell it. The distinct smell of alcohol sticks to him like a second skin—bourbon with subtle undertones of cinnamon and cloves. I want to push off the wall and rush into his arm and breathe in his scent, to bury my face into his chest and let his warmth seep into me, but I don't move.

Rigid like a stone, I remain staring forward.

"Go use the bathroom." His words are a little slurred, but not nearly as much as I figured they would be since his entire body is swaying. Is he going to be able to stay on his feet?

I get up and follow him to the bathroom, where I do my business quickly. I'm not sure about what to do. Should I try to use him being drunk to my advantage? Could I overpower him like that? Or at least outrun him? I just need enough time to make that stupid phone call. But that's exactly what I thought the other night too.

"Hurry," his deep voice booms through the door, making me jump.

When I exit the bathroom, he is leaning against the wall like he needs its support.

"I knew I never should've trusted you. You're nothing but a toy to me. Or maybe a pet, a misbehaving pet." His words cut through me like a dull knife.

This is the most he has spoken to me in days, and the hatred in his voice hurts more than I like to admit. He's still angry over my betrayal, and I understand why. We were headed somewhere better, and now... now we are headed nowhere.

"I'm sorry you feel that way." I really wish he didn't. Despite all of this, there is a part of me that wants him to like me, and not just out of survival instinct. "Can I have something to wear, please?" I dare to ask.

Markus's eyes immediately lower to my body, my nipples are hard like small diamonds, but it's not because I'm turned on. I'm freezing. Markus can't seem to differentiate that thought because his gaze turns heated a moment later.

"I think I like you like this. Naked and helpless. Besides, it wouldn't be a punishment if you were comfortable. How are you going to learn your lesson if I baby you?"

"I'm going to freeze to death," I point out, hoping he'll go for that.

"You won't. It's not that cold down there. Just enough to keep you uncomfortable. The only way you can earn clothes back is if you tell me what you were planning on doing?"

"I told you. I was just going to call my parents—"

"Liar!" He grabs my arm roughly.

He drags me back to the cell. My much shorter legs can barely keep up with his large strides, and I almost trip twice. Each time, he pulls me back up by my arm like a rag doll.

By the time we are back in the cell, my chest is heaving, and panic grabs me once more, but this time it's not because Markus is here; it's the fear of him leaving again. I'm lonely, so incredibly lonely.

Shoving me back in the room, he turns to leave, and I grab his arm and make a pathetic attempt to pull him back. "Please, don't go."

It's a feeble attempt, and I think the only reason he stops walking out is because he is so surprised by my begging.

That makes two of us.

But every time I think about him leaving, my pride goes out the window. I'm so fucking desperate for him not to leave. Desperate for his touch, his company. I've grown accustomed to him, and now he's gone. It's just me and the cold now, and I hate it.

"Please, just stay here with me. Just for a little while."

"Whatever game you are playing, you're not going to win," he half growls, half slurs.

"No game. I just don't want to be alone anymore. Please."

He shakes his head, but his body is leaning closer as if it has already made up its mind. He pulls his arm from my hold, and I immediately miss the contact. I step closer once more, reaching out for him, but he shoves me away like I'm nothing more than an annoying bug.

Stumbling backward, I crash into the wall, scuffing my shoulder against the brick wall. Even with the tears in my eyes, I can see the conflict in his eyes. He is one second away from staying, from rushing toward me, and checking my shoulder is okay.

"Please..." I beg one final time, and I see the resolve crumbling in his eyes. Those crumbles fall away completely when his eyes zoom in on my shoulder, where I now feel something trickle down.

I tilt my head down to look at my skin to find it cut open and bleeding. I don't even feel the pain that should accompany the wound.

What I do feel is Markus moving around in the cell, heading straight for me.

When I look up again, he is right in front of me, his fingers wrap around my arm once more, but this time his touch is gentler, kinder as he inspects the wound.

"It's nothing..." I tell him, and he must agree because he looks away from the wound and into my eyes. With a deep groan, he flops down onto the unforgiving ground, taking me down with him. I don't object or fight him at all.

Quite the opposite, actually. As soon as he is sitting on the floor with his back resting against the wall, I curl up in his lap like a fucking cat. It's sickening how drawn to him I am like a moth to a flame, like an addict to their drug of choice.

I might be able to chalk it up to the lack of human contact and my body being in a constant state of cold, but deep down, I know it's more than that.

He wraps his arms around me, and I sigh at the warmth. It feels like he's giving me a hug. I cuddle into him, unable to get close enough. I've never craved anything so much in my life as I'm craving Markus right now. I don't want an inch of space between us. I want to be engulfed by his body, by his warmth, and his strength. I want him to surround me in every way, and for once, I don't care about the consequences. I don't care about what may happen tomorrow. All I care about is the now and him being here with me.

~

THE NEXT TIME I wake up, that imaginary safety I was feeling when Markus was holding me is gone, and so is his warmth. I blink my eyes open, and I'm greeted with the familiar gray brick of my cell. The only difference is, I'm not shivering like normal. It takes me a moment to gather my wits and realize a large, heavy sweater is draped over my naked body.

Jackknifing into a seated position, I hold the sweatshirt out in front of me. It's dark gray, size extra large, and even before I bring it to my nose, I know it's his.

Taking a deep breath, I inhale his unique scents, letting them soothe me before pulling the sweater on over my head and down my body. Warmth encompasses me. I'm protected even without him here. A tiny brief smile tugs onto my lips, and I wrap my arms around myself.

He stayed with me.

Then left me his shirt.

It might not be much, but it's something.

It's enough to give me hope.

If that's a good or bad thing, I do not know.

20

MARKUS

One week. That's how long I've managed to keep her locked in the cell. It's been hell, and I've drunk almost every bottle of liquor in the house to cope with it. I don't want to admit it, but a part of me doesn't just want her. It needs her. I can still feel her fragile body pressed against mine as she nuzzled into my chest, seeking my touch. I tell myself it's because she's had limited human contact for days, but it's more than that.

It was like she threw caution to the wind completely and gave herself over to me. When I put her down, she shivered, the cold returning to her body, and as heartless as I am, as mean of a fucker as I've been known to be, I couldn't stand there and watch her slight body tremble. I took my sweater off and gave it to her like the gentlemen that I'm not.

I take some Advil to ward off the headache that's pulsing to life behind my eyes and make some breakfast. I take my time preparing it and think of what's coming today.

Lucca will arrive this evening and help me with the last-ditch effort of keeping Fallon in line. If this doesn't work, then I don't fucking know what will.

Cooking breakfast, I dish up the scrambled eggs and sausage

and place a piece of toast on the plate. Then, I pour a glass of orange juice and put it on the table.

I make myself a plate as well and do the same. Today will be the first time we've shared a meal together in days, and I won't lie. I'm eager for her company. With everything set up, I head downstairs. Retrieving my keys from my pocket, I unlock the door to the cell and push it open.

My heart clenches in my chest when I find Fallon lying on her side, the sweatshirt I left her encompassing her body. Fuck. A wound of possession reopens in my chest. Mine. All fucking mine. There is something about seeing her in my clothes, and it isn't an emotion I can even put into words.

Pushing the door open a little more, it creaks, and she wakes with a startle, pushing up into a sitting position, her sleepy eyes land right on me. Her brows pinch together in confusion as she looks at my hands, and I realize she thinks I'm coming to deliver breakfast.

"Have you learned your lesson?" I ask like a parent scolding their child.

Fallon pushes up off the floor, her legs a little unsteady. I clench my jaw and tighten my hand into a fist to stop myself from reaching out to her. I cannot treat her like a delicate flower, not when I'm the one that's going to pluck all the pretty petals off of her.

"Do I... do I get to come upstairs?" The hope that radiates out of her shatters me.

"If you've learned your lesson."

Rushing toward me, she nearly trips over her own feet, and this time I don't stop myself from catching her. My fingers connect with her hip, and I steady her as she crashes into my chest, hardly moving me with the impact of her body.

Peering up at me through her lashes, her gaze is a mix of disbelief and exhaustion. I can tell she is tired, the bags underneath her eyes are dark, and her skin is puffy from days of crying.

Her anguish is a pierce to the heart. I didn't want to have to keep her in the basement. Truly, I didn't. But she fucking betrayed me, she fucking broke my trust.

Taking a step back, I put a little distance between our bodies. "Come. I made breakfast, and then I want you to take a bath."

She nods her head almost stiffly. I start for the door and realize within a second that she isn't moving. Twisting around, I find her just standing there, staring at the open door. Did the solitude hurt that badly?

I extend my hand out to her. "Your breakfast is getting cold." The growl of my voice causes her to snap out of it, and her eyes dart to my hand. A visible shiver slices through her, and then she places her hand in mine. I shouldn't hold her hand, I know that. It will make her think things, but I don't really care right now.

Her hand feels so dainty in mine, soft and smooth. It takes great strength to stop myself from stroking the top of her hand with my thumb, but I manage.

Together we head up the stairs, and I ignore how perfect her hand feels in mine. It's stupid to even consider her being anything to me. I just locked her in a cold basement for a week straight for defying me. If she feels anything for me, it's going to be hate.

When we reach the table, I release her hand. She slides into her seat, and I follow, doing the same across from her. A symbolic feeling of normality washes over me, having her sit and eat with me. I guess I wasn't aware how much I'd grown used to having her here.

Fallon doesn't even blink. She picks up her fork and practically inhales her food. I eat just as fast and by the time she is done, I'm finishing up as well. She moves to pick up the plates, stepping right into her duties from before, but I shake my head, stopping her.

"No. We can clean up later. I want you to go take a bath."

"Okay… are you going to come too?" she asks, almost like she is scared I will.

I shake my head. "Not this time. I have something to do before my friend gets here."

"Your friend?" She sounds astonished.

"Yes, someone I trust and work with," I explain. She looks unsure and nervous about someone coming over. I'm guessing more so at the mention of him working with me. Fallon isn't stupid. She must have figured out by now what kind of work I do, which means my work associates are just as bad as me.

I gesture for her to lead the way, and she hesitantly does. I'd have given her a shower, but doing so would've made her comfortable, and the point of being in the basement was the opposite.

As she walks up the stairs ahead of me, I notice how thin her legs are. Did she lose weight while in the basement? She never finished her meals when I brought her food, but I didn't think anything of it until now.

She strips out of her panties and my sweater and eagerly heads for the bathroom.

While she is in the tub, I sit on the bed, going over the plan in my head. When I asked him for a favor a week ago, I wasn't really sure what I was going to do.

Now I do, and though I don't particularly want to do this, I have to. I need to know who she planned to call, who she risked her own life for because if I was anyone else. If she had been sold to any other fucker at that auction, she'd have been killed for doing that.

It's not like I can use my standard interrogation techniques on her. Her skin is thick, and even when afraid, she can manage to keep her secrets locked down. I need to go one step further. I need to cross that line, whether I want to or not.

I already know I'm an asshole for what I'm going to do to her. I've battled with myself all week over if I really wanted to follow through with it, but I have to know what she's hiding, what was worthy of tossing everything away.

Thinking about the private investigator, there is the possibility of her working for someone, that she was planted at the auction for a reason, but that's a far stretch. I'm apprehensive to believe that there isn't more to the story.

It's more likely she has a boyfriend that she's afraid to tell me about. That possibility is both plausible and infuriating—the thought of another man touching her, putting his hands on what's mine. I shake my head to rattle the thought away, but it sticks.

I've never been possessive over a woman before, but when it comes to Fallon, I will kill anyone who threatens to take her away from me. I know it. Feel it with every beat of my heart. No matter what happens, she will be mine till I say otherwise.

From my spot on the edge of the bed, I can see right into the bathroom. Fallon grabs a towel and starts to wrap it around her body, but before she can fully cover herself, I've gotten a view of her wet, slick body. My cock, of course, hardens to steel.

I've missed that, having her close to me, her whimpers of pleasure, of being inside of her. If she hadn't fucked it all up, everything would still be the same, and I wouldn't be preparing to hurt her.

Fallon steps into the bedroom, the towel wrapped securely around her body. Her long blonde hair is dripping wet, and my eyes latch onto a drop of water that glistens against her collarbone. My mind goes straight to licking that drop of water off her skin, to spreading her thighs and feasting on her clit, to sliding deep inside...

"Markus?"

"Yeah," I snap, her voice dragging me out of the lustful haze.

I can't be thinking about getting close to her or fucking her. Not until I find out what I need to. Answers before anything else.

"Why is your friend coming by?"

"You'll find out when he gets here," I tell her with a growl. She stares at me as if she knows something bad is going to happen. I wonder what she sees. What do I look like to her?

Like a monster? Like I want to ravage her alive?

"All I need you to know is that I want you to be on your best behavior. If you're thinking of trying something, don't. Lucca won't save you. He's bad, maybe even worse than me. Not only that, but if you do try something, the cell in the basement will be the least of your worries." There is so much malice in my words, it's almost hard for me to speak them.

Fallon's throat bobs, and she white knuckles the towel. She's afraid. I can see it, smell it. Like blood in shark-infested waters, she's leading me right to her, showing me right where to strike.

"Of course. I won't do anything stupid. I've learned my lesson."

I nod and stare into her azure eyes while I speak my next sentence, "I hope so because next time it won't be the basement you face. It will be me."

It's clear she is still scared, but instead of cowering at my words, she stands tall. In another life, she would be perfect for me, and I could treat her decently, maybe not with love, but I could care for her.

In this life, I don't know what we are or what there could ever be between us. Before I can figure it out, I've got to clear the air between us. Find out who she was calling, and why? And after tonight, I'll have my answer.

I just hope I don't have to hurt her too badly, trying to get it.

21

FALLON

Our conversation from earlier has weighed heavily on my mind through the afternoon. His threat looming over me like an ominous cloud. I don't know his next move, and that terrifies me. I should be able to read him better by now, but I can't. I wonder what secrets he's hiding, what kind of darkness lingers beneath the surface.

I get the feeling there is so much more to him than he lets on and that I've only seen a fraction of it. I wonder if he would actually hurt me. Everything he's done up to this point has been child's play.

Part of me refuses to think he could hurt me while the other part of me doesn't, not while knowing how dangerous he is. The thoughts linger even while I continue to push them away. It's like my mind won't stop conjuring up ideas.

The afternoon bleeds into the evening, and I get more and more anxious with every second that ticks on the clock. Markus's friend will be here soon.

I'm wary of having another man in the house. It's hard enough to deal with Markus, but another man... that thought leaves me in ragged knots.

An alarming ding-dong bounces off the walls of the house, startling me. I nearly fall off the couch in my haste to stand. Markus casually shoves off his seat, giving me a look that says *behave or else*. I clutch a hand to my chest to stop my heart from beating out of it. I didn't even know this place had a doorbell.

Markus's huge frame fills the doorway, making it impossible for me to see who is on the other side, but I assume it's his friend.

"Hey," a voice I've never heard greets coolly.

This is definitely his friend.

"Come in." Markus gestures and takes a step back, leaving space for the mystery man to enter. If I was smart, I would avert my gaze, look anywhere but at him, but I prefer to look my enemies in the eyes. He walks across the threshold and into the house, and if I thought the room was small before, it's even smaller now.

Tall, dark, and handsome. A true cliche if I ever heard one, but that's what he looks like.

At first glance, he looks like the all-American boy, but the way he carries himself tells me his normal appearance is a facade. Everything about him screams dark, in an evil kind of way.

His hair is dirty blond, unruly, and a little shorter on the sides than on top, almost military style. His eyes, a dark shade of blue, almost violent when they meet mine. I wonder what secrets they keep locked inside? I wonder how many people he's killed? In what way he's connected to Markus?

None of those questions will get an answer, though, so I don't dwell on them long. It's obvious he works out or does some type of physical activity. Where Markus is beefy, almost like a lumberjack, this man is slender, tall with an athletic body.

"Lucca, this is Fallon. Fallon, this is Lucca," Markus introduces us with a grunt, interrupting the stretch of awkward silence.

I can feel his gaze like a thousand pinpricks against my skin.

He's waiting for me to do something stupid, watching like a shark watches for blood in the water.

"It's nice to meet you," I reply meekly.

Lucca's eyes twinkle with excitement, and I don't like it. Don't like the way his gaze turns hungry as it drifts over me, almost as if he's interested.

Markus wouldn't dare to share me, would he?

"Fallon was just going to start the sides for dinner," Markus hisses through his teeth, his eyes shooting daggers at me. For whatever reason, he wants me to disappear for a while, and I'll gladly do that.

"Oh, yeah." I pretend as if I knew that. "I'll be in the kitchen if anyone needs me," I say with way too much cheer. Even though the kitchen is only a few feet away, I exit the room like it's a three-mile hike up a mountain, and I should've left a day ago.

I expel all the air out of my lungs. All I have to do is make it through this evening dinner, and then Lucca will leave, and with him will go the anxiety I'm feeling.

~

DINNER PASSES IN A BLUR, and I spend most of it pushing my food around on my plate. I can hardly stomach the steak, even though it smells delicious. All my attention is on Markus. Something is off about him.

I can't put my finger on it, but he is acting strange, and strange enough, I doubt it's because his friend is here. Throughout dinner, Lucca seemed to slip a mask over his face, similar to how Markus does. Concealing his emotions and feelings beneath it.

He watches me with this unreadable expression plastered on his face. He hasn't really talked to me at all, not since Markus introduced us, but I don't need him to talk to me to know he's here. I can feel his eyes on me all the time.

It's almost like he's waiting for something to happen. What that is, I'm not sure.

As I finish cleaning up the dishes, I wonder if Lucca expects me to ask for help, or maybe he wants me to be scared of him? It's almost like this whole day is a test, and tonight I'm going to be locked back up in that cell. I think Markus is distancing himself from me on purpose as if he is scared to get too close, too attached, because only he knows what's coming next.

Maybe I'm imagining things, or maybe he's preparing himself. Preparing to hurt me. I still haven't told him who I was going to call, and I'm sure he realizes that. I don't think Markus is the kind of person who gives up that easily or forgets.

No matter what, I'll do whatever it takes not to be put in that cell again.

While Markus seems cold and detached, my emotions are all over the place. I'm on edge because someone I don't know is here, Markus is acting off, and on top of that, I still haven't called them. I've been here three weeks now and haven't contacted them once.

What if they think I'm dead? What's going to happen to...

"Fallon," Markus's deep voice drags me from my dark thoughts. "Come here." The timbre of his voice sends shivers down my spine. This isn't going to lead anywhere good. I drop the dish back into the warm soapy water and dry my hands quickly.

When I turn around and head into the living room, both men are standing there and looking my way. Goosebumps pebble my flesh under the scrutiny of their cold-hearted stares. They are about to do something to me. I just know it.

My steps falter immediately. I'm tempted to run, to turn away from the wolves, and do whatever I can to escape. Markus's gaze turns angry. He knows exactly what I'm thinking.

"Come. Here," he orders, sterner this time. All I can see is the cell downstairs—the same four walls. No light, no sunshine. Coldness all around me. My insides knot a thousand times over. Swallowing down the golf ball-sized lump in my throat, I make my feet move. I force my feet forward because the alternative is worse.

"Stand in front of me."

With shaking legs, I follow his command and stop right in front of him. I'm a dog willing to do any trick for her owner. Lucca moves behind me, and suddenly, I'm sandwiched between them. My heart seizes in my chest. What's happening?

I turn my head to see what Lucca is doing, but Markus grabs me by the chin with two fingers and pulls me back, forcing me to see only him.

"Eyes on me, Fallon." His voice is smoke wisping through the air.

"What are you doing?" I ask, my voice small and unsure.

"We're going to play a game. I'm going to ask you some questions, and you're going to answer them truthfully. Each time I think your lying, Lucca is going to take one item of clothing off your body. If you are naked by the end of the game, you lose, and you don't want to be the loser in this game. Do you understand?"

I want to nod my head, but I'm frozen.

My whole body is petrified with fear. If I'm naked at the end, I lose. I'm too scared to ask what happens when I fail. Yes, *when*, because I already know I'm going to have to lie, and he is going to know when I do. It's a test, the biggest one yet, and I'm about to fucking fail.

"I'm going to take that as a yes," Markus says. He doesn't even skip a beat and jumps right into things.

"First question. Did you know the guy with the camera?"

"No." I shake my head. That much is true. I didn't know that guy.

Markus inspects me for a moment, his eyes narrowing. I'm so afraid I shake.

"I believe you," he finally says. "So you didn't know him. Fine. Next question. Do you know who sent him?"

Shit. Shit. Shit.

"No." I try to keep my voice even.

Markus shakes his head like he is disappointed in me. "Do you want to reconsider that answer?"

Pressing my lips together into a firm line, I say nothing and watch Markus look past me to his friend. They are both so much taller than me they can look right over my head. A moment later, I feel Lucca's hands grabbing the hem of my shirt and pulling it up. I raise my arms automatically, letting him take off my shirt. There's no point in fighting it.

He drops it on the floor next to us, leaving me in a pair of leggings and bra. Goosebumps spread across my upper body, and I'm reminded of the coldness I felt while in the basement. Tears prick at my eyes, but I force myself to hold them back. I will not cry in front of them.

"Next question. Do you have a boyfriend?"

"No." I shake my head, relieved that he is asking something I can actually tell him.

"Were you really going to call your parents from my office?"

"Yes," I lie again. This one falls from my lips a little easier since I've already told it a few times, but Markus still sees right through me.

Shaking his head again, he motions to Lucca, who quickly undoes my bra. He pushes the straps slowly off my arms and lets the bra fall to the floor carelessly. Cool air washes over my exposed breasts, and I'm glad Lucca is standing behind me and can't see. Though, I have the feeling that if I lose this game, he is going to do more than see them.

"Were you sent to the auction by someone?"

"No."

Another small shake of Markus's head, and Lucca is pushing his fingers into the waistband of my leggings, pulling them down my legs, leaving me in nothing but my thin panties.

"Did someone send you to get to me?" Markus's voice is nothing more than a growl now. He is angry. So fucking angry.

Each word penetrates deep through my skin, and I know at any second I'm going to be on the receiving end of that fury.

"No." I shake my head and squeeze my eyes shut.

Lucca dips his fingers into the sides of my panties, his touch burns me, and he pulls them down roughly, making me gasp. My knees are so weak, I think they might give out at any second. Every inch of my body is shaking at what's to come, and all I can think about is how I wish I could tell him the truth. But I can't. I can't tell him. The risk outweighs the reward. Tears threaten to fall from my eyes, all the emotions inside me push to the surface at once.

"Get on your knees," Markus orders, just as I hear him undoing his pants. I feel Lucca's hands on my shoulders, pushing me down gently, but instead of obeying and getting down on my knees, I shrug away from Lucca's hold and lunge myself at Markus. I have to try, try to get him to see that I don't want this. That I don't want to lie to him.

Wrapping my slender arms around his torso, I bury my face into his ironclad chest.

"I'm sorry. Please, don't do this. I'm sorry, I'm sorry," I repeat over and over again, hoping that he believes me. Hoping he doesn't go through with whatever he has planned.

I'm certain he is going to push me away. Push me into his friend's arms, but nothing happens. No one speaks or does anything. An eternity seems to pass before Markus wraps his arms around me, engulfing me completely while pulling me closer into his chest.

"Go upstairs to the bedroom and wait there for me. Don't do anything else. Don't fucking touch anything else. Go straight to the bedroom and wait on the bed. Do you understand?"

"Yes," I blurt out, nodding my head furiously.

I don't bother picking up my clothes, and I don't dare to look back at Lucca. I'm too afraid that Markus will change his mind. I simply untangle myself from him and run up the stairs like I'm being chased by a swarm of bees.

When I reach the bedroom, I climb onto the bed and sit in the center. Drawing my legs to my chest, I wrap my arms around my knees and wait for Markus. I don't know if Lucca is going to leave now, or what Markus will do to me next.

All I know is that I am grateful he stopped whatever he had planned downstairs.

22

MARKUS

I can taste her fear. It coats the air, leaving a sweet tang against my tongue. The way she rushed into my arms like I was her saving grace and not her damnation.

It made my chest swell. Fuck, her pleading, tears filling her eyes. Fuck it all to hell. I was sure I could do it. Sure, I could fucking push through her pleads, but somehow, she crawled under my skin. Weaseled her way in there slowly.

I felt like punching myself in the face right now.

"I knew you wouldn't go through with it." Lucca grins in front of me. I try not to look down at the floor where all of Fallon's clothes lay discarded. Thank fuck, Lucca didn't see anything but her ass.

"Shut up and get out of here." I point him to the door.

"Do you want me to do it? While you're gone, I mean." Lucca barely gets the words out before I'm pouncing on him. My hands wrap around his throat, and I growl into his face like a feral animal.

"Don't even fucking think about touching her again. This was a one-time thing."

Lucca laughs and shoves me away. "You told me to, stupid."

"I know!" I roar.

Fuck, I know. Just like I know he's only trying to be a good friend. Offering me help. "How would you feel about me offering to *take care* of Claire?"

Lucca's complete body stiffens, and every trace of a smile is wiped from his face. Not so fucking smug now, are you? "Don't even talk like that. It's completely different, and you fucking know it."

"Sure, it is." I withhold an eye roll. "Now get out. I have things to take care of." I open the front door, ready to shove him out on his ass, when he stops right in the doorway.

"Whoa, I didn't drive out here just to help you." A cocky grin lights up his face.

"I remember. I was hoping you would forget to bring up whatever it was you wanted to talk about."

"You're an asshole." He shakes his head.

"What do you need to tell me or better yet ask me?" I grip onto the wooden door tighter.

Lucca's face becomes serious in an instant. It's scary how quickly he can switch gears. It's also scary how infatuated he is with this Claire girl.

"Your brother, Felix. Are you still in contact with him?"

"Yes," I reply as if I'm annoyed, which I kinda am.

"Could you give me his number? I need help with something, and your brother is the man for hacking and tracking down people."

"First, he's not cheap. Two, if Julian finds out you're working with him—"

Lucca interrupts. "He won't. This is none of Julian's business, and it doesn't affect the family in any way. This is for me and me alone."

Regardless of my brother being my blood relative when he and Julian fell out, I choose to stay loyal to Julian. It caused discord between my brother and me I'm not sure will ever be resolved.

"I don't want to be dragged into this mess, so keep my name out of it. I'll text you his number, and only because I feel bad for you."

"You won't be. Thanks, fucker, if you need anything, let me know."

"We're not friends," I growl.

Lucca snickers. "Sure, we aren't, asshole."

As soon as he is gone, I make my way up the stairs. As a warning, I stomp my feet with each step.

I'm nowhere close to knowing the fucking truth, but I couldn't go further, not with her clinging onto me like I'm her lifeline, begging me not to do it. Fuck, I've gone soft. Julian would be disappointed in me, the other men would call me a pussy. I know Fallon is a weakness I can't afford, but she's also a drug I can't kick.

When I enter the bedroom, I find Fallon sitting in the center of the mattress, looking small and fragile. Her eyes are wide and wary. She's apprehensive about what's going to happen next, and rightfully so. I don't even know what the fuck I'm going to do. I should throw her back in the cell with the light off this time, but I can't bring myself to do that either.

Needing to expel some of the energy out of my body, I pace the floor in front of the bed. I feel her eyes on me, moving like a ping pong ball as I move across the floor.

What the fuck am I going to do with her now?

I need information, but I can't fucking bring myself to do what it takes to get it out of her. Hurting her isn't an option. I can't.

There is so much pent up aggression lingering inside of me, I feel like I'm about to burst at the seams. Plus, I haven't fucked anything but my own hand for a week, which is a dangerous mixture. Those are the perfect ingredients for a bomb, and I'm about to go off.

Stopping mid-step, I turn and look directly at Fallon. Like a siren, she sits on the bed, completely naked and exposed. She's looking up at me with her big blue eyes, almost pleading with me. My cock stiffens, and even if I didn't get the answer I wanted, I know that I've held off long enough. One more night without her, and I might fucking die.

I've got to have her. All of her.

Raw primal hunger for her pumps through my veins; I move closer to the bed, my eyes remaining on hers the entire time.

"Lie down on your stomach," I order, and to my surprise, she does it without questioning me. Her compliance only feeds the fucking beast that's ready to fuck her three ways through this mattress.

Grabbing a pillow, I slide my arm under her belly and lift her up enough to stuff the pillow beneath. Straightening back up, I take her in. With her ass up in the air, I can see her folds peeking out at me. Playing a ridiculous game of peek-a-boo.

I bet she is wet for me already, but that's not what I want right now. Her pussy might be good, but I want more. I need to claim something else.

"Don't move," I warn before I grab the rope off the floor on my side of the bed and start to tie her wrists together. Looping them around the headboard, I secure them. I test the rope, tugging on it, and make sure it's not digging too tightly into her wrists.

"W-what are you going to do to me?" Her voice is muffled by the sheets, but even so, I can hear the tremble in it.

"I want your complete submission tonight. I want you to trust me. Let me do whatever I want. Can you do that?"

"Yes... as long it's just you."

"Yes, only me. No one else is going to touch you." *Ever.* I don't know what I was thinking, asking Lucca to do this. The thought of him touching her again makes me want to put a bullet in his brain.

"Okay," she murmurs against the sheets. Even with her voice muffled, I can hear how relieved she is.

I retrieve a small bottle of lube from the side table and undo the cap. Her puckered little hole is calling my name.

Sitting down on the bed beside her, I pour a generous amount of lube in my palm, close the bottle, and toss it to the side. I rub my hands together before placing both on her ass. I massage her cheeks first, kneading her firm globes until they are pliant in my hands.

When I run my thumbs further down her crack, I feel her tense, and I know she just realized what I'm going for.

"Have you been fucked here?" I ask, circling my thumb over her tight hole.

"No," she mumbles into the bed.

Knowing that she's never been touched there only gets me harder, which I thought was impossible. Keeping one hand on her ass, I use my other to undo my pants and free my throbbing cock. When I look down, I'm not shocked to find it looking like it feels.

Painfully hard, the head almost purple. I can't wait to be inside of her. Fuck, I should prepare her more, make her come once, but I'm too far gone. Too close to the edge.

"I'm going to fuck your ass now," I tell her while pushing my thumb inside just a little. Pumping in and out slowly, I watch my thumb disappear.

"I'm scared." She's trembling, her tight ring of muscles squeezing my finger. I want to soothe her, banish her fear of what's to come away, but I can't. I'm so close to drowning in her, nothing short of a damn miracle is going to stop me.

"You don't have to be. Not about this. I'll make it good for you. I just need you to trust me, submit, and listen to what I say."

"Okay..." She sucks a shallow breath into her lungs, and I push my thumb in a little deeper.

"Keep that tight hole relaxed for me." I pull my thumb out and replace it with two of my fingers. I start with slow and shallow thrusts and work my way up to being able to shove my fingers in as deep as they will go without her tensing up.

Using my other hand, I massage her lower back until she becomes molten lava in my hands, and a soft little moan that's slightly muffled meets my ears.

Fuck. I'm going to make her love this. Make it so good she'll prefer that I fuck her in the ass over pussy.

When I think she's ready, I ease my fingers out and pour a generous amount of lube on my cock. Climbing up on the bed, I straddle her legs, so my cock rests perfectly between her globes. Her ass is fucking perfect, firm but with a little jiggle.

"I love your ass, and I can't wait to fuck it," I pant.

Grabbing her with both of my hands, I spread those cheeks apart and rub the tip of my cock over her puckered hole. I push the thick mushroom head against her tight hole, slowly working my way inside. I have to grit my teeth and breath through my nose as I work slower than I've worked for sex in my life. With it being her first time, I had planned on teasing her longer, but once her tightness grabs onto my dick, I can barely restrain myself.

Her little whimpers are the only thing keeping me from burying my cock all the way down in one thrust.

Don't hurt her. Make it good. I repeat the words over and over again to myself. I push in slowly, letting her get used to my thickness. With nothing but the head of my cock in her ass, she looks divine. Only when I move deeper does she tense a little, the tight ring of muscles in her ass closing around my cock, and I hiss through my teeth at the sensation. I want to plow into her, own her fucking ass... literally.

"Relax for me," I croak, my voice tight.

She whimpers, but after a moment, does just that, and the

death grip she has on my cock becomes nothing more than pressure.

I run my hands up and down her lower back to keep her that way. Then, I move again. When I'm mostly inside, I lean down and place a chaste kiss on her shoulder.

She tilts her head to the side, a tiny moan escapes her, and I continue kissing my way across her neck and back. I love how submissive she is, how trusting she is of me with her body. I want to keep her like this forever.

Snaking a hand beneath her, I find her slick heat. She's wet, and her little clit is engorged, waiting for me to touch it.

"Ohhhh... Markus." I rub gentle circles against it before upping my pace. When she starts bucking beneath me, seeking out her own release, I thrust forward and bury myself the last few inches inside.

Pure bliss. It feels like heaven just grabbed me by the balls. I've never felt anything of this intensity before, and for a brief moment, I remain still, sweat beading against my forehead, my lungs burning. Somehow, I manage to compose myself and continue working her clit.

"How does that feel?" I grunt into the shell of her ear.

"Full, so full."

"Does it hurt?"

"No... it's just weird, foreign, and full. I think you're too big." Her voice cracks at the end, a tiny sliver of fear appearing there.

"You'll adjust. Give it a minute," I grit through my teeth while holding onto my sanity by a mere thread. Her ass is gripping my cock so tightly, I can feel every fucking quiver her body makes. All I want to do is fuck her hard, rut into her like there is no tomorrow. Instead, I keep peppering gentle kisses along her skin and draw small circles across her clit, building the pleasure back up.

"I'm going to start moving now," I give her a little warning before I pull back my hips and thrust back into her.

She whimpers at first, and I clench my jaw wondering if maybe it does hurt after all, but that quickly turns into a moan when I increase the pressure on her clit.

"Ohhhh..." Fallon lets out a surprised gasp. "That's..."

"I told you I would make it good for you. I'm gonna make you come while I'm buried deep in your ass. You're going to come so fucking hard, you'll see stars, and because it feels so good, you're gonna beg me to shove my cock in this hole every night."

My dirty talk turns her on even more. I know because she grows wetter with each penetrating stroke. Before I know it, she is mewling into the sheets, tugging on her restraints, and pushing her ass into my groin. It's enough to make me explode right then, but I hold off. I want her to come first.

"Come for me, Fallon. Come while I fuck your tight holes..." Keeping the pressure against her clit, I dip a finger into her cunt, and that's what sets her off.

Her body stiffens beneath me. Her ass grabs onto my cock so tightly, my balls draw up, and I know my own release is about to come.

I let her ride out her orgasm before withdrawing my hand. Now that she's come, I can seek out my own release without worrying about hurting her.

Digging my fingers into her skin, I grab her hips and hold her in place while I fuck her roughly. She whimpers beneath me but doesn't ask me to stop. I'm delirious with need, using her, seeking out my release, and nothing else.

Driving into her over and over, I feel the rush. My heart thunders in my chest and my toes curl.

"Fuck. I'm coming... I'm going to fill your ass with my cum." I slap her ass hard, and she tightens further around my cock. Shit-fuckinghell. A second later, I explode deep in her hole. I come so hard and long, my vision blurs, and I stop breathing.

Wave after wave of pleasure rushes over me until I'm completely spent.

I collapsed on top of her and catch my breath. I can still feel her ass pulsing around my cock, and I wonder if she came again. She's squeezing my cock like she did.

When I realize she's not moving at all, my thoughts take a nosedive.

Did I hurt her? Is she okay?

Worried I might be crushing her with my weight, I push myself up and off her. I make quick work of the ropes, so I can turn her around and inspect her. Her eyes are closed, but her cheeks are flush, and her eyes are dry. She didn't cry. Still, I'm worried that I was too rough?

"Fallon?" She stirs, but her eyes remain shut.

Maybe I fucked her right to sleep? Lying down next to her, I slide my arms behind her head and turn her toward me. She sighs deeply and inches toward me. Maybe she is cold and seeking out my body heat. I pull her closer and tuck the blanket over us both.

"Go to sleep," I tell her and place a gentle kiss on her forehead. My heart expands in my fucking chest as the soft sigh she expels. That was good, too fucking good.

I can't believe this is how the night ended. I was sure it would be a disaster with Fallon crying her eyes out in the cell, and me drinking myself half to death.

Closing my own eyes, I'm about to drift to sleep when I hear her murmur something. At first, I can't make out what she is saying at all. It's a mumble jumble of words that make little sense. Then I hear them loud and clear, the words that will not let me sleep a single minute tonight.

"I'm sorry I have to betray you..."

23

FALLON

*A*nother three days pass. Things feel different and yet the same. I'm still nowhere closer to getting to a phone to call those people. I've thought about telling Markus the truth more than once, but the instructions were clear. I'm not to tell anyone, especially not Markus.

If I do, my sister will die...

Pressure forms behind my eyes just thinking about her. She's been held captive as long as I have now, but I don't know under what conditions. Somehow, I doubt it's in a cozy cabin like I am, and that makes me feel so incredibly guilty.

Markus has scared me more than once, threatened to hurt me even, but I'm sure he's done nothing compared to all my sister must have endured.

Switching gears, I think back to that night three days ago. He didn't get the information he wanted, but he still didn't hurt me.

His touch was gentle, possessive. He worshiped my body and drove out feelings I had no right feeling. He bought me, paid a million dollars so that he could fuck me however he pleased. The last thing I should be doing is giving in to these tantalizing feelings.

Captive falling for her captor. It was stupid and would surely end in either heartache or death. Markus wasn't the type to love or even care for another human, so why was he showing me compassion when he showed no one else it.

He hasn't asked me again who I was trying to call, which makes me wonder if he has something else planned or if he's simply given up.

I mull over my thoughts while eating breakfast, which Markus made. Homemade oatmeal with fresh fruit. Each bite I take lands in my belly like a brick. Across from me, Markus sits, watching me, his eyes glued to my spoon as I shovel food into my mouth.

As if he realizes what he's doing, he shakes his head and snaps out of it.

"Hurry and finish. We're going on a little trip."

Newfound excitement fizzles in my belly. "Where are we going?"

I try not to sound as eager as I feel but getting out of the house is just what I need today. I feel like a bird in a cage, never free, always longing for more. I need to feel the air beneath my wings just for a while.

"It's a surprise," Markus says, his voice icy.

It doesn't sound like a surprise should, but I don't say that. The last thing I want to do is piss Markus off. We've been on such great terms, and I don't want that closeness to go away. I'll keep my mouth shut for now.

Picking up the bowl, I place it in the sink. When I turn around, I find Markus standing a few inches away. *Jesus.*

"You know for such a large man, you move like a ninja," I blurt out.

Markus gives me as close to a smile as I've ever seen from him. "Let's go. We're going to be late for the surprise."

I grin excitedly. "I can't wait."

Markus only nods, and I wonder if it's a surprise for another test.

∼

IN THE CAR, Markus is quiet, too quiet. He grips the steering wheel almost as if it's someone's throat. We pass through a couple towns, and with each mile, I realize we're headed toward my hometown of Sun Valley. I chew on the inside of my cheek to stop myself from asking him where we're going. If I can keep the terror that's bubbling up in my stomach down, then I'll be fine. Maybe we're just passing through?

That has to be it. I never told Markus where I lived. It's merely a coincidence. Right? It has to be. Knots of fear develop in my stomach, twisting and tightening to the point of pain. Placing a hand against my stomach, I try to hide the pain.

Markus doesn't even look away from the road, and I see that usual cold mask fall over his face. As we enter Sun Valley, I stare out the window, anxiously waiting to see what will happen next. Markus slows and turns onto a side street, then another, slowly getting closer to my house. Turning into the subdivision, I start to tremble.

Once we reach my street, I'm a complete mess, and my throat is so tight I don't think I could speak even if I wanted to. My family home comes into view, and my chest starts to rise and fall so rapidly it feels like I'm having a heart attack.

Drive by, please drive by.

The car slows and pulls to the curb. I can see everything I tried my best to rebuild with Markus crumbling beneath my feet. He puts the car in park and reaches across the seat for the glovebox. I bite my lip to stifle the scream threatening to come out of my mouth when I see the shiny glint of the gun. *What's he going to do? Is he going to kill them… or me?*

All I can think is how my sister will never be saved. How my parents will either lose both of their children or lose their own lives.

"Please..." I beg, not even sure what I'm begging for. I do know he is not here to drop me off and let me go. He is going to use my parents against me because he can't bring himself to hurt me anymore.

Markus's cold eyes cut to me. There is no emotion there, just my own reflection. He's cold, heartless, a statue. My words will not reach him, and still, I have to try. I can't die here.

"Don't do this, please. I didn't do anything. I've been good." His huge hand comes out of nowhere, and I flinch, afraid that he's going to hit me.

All he does is place his hand firmly over my mouth. He shakes his head, all but saying to shut up. My eyes dart to the gun in his other hand, and the tears welling in my eyes finally fall, slipping down my cheeks without permission.

There isn't a single ounce of remorse in his eyes.

After everything, it comes down to this.

"I want you to think long and hard before you answer the question I'm about to ask you because the wrong answer is going to result in one of your parents dying. Got it?"

Shock. It rattles me to the core. I'm not sure why, but I never thought he would go this far, that he would find a way to hurt me without actually hurting me. Staring into his eyes, I know I have no options. It's either tell him what he wants or risk one of my parent's dying.

That's just not a risk I can take. He will do it. I know he will.

The Markus in front of me now is the cold, calculated one, not the man who was gentle and kind to me the other night, and not even the one who put me in the cell. This is the Markus you can't reach, no matter how hard you try. Left with no options, I nod my head.

"Who were you trying to call in my office?" I swallow at the intensity of his stare and words. I can't breathe, can't do anything. He pulls his hand away to give me a chance to answer. A lie forms on the tip of my tongue... would he really do it?

I look at the gun in his other hand. Yes, yes, he's going to do it.

"If you lie to me, I'm shooting both of them." He doesn't even blink.

I'm trapped in a corner, and even though the gun isn't pointed at my head, it might as well be. Telling him the truth will ruin my chances of saving my sister, but what choice do I have? None. I have no choice.

"Please, Markus, don't hurt them. They have nothing to do with this."

"Tell me, now!" he roars like a beast, slamming his fist down on the center console, the rage in his voice making me shudder.

"Okay." The air wheezes out of my chest, and I close my eyes and open them again, trying to calm myself enough to fully speak.

"They... they took my sister and forced me into doing the auction. When I went into the office, I was trying to call them so that I could let them know I was alive. I'm worried they'll kill her if I don't get in contact with them soon."

Markus remains staring at me, not saying a single word. He's quiet, and that scares me. Why isn't he saying anything? Does he not believe me? Is he still going to shoot my parents? I find it hard to breathe, my lungs burning as if they have no oxygen in them.

"Please, don't kill them. Please! You have to believe me, Markus." My voice rises with each word I say till it sounds like I'm screaming.

"Stop! Calm down. I'm not going to hurt anyone," he snaps, and immediately, I close my mouth. Why is it that even though he just threatened my parents' lives, I want to bury my face in his chest and have him soothe the fear that he put there.

I breathe deeply in and out of my nose a few times to try and get myself to calm down.

He's not going to hurt them. Everything is going to be okay.

Giving me a moment to gather my wits, he asks a second later, "Who are *they*?"

I shake my head. "They wore masks when they took me. They told me that they would kill her if I didn't do as they said. All I wanted was to call her to make sure she was okay…"

Markus puts the gun back into the glovebox and closes it. Even though it's put away, I'm still afraid. Afraid of what he threatened. Afraid of what might have happened. I'm shaken to the core, completely rattled, and I'm not sure I'll be able to piece myself back together.

Putting the car in drive, Markus pulls away from the curb and starts driving once more. I look back at my parents' house, wondering what they would think of me right now. I yearn to go in there, to hug my mom and tell her I'm sorry, but all I do is watch the house get smaller in the rearview mirror as we go further down the road.

I glance over at Markus, his features are unreadable, and I'm not sure what he's thinking or if he even believes me. I want him to hold me, take me into his arms, and tell me everything will be okay, but he won't. That's not the type of man he is. He's not going to comfort me or care for me. He's going to take and take until there is nothing left.

"When we get back to the cabin, I want you to write the number down."

All I do is nod. I'm not sure what he plans to do. Perhaps call them? I turn in my seat and look out the window, watching my hometown flash before my eyes as we drive away. How am I possibly going to save my sister now? I doubt Markus is going to let me call them. And even if I do… if he finds out that I only told him half the truth, I don't know what he'll do.

I squeeze my eyes closed and breathe deeply through my

nose. The walls are closing in around me, and there's nowhere for me to escape. I'm stuck, and the closer the walls get, the more anxious I become. Soon they'll squeeze the truth right out of me, and when that happens, I'm not sure Markus and I will be on the same side anymore.

Not once he discovers what I was sent here to do.

24

MARKUS

*Y*ou would think I would be used to despair, dealing with those with a broken soul, being in the business that I am but seeing Fallon so completely broken. So scared and frightened. It fucking ruined me. The guilt presses down on me, and with every thump of my heart, the pressure inside my chest grows.

Despite the guilt, I can't let her off the hook. Yes, she was forced to lie to me, but she lied to me, nevertheless. Matter of fact, she is still lying to me. Because there is no way she doesn't know more.

"What do they want you to do?" I ask, after driving for a while. I needed time to compose myself. Keeping myself from grabbing her and shaking all the information out of her. Luckily, Fallon stayed quiet, so I could calm down in my own time.

"I don't know. They said they would tell me when I called."

"How exactly did you end up at the auction, and how did you get that number? Be specific. I want every single detail you remember."

"I was walking home from class when two men, both wearing black hoodies, grabbed me. I couldn't even see their hair color or anything. The only thing I could tell from their voices was that one was an older man."

She pauses, and I glance over at her. She is looking out of the windshield, her forehead scrunched up like she is trying to remember that day.

"They showed me a picture of my sister. She was tied up..." Fallon's voice becomes shaky, "They told me to cooperate, or they would kill her."

"What did they ask you to do?"

"At first, they just gave me a piece of paper with the number on it and told me to memorize it. We drove around a little bit, and then we stopped at a building. The same one the auction was at. The older man brought me inside."

Fallon shifts in her seat, nervously. Clearly, she doesn't want to talk about this, but there is no other choice. I want answers now, not on her terms.

"Did the man seem to know the people who ran the auction?"

"He must have talked to them before because they were expecting us. They were talking about someone specific buying me, which I didn't understand. I still don't, really. How did they know you would buy me?" I can feel her eyes on me, waiting for my reply.

Fuck. What am I going to tell her? Not wanting to lie to her, I say nothing at all. Instead, I think about what this means. Whoever sent Fallon knew about Victoria. They knew I would want her. They also had to know I would be at the auction in the first place.

I get the feeling that Fallon has added this up already but hasn't said anything. She knows more than she is letting on, and I need the information she has to figure out who it is that sent her, but most importantly, why?

"Do you know anything else? Is there anything that sticks out to you?" I try to hide the anger in my voice.

I'm not sure how I'm going to get the answers out of her. I've done everything, used every tactic I can think of, minus physically hurting her, and I don't even want to think about going there. The thought of hurting her... of marking her flesh with bruises makes me sick to my stomach. I could never force myself to strike her, not even while knowing she holds all the answers. I can't.

Fallon shakes her blonde head. Her eyes are glued to the floor of the vehicle, and without knowing it, she's giving herself away. "No. I have the number I can give you, but aside from that, I already told you everything. I know as much as you do."

Thankfully, we pull into the driveway, arriving back at the cabin. Which is what I need, to put some space between us, give myself some time to digest the information that I just discovered. It's obvious that someone is after me and that Fallon was sent for a reason. She's a damn near spitting image of my past. A past that has haunted me for years, a past that shaped me into the man I am today.

I park the SUV and get out, walking over to Fallon's side. She slips out of the car and falls into step beside me. When we're inside the house, I walk straight to the whiskey cabinet. I'm tempted to grab the bottle and take it with me over to the couch, but instead, choose to pour myself a glass. I don't want to get drunk, not when I need to remain alert and focused.

Taking a massive gulp, I let the distinct burn of the whiskey resonate through me. It hits my belly like a weighted brick.

Twisting the glass in my hand, I find Fallon standing beside me, watching me. I'm almost angry because all along, she was doing this because she had to. She didn't run, not because she didn't want to, but because doing so risked her sister's life. Knowing she lied from the very start, at least to some degree. My grip on the crystal glass tightens. I don't know how I've kept myself from imploding on her.

She's so fucking brave and stupid. Brave for doing what it takes for her sister, but stupid for listening to someone who is obviously after me. But I suppose if the roles were reversed, I'd do the same, wouldn't I? Wouldn't any decent human?

"I want that number," I tell her before taking another gulp.

"Okay..." She wrings her hands together, nervously.

I pull out my phone and swipe my fingers across the screen to unlock it. When she doesn't say anything, I clear my throat. She jumps a foot off the ground, and I can see the moment her heart jumps into her throat.

After a second, she rattles off the numbers, and I punch them into my phone.

"Go start dinner," I order brashly.

Fallon looks down at her feet, and for a second, she stands there, just stands, and I wonder if I'm going to have to threaten her or if she has something more she wants to say, but the words connect, and she walks into the kitchen, disappearing from view.

Bringing the glass to my lips, I down the rest of the whiskey. I place the glass back on the little bar top and stare at the illuminated screen.

My thumb presses the green call key, and I bring the phone to my ear. I'm not sure what I was expecting... but before I get the chance to put together a reaction, the phone says: *the number you have dialed has been temporarily disconnected.*

It's by the grace of God that I don't whip my phone across the room.

She lied to me.

I fucking know it. There is no way they would give her a number and have it be disconnected. They wanted her to find a way to reach them, which is why they gave her the number in the first place.

That means that not only did she lie to me, she purposely gave me the wrong number. She might be trying to protect her sister, but she's going to end up getting herself hurt in the end. I won't stop till I know who is behind this. Barely talking myself off the cliff's edge, I walk into the kitchen. If she wants to play a game, then we both can play.

She has nothing here. Just me, and the only way to make it out of this is with my help.

"The number was disconnected," I say nonchalantly.

Fallon looks up from the vegetables she's cutting. "What? That's the number they gave me. How will I get in contact with them?" She tries her best to act shocked, and even a bit sad, but I see through her like an open window.

Her eyes skirt away from mine when I attempt to make eye contact.

She's just digging herself a deeper hole.

I move into her space and grab onto the counter. I've scared her enough today, pushed her to the edge already, but I want her to know I'm onto her. I want her to know that she's not safe playing this game. I won't protect her, knowing she is working with the person who is after me, even with her sister's life hanging in the balance.

"I know you think I'm stupid, but believe me, I'm not. You gave me the wrong number on purpose. You're afraid of what's going to happen, but if I were you, I wouldn't be worried about your sister. I'd be worrying about yourself because lying to me..." I lean down and pause. I can see the fear rising in her eyes. "If you are lying to me again, I can't be held accountable for what I'm going to do to you."

She's afraid of me. Afraid of what I might do, and now she'll be anxious and waiting.

"Please, Markus." Her lip wobbles, and I want to bite it.

I want to tell her she shouldn't have lied to me, but I don't. I press my lips into a thin line and shake my head, driving the urge to kiss her down.

"Don't worry, Fallon, by the time we're finished, you'll tell me everything I want to know without me even having to ask."

Her blue eyes grow impossibly round, and I run my thumb

across her bottom lip, all while wondering if I could kiss the truth right out of her?

"Get on your knees," I say in a brisk order.

She blinks, the fear still in her eyes, though it's diminished a bit. "What?"

My teeth grind together. "Don't make me repeat myself."

The little lump in her throat bobs, and she drops the knife onto the cutting board. Like the obedient little lamb she is, she drops to her knees. She peers up at me, her eyes shining with an unknown emotion. She is still afraid, yes, but there is something more.

"Undo my pants and free my cock."

"Markus." She tries to reason, but for every lie, every wrong move on a chessboard, there is a consequence, and this is hers. When she doesn't make an attempt to do anything, I attack.

Like a predator, I sink my hand into her soft golden locks and tug her head back. Soft, delicate features. Full plump lips. Everything about her makes me hungry. Makes me want to be better, do better. Maybe I could, but then again, maybe I couldn't. I'm not the man she makes up in her mind, whoever he is. I'm a beast, a monster, the villain.

Leaning into her face, I run my nose over her cheekbone, the bridge of her nose, inhaling her, wishing she trusted me enough to tell me everything. So soft, so perfect... a liar.

Pulling back, I growl, "Do it, or would you rather I fuck your ass without care?"

"No," she whimpers.

I release her hair. "Good, then undo my fucking pants, pull my cock out, and get ready to choke."

Her gaze drops to the swell in my jeans, and she flicks the button, undoing them, and shoving them down my hips. I bet she's wondering if I'm really going to hurt her. If this is a true punishment or not? Honestly, I haven't decided.

My thoughts fly out the window the moment her hands wrap

around my cock. Fuck, her touch undoes me. It unwraps me from the inside out, leaving all my protective insides vulnerable. Still, no matter how good her hands feel on me, it's her mouth that I want.

Swatting her hand away, I find myself gripping her by the back of the neck, my hold unyielding. "I want your fucking mouth," I grit out.

As if I'm not close enough to the edge of insanity, she drives me the last inch there when she places one hand on my thigh and leans forward, taking the mushroom-shaped head of my cock into her mouth. It's both heaven and hell. The warmth of her wet mouth surrounds me, and I have to remind myself that this is her punishment.

I'm using her for my own pleasure. Using her hot mouth.

"Open up wide," I groan.

With her trustful gaze on mine, she obeys, and I grit my teeth, knowing what's to come. Releasing the nape of her neck, I take both hands and cradle the side of her face, almost protectively. Without warning, I thrust to the hilt, my cock hits the back of her throat, and she gags like I anticipated, her hands pushing against my thighs in terror as I hold myself there for a moment before pulling back.

A wheezing noise meets my ears as she sucks a breath of air into her lungs like it will be her last. I allow myself to look down at her for one brief second and find that tears are already leaking out the corner of her eyes. Below me, she looks so delicate, so fucking perfect, a fragile flower pushing through the concrete, wanting to prevail no matter how damning the circumstance.

It makes me want to break her. No, I have to break her. I need her to tell me everything, need her to be broken and afraid. Need her to need me.

Forcing myself forward, I repeat the process again, but this time I move faster. I slide deep, relishing in the loud gagging sound she makes and the way her tiny throat tries to swallow around my cock. Saliva dribbles out the side of her mouth and down her chin, and I swear I've never seen anything more beautiful.

"You look so fucking pretty with my cock in your mouth," I say between my teeth, pulling back and diving in again.

She doesn't respond, but her nails sink deep in my thigh muscles, and I let out a hiss of pain. "Fuck, yes. Hurt me. I want to feel your anger."

From that point on, things get blurry. I fuck her mouth almost incoherently, holding her head in place, pistoning my hips faster and faster, using her mouth as if it were her pussy, and she lets me, knowing this is her punishment.

Hollowing out her cheeks, she tries to get me to come sooner by adding pressure, but I'm not ready to come yet, and this punishment ends when I say so.

"I'm in control." I snap my teeth together and hold myself at the back of her throat. She makes another gagging sound as I choke her with my cock.

Fuck, that sound is pure joy to my ears.

When I can't hold off any longer, and her silky mouth becomes too much for me to bear, I let go of her head and pull out. Taking my cock into my hand, I stroke faster, feeling the pressure in my balls, knowing I'm going to be coming soon.

"Fucking look at me. Open that pretty little mouth, and don't you dare look away," I grunt. Slowly, she does as she's told. Staring at her, I find her lips are swollen, her eyes are red as if she's been crying and not choking on my cock for the last five minutes.

She looks shattered and beautiful, but more than anything, she looks like mine. I can tell she's turned on, the lustful glaze over her eyes, giving her away. I almost feel bad... almost.

My orgasm nearly knocks me off my feet, my abs tighten, and I explode a second later. It's a sight to see and one that leaves my heart thundering in my chest.

Hot spurts of cum land on her lips and against her tongue. She remains that way, with her mouth open, and the proof of my orgasm right in front of me. Addicted to her fucking touch, I bring my cock back to her lips.

"Suck," I order, and like a submissive little mouse, she does. She sucks me hard as if she's trying to bring my cock back to life. "Fuck, yes," I growl, my voice sinister. I swipe my thumb over my release, rubbing it into her skin and lips, needing to mark her.

When I feel she's had enough, I pull back and tuck myself back into my jeans before buttoning them back up. I feel her eyes on me, and I already know she's wet. Her pussy weeping against her cotton panties.

"Are you..." She pushes off the floor, the words coming out in a stutter, and this is the part of the punishment I'm going to both love and hate.

"Get you off?" I finish her sentence while cocking my head to the side.

She swallows and nods her head to affirm that was, in fact, her question.

I shake my head. "Nope. As badly as I want your greedy little pussy, which I know is drenched and ready for my cock, this was your punishment for lying to me. Now you get to spend the entire day wanting something that I could easily give you, but you won't receive. Much like the phone number I asked for."

Anger rises in her features, overtaking the arousal that was there moments ago. I struggle to stop myself from ripping her yoga pants off and setting her ass on the edge of the counter right here in the kitchen to feast, but it has to be this way, even if I don't want it to be, even if everything in me says to give in to her wanton needs.

"I... I can't believe you," She hisses angrily.

"Believe it. Maybe next time you won't lie to me. Now, wash up and get back to making dinner." I turn around and head back into the living room for another glass of whiskey. I can feel her gaze on me. It's like knives piercing into my back.

Guess she shouldn't have lied.

∽

THINGS ARE quiet throughout dinner and as we get ready for bed. Fallon hasn't said more than a handful of words, but the best of all is that she hasn't denied that she gave me the wrong number on purpose. I'm stupid for being as pissed off about it as I am. It should be expected, but I keep hoping, thinking maybe because I treat her better than I know any other man at that auction would've. Maybe she actually wants this?

Before, the trust was growing between us, flourishing like a flower in the sun, but now that flower has been stomped into the ground. That thought makes me want to shake her.

"Do you have to go to the bathroom?" I growl, waiting at the edge of the bed.

"No," she whispers, not even fucking looking at me.

She's wearing one of my shirts and a pair of panties to bed. I don't dare admit to myself the pleasure I get from seeing her in my clothing. It's irrational and downright insane how much I want to make her mine.

"Good." I stomp over to the nightstand and turn off the light.

As badly as I want to push her away, I can't. My body won't fucking let me. She's an addiction I can't kick. I hated myself for leaving her so needy earlier, but I had to do something.

Rolling onto her side, I spoon her from behind and toss an arm over her, tugging her back into my chest. She molds to my body perfectly and lets out a soft little sigh. I'm tempted to bury my face in her hair, but I don't.

Trailing my hand down her belly, I brush against the waistband of her panties. A shiver ripples through her, and I bite back a chuckle.

"You're so fucking responsive to my touch."

"I don't want to be," she grumbles. "I wish I wasn't attracted to you."

"We all have things we wish were different. Life isn't fair, that's just how it is." I nip at her ear and slip my hand into her panties.

She makes a strange sound in the back of her throat, and I swear the sound has a direct line to my cock. "What are you doing?"

A husky rumble leaves my chest. "What I would've done earlier but couldn't because I had a point to prove."

My fingers dance over her smooth mound, moving lower and lower while her chest rises and falls faster and faster. She wants this. Wants me so badly, I bet she can taste the release on the tip of her tongue. Dipping a finger between her folds, I find her wet and grin like an asshole. I stroke her clit, rubbing gentle circles against it.

"I wish I didn't want you so much," I growl into her ear and suck on the tender flesh beneath it. Her breath hitches in her throat, and with each stroke of my finger on her clit, her body melts further into mine.

My cock stiffens, begging to be unleashed and let inside of her tight cunt, but she's not getting my dick tonight. Moving my fingers lower to her tight entrance, she lets out a frustrated sigh but shuts her mouth when I sink two thick fingers into her at once.

"So tight, so fucking perfect. You have no idea how jealous my cock is right now," I say against the back of her neck, pumping my fingers in and out, listening as the sound of her arousal fills the room.

"Oh, god. Please, don't stop, please, don't." Her hand latches onto my arm. Her tiny nails sink into my skin, and I kiss the side of her neck harder, sucking on her, wanting to imbed myself deep inside her.

Keeping my pace, I grind my palm against her clit, knowing it'll be the final blow.

"Come for me, squeeze my fucking fingers. Show me what my cock is missing."

Muscles stiff, her entire body locks up. I bet her toes curl. Her cunt tightens around my thick fingers, trying to push me out as she shudders against me, and her orgasm overtakes her, dragging her into the deep dark waters of pleasure.

Like a feather, she slowly drifts back down to reality. Her pulse thunders beneath my lips, and I gently kiss her flesh while continuing to hold her tight against my chest.

After a few minutes, I ease out of her panties and remain holding her.

"Thank you," she whispers.

"I don't like withholding pleasure from you. I want to make you feel good." The words are the most honest thing I think I've ever said to a woman.

"I know."

It's the last thing she says before she falls asleep, her soft snores filling the air a short time later. As I close my eyes, I wonder if there could be more to us. If the lies were pushed to the wayside, could we be something more? Could it be more than pleasure and pain? Captive and captor?

I feel myself sinking deeper and deeper into sleep, and then I hear it, a loud crash that has me shooting into a sitting position on the bed.

25

FALLON

I've never gone from a deep sleep to being wide awake so quickly. A crashing sound startles me, and my eyes fly open. In an instant, I know something is wrong. I'm on high alert, and so is Markus, who is already sitting up in the bed next to me.

He moves with lightning speed, pulling on some pants and grabbing something from beneath the bed. The moonlight coming from the window reflects against shiny metal, and I realize he is holding a gun.

There was a fucking gun lying just mere feet away from me this whole time?

"Go hide in the closet, and do not come out until I give you the all-clear that everything is good," Markus orders.

For a moment, my feet are lodged like sticks in the mud, and I stand there looking at his gun. I know chaos is taking place all around me, swirling like an approaching hurricane, but I can't bring myself to move.

When I don't follow his command, he takes matters into his own hands and grabs me by the arm. About that time, I snap out of it, but he's already dragging me across the room. He shoves me into the dark closet and shuts the door, the slam of it is deafening.

My heart is beating so loud and fast, for a few minutes, that's all I can hear—my own heartbeat thundering in my ear, and against my ribcage like a sledgehammer.

The walk-in closet I'm in is pitch black, besides the sliver of moonlight escaping through the narrow window. I sit and stare at that small sliver of light, hoping and praying that nothing bad will happen.

Then suddenly, there is a crash, something breaking, glass shattering, and males growling.

Markus is fighting someone. Somehow, that thought calms me a little. Markus is a big guy, muscular and taller than most men. If someone shoots him, he could die quickly, but in a fistfight, he probably has the upper hand... unless he is outnumbered.

Stepping closer to the window, I shove onto my tiptoes and peer down into the dark yard. I search for a car, but instead, find a man standing on the grass near the front door. He looks up and straight at me, almost as if he knew I would be standing here.

I suck in an unsteady breath before I seize to breathe altogether. I'm suffocating, drowning in a sea of terror.

Only when he doesn't react, do I realize he must not be able to see me through the window. That fact doesn't do much to calm me, though. There are at least two men here and only one Markus. He's outnumbered, which isn't good.

I don't know what to do... Should I go downstairs and warn him? Try to help him? Maybe I can grab a knife from the kitchen, but then what? Do I just stab him and hope I hit where I should?

Looking down through the window and at the man on the lawn, I wonder why he is not going inside. He looks up again, then to the other windows as if he is looking for something. No, not something, *someone*.

He pulls something out of his pocket, which I quickly realize is a phone. The screen lights up, illuminating a small amount of his face. I can't see enough to recognize him.

When he puts the device to his ear, I see it. The tattoo of a snake's head on the top of his hand, almost like it's crawling out of his sleeve.

I recognize it immediately. It's one of my kidnappers. He was the younger man who took me from the campus. I completely forgot about that tattoo until now, but I know it's him. He is talking to someone on the phone. Fear and elation swirl inside my stomach like a sinister cocktail. These men are here for me, not Markus, and they know where my sister is. I need to talk to him. I need to tell him I need more time.

When I make my next move, I don't think about the consequences. All I'm thinking about is my sister. I open the door and leave my secure hiding spot against Markus's wishes. Pulling open the bedroom door, I briefly stick my head out into the hallway. When I don't see anyone, I walk out, sticking close to the wall as if it will somehow protect me. Sounds echo from downstairs and into the hall.

I can hear two men grunting and the sound of more stuff breaking. They are still fighting.

With only one way downstairs, I have no choice but to go down the stairs. As soon as I reach the bottom, I see them. Two men, one Markus, the other I don't know. They are in an even fight, both getting in some good punches with neither one budging.

Markus's eyes find mine in an instant, and my heart stops. It's only a brief second that our gazes lock, but that's all it takes for me to know he is angry with me. I betrayed him *again* by not listening and putting myself in danger. The worst part of all and the part that has me second-guessing myself is that I know he's not going to forgive me this time.

No matter if he will forgive me or not, and minus whatever

feelings have been growing between us, my sister is the only thing that matters. I have to save her. I'm here because of her.

Shaking that dreadful feeling away, I dash through the open space and out the door without another glance.

The cool night air washes over my skin, and a shiver wracks my body in an instant. Only then do I realize I'm wearing nothing but a pair of panties and Markus' shirt.

Why didn't I grab something to wear?

"I see her. She is still alive," the man from the window's voice drags me from my thoughts. My head snaps up to where the sound is coming from. He lowers his phone and starts walking toward me. An evil grin spread across his face.

Even though every fiber in my body tells me to run away, I force my feet to walk toward him instead. The grass feels soft and cool against my bare feet as I step off the porch.

"I just need some more time," I tell him when I'm closer. "I can still get it."

"It's been more than three weeks, and you still haven't gotten it. We figured he had you locked up or already killed you, but here you are walking around without restraints. Interesting." His voice is low and threatening. The sound has the small hairs on the back of my neck standing. My mouth dries, and my knees start to shake.

He takes a step toward me, and I come to a sudden halt, not wanting to get any closer than necessary.

"He never lets me out of his sights, and there is no phone. I've been trying. I swear. Please, don't hurt my sister." My voice just as shaky as my legs now. I'd give up my own life at this point to protect my sister.

"I think it's too late for that. You didn't honestly think we would keep her for so long and keep our hands off her, did you?"

"No..." I shake my head, not wanting to believe what he is saying.

"Maybe I should give you a taste of what's been happening to her." He grins, and his eyes flash with lust and mischief.

He takes yet another step toward me, and that's when I snap.

Run—my brain screams.

Spinning my body around, I take off. As fast as my legs will carry me, I run across the yard and into the forest surrounding the property.

I hear the man following close behind, his heavy footfall getting closer and closer. I push my legs, forcing them to go faster. Adrenaline feeds my muscles, numbing my feet from the pain of rocks and sticks digging into the bottom of my feet.

Thin tree limbs whip into my face and arms as I dash through the darkness of the woods. I slowly start to register the pain, but I ignore it and keep running.

One moment, I am whizzing between trees, and the next, a body slams into me from behind, knocking the air from my lungs as he tackles me to the ground.

Gasping in pure terror, I try to free myself. With everything I've got, I buck, hoping I can get him off me, but he is just too heavy, too strong. Turning me in his hold, so I'm lying on my back, he straddles my chest and snatches my wrists, rendering me completely immobile.

"Stop!" I croak, pulling on my arms with all my might.

"Funny, that's what your sister keeps saying too." He chuckles, and the ache in my chest expands. My sister, my poor sister. It's all my fault. I should have tried harder, done more. I should have helped her. I let this happen to her, just like I'm responsible for this happening now.

Why didn't I stay in the closet like Markus told me?

After a moment of struggling, I free one of my wrists. Using the momentum, I lash out at my attacker, scratching across his face. I dig my nails into his skin until I feel warm blood running down my fingers.

"You fucking bitch," the man groans before pulling his arm

back. With a closed fist, he hits my face. Pain erupts across my cheekbone and spreads out all over my face like a wildfire.

My eyes roll back, and the dark night becomes even darker. I feel myself passing out, my vision blurring, but I force my mind to stay awake.

Suddenly, my wrists are free, and a hand wraps around my throat while the other tears my shirt from my body. I can't breathe, my head feels like it's about to explode, and I know I can't keep myself awake any longer. I'm going to die. I failed my sister, and now I'm going to be violated before I die. Worst of all, this evil man is the last thing I'll ever see.

Just when I think all hope is lost, the man on top of me is gone. All the weight is lifted from my body, ripped away like a tidal wave, leaving me on the forest floor, gasping for air.

It takes me a few seconds to regain my bearings, to even realize what's going on. Grunts and groans are coming from somewhere close by. I sit up and look around, and what I find has me both sighing in relief and shaking to the bones with fear.

Markus has the man who attacked me shoved up against a tree, pummeling his fist against his face and body like he's a sandbag. Like a wild animal, and without mercy, Markus beats the man to a pulp.

He continues his attack even after the man stops moving and slides down to the ground. Even after I'm sure, he is dead. Markus is crazed, unhinged, and without humanity. He keeps punching the now dead body until there is only one thought left in my mind...

I'm going to be next.

26

MARKUS

Warm, sticky blood coats my bare chest as if it's a second skin, and it takes me a moment to get my ragged breathing under control. War wages beneath the surface, threatening to eat away at my control. In my mind, I still see that fucker touching her, hitting her face while she is helpless on the ground, and I want to bring him back to life just so I can kill him again.

I quickly search his pockets, but there isn't a wallet or even car keys. My anger intensifies but diminishes a bit when I find a phone. It's not a complete loss. I shove the device into my pocket and return to Fallon's side.

The sight of her as she sits on the cold ground, her knees pulled to her chest, her arms wrapped protectively around them while she sobs, is enough to do me in. I have to get us out of the woods and back into the house. I know the last thing she wants me to do is touch her, but she's not going to move on her own, so I have no option but to pick her up.

"We have to get into the house and get cleaned up," I tell her, my voice thick.

She shakes her head and squeezes her eyes shut, like that's

going to make me disappear. I know she's going to struggle, so I move with rapid reflexes, snaking one hand beneath her legs while wrapping the other around her back and pulling her into my chest. Like a stallion, she bucks against my chest, but I hold her tighter.

"Please, don't... please..." Fallon cries while continuing to struggle in my grasp.

"Shhh, stop fighting me," I hush, but that only seems to make her fight me more. "I'm not letting you go," I growl like an animal.

The mere thought of her trying to escape makes me feral. I'm reminded that that's exactly what she did. I told her to remain in the closet, and she didn't. She ran right outside as if she couldn't get away fast enough. I'm tempted to fucking put her on the ground and rut into her a thousand times over, marking her body with my own while telling her over and over again that she will never be free of me, but I don't.

She is too close to the edge, too close to breaking, and I will not be the one that does that to her, no matter how tempting it is. When we reach the house, I jog up the stairs and into the bedroom. My thoughts are hyper-focused. I need to clean Fallon and myself, pack a light bag, and get the fuck out of here.

The cabin is no longer secure, and I was foolish for thinking that whoever is after me would stop at one person.

Placing her at the foot of the bed, I walk into the bathroom and retrieve a washcloth. When I return to the bed, I find Fallon in the same position I left her. Her chin is tucked into her chest, and she looks more scared than I've ever seen her before.

My shirt, the shirt she wore to bed, is tattered, hanging off one shoulder haphazardly.

The blood in my veins burns red hot as I drop my gaze, dragging it over her tiny body. Bruises have already started to form on her tender skin, and there is blood everywhere. It's hard to tell if she is bleeding or if the blood staining her skin came from me.

I look down at her legs, her thighs, where fingertip bruises have formed. I know he didn't rape her. I know because I got there just in time. If I allow myself, I can still hear her screams. The bloodcurdling sound may live with me forever.

"Did he hurt you anywhere?" I ask, not wanting to know but needing to know all at once.

When she doesn't move, doesn't even speak, I grip her by the chin and lift her face, so it meets mine. There is a turbulent storm brewing in her blue eyes. Pain, grief, and sadness consume her. She is lost inside herself right now. Unfortunately for her, things are going to get worse before they get better.

"Did he hurt you anywhere?" I repeat, this time a little slower.

Fallon stares at me for a long moment before shaking her time.

I nod and brush a few matted strands of hair from her face. She has a scratch above her eye and across her cheek that she must've gotten from a stray branch or twig. The other cheek is unscratched but swollen and red.

Using my thumb, I trace the cuts, making sure they're not deep. Her feet look to be cut up from running through the woods barefoot, but aside from bruises and the terror she is feeling, she will make it.

I release my hold on her chin, and her face falls once again.

She is broken, my beautiful flower, but she will prevail. I'm vaguely aware I should be punishing her right now, but what that fucker did to her is punishment enough.

I use the washcloth and clean the cuts on her face and feet. She has a little blood on her shoulder and arms, so I clean that off too.

"Take off your shirt," I order gruffly, my patience already shredded.

Fallon seems to fall deeper into herself, and I decide to take matters into my own hands. Leaving her once more, I go into the closet, find a shirt, yoga pants, and a fresh pair of panties. When I return, I dress her like a small doll, looking over her body for any injuries she may have been lying about. She reacts only briefly to my touch with a flinch, as if I'm going to hit her.

She should know better than that. I've had all the time in the world to hurt her, and I haven't. When I'm finished getting her dressed, I strip out of my pants, which are far less bloody than my skin. It looks like I bathed in the blood of my enemies.

I don't care about the blood on my hands or the death and anguish I've caused, but I know it scares Fallon, and the last thing I need is her becoming more fearful than she already is.

I remember the man's phone as I'm staring down at my jeans and retrieve it from my pocket. It's a burner phone, nothing special about it. There isn't even a lock on it. Stupid fucker. It's easy enough to navigate through, and I squeeze the phone hard enough to crush it like a pop can in my hand. In the messages is one single text, it's to a random number. The content of the message is a photo of Fallon.

I clench my jaw in an attempt to stave off the roar that wants to release from within me. I will get to the bottom of this. I will extract any and all information I can from Fallon, no matter the cost. If knowing the truth is going to protect her, then so be it. I'll be the big bad monster.

I'll do whatever I have to, to protect her, us.

Loosening my grip on the phone, I walk over and place it on the nightstand. The number will be valuable information for later.

"I need to rinse off quickly," I say through gritted teeth, the anger mounting. Fallon doesn't even acknowledge me, not even as I walk into the bathroom and start the shower. I pop my head out of the shower every few seconds to make sure she is still there while the blood swirls down the drain.

Once clean, I grab a towel and dry off. Fallon is quietly sobbing when I enter the bedroom. I'm tempted to go to her and console her, but such a thing will have to wait. We need to get out of here before more men arrive.

I pick out clothing in the closet, get myself dressed, and grab a duffel bag that I find on the floor. Shoving some clothes into it for Fallon and myself, I return to the bed. There is another gun hidden beneath the bed, and I run my hand along the frame until I find it.

It's a handgun, nothing fancy, but it will be good enough till we get where we need to be. I shove it into the back of my jeans, along with the phone from earlier, and walk over to Fallon.

"Let's go," I order, but she doesn't move. "Fallon," I say a little more sternly. She lifts her head and meets my gaze. She is frozen, an iceberg floating in a sea of endless emotions.

"We need to leave. There could be others coming."

"I... I wasn't running," she whispers, her bottom lip trembling.

Whatever patience I had left is gone. I'm in no way capable of having this conversation right now. Not without wanting to throttle her. She knew what she was doing, knew that her one and only chance at escape would've been right then. I don't for a second believe she wasn't trying to escape, but again, this conversation will be better suited for another day.

"I don't give a fuck right now, Fallon. Get up and pull yourself together. We need to leave," I order once more and decide this time if she doesn't obey that I'm simply going to pick her up and toss her over my shoulder.

She shakes her head, fear trickling back into her eyes. Of course, she tries to make a feeble attempt to escape me, crab walking to the headboard, but I'm past giving a shit, past all of it. This is survival now.

"I do not have the patience for your bullshit," I hiss through my teeth and grab her by the waist. I pull her to the edge of the bed, getting a better grasp on her, and then toss her over my shoulder. Likewise, she struggles, but her escape is futile. She would have better luck fighting off a starving bear than me.

"I have to save her. I have to, you don't understand, Markus."

She starts to scream while pounding her tiny fists against my back.

Her struggles intensify, and by the time I reach the car, I'm done. I have nothing left to give her. I'm hovering on the line of insanity, caught between crossing the line and standing on it. I drop the duffel bag to the ground and release my hold on Fallon at the same time. She slides down my front, her fists still raining fury down on me.

"I hate you and this place. I hate that my sister was taken..." She's crying now. Big fat tears slip down her cheeks. "They are hurting her, he told me. It's my fault... and your fault! You should have let me call them."

All I can do is stare down at her.

Her cheeks are red, and angry lines of fresh tears streak her face. I should care. I should wipe the tears away, cradle her to my chest, and tell her everything is going to be okay.

That would be the right thing to do, the good thing, but I'm not about to deliver false hope, and I'm not listening to this shit. If she had been honest and given me the answers I wanted, none of this would've happened.

I'm tired of playing nice.

Tired of protecting her.

Without even thinking, I grab her by the throat and push against the car, subduing her with my body. Panic flashes like a lightning bolt across her eyes, overtaking the sadness. Her pulse thunders beneath my hand, and I give her throat a hard squeeze.

I'm slipping into the past, slipping further away.

Brushing my nose against hers, I inhale deeply. I wish her scent could bring me back...

"Your sister is still alive. You're still alive. For how long, I'm not sure as you continue pushing and fighting me at every fucking turn. I've asked you to tell me the truth, and you've fought me with each step. The pain you're feeling right now is your own fault. I could protect us better, protect you better if you just gave me the fucking information, but you won't. I'm going to have to go back on my word. I told you I wouldn't hurt you, but I've changed my mind."

"Markus, please... I'm sorry." The words wheeze past her lips.

I'm grappling for control, grappling with myself over how to handle her.

There is no way around it.

I pull away a bit, watching her face, her struggle, the way her hands pry at mine, wrapped around her throat. I've never seen her more afraid of me before, not even the day I bought her. Her chest is rising and falling, but it doesn't seem like air is filling her lungs.

Guilt pulses to life in my chest, but I ignore the pang.

With my hand wrapped securely around her throat, I press my thumb firmly into the side of her neck. The blood supply to her brain is cut off immediately, and her fight-or-flight instincts kick in full force as she struggles harder. She digs her nails into my hands and tries with all her might to push me away, but there is no breaking the hold I have on her.

I keep the pressure there until her eyes flutter closed, and she goes slack in my arms, her body giving out on her. Like a rag doll, she slumps against me, and I hold her close to my chest while I maneuver her into the passenger seat of the car.

Once situated, I brush a few stray locks of gold hair off her clammy forehead. I'm tempted to kiss her rosy lips, but instead, press a kiss to the crown of her head. I can't grow anymore attached to her than I am. Not until I know the whole truth.

As I pull away, my gaze latches on the red and swollen fingerprints that were left on her delicate throat. My stomach knots, and the guilt I tried so hard to bury, to swallow down, starts to rise up again.

Before I can even think about it, I'm touching the spots, tracing them ever so gently with my fingers. I don't like knowing that I put those marks there, even though that's who I am and who I will always be. I'll always be the villain, the killer, walking on the wrong side of the law.

Pulling my hand back as if her skin is fire, I grit my teeth.

No! I won't feel bad. I won't let the guilt take me for a heinous ride down memory lane.

She ran from me.

She's hiding secrets.

She cannot be trusted.

Those three things weigh heavily on my shoulders and are the reminder I need.

If we're going to make it out of this on the same side, I will have to find a way to make her crack, and I have just the right idea.

27

FALLON

I wake with my heart galloping in my chest. I'm disoriented, my thoughts muddled, making it hard for me to piece together anything.

Sucking a full breath of air into my lungs, I exhale and swallow around what feels like a knot in my throat. My body aches as if I passed out or something. Sitting up a little more in my seat, I realize I'm in a vehicle that's being driven down the road. I dismiss that altogether when I swallow once more and feel the sudden rawness in my throat.

Instinctively, I lift a hand to my throat, my fingers press against the tender tissue, and I wince. *What happened?*

Everything comes barreling into my mind in an instant.

The men breaking in. The woods. Markus wrapping his hand around my throat. Strangling the life right out of me.

Tears prick my eyes. I shouldn't be surprised or let down. This is who he is, who he's been all along. Ever thinking that I could trust him was my first mistake.

"I'm going to have to go back on my word. I told you I wouldn't hurt you, but I've changed my mind."

Markus is driving, staring out the windshield, his penetrating gaze focused on the road ahead. He's white-knuckling the steering wheel just like he did my throat.

I want to say something, to lash out, but what good would that do me? It wouldn't change what's already happened? It wouldn't fix any of this or make my sister safe. I'm spinning out of control, and I'm not sure anything will be able to stop me.

With each swallow, I try my best to ignore the throb in my throat, but it's a reminder of what he did to me, of how everything he said was a lie.

I'm completely hopeless and afraid now. He told me he would never hurt me, and though he didn't *really* hurt me, it feels like he did.

Like a statue, he remains motionless and silent. That only enrages me more. How can he sit there so calmly? It's stupid to feel as angry as I do over this. I know that, but nothing he has done to me thus far has amounted to what he did earlier. I've never felt so afraid, never felt the real darkness inside of him, not until that very moment.

I half expected him to kill me. The coldness in his eyes... how uncaring he seemed, and how he took back his word on hurting me, truly hurting me.

The mere memory of it makes me shiver.

"How are you feeling?" His deep, robust voice cuts through the air.

I fold my arms over my chest. "Why do you care?"

"Honestly, I don't. I don't give a fuck if you're mad at me. I did what I had to do. My options were slim, and you wouldn't calm down. You should be grateful I didn't shove your ass in the trunk."

I refuse to admit it, but he's right. I was too far gone to care about anything, and the only way he was doing to get me out of that house was the exact way he did.

Markus isn't my main concern right now. My sister is.

Thoughts of what that man back at the cabin told me circulate through my mind.

She's being hurt and taken advantage of, passed around, and raped. Bile rises in my throat. By the time I get to her, she'll be a different person, her spirit broken. How will I save her and myself? I feel like I'm trapped between two canyons that are closing in on me more and more each day.

The car slows, and Markus signals, taking the exit. I'm tempted to ask him where we're going but press my lips together to stop myself from doing so. Whatever we shared back in that cabin ended there. It ended when he took back his word.

Off the exit, he pulls into a small diner that's connected to a gas station. Markus parks the car and turns the engine off. He lets out a sigh and turns in his seat to face me. He's a mammoth of a man, and the space inside the car seems smaller because of him.

"Here's how this is going to work." He pauses, and his cool amber-colored eyes briefly meet mine. "We're going to go inside and eat. You're going to listen and behave yourself. Ignore anyone who asks you questions. Believe me, you don't want to know what happens if you fail to listen to me."

"What, you'll strangle me and kill everyone inside?" I scoff, and then realize how much of a reality that truly is.

"I'll kill anyone who tries to take you from me, and I'll punish you greatly for misbehaving. Now, are you going to come in with me and listen?"

"I hate you, and I don't want anything to do with you," I growl.

Markus rolls his eyes. "I saved your fucking life back at the cabin, and I've been protecting you when I could've just been fucking you. I've been kind to you, the only way I know how. I'm a fucking criminal, Fallon, in case you've forgotten. I bought you—paid money for your body. That doesn't exactly say knight in shining armor, does it?"

I huff out a breath. "Fine, I'll listen, but not for you. For the people in that restaurant because I'm sure they didn't come to work today thinking they would die."

Markus chuckles. "Of course, not for me. Why make things easier for me, or us?"

Us? There is no us. There is him and me, and we're on opposite sides of the spectrum. I want to help save my sister while he wants to keep me chained to his side.

He climbs out of the car a second later and comes over to the passenger side. Opening the door, he grabs my hand and pulls me to my feet. My legs feel like jello and buckle beneath the weight of my body as I try to stand.

"I've got you." His voice strokes my ear.

Leaning against him for support, I grow angry. I don't want his help. I don't want to feel the feelings I'm feeling for him. All I want to do is save my sister, protect her, and make sure she is okay, but I can't even do that.

I've failed her and failed myself. Everything that is happening to her now is my fault, and I have to live with that. So no matter what Markus does to me, nothing will be worse than what I've already done to myself.

"I'm fine," I snap. "I don't need you."

Markus takes a step back, and I almost eat the pavement but catch myself at the last second. "Let's go."

He tugs me forward, and I let him. Together we enter the diner, where the smell of fried foods and coffee fills my nostrils.

"Sit wherever you would like," a middle-aged woman says as she pours a cup of coffee.

Markus obliges and drags me to a booth in the corner of the restaurant, away from the other patrons. He releases the hold on my wrist, only to shove me into one side of the booth before sliding into the other.

There are menus at the end of the table near the sugar and salt and pepper, and I grab one to give myself something to do.

A woman who looks to be about sixty-years-old with graying

hair saunters up to the booth. She looks like the mothering type. The kind that makes the best hot cocoa, crochets blankets, and stuff.

Her gaze bounces between us before coming to a stop on me. Her big eyes widen in horror. Oh god, are their marks on my throat? Do I have a black eye? Shit, I didn't even look in the mirror. I probably look like I just lost a boxing match.

"What can I get ya to drink?" she drawls, dragging her gaze away from me.

"Two coffees," Markus answers before I can even form a response.

The old woman seems to bite her tongue, nods her head, and whirls around, heading for the coffee pot. My heart skips a beat in my chest as anxiety swirls. The last thing I need is for Markus to do something to her.

I wouldn't put it past him to kill a little old lady.

I stare down at my hands, which are holding the menu with a death grip. Markus doesn't say anything, and aside from some late-nineties diner music, silence surrounds us.

The little old lady returns with our coffees, setting them down in front of us.

"We'll have two number one breakfasts," Markus orders for me, and I lift my gaze to glare at him. He gives me a toothy grin that says try me, and I'm tempted, but not enough to risk someone else's life. He'll kill everyone in here, even her, and I couldn't live with that on my conscience.

"Sure." She scribbles something down on her little notepad and then turns to me. It's then I see her name tag. *Minnie*. It's hard to appear normal under her microscopic gaze, especially when I know she can see right through me.

"Ya know, sweetheart, if you need help…"

I shake my head, fear rising up. "I don't need help," I whisper almost shamefully.

I do need help, so much help, but not from her.

Markus clears his throat, and I worry the second I look at him, he's going to have his gun out and pointed at this old lady's head. It'll be an image I won't soon forget.

"Listen, lady, you need to mind your own business," Markus growls like a bear.

Fear pulses through my veins like a second heartbeat. I'm sure the waitress is going to back off, scared of Markus, but instead, her wary gaze flicks to him. She shoves her notepad into the front of her apron before placing her hands on her hips, ready to give him a lecture.

"Everything becomes my business when it walks into my diner, *boy*. I know guys like you, seen 'em my entire life. Always causing trouble and hurting women. Thinking they're the king of the world. Your type doesn't scare me. You're nothing but a little boy to me. I've seen much bigger and scarier monsters than you."

Oh god. Please.

"I'm okay, really... everything is okay," I try to defuse the situation, afraid that Markus is going to lose his cool and flip his shit. My chest tightens, and I'm prepared to jump between this woman and him if I have to.

Strange enough, the opposite seems to occur. Instead of overreacting, Markus lets out a low chuckle and shakes his head. It's like he's amused and not at all threatened. The likelihood of her fighting him is slim, but she could call the police.

"I appreciate your concern and your bravery. Seriously, lady, you're hiding some gigantic balls under that tiny apron, but I can assure you, she's well taken care of. I'm not the one who did that to her face, and I'm not causing trouble, *yet*. I respect your need to check on her, but she's fine."

Her brows pucker together with disbelief, and I add for reassurance, "I'm okay. He's not hurting me."

She scowls, looking my face over once more. I know she doesn't believe us, and she shouldn't, however, after a second, she doesn't seem to care anymore.

"If you say so," she mutters and walks away to submit our order.

Once she's out of earshot, I peer over at Markus, giving him a dirty look. I find him sitting back in his seat with a smug look on his face. He thinks he's so smooth.

"You thought I was going to hurt her, didn't you?"

I shrug. "You hurt me, so what makes it any different?"

He leans across the table, his eyes bleed into mine, and I can't help but squirm.

"I didn't hurt you because I wanted to, Fallon. You left me no other option, and you continue to put yourself in danger again and again. As for the little old lady, I'm not always a violent person. I can be very understanding, given certain circumstances."

It's my turn to laugh, but I don't.

Even though this is a joke. All of it.

Him and me. What we're doing right now.

We're headed nowhere.

A car with no destination.

I have to focus my attention on finding the one thing that the person who took my sister wants. If I can find it, then maybe I can still save her.

Or at the very least, I'll have a bartering tool. Hope starts to bloom in my chest at the thought. I could still do this. I'll save her at any cost. Even if that means putting myself in danger.

He doesn't want to help me, anyway. He wants to keep me trapped, keep me as his for as long as he can. Soon he'll find out I wasn't made to be kept. This started as a job and will end as one.

28

MARKUS

I pull into my designated parking spot and cut the engine. The underground parking garage is silent and dimly lit. Still I feel like we're out in the wide open. I can't believe I'm bringing her here, to my place, my apartment.

I bought it because it's safe. But it's set up to keep people out, not to keep someone in. There is no way for me to keep Fallon here besides constantly having her tied up, and I know she isn't going to like that, not one bit.

"Where are we?" Fallon asks curiously as she peers out the window.

"My place. Come on." I get out and jog around the car quickly just in case she gets any ideas about running. I take a step back, giving her some distance so she can get out.

When she stands, I take her hand, close the car door, and lead her over to the elevator.

"Jesus, could you maybe slow down a bit. Not all of us are six feet tall," she complains, and I grunt in response. All I want to do is get us upstairs. Here in the city, anything could happen, and we don't need to be ambushed.

Inside, I punch in my code, and the door slides shut. When they reopen, we're looking into my penthouse. I tug her out of the elevator and into my living room. She digs her feet into the wood grain floor.

"Wow... this is your apartment?" The shocked tone of her voice meets my ears.

I nod and tug her further inside. "You want a drink?" I ask before forcing her to sit on the couch.

"Sure, why not?"

I pour us both a glass of bourbon and hand her one. Taking the seat across from her, I lean back and take a sip of the amber liquid. A sigh slips past my lips. I still feel uneasy, but nothing like I felt on the way here or coming into the building.

Fallon takes a hesitant sip, almost as if to make sure it's not poisoned or something. Once she is convinced it's not, she takes an actual drink, leaving the glass half empty. Her blue eyes gleam when they meet mine.

"How long are you going to keep me here?"

"Indefinitely," I reply, swirling the bourbon around in my glass.

She laughs. "I'm serious."

I look up from the amber waves in my glass. "So am I."

"You can't just keep me forever."

"We'll see."

She sighs heavily, as if the weight of the world is pressing down on her shoulders. "I need to help my sister."

"You can help her. Give me the number. Trust me."

"Trust you?" She laughs humorlessly. "How can I trust you? You tell me that you are a bad man. You point out how you bought me and how you're using me until you've had your fill. Hell, you told me just earlier today that you are going back on your word of not hurting me. Now you expect me to trust you?"

I shrug. "I've never lied to you, and none of today would have happened if you would have done what you were told."

She places her glass down on the coffee table. "I'm not a child, Markus. You can't just demand things and expect me to follow them blindly. I have my own mind, fears, and morals. I can't just override them. I can't change who I am, and I definitely can't risk my sister's life on a whim to trust the man who has not given me a single reason to trust him."

Logically, I know she is right, but what she doesn't realize is that's the only way this is going to work. She either tells me what I want to know and gives me the information so that I can help her, or she doesn't. I could easily make everyone disappear. Tie her to the bed and hunt down these people, killing them one by one, but she's stopping me.

Fallon is the moral compass I don't have.

She's the guidance I need, the rope tethering me to the rational side of thinking. Her sister would die before I could save her if I did things my way.

"So, tell me, Fallon. How do you see this working out? What do you think I should do with you?" I give her a moment to answer, but her rosy lips are set in a thin displeasing line. "Hold on, let me guess. I should let you go, but don't worry because you're not going to tell anyone what happened to you, right?"

"I wouldn't," she blurts out. To her credit, she sounds sincere.

Moving, I place my glass on the table as well. "Maybe that's what you think right now, but in reality, you will eventually give in. People are going to keep asking you. Your parents will know you're lying right away, and they will nag you about it. Not to mention, the police will get involved. Do you really think you would be able to lie to an officer's face in an interrogation room?"

Her eyes go wide, and the reality of everything sinks in. She knows I'm right.

"I hate to break it to you, but you're a shit liar. Any cop is going to smell your lies from a mile away, and then they're going to tell you stuff like, if you don't tell us the truth, we'll have no choice but to charge you for obstruction of justice—"

"They can't do that," Fallon gasps. It's comical how she assumes she'll be safe when all of this is over. Does she not fully believe me when I say I'm a bad man? Did she not witness me killing a man today? Maybe she's just blocking it all out, afraid to see the truth that's right in front of her.

"Yes, they can, and they will."

She shakes her head. "I don't care what happens in the future. I care about the now. About saving my sister." Despair drips from every word she speaks.

"I offered to help you," I add once more.

"And I declined. I don't want your help."

"Then I suppose there is nothing I can do for you. You'll stay with me, and I'll fuck you whenever and however often I want."

There is a long moment of silence.

"Will you ever admit that it's more than just sex?"

Her question surprises me and irritates me because the last thing I need her to think is that she has some kind of hold on me. I'm not ready to admit my feelings to myself, let alone tell her about them. I don't even know if what I'm feeling is real.

"Never. It's just sex. Nothing more. Your cunt is tight, and the fact you're attractive helps matters, but that's where it starts and ends."

"See, this is exactly why I can't trust you." She shoves out of the chair and turns to face me. "You say you never lie to me, but you do. You just did. Can you not admit the truth to me, or to yourself?"

The sides of my mouth tip up in an evil smirk. "Maybe it's you that's developing feelings? Is my cock that satisfying? Or are you afraid to admit that you're falling for a man that's on the wrong side of the law? Are you self-conscious? Worried what Mom and Dad will think when this all ends? I bet they'll love to hear how hard you came on my—"

My words are cut off, and before I can even grasp what is

occurring, her hand is flying and landing with a sear against my cheek. The force of her slap sends my head to the side. Nostrils flaring, I suck air into my lungs. I try and calm myself, but I can't. I'm ready to implode. Fists clenched and chest heaving, I turn my head slowly back toward her.

As if she realizes what she's done, her blue eyes grow wide, horror and fear overtaking her features as she takes a step back.

I barely manage to keep my voice even as I speak. "I've saved your ass, protected you. Fed you and offered to fucking help you save your sister, and you repay me with violence." I shove off the couch, anger vibrating through me.

Instinct kicks in, and she takes another step back, and then another. Her lips tremble, and she opens her mouth to speak, but I shake my head. I'm not sure what I would do if she spoke right now. I'm pissed, burning with rage.

"Mmm-Markus. I'm sorry. I didn't—" I'm on her in a flash.

Everything moves at a rapid pace from that moment forward. Like a fucking beast, I strip her out of her clothes, ripping them clean from her body.

She lets out a soft cry that barely registers in my mind.

My actions are careless, and my heart is completely disconnected from my body. In this instant, I'm relying on my most basic instincts, and those tell me to subdue her, to show her who the fucking alpha is. I'll deal with the consequences later, but right now, I need to put her in her place. The place she should've been in all along.

"You want me to show you what you mean to me? Want me to prove to you how good you had it?" I grit through my teeth.

"Markus... don't. I'm sorry. I didn't mean to—" I shove her into the couch face first, not wanting to listen to her excuses, and grab each arm, twisting them around, so I can hold both wrists in my grasp.

With little effort, I shove my pants down my muscular thighs.

My cock springs free, the organ as hard as a diamond. I look down at Fallon's slender body, the slope of her back, the goosebumps that pebble her flesh, the way she trembles, waiting for the worst to come.

I almost break down then but force myself to push forward. My cock slips between her ass cheeks and Fallon lets out a ragged sob.

"Is this what you want? For me to fuck you like a whore?" I growl and guide my cock down to her pussy.

Normally, she would be wet for me by now, but looking at her folds, I can tell she is dry. The fear outweighs the pleasure in this instance. It shouldn't matter to me. That's how I've treated all the others. I've fucked them regardless of foreplay, and yet try as I fucking may, I look down at Fallon, at her trembling body, at her dry cunt, and my cock deflates.

To fuck her now, like this, would destroy everything. It would break her, hurt her beyond repair, and she would surely hate me.

I can't fucking do it.

I can't hurt her, can't treat her like the others because she isn't like them. She's more, so much more, and that infuriates me. Rage bubbles up inside me, and I want to punch myself, make myself bleed for ever thinking I could go through with this. She's already bruised and experienced trauma, and here I am about to hurt her all over again.

Angry with myself and the situation, I pull away. I release her wrists and tuck my cock back into my jeans.

"Get up!" I order harshly.

Fallon slowly rises off the couch, tears cling to her blonde lashes, and her lips tremble. She's looking at me like I'm a monster, and I suppose that's what I am. What I'll always be. She isn't moving fast enough for my impatient ass, so I grab her by the wrist and tug her to her feet. She's unsteady on her legs, but I don't give her time to balance herself. Dragging her into the bedroom, I shove her toward the mattress and head toward the closet.

"I didn't mean it. I'm sorry..." she pleads, and her soft, sad voice unravels me. Thankfully, I find the handcuffs I was looking for and reenter the bedroom to find her sitting at the edge of the bed.

"Move your ass up by the headboard." She scurries back, and the fear in her eyes is astounding. I keep fucking up, keep hurting her, keep pushing her away, but it's not like she's making it easy. She doesn't give me the information I need. She doesn't want my help finding her sister. She expects me to let her go when I can never do such a thing.

"Markus," she pleads, and I snap.

"Shut up! I don't want to hear you talk."

Grabbing the handcuffs, I secure it around her wrist and bring the other part to the iron rod headboard, cuffing her to it. Shivers rack her body, and I pull back the comforter on the bed and pull it up and over her. She tugs against the cuffs and turns her face to me with pleading eyes.

"Please, don't leave me here."

I shouldn't touch her, not after what I almost did, but I can't help myself. Ever so gently, I cup her bruised cheek and turn her face up toward mine, so I can peer into her eyes. All it takes is one single look to tell she's confused.

"This room is the only safe place in the house. Until we leave, you will have to remain here. I'll get you some clothes in a little bit. You need to go to sleep." I pull away, and she shakes her head.

"No! I have to save my sister," she cries and thrashes against the mattress.

I start toward the door. "I know."

"Then why tie me to the bed?"

"I have to. I'm never letting you go, Fallon. Never. Not even after we find your sister." Her face falls completely, and I know she had hoped for a better outcome.

Maybe she thought I would grow tired of her? That I couldn't possibly want her, but the truth is that's exactly what's happening. I'm lying to both of us because the truth is, I'm falling for her even while knowing I'm incapable of love.

The only thing I can do is hope that by the end of this, her fate doesn't end similarly to Victoria's.

29

FALLON

The apartment is nice, but it would be nicer if I wasn't confined to one room for the majority of the day. Markus says it's for my own good, but I think he's lying.

I've been cooped up in this bedroom for days while he does errands and makes phone calls. It's frustrating because while he tells me to trust him, he seems to keep everything to himself, making it hard for me to want to put anything regarding my sister's life in his hands, and we won't even mention how crazy he acted when we got here. He almost fucked me on the couch before changing his mind and handcuffing me to the bed.

He's pent up here, much like a dog in a cage. The feeling is mutual. It's obvious he isn't used to living here, at least not recently. Every so often, I find him looking over his shoulder like he's waiting for someone to jump out and get him.

There is something different about him today when he walks into the bedroom with breakfast in hand.

"After you eat, I want you to get dressed. We have somewhere to go."

I just about leap off the bed, "That's all you're telling me? We have somewhere to go?"

"Don't get mouthy with me," he warns.

"Or what?" I don't know why I'm pushing him, probably because I'm on edge too. I'm past being obedient. It hasn't gotten me anywhere with him. I'm almost certain misbehaving would get me more places than being good has.

"You do realize I could treat you much worse, right? I could beat you, starve you, whore you out to men daily. You could have it much worse than being cuffed to a warm bed, being fed, and cared for."

"You're right. I could have it worse. I could be my sister. Who is probably going through exactly that. So save me your comparison because I would gladly trade spots with her," I scream into his face, not caring about the repercussions.

At the end of the day, I'm stuck with him no matter what. He won't let me go, even after all of this is over.

"You don't know what you are saying."

"No, *you* don't know! You don't know what it's like to be helpless. And for your information, just because there are worse people out there doesn't make you any better than them. Stop comparing yourself to awful people so you can make yourself feel better. Just because you have an ounce of compassion doesn't make you a good person. You have no morals and no grasp of reality. You are caught up in your own little dark world, watching everything slip by you."

"Are you done?" he asks, annoyed by my outburst.

Of course, he doesn't care. He knows all of this already.

At least I got to say my peace, which does make me feel a tad better.

"Yes," I huff, irritated by him patronizing me. "I'm not hungry. Can we just go wherever you want to go?" I won't admit it because he would probably cuff me back to the bed, but I need to get out of this apartment, this bed, this goddamn room.

"Fine, get dressed."

I do just that. It's not like there are many clothes to choose from, so the decision is basically made for me.

"Are you sure you don't want to eat something?" Markus asks as I walk past the plate of French toast he made for breakfast.

"I'm sure."

He shakes his head and grabs my hand. My treacherous little heart jumps in my chest as the warmth of his touch zings through me. At least he's not dragging me behind him like a lost puppy. We exit the apartment complex through the underground garage, and as soon as we step out onto the concrete floor, his entire body tenses.

I wonder how many enemies he's made to make him feel that he needs to peer over his shoulder, even in broad daylight?

Hitting the key fob, he unlocks the car, and we quickly walk across the garage. He glances over his shoulder like he expects someone to be there.

Once in the car, he starts the vehicle, and the engine purrs to life. He drives out of the garage and out onto the busy city street. I don't bother asking where we're going, not when I know he won't tell me, but also because I don't really care.

I need this reprieve, a drive to wherever to clear my head. Thankfully, that's exactly what I get. We drive through the city, and I stare out my window with my face glued to the glass. Turning in my seat, I glance over at Markus and find him white-knuckling the steering wheel.

"Is everything okay?" I ask, trying not to sound concerned for him.

"I'm fine." He slams his foot against the gas pedal, causing the car to exhilarate faster. Moving into the next lane, he darts around cars like he's in a Nascar race.

The rational part of me knows I should be scared, afraid we will slam into a barrier and explode into a raging inferno, but I'm not.

Using his turn signal, he takes the next exit off the interstate.

My stomach tightens as we slow and turn left at the stop sign. I have this really bad feeling for some reason, and it only seems to intensify as we continue driving.

I'm struck with fear when Markus parks the vehicle at the back of a building. Something tells me this is going to end badly.

"Where are we?"

Putting the car in park, he kills the engine and turns to me. "The auction."

I freeze. "N-no. I'm not going in there."

Markus grits his teeth. "Come willingly, or I'll drag you inside. The option is yours."

I knew this was going to be bad. I had hoped we were going to get out of the house, not go back to the place that he bought me. With a cringe, I look up at the building and weigh my options, which are none. One way or another, I have to go inside.

"I'm scared," I admit, turning to face Markus.

His face is a pane of glass, emotionless and cold. "Fear is normal. When we get inside, I need you to keep your eyes down on the ground and be quiet. I can't guarantee your protection in this place, not by myself."

I gulp. "That doesn't really help, but okay." That only scares me more.

"I just need you to know what to expect."

"Why are we here? Why bring me somewhere that you know I'm not going to be safe?"

"You'll see. Just do as I say, and everything is going to be all right."

"Okay. I'll listen."

Markus nods, and together we get out of the car and walk up to a door. My knees knock together with each step I take. Raising his closed fist, he knocks three times against the heavy wood, and then a little pocket hole slides open.

"It's Markus," Markus growls impatiently, his demeanor changing instantly.

The pocket hole closes. And a second later, the door is being pulled open.

Markus gives my hand a hard squeeze, and I do just as he instructs. With my eyes trained on the floor, we cross over the threshold.

"Take me to Tony," Markus orders harshly.

A man chuckles. "The boss sees who he wants to see."

Coldness whips through me when Markus releases my hand and steps away from me. I'm compelled to lift my eyes to see what he's doing, but in a way, I already know. The sound of a body hitting the wall meets my ears, followed by a gurgling sound.

I peek up through my lashes out of pure curiosity and find that Markus has the man pinned to the nearest wall, his hand wrapped around his throat.

The man's eyes bulge in his skull. "I said I want to see Tony. Do you think that's going to be a problem, or should I rearrange your fucking face before I find someone else to show me to his office?" The man's features fill with panic, and his lips start to turn blue. I should step in and put a stop to this, but I don't care enough to.

As if he realizes the seriousness of the situation, he shakes his head. Markus releases him like he's disgusted, and the man gasps, sucking greedy air into his deflated lungs.

"Past the bar, all the way down the hall," he gasps, "last door on the right."

Markus nods and grabs my hand, tugging me behind him as he trudges forward. Nausea builds with each step I take.

Why are we here? What's going to happen? The sound of our feet echo around me. I try to focus on anything but the bile rising in my throat.

Oh god, I think I'm going to puke.

Markus stops, and I nearly crash into him, stopping just short of burying my face in his back. He lifts his closed fist and pounds it against the closed door in front of us.

"Come in," someone yells on the other side.

Markus pauses, and I can feel his eyes on me even though I'm not looking at him. "Remember what I said. Eyes on the ground. Quiet. Be seen and not heard."

I swallow thickly and nod my head briefly. He doesn't waste any time after that, opening the door and waltzing in like he owns the place. With my eyes trained on the floor, Markus is my only source of guidance. Pulling me behind him, he drags me inside the room.

The smell of smoke and men's cologne clings to the air, and I hold back a cough. The legs of a chair come into view, and Markus gives me a gentle push in the direction of it. We both sit at the same time.

"What a pleasant surprise it is to see you, Markus."

This must be the man he was looking for.

"Tony, I would love to say I came here to thank you, but I didn't."

"What seems to be the problem?"

"You. I purchased her at your last auction. Not only was she bruised from one of your men when I got her, but I also found out she wasn't a virgin, which is essentially what I paid for."

My mouth pops open. I'm dumbfounded. No way did he drive all the way here to complain about me. Then it hits me. What if he didn't just come here to complain about me, but to return me? What if he's going to leave me here?

Fear latches onto me, sinking its nails deep into my flesh. He wouldn't leave me here, would he? The answer is yes, yes, he would.

"Virgin or not, she seems to have taken a liking to you. Are you looking to return her? We don't offer returns generally, but she's pretty enough, and she doesn't seem too damaged. We could definitely resell her."

Forget the rules. Forget what he told me to do. None of it

matters if he gives me back to them. I'll beg and plead if I have to, but I am leaving this place with him.

Latching onto his arm, I lift my head and find him staring at me. His expression is cold and deep like the ocean. Real genuine fear swirls in my gut.

"Please... I'll be good," I plead and grip him as tightly as I can. Disappointment flickers in his eyes. "Shut your mouth," he growls before looking away and back at Tony.

Tears well in my eyes, and Tony says, "We can take her and give you a new girl. A virgin, perhaps. You did pay a pretty penny for this one if I remember correctly."

A second passes, and then another, and I swear my heart stops beating. My hands tremble uncontrollably, and I can't even get a breath of air into my lungs. After everything, it comes down to this. I can see my one and only chance of saving my sister slipping through my fingers like grains of sand.

Finally, Markus answers, "No. I want to keep her, but I want another girl in return for my troubles." I tug my hand away and practically melt into my seat with relief.

"Mmm, I'm not sure about that. To lose a girl would be a huge hit on the books. I know she's not what you expected, but..."

"I want another girl," Markus roars and slams his fists down on the heavy desk, driving home his point.

"We don't have any new girls in yet. We do have one left over from the previous auction that never sold, but... I don't know if you would want her."

My heart grows wings in my chest, and it takes every ounce of restraint I have not to jump out of my chair and order him to take us to Julie.

"Let me see her," Markus barks.

I'm so shocked. I don't even know what to think. I can't believe he came here to get Julie. Or that he cared enough to remember me asking about her when he first brought me to the cabin. I'm not sure if I want to hug him or run away from him. When he does things like this, it's hard for me to remember how monstrous he is.

"We can take a walk down to the basement." Tony shoves out of his chair, and the feet make a scraping sound against the floor that makes me shiver. "I will be honest, I'm not sure what use she will be to you. My men have been fucking her since the night of the auction."

"Don't care. I want to see her." Markus ignores everything he's said and comes to stand as well, grabbing onto my hand and pulling me up with him.

My throat tightens, and my heart clenches at the words Tony has said. I can't imagine all that she has had to endure over the months, the pain, heartache, and loss.

By the time we reach the cell Julie is in, I'm paralyzed by sadness. Still, as soon as the cell door is opened and we enter, I tug my hand free of Markus's. I'm tempted to rush toward her still body, that's nothing more than a heap in the corner of the cell, but one look from Markus has me stopping in my tracks.

"Like I said, she's been thoroughly used. However, if you want her, she's yours. We don't usually do business like this, but I'm making an exception; the Moretti family has helped us a lot, after all."

I want to cut this man's tongue out of his mouth and feed it to him. The way he talks of Julie like she is nothing more than a piece of meat, and not a living, breathing, human with feelings. Markus takes a few steps toward her, and she doesn't even react.

Her face is tucked into her chest, and her body is nothing but bruised skin and bones. It's obvious they've been starving her and raping her repeatedly.

It isn't until I blink and feel wetness against my cheeks that I realize I've started to cry.

"I'll take her," Markus says, and I want to hug him.

He saved her. He rescued her even when he didn't have to. He went against everything he's been claiming and showed me a sliver of the human he really is.

Both elation and sadness encompass me in a tight hold. Even after doing this, I will still have to betray him. No matter what feelings I've developed or how much kindness he shows me, my sister must come first. I came here to save my sister, and that's all that matters. Rescuing Julie might have brought us closer, but none of that will matter when I find what I need to save my sister.

30

MARKUS

Placing the beaten girl carefully on the backseat, I try to ignore Fallon's continual questions.

"What did they do to her? How could they? Who are these people, and why did they not get her any help when she so obviously needs it?"

"Get in the other side and hold her head in your lap," I order, instead of answering her questions, and thank fuck, Fallon listens for once. She climbs into the backseat, carefully lifts the girl's head, and cradles it gently in her lap.

I get into the driver's seat and start the car, wasting no time in getting the fuck out of here. We're lucky we got out without there being a scene. Tony isn't usually as understanding as he was today.

"Where is the closest hospital," Fallon asks as I pull out of the empty parking lot.

"We can't take her to a hospital—"

"What? You have to be kidding me. We have to. Do you not see how badly hurt she is? If we don't, then this will have all been for nothing. She'll die without a doctor." I hate to tell her, but that's what was going to happen to her anyway. I hit the gas and drive back toward the interstate. Every piece of my plan has been put into place. Now I have to see if Fallon falls into line as well.

"I guess you're holding her life in your hands then."

"What's that supposed to mean?"

I grip the wheel hard. "Give me the number, Fallon. Give it to me, and I'll get her help. I'll have the best doctor in town come to the apartment."

Fallon snorts. "You're joking..."

I catch her shocked gaze in the rearview mirror. "Nope, that's the deal."

"Do you even know what you are asking? You want me to choose between Julie's life and my sister's." She shakes her head, looking utterly defeated, and I hate myself for doing this to her, but it's the only way. She's too stubborn to put her trust in me. It's either I force her or nothing.

"Either way, I'll be responsible for someone's death."

"I'm asking you to trust me, Fallon. Save Julie's life, so I can save your sister's."

I can see the turmoil she's going through; it's etched into the contours of her face. She's conflicted, scared, but most of all, she doesn't trust me.

"Markus, please, don't do this." Her voice is shaky and full of emotion, like she is about to cry. "Don't make me choose. I can't choose. I can't."

"It's not a choice, you can save them both. All you have to do is give me the number." My voice takes on a gentle tone, a tone that I've never used, not even once in my life.

Silence stretches between us for so long, I'm worried she might actually refuse. If she does, I'm not sure what I'll do. I guess my next resort will be threatening Julie as fucking shit as that sounds.

"Fine, I'll give it to you, but you have to promise... promise you'll help me save both of them. I don't care what happens to me when this is over, but I want both of them to be safe."

She's so selfless, so fucking caring, it's insane. She would gladly take a bullet for this girl, even though she hardly knows her. That single attribute makes me want her all the more.

"I promise I'll help you in any way I can."

"Okay." She nods in defeat. "I'll tell you."

"I'm going to trust you and call the doctor now," I'll tell her, mostly because I don't know if this girl is going to make it if I don't get the doctor there as soon as possible, but I'm definitely not telling Fallon that.

"When we get back to my place, you're going to write the right number on a piece of paper. I'm giving you the benefit of the doubt here, don't fucking play with me again. I'll send the doctor away faster than I called him and bring her back to the auction place to die in the basement. Do you understand?"

"I understand."

I get my phone out and dial one of the doctors we have on call. He answers on the second ring, almost like he was expecting a call. He agrees to come right away, no questions asked.

He better, for what I'm going to pay him.

Fallon remains quiet for the remainder of the drive.

The only sounds filling the cab are the quiet hum of the engine and the occasional whimper coming from the half-dead girl lying on my backseat. If I didn't have Fallon with me, I would've killed the girl just to put her out of her misery. I can only imagine what she's been through, and I wouldn't be surprised if she was keen to the thought of death. Hell, when all this is over, she just might try and do it anyway.

After what seems like an eternity, we arrive at the penthouse. I park in my spot, cut the engine, and get out of the car. Walking around quickly, I open the door where Fallon is sitting. She carefully gets out while keeping Julie's head cradled in her hands. I pass Fallon the car key before I awkwardly pull the girl's body out and lift her into my arms. A bag of flour weighs more than this girl does.

"Close the door and lock the car," I command.

"I'm surprised you trust me with the key," Fallon points out but does as she is asked. "What if I were to try and take off now?"

She's not dumb enough to do that.

"I know you wouldn't leave Julie behind. Now type in the code," I grumble once inside the elevator. She types in the numbers I rattle off, her hand shaking, and before I know it, the elevator is sailing north. As soon as the doors open, I carry Julie straight to the guest bedroom.

Fallon is following me like a shadow. With great gentleness, I place Julie's beaten body on the bed, and even the soft mattress seems to cause her discomfort. Her face distorts into anguish, and a pained cry rips from her throat. The sound is coarse, and one I know she has made a thousand times over given how badly beaten she is.

Standing up, I scan her body for any life-threatening injuries. Every inch of her skin is either covered in dirt, bruises, cuts, or dried blood. She is a mess, a disaster, and I know she'd be better off dead at this point, but for once in my life, I'm going to do the right thing. I'm going to help someone.

Turning to Fallon, I say, "Why don't you get a washcloth and start to clean her up a bit while we wait for the doctor."

Fallon disappears into the attached bathroom, and I hear the water running a moment later. Walking back out into the hallway, I grab a piece of paper and a pen from the entryway table. It's time for her to uphold her end of the bargain.

When I return to the room, Fallon is already running a washcloth over Julie's forehead and cheeks. She's watching her with hawk eyes; the concern she has for this girl is everlasting.

"Here," I hand Fallon the items in my hand, "write the number on it." She hesitates for a brief moment, then drops the washcloth on the nightstand and proceeds to write the number down. "I'll be right back."

Fallon's gaze flicks to mine, searching for confirmation in my eyes. I give her a tiny nod, hoping to ease her mind, but I'm not sure there is anything I can do to convince her right now. Until I can actually deliver, Fallon is going to doubt me and my intentions.

I quietly slip out of the room, closing the door behind me. I walk to the end of the hall, where I can still see the door, but where I know Fallon won't be able to listen in on my conversation with whoever is going to be on the other line.

Eagerly, I type in the number from the piece of paper and hit the green call button. I hold the phone to my ear and suck in a calming breath. I'm not the nervous type, never have been, but for some reason, there is an anxious feeling that washes over me as I wait for the person to pick up the phone. The phone rings exactly four times.

With each ring, my patience draws thinner, and dread weasels its way up my spine. Then the ringing stops.

"Hello," a familiar gruff voice filters through the speaker, "Fallon, are you there?" I almost drop the sleek device, barely stopping it from sliding out of my hand.

No, this can't be. It can't be him.

Pulling the phone away from my ear, I look at it instead, as if that would explain why Victoria's father kidnapped Fallon and sent her to the auction for me to buy. Before I do something stupid like talk to him, I hang up the phone and slip it back into my pocket.

All I can do is stare at the floor—shock coursing through my veins. I've expected all kinds of people behind this, but not him. I know he hates my guts, but Timothy is not the kind of guy capable of something like this... or so I thought.

My mind is spinning as I try to form a plausible explanation. Victoria's father loved her. He was a good dad, an outstanding citizen. How could he do this? Kidnapping? Sending a woman to an auction? A woman who looks like his dead daughter, no less.

Regardless of how this happened, one thing is clear. This is bad.

Really fucking bad.

∼

"I'm going to give her some antibiotics and morphine through the IV for now. I'll probably do this for the next few days to keep her comfortable, then we can switch to oral medicine. I don't see any injuries that will require surgery, but the amount of superficial trauma is so extensive that it will take her awhile to recover," Doc. Schwarz explains. "She is also dehydrated and malnourished. I'll leave some supplements for when she wakes up."

"So, she is going to be out for a while longer?" I ask the doctor while he cleans the final few wounds. He has been here for over an hour, examining and cleaning every cut and bruise.

"For her sake, I hope, yes. The longer she is out of it, the quicker she can heal. The physical trauma in itself is a lot, but the mind is going to be the biggest burden. Your bones and skin can heal, but what's done to you, the things you remember…"

I know what he's referring to. The fact that she was obviously raped, repeatedly. Like I said before, putting a bullet in her head would be doing her a favor.

Fallon has been sitting on a chair in the corner of the room, watching the doctor take care of her friend. She watches him meticulously as if to make sure he's not doing anything wrong.

"What about those cuts on her legs? Won't you stitch them up?" I switch gears.

"It's too late. Stitches have to be done within twenty-four hours of the injury. These seem to be older, and the skin is already healing itself. At this point, it's better to just keep the wound clean and let her body do the rest."

"Oh." Fallon lowers her head.

"I told you, Doctor Schwarz is one of the best in the city. Julie is in good hands."

"Her scarring will be very visible since it wasn't stitched up, but that's something she can have revised later. Right now, we'll just make sure she doesn't get an infection, so she can recover and get back on her feet."

"Thanks, doc." I watch him pack up all of his stuff.

I walk him out to the door and hand him a wad of cash before sending him off. When I get back to the guest room, Fallon is sitting on the edge of the bed, holding Julie's hand. The floor creaks as I walk in, and she looks to where I'm standing.

"What kind of doctor is he that he doesn't even ask how this happened or demands we take her to the hospital and call the police?"

"The kind that is paid handsomely and told not to ask questions."

Fallon shakes her head in disbelief, her eyes dropping back down to Julie's hand. "Did you call the number?"

"I did." I nod, taking a seat on the chair Fallon sat in moments ago. My chest tightens. "I know who has your sister."

That has her interest peaked. Her head snaps up and her eyes connect with mine—the purest blue, soft like little waves that crest against the shore.

So trusting and kind. I can't let her down. Not just because I don't want to but because I already let another woman down once before.

"Who?" she croaks.

"His name is Timothy Brent, and he thinks I killed his daughter."

"Did you?" Fallon looks me straight in the eyes. Emotions I have been trying to keep buried rush to the surface, bubbling over the sides and pushing past the walls I carefully constructed around myself.

Did I kill her? I didn't pull the trigger, but I might as well have. Her connection to me is what inevitability got her killed.

"It's my fault she is dead," I admit.

"Do you know where my sister is? Can you save her?"

"I don't know, but I'll try." My words seem to calm her down enough to drop the subject for now, but I'm sure it won't be for long. One thing is clear, I can't find her sister and take care of Julie at the same time. She'll need around the clock care if she is going to make it. I'll need someone I can trust to help me with this shitshow.

Tugging my phone from my pocket, I unlock the screen, navigate to my messages, and click on the one contact I know I can count on one-hundred percent.

Me: I need you to come to my place no matter how long it takes you. Get on a plane and get here. I need your help.

The answer comes only seconds after I hit send.

Felix: I'm on my way.

31

FALLON

It's been three days, and I haven't left Julie's side, other than to sleep. I would stay with her at night as well if Markus would let me, but I don't want to fight him on it since he lets me take care of her the rest of the time.

She's opened her eyes a few times, but I don't think she has fully woken up yet. The times she looked at me, there was no recognition in her gaze. Actually, there was nothing in her gaze, only emptiness, and pain.

We tried to get her to eat, but she refused, turning her head away and squeezing her eyes shut before falling back into a deep sleep.

I'm so worried for her, not only because of the physical wounds, but about the trauma you can't see. Her body will heal, but her mind is a different story.

I can't imagine what she's been through, and I don't think I want to either.

"Are you hungry?" Markus's voice drags me from my thoughts. "I'm going to order some Japanese food."

I look up and find him leaning against the door frame with

his arms crossed over his chest. The sight of him causes a ball of warmth to form in my belly.

"A little. I love Japanese."

"Anything in particular?"

"Not really," I shrug, "I'll eat whatever... except maybe like raw squid."

"No raw squid, got it." Markus disappears into the hallway, and I go back to holding Julie's hand. It's not much, but at least I feel like I'm doing something.

I hate not being able to take her pain away. At least she knows I'm here, or I hope she knows anyway. I don't want her to feel alone.

"Do you know that you are safe now?" I ask quietly.

Reaching out, I brush my fingers gently over her beautiful face. She doesn't flinch, doesn't move, not even her breathing changes. The bruises on her cheek have turned from a dark blue to a light purple, and hopefully, they will soon fade altogether. Maybe it's best she stays asleep for a few more days. Once awake, the mental wounds will take over, bringing with them a whole new level of pain.

The thought has barely left my mind when Julie pulls her hand from my hold. I look up to find her eyes wide open, fear reflecting back at me as she takes in her surroundings. I'm almost glad I see fear in her eyes because even that is better than the void of emotions I've seen until now.

"Julie, it's okay. You're safe now." She shakes her head as if she doesn't believe me. "I promise, Julie, no one is going to hurt you here."

I try to take her hand, but she pulls away yet again. I let her. I won't do anything she doesn't like.

"Julie, you've been out for a few days. You need to eat something. It will make you feel better." I grab the bowl of oatmeal I made for her earlier from the nightstand. Using the spoon, I get a tiny amount of oatmeal and hold it to her lips. "Please, Julie, just a tiny bite," I beg, but she turns her head away, like she's been doing.

Sighing in defeat, I put the bowl back onto the nightstand. It's like she has just given up.

The loud ding-dong of the doorbell startles me. I sit up a little straighter, wondering if that is the fastest food delivery service in the world or if I have been sitting here much longer than I thought. It only feels like a few minutes have passed since Markus walked in here.

I could be wrong, though. Time seems different when you're waiting for someone to wake up and heal.

Curiously, I look at the cracked door. If it's not the food, then who else could it be? The doctor already came by to check on Julie this morning, and he's only been coming once a day, so I don't think it's him.

A few more moments pass, and I hear the *ding* of the elevator door echo through the apartment. Two male voices fill the space. They are hushed like they don't want me to hear, which confirms that this is not the food delivery.

My heart hammers in my chest. Markus didn't tell me anyone was coming, and the last time he invited a friend over, things did not end well. I glance at Julie, and her eyes are still open. She is staring at a spot on the ceiling, almost like she is in her own little world, oblivious to what's happening around her.

I take her hand again, and this time she lets me. The door creaks open, and I hold my breath. For the last three days, I've held Julie's hand for her comfort, but right now, I feel like our roles are reversed.

Suddenly, I'm clinging to her, so I know I'm not alone.

Markus enters the room first, a stern look on his face, which does nothing to ease the tension festering in my gut. Then another man steps in, he's big, and with the two of them inside, the room seems to shrink. The nameless man peers around the room until his gaze stops on me.

He pins me with a glare, and I recognize a familiarity almost immediately—dark eyes, dark hair, tall, and bulky build. The man looks like an older version of Markus.

"Fallon, this is Felix, my brother," Markus introduces the man beside him.

Brother... that makes sense. "Um, hi," I say awkwardly.

He answers with a grunt. Great, he is just as big of an asshole as his brother.

Walking into the room, he stops a foot away from the bed. Now that he is closer, I can see he already has some gray streaks in his hair and his forehead has wrinkles that set his face into a permanent frown. He's still very much attractive, but more so in a silver fox kind of way.

"What do you think?" Markus asks, and I'm not sure what exactly he is asking, or even who. Me? Felix? I don't understand.

"I'll take her," Felix growls, looking down at Julie, who is still looking at something on the ceiling.

What the fuck? Every alarm goes off in my head.

"What do you mean by *take her*? Take her where?" I clutch on to Julie's hand a little tighter.

"Felix is going to take Julie off our hands for a while," Markus explains, like he is talking about a pet that has become too much to handle.

"She is not a dog, you can't just give her away, or sell her, or whatever it is you just did. She is not a form of currency. She is a goddamn human." I enunciate each word clearly, my voice filled with determination and passion. I won't let her be hurt anymore.

Felix's eyes slide back toward me, his face a blank mask. I can't read him at all.

I have no idea if he is good, bad, or something in between. All I know is that I'm not just going to let him take her.

"Julie should stay here until she is better. She'll be scared with you, and she knows me. We're friends. I won't just let you take her, so you can do whatever you want with her."

Without saying a word, Felix takes another step toward the bed, then sits down on the edge. Julie doesn't move, does not react like I thought she would.

"Hand me the bowl of oatmeal," he orders in the same demanding tone his brother uses on me. I almost roll my eyes but manage to hand him the bowl without doing so.

"She won't eat," I point out, but that doesn't seem to stop Felix from trying.

Just as I did, he shovels a tiny morsel of food onto the spoon, then holds it to her lips. She doesn't move an inch. Doesn't even blink.

"Look at me," he demands, his voice deep and commanding. To my utter shock, Julie does. Her eyes go from the ceiling to where Felix is sitting. "Good girl, now, open your mouth. You need to eat, doll."

My jaw drops to the floor when her lips part slowly, her eyes never leaving Felix as he gently slides the spoon into her mouth.

"See, Felix is going to take good care of her," Markus says. "She'll be safe with him."

"No, this means nothing. It's just a bite, she was probably scared. You can't just give her to him," I argue, but my pleas don't reach anyone.

"Fallon, Julie is leaving today, whether you like it or not. You can either help me get her ready and enjoy the last few moments you have with her, or you can wait in the bedroom."

"I won't let this happen! You can't—" I gently place Julie's hand on the bed and shove up from my chair.

"Bedroom it is," Markus declares. "You can either go there yourself, or I can drag you there by your hair. Your choice."

My gaze zips between an upset Markus, an unreadable Felix, and an incoherent Julie. *Fuck*, Markus is not going to budge on this. My heart is breaking for Julie, but what can I do? Fighting Markus won't change anything. She's still leaving here, regardless.

"Can I at least say goodbye?"

Markus nods, but I can tell he is annoyed, and his patience is running low. I'm on thin ice right now. Cradling Julie's hand between both of mine, I lean in and carefully kiss her cheek.

"I promise I'll see you again soon," I whisper. "Goodbye, for now."

I stand quickly, not wanting to cry in front of either of these men. I briskly escape the room and head toward Markus's bedroom. I'm almost inside the bedroom when I realize this is the first, and most likely, last time, Markus has let me out of his sight without me being tied to the bed. Could this be my only chance? I know Markus said he would help me, but how much can I count on that? Am I willing to gamble on my sister's safety? *No.*

Darting a look over my shoulder, I make sure Markus didn't follow me before I bypass the bedroom and venture further down the hall. I open the first door I find and peek inside. It's a gym. I don't think I'll find what I'm looking for here, so I close the door and keep going.

I open the next door and pop my head inside. The first thing I see is a wall of books. A bookshelf that stretches from the bottom all the way to the ceiling. I scan the rest of the room and find a large desk sitting in front of a vast window that overlooks the city. *Bingo.*

Sneaking inside, I close the door behind me and start my scavenger hunt. I pull open every drawer, look in every small space, nook, and cranny only to come up empty time and time again. With every passing moment, my heart beats faster, knowing that Markus is going to find me soon. It's inevitable. He is going to find me and punish me.

I know it, but I also know that I couldn't live with myself if I didn't try.

I have to at least try. I have to…

"Looking for something?"

I freeze. My whole body just stops as if my operating system just got fried by lightning. Fear holds me prisoner, tossing away the key. The only movement my body will allow is my eyes lifting to where Markus is standing.

To my utter shock, he seems... *calm*. Which is extremely alarming. With his arms folded across his chest, he leans against the wall casually, almost identical to the stance he took earlier when he asked me about food. But this isn't takeout. This is life or death for someone I love, and as much as I don't want to hurt Markus, my sister means more to me.

Still unable to speak, move, or even breathe, I do nothing. Silence stretches between us as I wait for the moment Markus will snap.

He'll drag me out of the room by my hair, tie me up, and lock me away for weeks. The images running through my head already look like the preview of a movie, a promise of what's to come. I feel like a mouse that's seconds away from falling into the trap.

Instead of all the things I'm conjuring up in my mind happening, he leisurely unfolds his arms and strolls across the room. He stops in front of a modern-looking painting hanging on the far side of the wall. Using both hands, he pulls it from the wall and deposits the picture on the floor next to him.

A safe was behind the picture. *Of course.*

Markus types in a combination, and the safe door clicks before swinging open. My entire mouth goes dry, and I wonder what is inside. What's he going to do? The suspense is killing me.

Markus reaches inside, and I'm almost positive he is reaching for a gun. When he turns around, I nearly flinch but discover that there is something small in his hand. Stretching his arm out to me, he shows me the small item lying in the palm of his hand.

"Take it. That's what he wants, isn't it? The footage from that night."

My lungs burn, and I realize I'm still holding my breath. I

suck in a tiny bit of air, still unable to get my body to move or act normal.

"Take. It," Markus repeats, his tone more insistent this time.

It's a trick. It has to be. After everything, he's willingly giving me the one thing I need to set my sister free?

He sighs deeply and closes the distance between us in two large strides. Before I can spiral into a full-blown panic, he grabs my hand and shoves the thumb drive inside. Then steps back again.

He reaches into his back pocket. "Here is some cash for a cab or whatever you need." He takes out a wad of bills, that must be at least a few hundred dollars from his wallet and hands them to me. I can't seem to comprehend what is happening. Why is he doing this? Why is he offering to help me? He asked me to trust him, and now he's giving me what I need and letting me go.

On autopilot, I lift my hand and take the cash.

"You're letting me go?" I ask in disbelief. "You said you would never let me go."

Markus shrugs, a cold mask sliding over his face. "Changed my mind. Getting rid of Julie is such a relief. Made me realize how much work you are. I've got better shit to do. Plus, I've grown tired of your pussy. I'm going to buy something better next auction, someone prettier and less mouthy."

His words slice through the thumping organ in my chest. I feel myself bleeding out. Fading.

"You don't mean that." I don't know why I say it. I should be glad he changed his mind. I should be running out of this apartment as fast as I can.

Trick or not, I need to take the chance to get away. Instead, I'm hurt by his words, hurt by the thought of him replacing me as if I were nothing to him.

"Let's go. I have better things to do. Get out." He points toward the door.

"Are you serious?" I swallow around the ball of emotion in my throat, around all the words I want to say but can't.

"Out!" Markus roars, and my limbs spring into action.

He doesn't move as I head toward the door, and I don't hear him following me to the elevator. Even when I step inside, I am convinced he is about to jump around the corner and pin me to the ground, but nothing happens when the door closes, and nothing happens when it reopens into a large foyer downstairs.

The front of the building is all glass, and I can see the busy street ahead of me. Still unable to trust this whole situation, I take a hesitant step out of the elevator. I'm prepared for something bad to happen but again, nothing.

Clutching onto the thumb drive, I speed walk toward the exit. I push the front door open, and the sounds of the city wash over me. People talking, laughing, cars speeding by, and honking somewhere down the street. The onslaught of sounds is almost overwhelming. The only thought keeping me sane is the one where my sister needs me.

I take one more glance back and into the foyer. It's empty... Markus didn't follow me.

A mixture of relief and disappointment floods my veins. Maybe he was telling the truth? Before I allow myself to dwell on the thought, I shove both feelings down into a deep corner of my mind, spin around and hail a cab.

Someone stops in a matter of seconds, which isn't surprising seeing that every other vehicle seems to be a taxi. I get into the back, stuffing the cash into my pocket but keeping the thumb drive in my hand.

"The library, please."

"To the library," the driver confirms and takes off. Thankfully, he doesn't try to make any small talk with me since I don't have the nerve for that right now.

He drops me off in front of a large gray building, and I pay him with one of the twenty-dollar bills Markus gave me. "Keep the rest," I call on my way out and slam the door shut behind me.

Walking up the stairs to the front door, I wonder if this is the right move. Maybe I should just find a phone and call the number myself? No, I need to see what's on this drive.

Inside, I bypass every single bookshelf and find a public computer instead. Luckily, they have one available all the way in the corner, away from prying eyes.

I shove myself down into a seat and plug the thumb drive into the USB port.

A few seconds later, a folder appears on the screen. It reads **Victoria**.

Sucking in a shaky breath, I move the mouse over the folder and click on it. Two sub-folders open, neither one is labeled, so I just click on the first one. My heart clenches so tightly in my chest, I wonder if I'm having a heart attack.

What I see has my blood turning ice cold. Bile rises in my throat as I take in the image before me. It's a picture of Markus holding a woman in his arms, cradling her, a woman who seems to be dead, killed by a gunshot wound to her head.

A woman who looks very much like me.

32

MARKUS

I watch Fallon as she rushes into the library. Her heart-shaped face is etched with sadness, and her plump lips are turned down in a permanent frown.

Telling her to leave when all I wanted to do was take her into my arms was the hardest thing I've ever had to do but necessary since this is what would've happened anyway. She was always going to run, always going to try and help her sister. Admitting I wanted her in any way wouldn't have changed the outcome. We were headed here from the beginning.

Brave, and so beautifully selfless. She was willing to endure my wrath again and again to save her sister. Pushing her away was the only way for me to get the full picture. It hurt like hell. Her walking away was like a bullet being embedded into my skin.

She wasn't ever going to trust me enough to help her any other way. Maybe she would after this, or maybe she wouldn't.

What I do know is that now Fallon will lead me right to Timothy. It's not the most ideal situation, and definitely more dangerous than I'd like it to be, but it is what it is. I'll make sure Fallon gets out of this unscathed.

I'm across the street from the library. The busy city surrounds me, and no one seems to notice me sitting here in my car. I kept my distance, stayed far enough back that any time Fallon looked over her shoulder, there was no way she would've seen me or the car.

A few minutes pass, and she appears again at the entrance of the library. I'm guessing she watched the video on that drive.

I wonder what she thinks of me now. If it changes how she sees me.

Looking out into the street, she descends the steps. She pauses when she reaches the bottom step and glances over her shoulder like she's expecting to find me there.

No, baby... I'm right in front of you.

Rushing across the street, she heads straight for *Beans,* the coffee shop.

From the spot I'm sitting in, I can see the door to the coffee shop perfectly and inside through the immense glass windows that overlook the street.

Fallon goes up to order a coffee and drops into the first seat she can find—in front of the window. She looks so incredibly sad. I wish I could take all the pain I've caused her away. I want to be better for her, but is it even possible?

When all of this is over, is she even going to want me? I've broken her and held her captive. She could never want me... never want to stay by choice.

As I stew in my own misery as I watch Fallon. She occasionally sips on the liquid in her to-go cup while staring out the window like she is waiting for someone.

Of course, she called Timothy to let him know she had the thumb drive. All that hassle he went through for a video. So stupid, so fucking stupid, but his stupidly is what's going to get him killed. I'm doing this for Fallon, for her sister.

My blood pressure spikes, and I have to force myself to remain in the car when a white van pulls up. The moment she sees the van, she hurries from her seat, leaving her cup behind.

The front windows of the van are tinted, so I can't make out the faces of the men inside.

She walks up to the passenger side door. Whoever is in that van exchanges words with her because the frown on Fallon's face deepens. She nods apprehensively, and the side door on the van opens. She's devoted to finding her sister, and I'm devoted to protecting her.

I might have said she could leave, but I never meant it. In every physical way, she is mine. She will always be mine.

Fallon climbs inside the van, and the door closes behind her. My heart sinks into my stomach. I hate not being inside that van, hate not being able to see her. I swear to god if they touch her, I will rip every appendage off their bodies and feed them to them.

The van pulls away from the curb, and I start my car, the soft purr of the engine fills the cabin. I keep a safe distance behind them. I don't need to blow my cover, not yet. The drive isn't a long one, but it feels like it is. Turning into the business district, we drive a little further. The van turns into an old parking lot with an abandoned warehouse on it.

I stall and pull to the side of the road, waiting for them to head inside. Two men climb out of the front seats and together walk over to the passenger side door.

A second later, Fallon is being pulled out of the van. One man holds her by the arm while the other points his gun at her. I can only imagine what line of bullshit he is telling her. And even though it's obvious she is afraid, she still holds her head high.

They disappear through a side door on the building, and as soon as they're gone, I get out of my car. I'm not sure what they plan to do with Fallon, but protecting her is the most important thing to me. I move with grace and precision, pressing my back against the brick exterior of the building.

I spot the door they went through and consider going in that way, but choose not to at the last second. The element of surprise is what's going to get me further. I can't let these idiots or even Fallon know that I'm here.

Walking around the building, I find another door. It takes me all of ten seconds to pick the flimsy lock and slip into the building unnoticed. As soon as I'm inside, I hear voices. They carry through the air, a beacon of guidance. The building itself isn't that large and looks like the type of property used for the overstock of equipment.

"Where is my sister? I did everything you wanted. I showed up alone, brought the drive. Please, just let my sister and me go. We won't tell anyone," Fallon pleads.

Sadly, there is no point in begging with these men. They don't care.

One man laughs. "Your sister isn't here, bitch, and we're not letting you go. The plan was to kill you, but we changed our minds when we saw you at the coffee shop. You're much too pretty to waste a bullet on."

Radio static fills my head. I slip into the darkness. The place I feel most at home. These bastards will pay for touching her, for even *thinking* of putting their slimy fingers on her.

"No, no. This wasn't the deal. I just want to save my sister!" Fallon starts to cry, and the last of my resolve snaps.

I descend into my mind and pull the gun from its holster at my side. Slipping between the racks, I wait until I'm closer before showing myself. Both men are standing right in front of Fallon while she sits on what looks like a chair with her hands tied behind her back.

"There's no saving your sister. There isn't even any saving yourself..." One guy leans in and touches Fallon's face. She turns her face and tries to move away from his touch, but he crowds her. "I can't wait to taste you... see if you're as sweet as..." I don't allow him to finish his thought. Lifting the gun, I point the barrel at him. He tilts his head to the side a smidge, and I take the shot.

Pulling the trigger, the deafening sound of the bullet leaving the chamber ricochets all around me. A soft gasp leaves Fallon's lips as the bullet embeds in his forehead, and he falls backward, landing haphazardly against the concrete.

One fucker down, one to go.

The other man is so shocked, he hasn't even reached for his gun yet. He's still staring at the space his friend was just standing. I waste zero time and move a little to the left. I pull the trigger again. The bullet goes straight into his head, and much like his friend, he crumbles to the floor a second later. I rush forward and undo the rope binding her hands at her back. Fallon twists in the seat and audibly sighs when she sees me.

"I'm sorry, Markus. I just wanted to save her."

Big fat tears tumble down her cheeks. She's utterly defeated. I want to make it better, but the only thing that will make her happy is saving her sister, and that's going to take a little more time.

"I know. It's okay. I promised you I would do whatever I could, and I will," I say as I pat down the two bodies.

"Why did you tell me to go? Why did you let me go if you were just going to follow me anyway?" Her voice cracks with unspoken emotion.

"I had to. They wouldn't have come for you if I was there with you, and you didn't trust me enough to let me help you. Now I've proven myself. Proven that I won't let anyone hurt you." I want to take her into my arms, but we need to finish this. We need to give Timothy what he wants, so we can save Fallon's sister.

In my search of the bodies, I find a phone. Again, it's a burner phone, and I navigate through the recent call history. Timothy's number is the last number called, and I hit the green call button and put the phone on speaker.

The phone rings twice. "You better have her."

"Your men are dead. It's time to end this, Timothy. I have the footage right here, on a thumb drive. Just tell us where Fallon's sister is."

"You don't call the shots, Markus." The disdain in his voice is suffocating. "There is a laptop on one of the shelves. Open it and upload the drive to the computer."

"Fallon," I whisper, pulling her attention back to me. Her gaze snaps to mine, and I extend my hand out to her. "I need the thumb drive."

With a nod, she reaches into her pocket and retrieves the tiny object. She places it in the palm of my hand with trembling fingers. I want to cover her hand with mine and tell her everything will be okay, but the truth is, I don't know what's going to happen next.

I spot the computer sitting across the room. My boots slap against the concrete as I walk over to it. The screen lights up, and I click *guest* on the welcome page. The process to upload the video takes less than five minutes.

"It's done," I growl into the phone and slam the laptop closed. "Now, tell us where Fallon's sister is."

"I told you... you don't call the shots, Markus. This is my game, my rules. I'll be in touch about the sister."

The line goes dead, and I grit my teeth before tossing the fucking phone at the nearest wall. He got what he wanted. He got the fucking video, so why is he still holding her sister hostage? Fallon lets out a ragged sob, and it's soul-shattering and heartbreaking. I've heard a lot of crying, begging, and pleading in my life, but nothing that's ever sounded like this.

I walk over to her and take her frail body into my arms. I hold her tightly to my chest and let her cry, knowing she needs me, knowing that for once... we're on the same page.

"I will get your sister back for you, Fallon. I will. I don't care what I have to do. I'll get her back for you," I whisper and brush a kiss against her forehead.

I won't let her down.

Timothy is going to pay.

33

FALLON

I didn't know the gaping hole in my chest could get any bigger until the moment I heard Timothy say he wasn't releasing my sister. Now every time my heart thumps, it feels like it's only half working, half supporting my body. I'm disoriented and confused. I did everything he asked.

I betrayed Markus, brought the video, endured pain, fear, and humiliation, and I'm still no closer to finding her. Thankfully, Markus showed up when he did. Part of me knew he had to be following me while the other hoped he wasn't.

Utter defeat overtook me when Timothy said he would be in touch. I won't lie. Part of me wanted to die. I knew my sister was going through a fate much worse than I, and even after all I've done, she was still going to continue to endure the poor treatment. It was a slap in the face.

Arriving back at the penthouse, Markus holds me in his arms and carries me to the elevator, holding me to his chest, cradling me like a baby, and only releasing me once we're safe inside the protective walls of his apartment.

He places me on the couch, and the loss of warmth from his body makes me shiver. I tuck my knees to my chest and wrap my arms around my body. I hate myself right now. Hate that I have him here. That I am protected and safe while Amelie is still out there. Markus sits beside me, his penetrating gaze moving over my body like he has x-ray vision.

"Did you look at what was on the thumb drive?" His voice is deep, like a canyon with jagged peaks.

I nod my head. "I saw Victoria. She looks like me."

Somberness creeps into his features. "That's how he knew I would want you. You're the spitting image of each other. Beautiful, blonde, and a smile that lights up the room."

It was a bit shocking to see how much we resembled each other, and it hurt to know that he only bought me because I looked like her... a ghost of his past.

My throat tightens. "I'm sorry, Markus. I didn't want to leave. Aren't the police going to come for you now? With those images out there, surely, he's going to hand it over to them."

Markus's thick brows furrows. "I thought you watched the video?"

"I only looked at the pictures on the drive. I was afraid to watch the video. I didn't want..."

"The image you have of me inside your head to change?" he finishes my thought.

I nod my head and look away shamefully. It's a complete contradiction for me not to watch the video. I know the type of man he is and have experienced it firsthand. Still, I don't want to see him in a worse light than I already do. The thought of him killing a woman that looks just like me makes me want to run away instead of seeking comfort in his arms.

Markus shoves off the couch and disappears down the hall. I sit up a little straighter, wondering what he's doing. A few moments later, he returns with a laptop in his hands. I stare at him, a bit puzzled.

He sits back down beside me and opens the laptop, placing it on the edge of the coffee table. My stomach twists, a knot forming there. I know what he's doing. He's going to make me watch the video, make me see him in a different light.

"Markus," I whisper.

He turns to me, his eyes pleading, and shakes his head. His fingers move over the keys as he types his password into the computer and navigates to the files. Maybe it's for the best that I see the video. Perhaps then I can be reminded of the sinister man he is. A couple more clicks and a video pops up. It's grainy, not of the best quality, but you can make out Victoria perfectly.

Her face is bright and joyful. She seems to be calling out to someone, her lips moving. My heart skips a beat in my chest, knowing that something bad is about to happen. All the joy in her face disappears, and she looks down at the ground. In the next instant, a car pulls up.

You can see it in the corner of the video. A second later, shots are fired, and Victoria hits the ground. Markus rushes to her side, clutching her to his chest, but it's too late. She's gone. Nothing can bring her back, and it's obvious from his anguished face that he knows this.

In the matter of one single second, he fractures, the despair in his eyes, the loss. I can tell that this single moment shaped him into the man he is today. He loved her. She wasn't just a friend. She was something to him, and when he lost her, he lost a piece of himself.

The video ends, the screen going black.

My throat tightens, and I feel tears prick at my eyes. I'm in love with a man who is still holding onto the ghost of a woman that looks just like me.

Markus closes the laptop and turns toward me. There is a chip in his armor, and I can see right inside, see into the good parts of him, the person he hides from the rest of the world, that he covers up with pain, despair, and bloodshed.

"She was the only person I ever loved..." His voice is gravelly, broken, and I want to take him into my arms and tell him everything will be okay, but will it be? I suddenly can't breathe when our gazes collide. I'm suffocating in his grief, drowning in it. "Losing her... it hurt so bad. It felt like someone ripped my heart out of my chest and stomped it into the ground." He presses a fist against the organ thundering in his chest.

"It's because of me that she died, and I've never allowed myself to forget it. Her memory haunts me, the words I spoke to her just seconds before she was viciously taken from me." His liquid amber eyes shimmer. "She would still be here if she hadn't gone out looking for me that day. If I'd been a better man, who didn't get involved in crime."

I can see him slipping into the past, filtering through his thoughts. Part of me feels that I should reason with him and tell him you never know what the future holds, but I know all too well about guilt. Wondering if you had made a different choice, would the outcome be the same or different.

Instead of giving him some mediocre bullshit sob-filled paragraph, I say to him what no one has probably ever said to him. Reaching for his hands, he lets me gently clasp them in mine. It's almost like he too needs the comfort and touch of another human in this moment.

"I know you won't believe me, but it wasn't your fault. It really wasn't. We all make choices, and she made a choice to come and find you that day. It was a wrong place, wrong time kind of thing. Neither of you could've expected it to end the way it did."

I can visibly see his chest heaving, his mind swirling with a thousand thoughts. I understand why he chose me, why he never hurt me even though he could have. He was reliving a memory, but I turned out to be someone else entirely.

I'm not her, and he knows that.

Reality slowly seeps back into him, and after a second, he tugs his hands away from mine. I wince at the loss of his touch. He makes me feel secure and safe, and without him, I'm in a constant tailspin of fear.

His jaw clenches, and he looks like he wants to apologize, but that's not Markus. He doesn't say sorry. "I let myself love once before in my life, and I promised never to love another the day that I lost her. Love is fragile, and I don't have it in me to endure another loss."

I know what he's saying, and the point of his words pierces my heart.

He will never allow himself to love another, including me. It hurts to hear him say it, and I wish things were different, but it's for the best. At least, it isn't that he isn't capable of loving me. He just chooses not to, and now I understand why.

"I understand," I whisper, letting him know I get what he is saying. He stares at me for a long second, his gaze holding me in place.

I can see the turmoil-filled battle beneath the surface.

He doesn't want to want me like this, but he can't help it.

He's afraid of getting hurt, but he doesn't know that losing him now would gut me, leaving me to bleed out on the cold ground.

This might have started as someone else's revenge, but it's ending as something entirely different for us. Something neither one of us can stop from happening, no matter how much we wish we could.

34

MARKUS

Two fucking weeks and still not a damn word from Timothy. Every day I grow angrier, and Fallon more worried. I don't tell her what I'm thinking, but the truth is her sister is most likely dead... or she wishes she was.

Leaning back in my chair, I click through Amelie Brice's social media again, looking for some clues I might have missed the first twenty times I checked. Fuck, I'm not good at this shit. I don't do research and find people like Felix. I just kill them. We would be the perfect team... if it wasn't for that one thing keeping us separated... there are things Felix won't do, lines he won't cross. I think back to the last time he worked with Julian.

"Felix, find out where she is hiding, hack into whatever database you need to find her. As soon as we get an address, bring Sophia in for questioning, Markus. Her husband hasn't spilled the beans yet on where he hid our last shipment of guns. Perhaps a little encouragement will help..." Julian grinned like the devil. All that was missing was his pitchfork and devil horns, and he would have the image down pat.

"I'm not doing it. I'm not helping you bring in an innocent woman," Felix piped up.

All I could do was shake my head. It seemed like he was fighting with Julian on everything, every step of the way. He was going to get us both killed. It was only a matter of time.

Julian snarled, "You'll do whatever the fuck I tell you to do. I'm the boss. Not you."

Anger was seeping from his pores. Julian was unhinged often, one second away from losing control. If I didn't get Felix out of here soon, he'd end up buried in the ground.

"I'm not doing it, boss... you can kill me if you want, but I'm not hurting an innocent woman." Felix shook his head with a determined scowl on his face.

Julian turned toward me. His dark eyes were vicious and promised pain. "Get your brother out of here and talk some sense into him before I kill him."

"Of course, boss." I did as I was told, knowing that Julian really would kill him. Grabbing Felix by the back of the neck, I dragged him out of the office. Felix was just as big and strong as me, but he didn't even struggle. It was like he didn't care what happened.

"Do you have a death wish? He could've killed both of us," I scolded as soon as we were outside. Felix stared at me for a long moment; his dark eyes seemed to look right through me.

"I'm not doing it, Markus. I'm not killing a woman. I'm not hurting one either. I have boundaries and shit I won't do. Unlike the rest of you, I have a moral compass. I'm not doing it."

I gritted my teeth. "You are, or we will both die."

Felix never even tried to find her. That was the night we were forced to go our separate ways. He knew making that choice meant he could no longer stay in the city.

I was sure Julian would kill me that night when I returned to the mansion without the woman, but he directed all his anger to Felix instead.

I pull from the memory of that night. The day my brother chose to be a better man than me. My finger stops, hovering over the mouse as I direct my attention to the image on the screen. Amelie is only a few years older than Fallon, but they couldn't be any more different. They don't look alike. Amelie is tan with dark hair and hazel eyes, and from what I'm seeing on her profile, they don't act alike either.

But in this picture, the one posted most recently, Fallon and Amelie have one thing in common. A sense of deep, radiating sadness in their eyes.

I flip through the pictures again, paying more attention to her facial expression instead of the people and places surrounding her. I notice that even ones she smiles in, it never reaches her eyes. In some of them, I can see more than sadness... fear. She was scared of something, even before she was kidnapped. Is it possible someone was watching her before? How long has Timothy been planning this?

So many fucking questions. I still don't understand how Timothy got caught up with these men. He wasn't involved in anything criminal when I was with Victoria.

In fact, it was the opposite. He hated that I was in the mob. He pushed her to break up with me and find someone else.

A good guy like himself.

Apparently, her death changed not only my soul but his as well.

My phone buzzing in my pocket pulls me out of my dreadful thoughts. I grab it, expecting to find another update from Felix. Julie has been doing well, considering everything. She's been eating and started talking a few days ago. I knew Felix would take good care of her; he's always been more caring than me.

Checking the phone, I'm surprised to see a text from Lucca.

Even more surprising is what it says: **I'm sorry. I had to.**

What the hell is he talking about?

I'm about to text him back when my phone rings in my hand. This time, it is Felix calling. I push the green answer button and lift the device to my ear.

"Hey, any news?"

"Yes, I got a solid lead on Timothy." Felix gets straight to the point.

I sit up straighter. "Spit it out."

"Looks like he is in France, close to where the sister used to live. They never left the area. He is holding her there."

"Fuck, I figured they would have moved her by now. They could have been anywhere in Europe. Why stay?"

"I was wondering the same. Are you going to send someone to get her?"

I almost laugh. "No, I'm going by myself."

"You sure about this? Those men he is working with are hired guns but well trained. I've got a bunch of intel on them, and it's not good. You definitely shouldn't go in alone."

"I'll figure something out. You have a location?"

"Yes, I'll email you everything I have. I would offer to come with you, but..." I already know what he's going to say.

"You can't leave Julie alone. I get it. Don't worry, you've done enough. Thank you again."

"No problem, I'm glad you called me for help."

"Yeah, me too. Talk soon," I end the call just as I feel Fallon's presence enter the room. When I turn around, I find her standing at the entrance of the room.

"Was that Felix? How is Julie?"

"Yes, that was him, and she is doing better. Also, Felix found your sister."

"What!" Fallon squeals while running toward me. "How? Where? When can we get her?" Questions shoot from her mouth like bullets from a machine gun.

"She is still in France, close to where she used to live with her boyfriend," I explain. Fallon moves next to my chair, her hand landing on my shoulder like she is trying to hold me here, so I can't get up and run off.

"She was there the whole time? So, wait, that means those guys lied. They said that they... they hurt her. If she was in France this whole time, then there is no way that's true. I mean, unless they were there in Europe, but that's unlikely, right?"

"Fallon, I don't know. I want you to be prepared for the worst. Even if those guys didn't hurt her, she has still been their prisoner for two months."

Fallon takes in a sharp breath. "I know." She nods, turning her head away to hide the pain etched into her features. Grabbing her wrist, I pull her down onto my lap and wrap my arms around her. The motion feels both foreign and natural. Two opposite emotions that shouldn't go together, but somehow, they do.

I know she isn't going to like what I say next, but I can't risk her getting hurt. Her safety is my biggest priority, and I can't focus on both her and her sister.

"I'm going to make some calls and get a plane to France. I'll find her and deal with the rest."

She pulls back from me, her eyes wide with shock. "What do you mean *you*? Wasn't the plan all along for us to go together?"

"Fallon." I sigh. How can I say this to her without her getting the wrong idea? Without her thinking deeper into things?

"Don't Fallon me," she growls, and it kind of reminds me of an angry kitten. "I'm going. She is my sister, and I want to be there when she is rescued. I didn't come this far just to sit on the couch while you finish the job."

I can tell she isn't going to let this go, and I guess I never expected her to. If I've learned one thing about Fallon during our time together, it's that she cares and loves with her whole heart, and she is going to see this through whether I want her to or not.

"I'm only taking you if you'll listen to every single thing I say. I can't be worried about you following my commands while we're doing shit like this."

"I swear, I'll do whatever you say."

Giving up, I pull her back into my chest. "Fine. Pack some clothes, the essentials only. We'll leave as soon as you're ready."

The smile that graces her lips makes me want to kiss her until the world around us fades away. "Okay..." Straight white teeth sink into her bottom lip. "Thank you for doing all of this."

"Don't thank me yet. Wait until we bring Amelie home."

If we bring her home. I add in my head. Fuck, I really hope we bring her home. I hope that I can be Fallon's hero for once, even if it will only ever be this one time.

35

FALLON

A few hours later, we are boarding the private plane Markus was able to charter at short notice. I take a seat in one of the large leather chairs, buckling up immediately.

Markus sits down across from me. I can feel his eyes on me, watching my leg bounce nervously. My gaze darts around the room as I try to locate an exit.

Would it be so bad to throw myself out of a moving plane?

"Are you scared of flying?" Markus asks while buckling up.

"A little, but more nervous about getting my sister back than anything."

It's much more than my fear of heights that's got my gut twisting into worried knots. We're on our way to get my sister, to rescue her. After all this time, it's finally happening. I'm bringing her home. Everything worked out.

The joy I feel flips to fear when I think of all that my sister's had to endure. She probably won't be herself anymore. She's probably a shell of herself. The more I think about how they hurt her and used her, the higher the panic becomes.

"Hey, you okay?" Markus's deep voice reaches for me, but I'm already creeping toward the sky. My chest rises and falls, but it doesn't seem like I'm taking in any air. I can't breathe, can't think. In my mind, I see my sister, beaten and broken. Used and abused.

"Once we take off, I'll get you a drink. That will calm you a little, take the edge off, at least." The plane is already moving, getting ready to take off, and my fear switches. I'm caught between a rock and a bolder.

I can feel Markus staring at me, watching me like I'm a crazed person. The plane picks up speed, the humming of the engine becomes loud, almost high-pitched, and the force of taking off pushes my body into the cushioned leather. I squeeze my eyes shut and grip onto the armrests to hold myself in place. A moment later, we're in the air, light like a feather. I'm not so sure, though, so I remain with my eyes closed and a death grip on the armrests for a little while longer.

When the roar of the engine turns into a calming hum, I relax more.

After a few more minutes, Markus unbuckles and walks over to the bar. He moves bottles around before finding a decanter of whiskey and two glasses. He pours us each a small amount, but before he even steps away from the bar, he downs his like a shot. Placing his glass back down on the bar, he turns and returns to my side with a glass for me in his hand.

"It will help take the edge off."

I take the glass with trembling fingers. "I'm afraid she's going to look like Julie or worse, and I can't..."

"Shhh, everything is going to be okay." He tries to soothe me, but there is no soothing what my mind already knows. I don't know the condition my sister is going to be in, but after two months, I would assume it's not going to be much better than Julie.

"I'm also afraid of heights... and I just..." I'm spiraling.

Markus drops into the seat beside me and takes my hand into his.

"Breathe. It's going to be okay..." He assures me.

But is it really? Is it really going to be okay?

Doubt clouds me. "What if it isn't? What if everything is falling apart, and there is no way to fix it? What if my sister is dead?" The words hurt so much to speak aloud, and the panic closes in around me.

Oh god. I'm waiting for the moment I pass out, but it never comes. Instead, a different feeling encompasses me when I feel Markus's lips against mine, kissing me with a feral need. He's kissing me. His firm, gorgeous lips are on mine.

My eyes pop open, and I'm tempted to pull away and tell him no, but his hand sinks into my hair, bending my head to a different angle, and I melt into a puddle of mush. Thoughts of my sister and the panic I was feeling moments ago fade away.

All I feel is Markus, his hot kisses, and his firm grip in my hair. His lips move down my neck and across my collarbone.

"I thought you didn't kiss," I pant breathlessly.

"I'll make an exception for you today," he whispers against my skin.

He devours me, licking and sucking my flesh like he wants to crawl inside of me. The warmth in my belly moves outward through my limbs. I want him badly. I want him to fuck me, hard and fast with bruising force. I want him to own me like only he can, to remind me who I belong to.

My core tightens, and I can feel wetness against my panties at the thought.

"Stand up and strip. I'm going to fuck you, right now, hard and fast."

I almost smile but hide it at the last second. It's scary how well he knows me, how he knows exactly what I need, and what I crave. Eager for his cock, I do as I'm told and strip out of my clothing. He watches me, his dark gaze drifting over the length of my body, my breasts, smooth belly, and shapely hips.

"I want to devour every fucking inch of you. Mark every single inch of your body. Every time someone looks at you, I want them to know it's me you belong to…"

He licks his lips, and a hunger takes over his features. That singular look gnaws at my resolve for him, and like two hungry animals, we collide.

Like the beast he is, he pins me to the leather couch across the plane. For one brief second, worry develops in my mind.

"Wait… what if someone comes out here?" I peer at Markus over my shoulder. He's just popped the button on his slacks and is shoving them down his thighs. He looks at me with liquid molten in his eyes.

"No one will come out here. The only other person on this plane is the pilot, and for the price I paid, he better keep his ass in the fucking captain's seat." That's the only response I get, and that's fine because the thought becomes a distant memory the instant I feel Markus press the thick head of his cock to my entrance.

In one swift move, he plunges inside me. The air in my lungs escapes on a gasp, and I sink my nails into the leather to stop myself from sliding forward with the momentum of his thrust. *Oh god.* My core clenches around him, squeezing him tightly, and I know what's to come. The anticipation bubbles up in my stomach, feeling like tiny little butterflies.

Fingers dig into my hips, and for the next few minutes, Markus owns me. He worships my body, claiming me with his cock. Each stroke, every touch, it sends me higher and higher, coaxing me closer to the edge.

"So fucking perfect… I wish you could see the way your pussy swallows my cock, it's an incredible sight." All I can do is whimper in response, the pleasure and pain ravaging me, stealing the words from my mouth.

My brain and body are in two dimensions. My nipples rub against the leather, heightening my pleasure. The slaps of our bodies coming together fill the room. His manly scent washes over me, blanketing my senses. He moves faster, grinding his hips into me, pushing my pleasure to a new height. I'm close, so fucking close.

"Beg for it. Beg to come..." He growls.

I'm so caught up in the pleasure, in the movement of his hips, the slap of his balls against my clit, and the way his cock enters me with punishing strokes, that if I don't come soon, I swear I will die.

"Fucking beg," Markus commands as he sinks a hand into my hair, fisting the locks and pulling me backward. The movement brings us closer together, and I feel him deeper in my stomach, in my fucking soul.

"Please... please, let me come..." I gasp as he grinds against me.

My orgasm sweeps through me, and my pussy clenches, gripping him so tightly it has to be near pain. Every muscle and cell in my body ceases to exist as pleasure overtakes my most basic instincts. I'm a slave to the pleasure he gives me.

Markus continues to fuck me, pressing deeper and moving faster as I float down from the high of my orgasm.

"You're mine... forever... mine," he growls each word, and I bet if I looked over my shoulder, I would find him with his teeth bared. I feel each word being burned into my soul. The idea of being with anyone else makes me sick.

Markus is it for me, and that is both terrifying and sad because I know he will never truly be mine. A second later, his entire body tightens, his movements cease, and the warmth of his release spills inside of me. Collapsing against me, he presses his body into mine, and the weight of him makes me feel safe, secure, cocooned.

I sigh and stretch out beneath him. His cock slips out of me, and I can feel our juices dripping out of me. Still, we remain where we are in a bubble of post-orgasmic bliss.

Stroking my hair, Markus whispers softly into my ear, "Everything is going to be okay. I've got you, Fallon. You're mine, and I protect what is mine."

He says it like I'm his treasure, something he values and cherishes forever, but I know the truth. When he is done with me, once I've reached my maxim use, he will toss me in the garbage and move on.

I'm nothing special to him.

Everything is not okay, and even after I rescue my sister, it won't be. I never anticipated falling for my captor, and now that I have, the idea of walking away is earth shattering.

36

MARKUS

Handing one of my guns to Fallon, I watch as she simply stares at it. Instead of reaching for it, she looks at it like it's some kind of alien device.

"Have you shot a gun before?"

"No."

"If everything goes as planned, you won't have to, but I need you to at least have this. If I go down, you start shooting."

"If you go down?" she asks in a high-pitched voice. "What do you mean?"

"Fallon, you know what we are walking into. I might get shot. Fuck, you might get shot." Even though I will do everything I can to prevent that. Just the thought of her getting hurt has my chest aching, but I know she won't stay behind.

The only thing calming my nerves right now is knowing that she is wearing a bulletproof vest underneath her sweater. Of course, that won't save her if someone aims for her head. Fuck, I can't think about this, or I won't go through with it.

I'm already contemplating calling this whole thing off, throwing Fallon over my shoulder and taking her back home, where I'll keep her chained to the bed. Yes, that would be much safer.

"Okay, I'll take it." She reaches for the gun. It looks much bigger in her hand. Her fragile fingers wrap around the sleek metal tentatively.

"It's loaded with a bullet in the chamber. There is no safety. All you have to do is point and shoot, that's it. Aim for the chest if you can."

"Got it. Point at chest and shoot," she repeats, but her voice is shaky, making me wonder if she could really go through with it.

Would she kill someone if her life depends on it? I already know she would risk her life to protect someone else, but would she take a life to protect her own?

"Just stay behind me and follow my lead."

Felix was able to get me the blueprints of the building, and the intel says there are only three guys guarding her. We should be able to take them down easily since we have the element of surprise on our side.

"Ready?" I give her a final once over.

"So fucking ready," Fallon answers right away, making me smile.

She was nervous on the flight, she was scared on the drive over here, but now her head is in the game. Her hands are steady, and her voice is determined.

"Let's go," I nod and lead her down the alley.

I parked the rental a block away, so they wouldn't hear a car approaching. This whole block consists of abandoned buildings, most of them condemned, which means besides the occasional homeless person, you won't find anyone here. Especially not in a fifty-thousand-dollar SUV.

Staying close to the wall, I walk down the small back road with Fallon following close behind. When we get to the building, I spot the camera above the door, right where Felix said it would be. I don't know how he was able to figure out all this shit, but I don't care. I'm just glad he did.

Before we're close enough for the camera to pick us up, I raise my gun and fire the shot, shooting straight into the lens.

"Hurry," I urge as I quickly make my way to the door, holster my gun and get the lock pick kit out. The door is older, and it only takes me a minute before the lock clicks open. In one swift move, I pocket the kit and retrieve my gun.

I open the door slowly, staying low just in case someone is already in the hallway. Sticking my head in, I see nothing but an empty space.

"It's clear," I whisper and move inside. Fallon is so close, I can feel her body heat behind me, and I let that calm the fear coursing through my veins. The fear of something happening to her tonight.

The place is dark, apart from some outside light coming from holes in the ceiling. The floors and walls are cracked and wet, which explains the mold and mildew smell filling the air.

When we get to the end of this hall, it splits into two corridors. I knew this from the plans, but I do not know where they are keeping her. Luckily, the idiots start to talk somewhere down to the right, giving themselves away.

I follow the voices with my gun raised. As we get closer, I can make out some of what they're saying. My French is rusty, but I do know what *la fille* means... *the girl.*

I glance back over my shoulder at Fallon one final time, giving her a small nod. I told her what to do. Hopefully, she'll listen to everything I said.

Positioning myself in front of the door, I suck in one deep breath before I lift my leg and kick in the door. The old, rotted wood breaks with ease. Small and large pieces fall away as I step into the room with my gun raised.

Time slows down as adrenaline floods my veins, and I become hyper-aware of everything around me. Two men are sitting at the table, their eyes wide with shock. One gets up while the other drops to the floor, but both reach for their guns.

I don't think. I fire the first shot at the idiot who gets up instead of down. The bullet hits him right between his eyes, and his body crumbles to the ground.

I lower my gun and shoot again. Unfortunately, the other guy is fast. He rolls away, and the bullet hits his shoulder instead of his head.

Reaching behind me, I grab ahold of Fallon and drag her with me as I take cover behind the wall. The guy shoots at us twice, and I can feel the impact of the bullets through the concrete wall, but luckily, it's not thin enough to penetrate.

Then I hear nothing. Silence. He's going to have to come out eventually, and I have time. It doesn't take long for him to get impatient. I hear him move around the room with a groan. That's when I make my move.

I come around the corner and fire into the room. He doesn't have a chance this time. The bullet hits his chest before he can raise his gun at me.

The man joins his friend on the floor, and I watch the life drain out of his eyes before turning my attention back to Fallon. She's hot on my heels, staring at the man I just killed. Surprisingly, she doesn't look scared or satisfied. She really doesn't look like anything right now. As if she has shut her emotions down, which might be a very good thing, depending on what we are about to find.

"You okay?" I ask as I look around the room. There is no sign of Fallon's sister, but there are two empty food trays with half-eaten meals.

"Yeah. Didn't Felix say there should be three guys?"

"He did. So still be on high alert. Let's continue down the hallway," I say and go back to leading the way through the building.

When I hear footsteps approaching from behind us, I quickly

spin us both around, shoving Fallon behind me. As soon as I see a figure appear around the corner, I aim my gun at him.

"Stop right there, or I'll blow your head off like I just did your friends."

The guy stops dead in his tracks, his face goes pale, and his eyes go wide. He even puts his hands up, showing me his palms as if that will save his life.

"Where is the girl?"

"S'il vous plaît... please," he begs for his life. What a pussy.

"Where is the girl," I repeat, my patience dwindling away.

He slowly raises his hand and points to the hall behind us. "Last room," he says with a heavy French accent.

"Merci." I thank him before I pull the trigger. The shot echoes through the hallway. Before I can turn around all the way, a second shot rings out.

Panic seizes every fiber in my body, and I spin around in terror. Did someone shoot me? Or worse, Fallon. What did I miss, who did I not see coming? If something happens to Fallon, I will kill everybody in this fucking country.

In the single second it takes me to turn around, my head is swarming with all of these questions. When I'm finally turned enough to see what's going on behind me, I'm even more shocked than I could have imagined.

Fallon is standing with her back to me, but she is angled enough to where I can see that she is holding her gun with both hands. A few feet away from us is a man, gripping at the center of his chest. Blood is seeping out between his fingers, where Fallon must have shot him.

He falls to his knees, then collapses to the front and falls lifeless to the floor.

The space falls into a dead silence, and for a moment, I just stand there, unsure of what to do. She killed someone. My innocent Fallon killed someone. She put her life before someone else's, and I couldn't be prouder of her.

Taking a step forward, I look into her face, expecting to see shock or remorse. Instead, I see relief.

"He was going to kill you," she tells me, and my jaw almost drops to the floor.

Did she just kill someone for me? I won't lie, now isn't really the time, but my cock grows rather hard at the realization.

I don't have time to dwell on that thought because Fallon is already on the move. Heading toward the end of the corridor.

"Wait," I call after her, but she sprints further down the hall. "Let me go in first!"

Fearless, like a fucking warrior, she runs to the last door in the hall and slides the large deadbolt open. I'm right next to her as she pushes the door open. I raise my gun, pointing it into the room.

"It's her," Fallon gasps and runs into the room. I curse, trying to grab her, but she slips away. Growling, I quickly scan the room and find it empty besides a small woman sitting on a mattress in the far right corner.

"Fallon?" Her sister's voice fills the space.

"It's me." Fallon sinks to her knees in front of her sister. The two immediately fall into each other's arms.

"I can't believe you're here." Her sister's voice cracks, relief flooding out of her.

"Everything is okay now," Fallon speaks softly to her, pulling away to assess her a little. From where I stand, I can see nothing that would lead me to believe she was beaten.

She seems thin, almost frail-like, but not beaten or abused. She looks nothing like I expected.

"We need to go," I growl, not wanting to cut their reunion short but also worried that we're sitting ducks by staying here any longer.

Fallon nods and helps her sister to her feet. When she faces me again, there is a twinkle in her eye that wasn't there before. I'm unable to deny the joy that seeing her happy brings me. I want to see her smile all the time, but how? This was always supposed to be temporary.

Now, I'm not so sure...

Amelie looks right at me, her hazel eyes are guarded, and her slight body trembles. She doesn't really seem afraid of me, just unsure.

"That's Markus. He helped me rescue you." Fallon pauses and peers up at me, her big blue eyes bleeding into mine. "He isn't going to hurt you. He's one of the good guys."

I almost snort while hurrying the girls into the hallway. *One of the good guys?* I wish. If only Amelie knew the shit, I put her sister through to get here.

"It's time to get out of here," I say over my shoulder and lift my gun.

Fallon nods her head, and together, we head out of the building.

37

FALLON

The reunion with my sister is filled with both joy and sadness. I hug her fiercely, wrapping my arms tightly around her, never wanting to let her go. Like I expected, she is quiet, her usual bubbly smile gone.

I'm afraid to ask what happened to her while she was being held captive. Did they rape her? Beat her? On the outside, she looks okay. A little thinner than before, and there are bags under her eyes, but it doesn't look as if she was abused or anything.

"Are you okay? Did they hurt you?" I ask once we're finally alone and on the plane.

Amelie shakes her head. Her heart-shaped face is paler than normal, and her mahogany brown hair falls in soft waves down her back. Its color is dull and lacking its normal robust products. Overall, she looks the same, which is a relief. I expected her to look like Julie, beaten and broken, but she doesn't. She looks *normal*. At least on the outside.

"Do you need a doctor? I can have Markus find one and have them there as soon as we land." Again, she shakes her head, and when she speaks, she looks out the window instead of at me. I feel like she isn't telling me something. In fact, I feel like she isn't telling me a lot.

"No doctor is needed. I'm fine. I just want to go home."

"Okay... do you want to call Leon—"

"No! Do not call him," she blurts out, borderline yelling.

I'm flabbergasted by her small outburst, and I take the seat beside her. Leon has been her boyfriend for two years. She's been head over heels for him, spending every free minute with him. Heck, she dropped out of college for him. "Just to let him know you're okay, I mean. You don't have to talk to anyone about what happened while you were there."

"Fallon, I told you I'm fine. No one hurt me. They didn't touch me."

"They didn't hurt you?" I repeat, making sure I heard her right. I'm glad she is okay, relieved beyond measure, but she might be lying to me, and I don't want her to face this alone.

She turns in the seat to face me. Her green eyes are sad, her expression heartbroken. "No. I'm fine. I just want to go home to Mom and Dad, and I don't want to talk to Leon ever again." I'm unsure of what I should say. Did Leon have something to do with this? Why is she so upset?

I decide to leave it alone for now, but the questions linger in the back of my mind. The plane takes off, and I stick to her side. Markus takes a seat across from us after a short while, and we ride in silence.

Eventually, she falls asleep, her body curled into a tight ball, her face pressed against the glass of the window like she wants to escape us. I know Markus told me to prepare for the worst, and I did, but I over-prepared.

I move to the seat beside him and grab his hand. I know he can never love me, but I need to anchor myself to someone right now—anchor myself to him. Neither of us wants to admit that we're falling deep into each because that would change everything. That would take our relationship from captor and captive into a strange new territory.

"What's wrong? I thought you would be happy to see your sister?" Markus asks in a hushed whisper. It's like he can see the worry developing inside of me.

"I am. It's just... I don't understand. They had her that whole time, and they never touched her. How? I mean, I'm grateful that she is okay and unharmed, but I was expecting worse, like you said earlier."

"She's lucky, that's for sure." Markus squeezes my hand. The warmth of his touch soothes some of my fears of the unknown away.

"Also, she is acting weird about her boyfriend. She said she didn't want to call him at all."

"I'm sure she'll come around and tell you more. Give her some time. She's been through a lot."

"Yeah. I guess," I nod, "I never got to tell you... thank you. For making good on your word."

"I gave you a promise, and I don't go back on them. You trusted me, so I put my trust in you." I shake my head and smile, really smile. She's safe, and everything I did to get to her no longer feels like it was for nothing.

For the first time, my heart is filled with joy instead of sadness, and I wonder how long this feeling will last. Timothy is still out there, doing who knows what? Would he try to come for my sister and me again? Markus? Every bone in my body says yes.

No one will be safe until he is gone.

∽

WHEN WE LAND, I'm unsure of what to do next. This is where mine and Markus's road should end, where we should part and go our separate ways.

What else is there to do? My sister knows where I am, and he already said it was okay for her to go home. He can't keep me prisoner now.

The question is... could I? Could I walk away from him? Turn my back on him, after all, we've been through? Resume my mundane college life after what I've experienced?

To walk away from him now, after everything he's done for me, seems like the ultimate betrayal.

But if he can never love me, what future is there for us?

As we walk to Markus's car, his phone starts to ring. I hold on to my sister's hand a little tighter, worried she will disappear if I don't. Markus unlocks the car, and we climb inside while he remains standing outside on his phone.

"He's just like the others. The men who took me... a criminal," my sister states as if she knows the truth. I nod my head because, at this point, why lie?

"He..." I start, contemplating if I should tell her the whole story or leave the worst part out. I decide after everything, Amelie deserves the truth. "He bought me at an auction. Paid one million dollars for me."

Even in the dark, I can see the shocked look flick onto Amelie's face. "I don't know what to say..." For a moment, she just stares at me, maybe waiting for me to say more, but there is nothing else to say. "An auction for people? Like... wow... was it just you there?"

"No." I cringe as the image of Julie's beaten body pops into my head. "There were other girls. We were able to save one of them, but I don't know about the rest."

"I can't wrap my mind around that. How could people do that? And what kind of man is Markus that he bought you?" She shakes her head.

"These people are bad, Amelie. Bad. Including Markus, but he is not evil like some of them. He didn't hurt me."

"He didn't hurt you? He just kept you as his prisoner?"

Before I can respond, the car door opens, and Markus climbs

into his seat. His posture is stiff, and like a sixth sense washing over me, I know instantly something is going on.

He starts the engine and pulls out of the parking lot without a word. I decide to wait until we arrive at his penthouse before I press him with questions.

My sister has been through enough and doesn't need to hear anything more about Timothy, whom I assume the call was about, and what has Markus so tense and worried. I do my best to abate my own worry and bask in the presence of my sister, who I have been without for two months.

"What happens next?" Amelie leans into my side and whispers in my ear.

I lick my dry lips. "I'm not sure yet. We're going to Markus's apartment. Then, we can figure it out from there, after a shower and good night's sleep."

Amelie's pink lips press into a thin line. She doesn't believe me. I can't imagine what she thinks. How does she feel? She probably thinks she's being pushed from one cage and into the next, but she's not. I won't let that happen. I won't let her be trapped, not ever again.

"We will leave soon. I'll take you home. We just have to make sure it's safe," I assure her.

She nods, and I look away, only to meet Markus's gaze in the rearview mirror. Those amber eyes of his are punishing, their depths ice cold. I shiver at the intensity of his stare and look away.

When we arrive at the apartment, Markus still hasn't said anything, and the tension stretches between us. I show my sister into the guest room and give her a pair of fresh pajamas and a towel.

I leave her to shower and go to track him down. I find him sitting on the edge of the bed. He looks up as I walk into the room. My throat tightens when I notice the anguish in his eyes. Whatever he has to say is going to hurt me.

"Felix called me. He found something else out while looking for your sister and Timothy."

I'm almost afraid to ask him to continue. "Yes?"

Markus runs a hand through his dark hair. "I don't even know how to say this because it's so hard for me to believe. I can't imagine what you're going to think when I tell you."

That sends my heart into my stomach, and I grip the edge of the doorframe to keep myself from sagging to the floor. "What is it?"

He swipes his tongue out over his bottom lip, and while the movement itself is sensual; it doesn't distract me away from the feelings rippling through me like it normally would.

"There is a reason you look so much like Victoria."

"I don't understand..." How could I possibly be connected to Victoria?

"Fallon, you're adopted. Apparently, your mom... your adoptive mother had lost a baby. It was stillborn. Through your father's connections, he was able to adopt you quickly, making everyone think you were the baby she had carried."

My mouth pops open, but no words come out. I just stare at him blankly. Everything is a lie. Every. Single. Thing.

Markus continues, "When Felix looked into Victoria's mother's whereabouts, he found out..." He pauses, and his eyes dart away for a moment before coming back to mine. "Just hours after you were born, your mother gave you up for adoption. From what Felix found, it wasn't willingly. It looks like she had cheated on Timothy. When he found out you weren't his, he forced her to give you up, threatening to take Victoria away if she didn't."

The shit keeps getting deeper and deeper.

"Oh my god, that's awful." An impossible decision. "He made her choose between the daughter she already had and the one she just gave birth to?"

"If what you're saying is correct... that means I have to find her."

"I'm sorry, Fallon. She is gone. Losing you was too much for her to bear. She left the hospital hours after you were born and committed suicide."

My hand slips from the door, and my knees give out on me. Like a rag doll, I head toward the floor. I don't have the strength to stop myself from falling.

Luckily, Markus catches me before I contact the floor. He pulls me into his broad chest and wraps his thick arms around me, holding all my broken pieces together.

I can't even wrap my head around everything he's just told me.

Everything crumbles around me. Amelie and I aren't even related. My parents, my mother and father, the people who raised me.

I'm on a damn rollercoaster that refuses to stop and let me off. I want to scream, to hurt someone or something, but that won't change the outcome, won't change what's already happened. I'm adopted, and the only girl Markus ever loved is my sister. As badly as I want to turn in on myself and disappear from the rest of the world, I can't. Amelie needs me. After all that she has been through, I have to be there for her. I'll make sure she is okay first, and then I'll break down. After a few moments and some calming breaths, I muster up the courage to speak.

"What do we do now? My sister wants to go home soon."

Markus holds me tighter, like he's not going to ever let me go, and I almost wish he wouldn't. That I could be his, and he could be mine forever.

"You and your sister aren't safe until Timothy is dead. He could come back for you at any time, and I don't know... If you died because of me, because of something stupid that I caused, I would never forgive myself. I've already lost so much."

"But... you said Amelie could go home after this."

"I thought Timothy would be there, or at least we'd get a lead to find him. We have nothing, and he might come after you to hurt me. He thought I was the one who killed Victoria, that's why he wanted the tape so badly. He thought he could put me behind bars with it. Now that he has is, he knows it wasn't me, but I think he still blames me... and fuck, he isn't wrong. It was my fault she was there that day."

I lift a hand and touch his cheek. It's rough beneath my palm. A mere contrast of how different we are. Rough and soft. Dark and light. We shouldn't be, but we are, and it feels like our fates have already been sealed.

"It's okay... we will stay until it's safe."

"I was hoping you would say that," he whispers as his lips press against the side of my head. I know he would tie me to the bed and hand-feed me if he had to. The possessive nature in him won't let me go, so I wonder how this is all going to pan out in the end. Will he let me leave?

"I need to go talk to my sister. Tell her we have to stay here for a while. I don't know how well she is going to take it, but I'll try."

Markus slowly releases me, like he doesn't want to let go yet. My heart begs me to return to the warmth of his embrace, but this isn't good for me. Pretending that we could be a couple when we most definitely aren't. Now would be the time to start putting distance between us, but the thought leaves me even more distraught than I already am.

I've just reached the doorway when he says, "If you need anything... I'm here for you, Fallon."

I peer at him over my shoulder. "Strange how foes become friends."

His face falls. "You don't need anything else added to your plate, but if I could... I would... with you, Fallon. It would be with you. And that has nothing to do with your connection to Victoria."

I know he's referring to loving me. How he can't because he gave all his love to the woman I now know is my dead half-sister. I hold back the river of emotions threatening to break the dam and destroy everything in its wake.

"I know," I whisper and walk out the door before I cry.

It isn't until I'm halfway down the hall I'm able to force myself to calm by taking slow and steady breaths. The last thing I need is to project my emotions out onto Amelie. None of this is her fault, none of it, and I'm not going to drag her any deeper into it.

The guest bedroom door is ajar, and it creaks as I push it open a bit more. Amelie looks up from where she sits at the edge of the mattress.

She is wearing one of my nightgowns, and even though she's taken a shower, she doesn't look any better. I walk into the room and close the door behind me.

She isn't going to like what I tell her.

"Did you find out when we can go home?" The look of agony on her face makes me want to turn around and walk out of the room.

"I talked to Markus, and until things with Timothy are over and they find him, we both agreed that it's probably best for us to stay here. Mom and Dad still think you're in France." Her face falls, and she looks like she's going to cry. I would expect it. She's been too calm, too quiet for someone who has been held captive for the last two months.

"I mean, I really want to go home, but what does it matter?" She shrugs. "I've gone from being held captive by someone else to being held captive by my sister."

Her words sting. "You're not being held captive. It's safer here, for both of us. I didn't go through all the trouble of getting you back just so we could end up in the same situation again." My voice rises, and I do my best not to scold her, knowing her head isn't in the right place, but I'm not letting her leave here.

Amelie tilts her head to the side, and her green eyes become luminous. "You like him, don't you? That's why you don't want to leave."

She's pulled the rug right out from underneath me. "No. That's not it. It's not safe. As soon as it is, we will leave. Markus means nothing to me," I lie. The words feel like acid on my tongue as I speak them.

"Whatever. I'm tired." She's starting to shut down, and still, I want to help her. All of this is my fault—all of it.

"Do you... want to talk about anything? About what happened while you were held captive? I'm here for you, Amelie."

"I want to sleep," she answers in a monotone voice.

I let things be and don't push her any further. "Okay. You can stay in here. If you need anything, I'm right down the hall."

Amelie doesn't respond, and I force myself to walk out of the bedroom. Everything feels like it's falling apart. My entire life is a lie. Everything I've come to know, a lie. It's like I don't even know who I am anymore.

I head back to the bedroom, and thankfully, Markus isn't there. Stripping out my clothing, I turn the shower to hot and wait for the bathroom to steam up. I step into the shower, and like a faucet being turned on, everything I've been holding in breaks free.

It comes barreling out of me in the form of tears.

My body shakes and trembles, so much so I lean against the tile wall to keep myself upright. I'm in love with a man who can never love me, a man who paid a million dollars for me, a man who is a violent, dangerous criminal.

I'm adopted, my entire life a lie, and the whipped cream on top... I'm the spitting image of my dead half-sister, the only woman that Markus has ever loved.

I'm so caught up in my self-loathing that I don't notice someone else is in the bathroom until the glass door of the shower slides open, and Markus's naked physique appears in front of me. I try to pull myself together, but it's not happening, and all it takes is one look for him to know that I'm shattering.

"I'm here for you, Fallon." His gravelly voice washes over me, and my nipples harden at the sound.

"I've been strong for so long... I'm tired of being strong," I sob, and he takes me into his arms, holding me to his chest like a piece of glass that's going to crack right down the middle.

"You don't have to be strong. I'm here, you can lean on me. Let me be your strength." His breath tickles my ear, and I shiver.

"You would do that?"

"I care about you, Fallon. Maybe not in the way you want or need to be cared for, but I'll try my best. I want to help you through your pain, through the secrets that we uncovered. We can be the same without all the bullshit, without the auction or money that I paid for you hanging over our heads, and when this is over... you can leave, if that's what you want."

His confession only makes me unleash a new wave of tears, and I suck a ragged breath into my lungs. I knew he would do this, push me away, eventually. He's giving me an out, letting me leave when he said he never would. Little does he know, I don't want to leave.

I want to stay forever, but I'm afraid... afraid of what happens when this is all over. Afraid that we may fall apart before we have the chance to become whole.

"I want that. I want you, even if it's not fully. Whatever you can give me, I'll take it." I bury my face into his muscled chest and sink deep into my mind. I think of all that I've discovered, how twisted and thorn-filled our lives have become.

I don't know what tomorrow will bring, but I know that I've done all I can do. I've saved my sister, and we're safe here with Markus as long as we stay put.

In the end, that's all I want. I can't make Markus love me. The only thing I can do is hope that when the time for me to leave comes... he doesn't let me go.

38

MARKUS

Three Months Later

Three months come and go in the blink of an eye. Life with Fallon is normal, real. It's everything I could've asked for and more.

Over the months, we've grown closer, and things have changed. My emotions and feelings toward her have matured tremendously, and the thought of her not being here tomorrow or for the rest of my life terrifies me.

I don't want to let her go... I really fucking don't, but I told her at the end of all of this, once it was safe, she could leave. I'll make good on my word and let her, even though it's going to kill me. I do my best to stay busy every day, to take my mind off the thought of her leaving. Sometimes, I pray that Felix never calls because the day he does, I know everything will change. I've just finished up lunch and a game of scrabble with Fallon and Amelie when my phone starts to ring.

If someone had told me a year ago, I would be sitting in an

apartment with two women, playing board games and cooking like I was anything but a higher up in the mob, I would've told them to fuck off. But here I am, domesticated as fuck.

Amelie has adjusted surprisingly well. It took her awhile to get used to me, to trust me not to hurt her or Fallon, but we somehow got there.

Julie ended up staying with Felix permanently. Even after she recovered, and we offered her a fresh start, she chose to live with Felix. I'm not sure if that's the best outcome for either of them, but that's a story for another time.

Glancing at the phone, it's as if he can hear me thinking about him. Felix's name is lighting up the screen.

"Hello, brother—"

"He's here. In town," Felix says with no preamble. There is no further explanation, not that I need any.

"Where?"

"I'll send everything to your email, but before I do, I have to tell you not to go in alone. I know you didn't listen last time, and you got fucking lucky. This is different, though. Just please fucking listen to me when I say do not go in alone," he repeats.

My lips tip up at the sides. He's showing such brotherly love.

"I won't, and thank you for finding him," I say before ending the call.

Without taking a second to think about it, I call the one person I know I can count on to help me.

It rings a few times before Julian answers. "Nice to hear from you, how is your—"

"I need your help, and it can't wait," I say, hoping he'll do this for me. Especially after I practically abandoned him.

"What are you talking about? Wait..." He trails off, probably putting one and one together. He knows I've been looking for Victoria's father.

"I found Timothy. He is here, in town. I need to move now. Can you help?"

It doesn't take Julian long to respond. "I see. Yes, I suppose I can help," he says, all nonchalant, probably because Elena is close by and listening to his every word.

His voice is calm, almost uninterested, but I don't miss the note of excitement. Since his marriage to Elena, he rarely goes out and gets his hands dirty anymore, that doesn't mean his need for bloodlust has disappeared. He's just better at hiding it.

Like all made men, he yearns for violence, and tonight, he will get his fill.

"I'm on my way."

I quickly pull up Felix's email and go over everything he sent me. Location, blueprints, etc. It doesn't take me long to get ready. I've been waiting for this day for three months, welcoming it with open arms and not wanting it to come at all.

Only when I'm dressed in Kevlar and tactical gear from head to toe do I leave my office.

Fallon and Amelie are curled up on the couch. I notice a chick flick playing on the large flat screen as I pass them in the living room. They are both asleep, but Fallon's eyes fly open when she hears me approach.

"Where are you going? Work?" Her voice is sleepy.

She knows that sometimes that's all I can tell her.

"No, Felix called. We found Timothy. He is close by, in the city. I'm going to kill him tonight," I whisper, trying not to wake up Amelie.

"Oh..."

Worry lines crease her forehead, and I itch to smooth them away. "Don't worry. I'll be back by the morning. He's not getting away this time. By tomorrow you'll be safe... and free." I force the last word past my lips.

"Okay." She nods, but her eyes tell me she is unsure about this.

She is worried about me, which is still an odd feeling to

process. Having someone care for me like that is something I never expected to happen again, especially from Fallon.

Leaning in, I give her a chaste kiss before I pull away. She forces a smile, and I almost stay a few minutes longer just to make sure she is okay, but I'm on the clock.

Time is running out, and I can't miss this window of opportunity.

"Go back to sleep. I'll be here when you wake up," I promise her before slipping into the elevator. The doors close slowly, and our gazes remain on one another until we can no longer see each other.

By the time I reach the parking garage, I'm in hunting mode. I jog to my car and get inside in a hurry. I break about every traffic law in the city, speeding across town to Julian's place. I'm not concerned in the least bit about the cops pulling me over. Julian pays them a fortune to turn a blind eye to our shit.

When I arrive at Julian's mansion, he is already waiting at the gate for me. He's dressed similar to me. All black, tactical gear, and I'm sure armed to the teeth. Without his expensive suit, he looks more like a mercenary than the head of the mob.

"Eager for a night out?" I grin as he climbs into the car.

"You have no idea."

"Good, I can't wait to get this done. Felix sent—" *Fuck!* As soon as Felix's name leaves my lips, I know I've fucked up. I'm so consumed with the thought of finally getting Timothy that it just slipped out. I glance over at Julian, planning to see an angry scowl or the chamber of his gun, but instead, find him staring at me with his eyebrows raised.

"I don't know what I should be angrier about, you not telling me that Felix has been back in your life for months now, or the fact that you thought I didn't know all along?"

Gripping the steering wheel a little tighter, I say, "I didn't know how to tell you."

"He is your brother by blood, and he was never cut out for

this life. I know you're loyal to me. You are one of the only people I still trust." That means a lot coming from Julian, especially after the whole Lucca fiasco. He's trusted basically no one since his betrayal.

"I'll always have your back. I don't know what drove Lucca to do what he did, but there is nothing that could make me turn on you." I often think about that text Lucca sent me while I was on my way to France. *I'm sorry. I had to.*

I didn't know what it meant at the time. Only later did I find out Lucca had double-crossed us, all of us, but it hit Julian the hardest. I still don't understand why he did it, but I'm almost certain it has something to do with that little redheaded girl he sent me after. *Claire.*

"Enough with the traitor. What's the lowdown on this guy we're killing?"

"He's at a poker game happening in the basement of Giovanni's place. Felix said there are five guys inside, but no one is guarding the entrance. No cameras, either."

"So... they're really stupid or just arrogant. This is going to be a walk in the park, like taking candy from a child." He sounds almost disappointed, like he had hoped for something more challenging.

"Probably a bit of both. I want to kill everyone quickly, except Timothy. I want to know what his endgame was, and then I'll make him suffer for what he put Fallon through."

Usually, Julian makes all the rules and decides how the fucker will be handled, but he knows I need this. This is my kill, my chance for revenge.

"Sounds like a plan," he agrees.

"Here, that's him." I pull up a recent picture on my phone and show it to Julian, so he knows which one not to kill right away.

"Perfect. I'll make sure I save him for you." Julian grins, and truthfully, it's scary to see him this joyous over spilling blood.

Ever since getting married and having a kid, he's been more reluctant to leave the house.

That, and the fact he trusts no one, Lucca really did a number on him.

Twenty minutes later, we pull up to Giovanni's place. It's a rundown house next to his garage, where he sells stolen auto parts. He is a small-time criminal, petty theft, and shit. Usually, we stay out of his way, but not today.

We're in a bad part of town, so we're not worried about being seen or heard. Nobody will call the cops here. Screams, fighting, and shootouts are a common thing here.

We make our way around the house. Just like Felix said, there is no one standing guard. I pick the lock on the back door, and we are inside the house with no trouble at all.

As soon as we step into the kitchen, we can hear laughter echoing up the stairs from the basement. At least some of the men are down there. Julian and I walk through the house quietly with our guns drawn. This seems way too easy. A toilet flushes, and we both look at each other.

A moment later, the bathroom door swings open. The guy steps out into the hall, still zipping up his pants. I'm on him before he can react.

With my hands around his throat, I press him up against the wall. He wheezes for air, his hands desperately trying to get me away. He makes a feeble attempt to hit me in the chest, but he's already so weak it barely hurts.

His eyes start to bulge in his skull, small veins burst, turning the white in his eyes blood red. His lips turn a sickening blue, and I watch as the life drains from his body before I slowly lower him to the floor.

"One down, four to go," I whisper when I turn around.

Julian nods, and we make our way down the stairs.

The basement smells of smoke, sweat, and booze. The

laughing gets louder with each step we descend. The men are so drunk and distracted, they don't even see us coming.

"Good evening, gentlemen," Julian greets cheerfully, announcing us to the four men sitting around the round poker table.

The laughing stops immediately. The men scramble off their chairs, reaching for weapons, but their moves are sluggish from the alcohol they've ingested, and they don't stand a chance against us.

Julian fires two shots, hitting the two men to the right, right between their eyes. I kill the one on the left just as his fingers ghost against his gun.

After the echoes of the gunfire cease, the room descends into silence. All I can do is stare at Timothy, the father of the girl I used to love.

Even the recent picture I have of him didn't show how terrible he looks. His leathery, pale skin is covering his thin face, which is set in a permanent frown. Deep wrinkles are etched into his forehead and around his mouth, making him appear older than he is. The dark circles under his eyes make his already dark brown eyes seem black.

He looks to be twenty years older than he actually is. For a split second, I feel sorry for him, knowing what he lost, knowing that he lost everything he ever loved. That feeling quickly vanishes when I'm reminded of all he did to Fallon.

"This is all your fault," he sneers at me. "You're the reason she is dead. She was a good girl. Had her whole life ahead of her, and you destroyed that. Ripped it all away."

"Kind of like you ripped Fallon's life away from her? Like you destroyed Amelie's?"

"Amelie was collateral damage, and Fallon deserved it. It's her fault my wife killed herself. She was nothing but a mistake. If I had it my way, Fallon never would've been born."

Anger surges inside of me, making my muscles quake. "I can't wait to kill you, old man. It'll be the highlight of my life to see you perish. But first, let's make one thing very clear. You started this. You are the catalyst that set everything into motion."

With my gun pointed at his head, I take a step toward him. "I always thought you were a good guy, single dad, hardworking, no trouble with the law. It took me a while to see you for who you really are. The kind of man you are hiding inside. Tell me, why did your wife cheat on you? Because you were such an outstanding husband? Why did you have to threaten her with taking Victoria away? Because she loved you so much?"

"You know nothing!" he spits, gritting his yellowing teeth.

He doesn't like that I'm giving it all back to him. That I'm not backing down like all the others in his life have.

"I know Victoria wanted to move in with me. I know she didn't want to go home most nights. I was too young and dumb back then to see why. You were never the good guy you pretend to be, were you?"

"Funny coming out of your mouth. Like you're such an outstanding citizen?"

"I've never pretended to be good. I'm a killer, a criminal, I'm selfish and arrogant. I've never pretended to be anything else. I don't hide it either, never have, never will. And I'm not going to pretend that I feel any remorse or that I won't take great pleasure in killing you... killing you very slowly."

All the blood drains from Timothy's already pale face, making him look... well, dead. His legs give out on him, and he sits back down on his chair. I can see his hands shaking from here, fear overtaking his body. He knows his clock is up. The only way he's leaving this building is in a body bag.

Out of the corner of my eye, I see Julian take a step closer. Without glancing over my shoulder to see his face, I know he is excited and ready to start.

Grinning, I say, "Let's begin..."

39

FALLON

Since the moment he walked out that door, I've been sitting on the couch staring at it. I'm afraid he won't come back, afraid I gave up the chance to tell him I want more, need more. The minutes tick away, but the ache in my chest never eases.

"He's coming back," Amelie says, walking into the living room.

"I know he is." I try not to sound as desperate as I look and feel.

"Then why are you staring at the door like he isn't?" She lifts the cup of tea she just made to her lips. Amelie knows some about Markus but not everything, and even though she was held captive by Timothy and his men, she doesn't know just how bad this could go.

Markus isn't invincible. He is human. A bullet will kill him just the same.

"I'm not," I lie. I already know that she thinks Markus and I are dating, even though I've told her many times it's not like that. The last six months have been a whirlwind, and when he got the phone call this morning, I almost sagged to the floor.

"Whatever, you can lie to yourself but not me." She walks away, shaking her head and leaving me alone with my thoughts. So much still hangs in the air between us. I haven't told her I'm adopted yet, and she hasn't told me what happened to her while in confinement. I do know that someone had to be protecting her or caring for her. Otherwise, she would've been dead.

I stare down at the paperback on the coffee table. I've tried reading the thing three times, and I just can't focus.

Markus didn't tell me where exactly he was going, and I have no way to contact him. I just hope he didn't go face Timothy alone. Running my fingers through my hair, I tilt my head back and rest it against the couch. I stare at the ceiling, wondering how I'll move on from him if he doesn't return to me.

The sound of the lock disengaging has me bounding from the couch, and by the time the door opens, I'm standing in front of it. Markus appears in front of me, and I can't stop myself. I lunge for him, wrapping my arms around his middle while burying my face into his chest. He smells of sweat and gunpowder.

"Well, hello to you too."

"You're back." I sigh and pull back a bit, so he can come inside.

"Did you honestly think I would lose in a gunfight?" He raises a thick brow.

I shake my head. "No, but things happen." I do my best not to frown or show how sad this moment makes me. He is back, and after tonight, nothing will ever be the same for us. This is where we go our separate ways, where we stop pretending and move on.

Can I end it, or do I try...

"They do, but today they didn't."

I nod and untangle myself, walking backward toward the couch. "Is he... dead?"

"Yes. It's over. You and your sister are safe now. No one will ever try to hurt you again." Knowing his next set of words, my chest tightens, and I swallow around a grapefruit-size knot in my throat. "You can go back home, back to your life... if that's what you want."

I look from the floor and into his steely gaze. *Is that what I want?* Of course not. My home is here. My life is with him. There is nothing for me out in the world anymore.

"What would you say if I told you I didn't want to leave... that you're my home now, and that the last six months have been incredible. I've seen a side of you I never expected to see and..." I want to say the words, but they stick to the roof of my mouth. I'm so scared of his rejection, but I force myself to say them anyway, "I love you."

Markus crosses the space separating us in a flash. His mammoth hands reach for me, and he cups me by the cheeks, pulling me closer to him and into his face. I have to crane my neck back to see his whole face, but it's worth it. Even in the aftermath of bloodshed, he is gorgeous beyond measure.

"These last three months have shown me how wrong I was. I dreaded this day and prayed that my brother would never call, and not because I didn't want Timothy to die. Because I knew the day he called was the day everything between us would end. I would have to let you go, even if it's the last thing I want to do. I love you, Fallon. I never thought it was possible that I could love again after losing Victoria, but you opened my eyes. I want you here with me. Want you to stay and be mine, and I yours."

Tears form in my eyes, and when I blink, they fall, sliding down the apples of my cheeks.

I feel... whole and full of love. I knew he felt different, could feel it in the way he cared for me. He made love to me, pampered me, and made me his equal. Not once did I feel like I was his captive, not since the day we rescued Amelie.

"You mean it?" My voice cracks.

"Yes, every fucking word. I want you, Fallon. To be mine. Forever. As my other half. We didn't start things out in the most conventional of ways, and I'm an asshole on even my best days, but I want you. All of you."

"Yes!" My lips are trembling, my thoughts swirling. "I want to stay. I want you too."

Pressing his firm lips against mine, he steals the air from my lungs. Fire and passion encompass us. I part my lips, and his tongue slides inside, tangling with my own. He tastes like sin and mint. I crave his kisses, his touch, every single thing about him.

I run my hands through his dark hair, tugging on the strands. If we don't end this, we'll end up fucking right here on the couch, where Amelie could come out at any second. As if he's thinking the same thing, he pulls back, his nose grazing mine, and his chest rises and falls at a rapid rate, matching the tempo of my own.

Our breaths are ragged, our lips aching.

"We're doing this?" he finally says, his voice thick.

Does he not believe me or think I am serious? I've already fallen for him. There is no undoing what's already done.

"Yes?"

"Just making sure because after today, I'm never letting you go. I will kill anyone who tries to take you from me and tie you to the damn bed if you try and escape on your own. This is your only chance to leave for the next however many years we have together."

I smirk, feeling like I've won the lottery. "Then so be it because I'm not going anywhere."

Markus grins and grabs me by the back of my legs, hiking me up his firm body. I let out a small squeal that he silences with his lips. He kisses me with so much passion, he steals the air from my lungs.

Caught up in his touch and the fire he stirs in my belly, I don't even realize we've made it to the bedroom until he places me down on the mattress. He releases me and goes to the door, closing us inside.

Those full lips of his turn up at the sides, and it's such a seductive grin that my nipples harden at the sight of him. Pulling his shirt over his head, he tosses it to the floor. By the time I've gotten my leggings off, he's already naked and stalking back toward the bed.

"I can't even describe how much I need you right now." His lips brush against mine, and his hand snakes beneath my back. He lifts me, cradling me to his chest while his thick cock swings like a sword between our bodies.

"I need you too, so shut up and fuck me," I order, wrapping my legs around his middle and digging my heels into his ass cheeks.

I'm wearing a thin cotton T-shirt and no bra since I've spent the entire day lounging around waiting for him to return home. Of course, I'm bare from the waist down, and Markus uses that to his advantage, brushing the head of his cock against my entrance.

"Are you ordering me around?" His lips trail down my throat and over my throbbing pulse. My blood hums in my veins, and I lift my hips, seeking the pleasure I know only he can bring me. One of his hands moves beneath my head, and it's like he's cradling me in his arms. His fingers move through my hair, and he fists the strands tightly, causing a sting of pain to radiate across my scalp. "Are you?" A deep growl emits from his chest.

My core tightens at the deepness. I want him to fuck me already, to show me who is in control.

"Yes." I curl my lip and lift my head, pressing my nose against his. "Now fuck me like you claim to love me."

Without warning, he slams into me, all the way to the hilt, his hips kissing mine. Our bodies connect, bringing a jolt of pleasure mixed with pain.

He fucks me brutally, and not like he loves me but hates me. It's raw, powerful, and consuming.

The air in my lungs wheezes out past my lips, and my toes

curl with each thrust. I dig my nails into his shoulders, dragging them down his back.

"Fuck, yes. Make me bleed," Markus grunts and bares his teeth, the corded muscles in his neck tighten, and he looks like a wild animal about to dig into his prey.

The hand that was cradling my head moves to my throat. Staring into my eyes, he gives my slender throat a tight squeeze, and I feel lighter—like I'm flying. It's an adrenaline rush to know he holds all the power, that he could hurt me if he wanted to, but knowing that he won't.

With that single hand, he pins me to the mattress and fucks me like a savage beast. While his other hand moves beneath my shirt, finding my tit and tweaking the hard peak. Each stroke makes me hotter, and soon I'm ready to combust like a shooting star in the night sky.

All the muscles in my body tighten, and I become as straight as a board.

"I'm..." I sink my nails harder into his skin. "I'm coming." I finally get the words out just as my orgasm crests, and the world around me fades. My entire channel convulses around Markus's cock, and he lets out a hiss as I bear down on his length.

Waves of pleasure still lick at my sensitive flesh as he pulls out of me. I whimper and give him a displeasing look because I know he didn't come yet. Before I can voice my concern, he flips me onto my stomach. The drawer on the nightstand opens, and the sound of a bottle opening meets my ears.

I feel the cold lube between my ass cheeks a moment later and shiver at the contact. Markus climbs back onto the bed and moves, so he's right behind me.

With two fingers, he spreads my ass cheeks and groans. "Your ass was made to be fucked by me." Landing a harsh slap on my ass, he slips a finger into my tight puckered hole at the same time.

I whimper into the mattress and claw at the bedsheets at the intrusion. My ass tightens around that digit, and Markus places kisses across my shoulder and neck, helping to loosen the tension. As soon as he can start to move, he does. Very slowly he fucks my ass with his fingers until I'm a writhing mess.

"I-I need you."

"Now you *need* me," Markus replies cockily.

"Markus." I groan, feeling like I might die if he doesn't fuck my ass soon.

He chuckles and replaces his fingers with his cock, slowly slipping into my tight hole. I breathe deeply through the transition, and once he's fully seated, I sigh as delicious pleasure ripples through me. His hand ghosts over my backside, and then he moves, his thrusts shallow at first. Over time, he moves faster and faster, his balls slap against my clit, and like a match being lit, I burn up in the flames of pleasure, my orgasm grabbing me by the throat.

I can't breathe, can't see. All I can do is feel. Feel the love Markus has for me. Feel the intense pleasure. Feel our connection, growing, becoming deeper.

Markus lets out a roar that rattles the walls, and I feel him still behind me. I've barely just caught my breath when his release floods my asshole. I'm content, joyful, and happier than I've ever been. Timothy is dead, my sister is safe, and Markus is mine.

"I love you, Fallon," Markus whispers before placing a kiss on my shoulder.

"I love you too." I sigh.

There is nothing that could take the joy I'm feeling away. I've got it all. Now, I just have to make sure no one tries to ruin my forever.

40

MARKUS

I've come to care for Amelie, I really have, but the entire time she's been staying with us, something has been nagging me about her. She is keeping things from us. I can see it in her eyes when she thinks no one is looking.

The way she flinches at a loud noise. The way she looks over her shoulder like she thinks someone is following her. The way she looks out of the window as if she expects someone to be standing there.

At first, I was convinced it was PTSD from being held captive, but the more I watch her, the more I think there is something else... something deeper going on. No matter how many times Fallon and I have tried to talk to her about her time in captivity, she refuses to talk about it.

She shuts down completely and turns in on herself. I think Amelie has been scared for a long time. A lot longer than the time she spent in that cell.

The fact that she didn't want to go back to her boyfriend only adds to my suspicions. I just can't figure out what exactly happened. Was her boyfriend involved in her kidnapping, or was he just an abusive asshole before?

I know it's bothering Fallon, not knowing what happened, not knowing how to help her.

I wait for Fallon to take a bath before I make my way to Amelie's room. The door is wide open, so I step in. Her back is turned to me, and she is folding clothes and neatly stacking them into her suitcase, which is propped up on the bed.

"Ready to go home?" I ask, making her jump and drop the sweater she was holding.

"Jesus, you scared me. You move awfully quiet for a guy your size."

"So I've been told." I chuckle.

"And yes, I'm ready to go back home and be with my mom and dad for a while. I've missed them so much." She picks up the sweater and places it back on the bed.

"How come you never visited or had them come and visit you?" I ask, trying to keep my voice casual, so this sounds less like an interrogation. I could easily get the information out of Amelie, have her crying, and telling me everything I want to know, but she's Fallon's sister, and whatever happened to her when she was being held captive is something she will talk about when she wants to.

She shrugs. "You know... everyone is so busy."

I know that's a lie. Her parents have asked multiple times to come over while she's been here. I don't doubt that they would have closed the store to fly over to France to visit her. Amelie dropped out of college and moved in with her rich boyfriend. Neither time nor money should have been an issue for her to visit them either.

Something else kept her from seeing her family, and I'm going to find out what.

"You know what I do for work, right?"

Amelie's body tenses at my question and her next words are hesitant, almost scared, "Yeah, I mean, kind of. Not exactly, but you work for the mafia, I know that much." She swallows thickly. "If you are worried about me saying anything, I would never."

"I know, that's not where this is going. I just wanted to let you know that if you ever need anything, you can ask me. I'm in love with your sister, and I'm planning to be with her indefinitely. That makes you family, and I protect my family. I won't tolerate someone hurting my family."

"Um, thanks." She bites her bottom lip nervously like she is unsure of what to say. I decide to come right out with it.

"Did someone hurt you? Before you were kidnapped? Maybe your boyfriend?"

She looks at me out of the corner of her eye. "What if he did?"

I don't even hesitate with my response, "Then, I would hunt him down and kill him for you."

She shakes her head. "You can't."

"Why?"

"Because he's already dead."

"Already dead?" It takes a lot to shock me, but her response does. "Did you kill him?"

Amelie is a small thing, short with little muscle mass. I doubt she could fight off an aggressor, let alone kill someone.

She shakes her head again. "No. I didn't kill him."

"Then who did?"

"I don't want to talk about this," she whispers and squeezes her eyes closed.

"I understand that, but if you didn't kill him, someone else did. Who are you protecting? I'm not asking you to tell me your darkest secrets. I just want to know who did it. Maybe I can send him a thank you card or something."

Amelie doesn't laugh, so I figure I've missed my chance at convincing her to tell me, but then she says, "It was one of the guys... the men who held me prisoner."

She doesn't continue, but I know there is much more to this

story. I try to think of a reason why they would kill her boyfriend, and only one comes to mind.

"Did he try to come for you?"

Her eyes flicker away before returning to me. "Yes, that's what happened," she explains, nodding her head. I didn't think it was possible, but she is an even worse liar than her sister. Something else happened, something she doesn't want to talk about.

I decide to let it go for now. I'd rather have Felix do some more digging on the boyfriend.

"Please, don't tell my sister... about Leon. I don't want her to be upset. She's been through enough, and I know she would feel bad."

I had to agree with Amelie. Fallon would be upset. The idea of not telling her didn't sit well with me, but I could always explain later to Fallon what her sister had told me.

"Fine, but you need to make me a promise."

Amelie nods her head profusely. She didn't want to hurt her sister any more than her sister wanted to hurt her. They were both selfless when it came to each other.

"What promise?"

"If you need anything, you come to me. You get into any kind of trouble, you call me. I will destroy anyone that fucks with you. Anyone, do you understand?"

"Yes," she whispers and looks me right in the eyes. "I'll call you if I need anything."

I can only hope that's the truth because if anything happens to Amelie again, I'm not sure Fallon will survive.

EPILOGUE

Fallon

One Year Later

We get married on a Sunday. The sun hangs high in the sky, shining down on us. Waves crash against the private sandy beach, and the wind blows through my hair. There couldn't be a more picturesque moment. My dress is perfect, white, and elegant. Markus looks dapper in his tux, his hair sculpted perfectly against his head.

He looks as much the growly bear now as he did the day of the auction.

My parents, sister, Felix, Julie, and Markus's close friends, Julian, Elena, and their daughter, join us in our celebration.

With our hands joined, we stare into each other's eyes. We recite our vows, and Markus grabs onto me, pulling me into his chest, planting a possessive kiss against my lips when we are announced as husband and wife.

Everyone smiles, and I'm sure I'm going to implode with happiness.

"Now you're never going to get away," Markus whispers into my ear.

I shiver from the possessive tone he takes.

"I wouldn't even try to leave. I was yours before I even realized it," I reply, my eyes catching on the diamond ring on my finger.

"You've always been mine." He pulls me even closer to his side, and I squeal as I trip over the end of my dress, only for him to catch me around the waist.

It's still surreal and crazy how our lives have changed over the last year. We walk up the beach and toward the condo where we have dinner and drinks set up. We both agreed that something small and private would be perfect.

"I can't believe we're married and that this year passed by so fast," I announce when we reach the entrance to the small reception area. There are light decorations, flowers, and candles lit. It's intimate and totally us.

"This year has been a wild one." Markus hands me a flute of champagne. "I personally can't believe I convinced you to marry me."

"There was no convincing," I reply just as everyone else comes walking into the backyard.

My parents are the first to arrive. They don't know that I know about the adoption. Amelie doesn't know either, and I don't want her to. I don't want anything in my life to change. They might not be my family by blood, but they are my family in every way that counts.

Everyone takes a seat, and we have a buffet-style dinner. There are laughs, tears, and joy. The sun starts to set, the sky turning a hazy orange as it kisses the horizon.

Felix and Julie end up leaving right after we eat. Not that a fight would break out or anything, but the tension between Felix and Julian is noticeable.

"Let's make lunch plans," Julie says as she wraps her arms around my middle.

"Yes, let's go next week. We need to catch up, and I have no idea when Felix is going to run back to the island with you."

Julie laughs, and it makes me happy to see her smile. She's healthy, cared for, and I'm so happy for her. "Who knows, but yes. We will catch up."

"You're so fucking beautiful. Have I told you that?" Markus's voice dips seductively, and my core tightens. I swear I could get pregnant just from the things he says some days.

"Only a handful of times, but please, tell me again because there is nothing like being told how beautiful you are by the man you love."

Markus chuckles, and we move on to cut the cake.

My parents leave not long after that, and though it saddens me, I know they don't approve. My mother said I was too young to get married when she found out, and my father told me he didn't feel Markus was good enough for me. Little did he know, the man he claimed wasn't good enough had saved both his daughters on more than one occasion.

We part ways, me kissing them goodbye and sending them on their way. Amelie, of course, stays behind. For the most part, she is stuck to my side. She's attending college downtown, and even though she's never really spoken about her time in captivity, I know something happened. I can tell just from the constant paranoia she exhibits. Always glancing over her shoulder as if someone is going to come for her.

Markus squeezes my hand, and his deep voice drags me back to reality. "I'm going to step away and talk to Julian for a couple minutes. I'll be right back."

"Okay."

Grabbing my fork, I slice through the piece of marble cake in front of me.

Elena, Julian's wife, catches my eye as I shove a forkful into my mouth. She's beautiful with long dark brown, almost black hair, and piercing green eyes. Markus told me a little about how she and Julian came to be.

Julian took her as revenge, forcing her to marry him. Obviously, it all worked out, judging by the happiness that radiates off her. She cradles their sleeping daughter in her arms.

"Congratulations." Elena smiles sweetly.

"Thank you. Your family is beautiful."

The fact that they have a daughter and seem to have overcome their circumstances, giving in to love, gives me hope. I'm not sure if Markus and I will ever have children. We've discussed it briefly but decided now wasn't a good time. We want to have some time for us before we add any small little humans to the mix.

"Thank you. She is a true blessing, and don't tell Julian I told you this, but she definitely has her daddy wrapped around her finger."

We both smile at her reply.

"I am not surprised. She is beautiful."

Elena strokes her full head of hair. "Thank you. With Christmas coming up, we're going to be going to a few fundraisers. It will be our first time without her." Elena frowns.

In the world we live in, I cannot imagine leaving any kids we might have with someone even for a few hours.

"I can't even imagine how scary that is going to be," I say. "Markus and I aren't sure if we will have children yet. We just want to enjoy each other."

Elena nods and smiles. "Of course. Enjoy your new marriage and time together."

Right on cue, Markus and Julian come walking back into the room. They are both smiling, and when they reach the table,

Julian slaps a hand on Markus's back and looks me right in the eyes. His gaze is penetrating, powerful, frightening, and I have to stop myself from looking away.

"I want to congratulate you. One for reeling this guy in, and two for putting up with his shit. He's a tough son of a bit—"

"Julian!" Elena scolds, cutting him off.

He looks away for a second and winks at her. "Sorry, beautiful." Julian is the kind of man that could convince you that the sky wasn't blue. He's dangerous and decadent, and he only has eyes for one woman.

Elena merely shakes her head, but I can tell they're in love; that one look makes her weak in the knees. She loves him wholeheartedly.

He continues, "Like I was saying, congratulations. He's your responsibility now."

Markus chuckles, his eyes sparkling with joy, and his happiness is contagious.

What started as someone's revenge bloomed into love between two unlikely people, and I couldn't have asked for a better outcome. He's everything I could ever hope or wish for. He takes his seat beside me, and I lean into his side.

"I love you," I whisper.

"I love you too, beautiful."

And there is nothing like hearing him say, *I love you*. Especially when I was sure he could never love again.

***

Thank you *for reading Violent Beginnings. Lucca's story is coming soon.*

ABOUT THE AUTHORS

J.L. Beck and C. Hallman are an international bestselling author duo who write contemporary and dark romance.

For a list of all of our books, updates and freebies visit our website.

www.bleedingheartromance.com

About the Authors

Beck and Hallman
BLEEDING HEART ROMANCE

- CASSANDRAHALLMAN / AUTHORJLBECK
- CASSANDRA_HALLMAN / AUTHORJLBECK
- CASSANDRAHALLMAN / JLBECK

ALSO BY THE AUTHORS

North Woods University
The Bet
The Dare
The Secret
The Vow
The Promise
The Jock

Bayshore Rivals
When Rivals Fall
When Rivals Lose
When Rivals Love

Breaking the Rules
Kissing & Telling
Babies & Promises
Roommates & Thieves

The Blackthorn Elite

Hating You
Breaking You
Hurting You
Regretting You

The Obsession Duet
Cruel Obsession
Deadly Obsession

The Rossi Crime Family
Protect Me
Keep Me
Guard Me
Tame Me
Remember Me

The Moretti Crime Family
Savage Beginnings
Violent Beginnings
Broken Beginnings

The King Crime Family
Indebted
Inevitable

STANDALONES

Their Captive

Convict Me

Runaway Bride

His Gift

Also by the Authors

Two Strangers

Printed in Great Britain
by Amazon